The Rain Forest Mystery

Books in the Choice Adventures series

THE RAIN FOREST MYSTERY

O'Ann Steere

Tyndale House Publishers, Inc.
Wheaton, Illinois

Cover Illustration copyright © 1991 by John Walker
Library of Congress Catalog Card Number 91-65081
ISBN 0-8423-5028-4
Copyright © 1991 by The Livingstone Corporation
Printed in the United States of America
98 97 96 95 94
9 8 7 6 5 4

It was hot, and Willy wiped the sweat from his brow. He couldn't believe how hot it was. "Isn't there any place around here where it isn't so humid?" he mumbled.

"Willy! Look!" shouted Jill, pointing. Through the dense jungle they could barely see the outline of a dark cave. "It's cool inside caves you know," she continued, more to calm her nerves than to tell Willy. Birds and other strange animals made sounds in the distance. Willy and Jill were alone. And scared.

They gulped and headed for the cave. Willy led the way into the darkness. Fortunately he had a flashlight with him and a canteen full of water. The walls of the cave were black and jagged. Jill was close behind.

"How far do you suppose it is to the falls?" she asked.

"Don't know," he replied. "We'll just have to keep going till we get there. It's gotta be at the other end, though."

Just then a swarm of bats came flying out of the cave by the thousands. Willy and Jill ducked and covered their heads, Jill screaming full force. Willy started screaming, too. The commotion stopped almost as soon as it had begun. "I don't like this place," whimpered Jill.

"You think I'm having a good time?" replied Willy roughly. He pulled out his jungle knife and started to . . . .

"You want Coke, 7-Up, or coffee?" asked Jim.

"Huh?" Willy replied blankly.

"Coke, 7-Up, or coffee?" Jim repeated, bringing Willy back to reality.

"Oh, uh, 7-Up."

"You looked like you were in dreamland," said Jim.

"Oh," replied Willy a little embarrassed. "Just thinking about what Brazil will be like." Jim took Willy's cup from the stewardess and handed him his 7-Up.

"I'll bet it's nothing like what you're expecting," said Jim. "Most Americans think Brazil is nothing but jungle and rain forest. We do have that, but we have other stuff, too. It's great. I'm going to show you all the great places. You're going to love it. And you're going to love my parents, too. They're great. You'll fit right in. Don't worry about not feeling at home."

Willy had heard all this before, but the plane was going to touch down in about an hour, and Jim was getting excited. Willy himself was getting tired from his heart beating so fast from the excitement. He had never been on a plane before, much less out of the country. It was almost too much.

Willy let his thoughts wander for another hour, too nervous to talk. Tightening his seat belt again just to be sure, he glanced over toward the three people seated next to him: Tina, Jill, and Jim. All were part of the Ringer gang. He thought about how each one of them had come to be on this flight to Brazil.

Tina and Jim were sister and brother. At thirteen, Tina was one of the youngest members of the gang, and the shyest. She was practically afraid to speak to her own shadow. For Jim and her, going to Brazil meant going home. They'd been living in the Washington, D.C., area at their grandparents' home. Their parents lived and worked as missionaries in Brazil, and by late tonight they would all be together again as a family.

Next to Tina was Jill, also thirteen. She was Chris's cousin, Willy's best friend. Willy still felt bad that Chris, Sam, and Pete hadn't been able to come on this trip, but the decision had boiled down to Jim and Tina each asking one person to go. Willy felt glad that Jim had asked him. Jill and Willy liked to tease each other a lot. He admired the way she loved adventures and the special things she knew about—like electricity, for instance.

In the seat beside Willy sat Jim, a year older than Tina. Willy wondered how Jim could shift from Portuguese to English and back in the same sentence. Sometimes with his Ringer friends he would forget English and just substitute Portuguese, the language his family spoke at home. Willy had learned a few words from Jim, but not anywhere near enough to be able to understand it! He'd have to stick close to Jim once they got to Brazil.

Willy himself was one of the original Ringers. He and his friends had discovered some amazing secrets in an old church in Millersburg. They also had met Jim and Tina's grandparents, who were reopening that church after it had been closed for awhile. Now Willy was flying to Brazil. *Wild,* he thought.

The plane soon touched down and taxied to the terminal. Once it had stopped, Jim and Tina disappeared almost as soon as their seat belts were off. Willy lost sight

8

of them in the crowd leaving the plane as he and Jill waited to get their stuff from the overhead compartments. "Hello, Brazil," Willy said, smiling at Jill. He was determined not to lose sight of her, too, since she was now the only familiar face within eyesight. They got their bags and started down the aisle.

Just then someone tapped Willy on the shoulder. "Excuse me, young man." Willy turned around and saw an older woman hunched over a large black suitcase and pointing to the overhead compartment. "Would you help me carry my bags? I'm not used to flying on such long trips, and my rheumatism's got me in sore condition. I can't move very well right now, and, oh my goodness," she finished laughing, "I could really use some help." She looked at Willy through thick glasses. With the other passengers bearing down on them, he barely had time to think.

 CHOICE

If Willy helps the woman, turn to page 28.

If Willy catches up with the others, turn to page 76.

"Jim's right," Willy said, looking at the others with determination. "We can't just run away and hide. Let's at least see if we can get a good look at this guy and at what he's doing. If nothing else, we can give a description of him and his plane to Clay when he gets back. He'll know what to do about a smuggler."

"That's true," Jill said. "Besides, we should be able to hide in the forest for as long as this Barros guy will be here. From what Jim picked up from the natives, Barros doesn't stick around too long."

"That's three votes for catching the smuggler," Jim said triumphantly. It was great to see how his friends were willing to take a risk so they could help stop a bad situation. He was really proud of them. Then he glanced over at Tina. She was sitting silent, a concerned and frightened look on her face. Jim reached out to touch her arm.

"Hey, Tina," he said quietly, "it's OK. If you don't want to do this, we won't." Tina and the others looked at Jim in surprise. Frankly, Jim was surprised at himself, too. But suddenly he knew it was more important to take care of his sister than to try to be some big smuggler-busting hero. "If you're really scared, we'll just hide out until the smugglers are gone. We won't even try to get close enough for a look."

10

"Do you mean it?" she asked him. When Jim nodded, she looked away for a minute. Then she shook her head. "No, I don't want to let these guys get away."

The others all let out their breath, as though they'd been holding it in suspense, waiting for Tina's response. She looked at them and flashed a smile.

"Let's go out there and catch ourselves a smuggler!" she said.

The next morning, the four Ringers were ready. When the first humming whir of a distant airplane engine broke the quiet, all four jumped to their feet. "Quick, it's time to go!"

Jim pushed out of the back window the screen they'd loosened the night before. Tina was already standing on the boxes they'd piled up below the opening. As soon as he backed out of the way, Tina jumped through the hole and started for the stand of trees near the hut. Willy and Jim followed her quickly.

They huddled silently. The whir had become a full-fledged buzz. An airplane landed on the "abandoned" strip.

"OK, everyone," Jim whispered, "take note of everything you see. We need to remember all of this to tell Clay."

The kids peered from their hiding place, watching the men who stepped out. Suddenly Willy said in a harsh whisper, "Hey! I saw that guy at the airport when we landed in Belem."

The man Willy recognized leaned against the plane and lit a cigarette. The other men fanned out, looking all around. "They should be here with the birds soon, Boss," one man called out. "They knew we were coming."

So the man from the airport was Senhor Barros! The kids strained their eyes to see as much as they could. *Black hair, a scraggly moustache, dark eyes, crumpled safari clothes, and one mean-looking face,* Willy noted to himself. *This guy looks like real trouble.*

Suddenly Senhor Barros waved toward Clay's Cessna and said in a gruff voice, "Search that plane! And make sure no one is in the hut." The men rushed to follow his orders.

Soon another voice called out, "There's been somebody sleeping in the hut! They were here recently. They musta gone out the back window."

Barros threw his cigarette down and stomped it out angrily. "Check the woods!" he barked. "They can't be far. Last thing we need is witnesses."

The Ringers started to scramble deeper into the forest. Just then, Jim tripped on a tree root and crashed to the ground, letting out a grunt as the air was knocked out of him. The other Ringers grabbed him and tried to help him up, but they suddenly found themselves surrounded by several large, unfriendly looking men.

A scruffy man grabbed Jim, pulled him to his feet, and grunted to the rest of them, "Get out there by Senhor Barros."

Turn to page 125.

12

The visitors followed the Ringers back to the hut. From the confident way they walked, the kids got the distinct impression that they had been here before. Each visitor kept a close eye on his package of parrots. Entering the hut they sat down, but they kept their parrots between their crossed legs or used the cages as a backrest.

Our four heroes didn't have any special treats to offer their guests, but at least they had plenty of water. By taking turns and sharing the cups, everyone was able to have a drink before the conversation began again in earnest.

Jim wasn't able to catch every detail, but basically here's what he found out: The guests were as surprised to see the Ringers as the Ringers had been to see them. They'd come here expecting to meet someone called Senhor Barros. The parrots were for him. Barros came here once a month and paid cash for every parrot they were able to bring to him. He flew in, bought the birds, and flew out immediately. They hadn't been expecting him until tomorrow, but when they heard the plane land this afternoon, they'd loaded up their bounty and headed for the hut.

The visitors excused themselves. They thanked the Ringers politely for the water and said that they would be back when Senhor Barros arrived. Then they disappeared into the night.

"You know," Tina shuddered when they were alone again. "There is a major trade in exotic animals these days. Some people think it's a status symbol to own an unusual pet. So they buy a cheetah or a toucan or a parrot. Some of those animals have been imported legally, but the demand is big, so smugglers have started to move into the trade, sneaking animals out of places like Brazil. A lot of the animals are so poorly cared for that they die on the way, but the ones that make it are sold for good profits. I wonder if this Senhor Barros is a smuggler?"

"What I wonder is why anybody would get involved in that in the first place," Willy threw in. "If the animals are mistreated so badly, why would anyone be willing to participate in the trade?"

"We know people are responsible for caring for the earth and the things that God created to live on it," Tina answered. "And people should be willing to do an honest day's work and get an honest day's pay too. Unfortunately, one of the real problems facing Brazil right now is an inflation rate of nearly 2,000 percent. That means that a baseball mitt that cost ten dollars in June would cost twenty-three dollars when school started in September, and over fifty bucks by Christmas! If you want to buy a mitt, that's frustrating. If you need to buy things like milk and eggs, it's a nightmare! So as long as the animals are out there, some people are bound to see them as one way of coping with the need to feed their families."

Willy thought about it for a minute and answered, "Well . . . maybe. But what about a guy like Senhor Barros?"

"I have a feeling," Jim said, "and it isn't good. The guy

flies in and out of what is supposedly an abandoned airstrip. He pays in cash and leaves right away. I'm afraid we've run into a real live smuggler."

"If he is a smuggler, he's likely to be armed and dangerous," Jill said. "What could four kids alone in the jungle do about it anyway? Maybe the part of God's creation we need to take good care of right now is ourselves!"

"I agree we should be very careful. But, since we're stuck here anyway, let's try to find out what's going on, OK?" responded Jim.

CHOICE ➡

If the kids choose to confront Senhor Barros in the morning, turn to page 9.

If the kids decide to hide when Barros arrives, turn to page 67.

It was a beautiful warm and sunny morning. The kids put on their shorts and running shoes and joined Mr. Whitehead in the car. "I'm sure glad you decided to come along today. We really could use the help in publicizing our film ministry. We have a wonderful Christian film to show tonight. Your job will be to distribute these pamphlets inviting people to attend. I think you'll be surprised at how interested people are when they hear about a free film. We'll all meet back at the car at 3:00."

Each Ringer took a sack of brochures, and they headed off together. Willy whistled and commented, "This reminds me of my days as a paper boy. Too bad we have to hand deliver these. If we could just sling them toward people's front door, we could really make some time. We could invite half of Belem, I'll bet!"

Tina had her doubts. "Belem's a pretty big place, Willy. Besides, if you didn't give the invitations to people face to face, they probably wouldn't come."

The first hour went smoothly. The kids took turns approaching the houses or apartments and handing the paper to whoever answered the door. Jim and Tina could carry on some conversation with the people they invited, while Willy and Jill depended on the international language of a big smile.

By the second hour, things were beginning to drag.

16

The kids were hot and sweaty. The newspaper sacks seemed heavier and heavier, and they dug into the kids' shoulders. It looked like they had nearly as many invitations left to deliver as they had to begin with.

"When I thought of missionary work, this isn't really what I had in mind," Willy grumbled.

"Yeah," said Jill with a sigh, "anywhere else I would call this just plain work!"

"I'd forgotten how hot the sun gets here," Tina murmured. "I feel like a popsicle that's just melted."

They continued for another block: approach the residence, smile, hand over the flyer, go on to the next door. Over and over while the sun continued to climb in the sky.

When they got to the next corner, Jim made a suggestion. "I can't take much more of this. I really need a break. Let's go get a cold drink at that little stand, and then we can get back on the job."

They dropped their heavy sacks, ordered drinks, and sat down in the shade of a tree to enjoy them. Jill noticed that two young men ordering at the drink stand were staring at them, apparently sizing them up. One seemed to be telling the other something about Jim. They were trying to be discreet but weren't doing a very good job. Jill was about to ask Jim to look at them when they suddenly approached.

"Aren't you Tina and Jim Whitehead?" asked the one with the big USA on his T-shirt. It was obvious that he was an American.

"Yeah, we are. Who are you?" answered Jim.

"I'm Nathan. This is Hector. We were all at the American school a couple of years ago. My dad had to make a trip back to the States when all the diplomats were getting anti-terrorist training, and by the time he'd completed the course and we got back here, you guys had gone back Stateside to live with your grandparents."

"I think I remember you guys," said Jim. "You were in the class behind mine, right?"

"Right," said the boys in unison, obviously glad to be remembered.

Hector continued, "So, what brings you back to Brazil?" His English was good, but he had a Brazilian accent.

"We're down visiting our parents. We'll be going back for school in the fall," answered Tina. She took care of the other introductions. "This is Willy and Jill. They're friends from our town near Washington. Actually we're all part of a big gang that hangs out together. We wanted them all to come along this summer, but only Willy and Jill could make it." As everybody said hi, Tina changed the subject. "Things sure seem different in just a year!"

"You'd better believe it," agreed Nathan. "All kinds of things have changed since you were here last. How 'bout if I take you on a guided tour of our old haunts and the newest places around town?"

Hector also had an idea, "Why don't you guys also come out to my family's *fazenda* for a visit?" he suggested.

Jill couldn't keep from blurting, "What's a *fazenda?*"

Tina explained, "*Fazenda* is a word for ranch or farm in Portuguese."

18

CHOICE

If the kids decide to go with Nathan, turn to page 124.

If the kids decide to continue passing out pamphlets, turn to page 24.

If the kids take Hector up on his invitation to visit the *fazenda*, turn to page 51.

After some time to talk over the options, the Ringers decided they would stay at the hut while Clay went for help. They stood side by side and watched until Clay completely disappeared in the bush. They waited until no sound or motion gave any clue at all that the pilot was out there in that vast sea of green. Silently the gang turned and filed into the hut. Now there was nothing to do but wait. . . .

They sat in the hut staring at the walls, the floor, the ceiling, and each other.

Jim got up to stretch. "I gotta move around a little bit. This is driving me nuts already. If I just sit here like a bump for three days, I'll go crackers! I'm going to take a short walk around the area. I won't go far, and I'll be back before dark. Anybody care to join me?"

It occurred to Tina that her brother could be depended upon to be back before dark because he was probably as uncomfortable about the idea of spending the night alone in that huge forest as she was. She didn't bring it up. Instead she said, "Sure, let's all go."

If the Ringers were feeling nervous before the walk, their discoveries didn't help calm them at all. Out behind the hut they found a pile of tin cans that hadn't been buried. They hadn't rusted either, which meant they couldn't be very old. At the far end of the runway was a torn blue oxford shirt. It had been left lying in the grass and didn't show any sign of mold.

The discovery of those cans and shirt gave all four Ringers the creeps. Maybe this place wasn't as deserted as Clay thought. Nobody wanted to say out loud that they were feeling frightened, but when Tina suggested heading back to the hut, everyone else was more than willing to go.

Inside the hut, they went back to the silent staring routine for about an hour and then ate dinner. "Dinner" might be too fancy a word for what they ate. They had some basic survival food that could be eaten right out of the tin and water to wash it down. It was hardly gourmet cuisine, but at least they wouldn't go hungry during their wait.

They were gathering their cans when Jim stood straight up. "Did you hear that? What was it?" They froze and listened. There it was again. Someone or something was outside the hut!

It took every ounce of courage Jim could muster to walk to the doorway and peek out. "Somebody is in the clearing. Maybe more than one somebody."

"Let me see," Willy said, pushing Jim aside. "Holy cow! There's a bunch of them."

"What do they look like?" Tina asked.

"Well, they look like natives, and they look like they're looking for someone. What are we going to do now?"

CHOICE

If the Ringers decide to hide in the hut, turn to page 83.

If the Ringers decide to go out and meet the visitors, turn to page 102.

"**T**his place hasn't changed that much," Tina said as the five of them stood in front of the Ver-o-Peso Market. Hector had left for home.

"What does the name mean?" asked Willy.

"It means 'See-the-weight,'" answered Jim. "It's a way of saying that you sell things honestly."

Nathan started into his tour guide routine again, even repeating things the kids already knew. "This whole market was designed and built in England and then transported to Brazil. Its name, Ver-o-Peso, comes from the fact that, during colonial times, officials of the crown were stationed here to 'see the weight' and set the amounts of taxes to be charged. By six o'clock every morning, vendors are converging here by boat and on foot with items to sell. The old sellers' stalls and stone archways have remained unchanged for hundreds of years. Look. You can still buy almost anything here: fruit, vegetables, fish, crafts, medicines . . . ."

It was a beautiful market. The small stands held every type of product. The sellers had thoroughly polished their wares so their colors gleamed in the tropical sun. Willy was fascinated. This was totally unlike the mall. Shops were open air. Goods were piled on tables, and prices were haggled over. Some of the food was still alive! Chickens danced in cages waiting to be purchased. You could pick a fish out of a bucket and have it filleted while you wait. There were foods Willy had never heard of, let alone tasted.

Willy was engrossed in the drama of a shopkeeper and bargain hunter "arguing" over the worth of a potential purchase. He was trying so hard to walk and watch what they were doing without appearing to stare that he bumped into a stall.

Well, maybe it wasn't so much a bump as a serious collision with stacks of cages full of chickens. But not for long. By the time Willy recovered from his accidental demolition derby, there were chickens escaping in all directions. The shopkeeper was shouting, and Willy was wondering how he could possibly have been so careless—and how he could disappear. It was a moment of panic.

CHOICE ⇒

If Willy tries to make himself invisible in the crowd, turn to page 113.

If Willy tries to figure out some way to clean up the mess, turn to page 128.

It would have been fun to go with Nathan and Hector, but the kids had promised that they'd help with the film publicity, so they got back to their work.

It would be nice to say that something tremendous and exciting happened to them, like at the very next house a famous rock and roll singer who happened to be vacationing in the area answered their knock and invited them in for tea . . . or they found a fifty-dollar bill in the street . . . or that just by being in the right place at the right time they prevented a bank robbery and were featured on the evening news that night. But nothing like that happened.

They spent the next four hours hauling those heavy packs from door to door. They were hot, and their shoulders ached, and it wasn't exciting at all. At one low point Willy grunted, "This reminds me of a story I heard."

"What story is that?" Tina asked.

"The one about the man who kept banging his head against the wall. When someone asked him why he did it, he answered, 'Because it really feels great when I stop!'"

They kept walking and doing the work they had promised to do. Ring bell, deliver note, go on to the next house. Door after door.

Finally, 3:00 came. They trudged back to the car. When they got there, they took off their shoes and rubbed their tired feet while they waited for Mr. Whitehead.

That night the park was packed. More than 150 people turned out to see the film. The Ringers recognized some of them as people they had handed notices to. When the movie ended, Mr. Whitehead stood and asked if there was anyone in the crowd who would like to give his or her heart to Jesus. Even though Willy didn't understand the words, it was impossible not to understand the look of joy on the faces of the people who made that decision. They were becoming part of the greatest adventure of all—life with Christ!

Suddenly, the hard work in the hot sun seemed worthwhile. By spending a day working even when it got boring and difficult, the Ringers were part of bringing people to the place where they chose to spend eternity in heaven. The Ringers were glad they had stuck it out.

Several men stayed after the meeting to help clean up the park. As they were working, one of them, Miguel, said to Jim, "You four were a big help in getting the word out. Without your leg muscles we would never have had such a large group tonight. I was thinking you might be ready for a break. I'm planning to go to a big soccer match day after tomorrow. I'd love to take you along. What do you think?" Jim translated what he said for Jill and Willy.

CHOICE

If the Ringers choose to go with Miguel to see the soccer match, turn to page 131.

If the kids turn down Miguel's offer, turn to page 63.

Four petrified Ringers waited. They couldn't risk moving anywhere until they were *sure* that Pedro was sound asleep. A false move could mean terrible trouble.

Pedro resettled in his chair. The Ringers forced themselves to wait it out. He wasn't alert, but was he asleep? And if so, would he stay asleep?

Then, like the most beautiful symphony ever written, came the sound of gentle snoring. After ten minutes, it crescendoed into a consistent drone. The late hour and liquid dinner had done their work. Pedro was in dreamland, somewhere between "out cold" and hibernation.

The kids began a stealthy progress toward the door. Getting by Pedro was like carrying a hornet's nest. One false move and they'd get caught. But Pedro kept snoring.

When Jim reached the door, he was so thankful he could hardly keep himself quiet. It swung open with only the slightest pressure. The four stood out in the fresh night air at last.

They didn't stand there long. Jim immediately knew they were at the airport in Belem. With the moon as a lantern, they took off at a full run toward the terminal. When they got there, they raced to a phone and called the Whiteheads. They had been praying for the kids' safety, but they had no idea how much danger the kids had been in!

A while later, it was another one of those wonderful reunions at the airport: hugging, kissing, and talking. And this time Willy and Jill were included. Now they began to pray for Clay's safety, as he was still trudging back to civilization through the jungle.

The Whiteheads notified the local authorities who immediately arrested the slumbering Pedro. Then the police hid inside the hangar and were waiting there when Senhor Barros returned the next day. The evidence was right there in the plane with him. Thanks to the bravery of the Ringers, the parrots were released and the smuggling ring was broken.

Imagine Clay's surprise two days later when he emerged from the jungle and was greeted by the same gang he had left stranded back in the isolated hut. "You Ringers really get around!" he said.

THE END

Turn to page 141.

"**S**ure," Willy found himself saying as he nervously tried to keep from losing sight of Jill. He put down his own bag and reached for the woman's bag. It was heavy. She smiled.

"Oh, thank you so much, young man," said the woman. "So many young people these days won't lift a finger to help you; they just go on their way and ride their skateboards and listen to that music, but you're a nice young man I can tell." She patted Willy on the shoulder as he struggled down the aisle with the two bags. His heart was racing again—he had lost sight of Jill.

I am alone in the country of Brazil, a large, very large country where they don't speak English, and I don't know anybody within a thousand miles. Oh man, where are Jim and Tina and Jill? Willy's thoughts ran wild as he struggled for what seemed like forever down the aisle and out the plane. Finally he got to the exit, said good-bye to the stewardess, then picked up the pace as he headed toward the terminal.

"Don't lose me, young man!" the woman said. Willy felt his heart rate pick up even more as he slowed down to let the woman catch up. He started looking around for his friends, growing more and more frustrated.

Finally he and the woman reached the terminal. "Thank you so much," the woman said, patting Willy's arm like it was a poodle. "You can put it down now; the porter will help me. Thank you so much." The woman smiled at Willy again. Willy smiled back dutifully and said good-bye while frantically looking around for someone he recognized. He couldn't see Jim, Tina, or Jill anywhere. His head was spinning.

"We're going to have to put a leash on you," a teasing voice said from behind him. "You're not safe in airports." It was Jill! Willy turned around to see the whole gang standing next to two people who had to be Mr. and Mrs. Whitehead, Jim and Tina's parents. He breathed a huge sigh of relief.

Willy tried to explain the delay, but got interrupted. "Where'd you get that?" asked Jill, pointing to his hand.

"What?" Willy replied. He then noticed a five-dollar bill in his hand. "Hey, she must have . . . ." He looked around for the woman he had helped, but she was gone. He shook his head, then turned as the Whiteheads introduced themselves. Soon they were heading for the Kombi.

CHOICE

Turn to page 43.

After some thought and discussion, the gang decided they would hike out with Clay. He nodded his head, then opened the cargo bay and began to pull out boxes. "Like other missionary pilots, I often cover rugged or dangerous terrain. So I never fly without basic survival equipment. That's just God-given common sense.

"There's a compass, insect repellent, and nets, and enough tinned meat and water to make it if we're frugal. But we'll have to be careful. I'm not sure exactly how long this will take. We might run into help along the way. If we have to walk all the way out, drinkable water is going to get very scarce."

Soberly they picked up the provisions Clay had distributed to each of them. It wasn't going to be easy, but at least they were all together. With one last look toward the damaged airplane and the hut, the group hit the trail.

From the airplane, the jungle had looked to Willy like a solid sea of green. Now he had visions of having to hack their way through with a machete, inch by inch.

It wasn't like that at all. The tree tops formed an almost solid umbrella, blocking out 90 percent of the sun's light. In fact, it was hard to be sure where the sun was.

Once Willy's eyes adjusted to the dim light he saw that there was plenty of room to walk. Without the sun, plants don't grow well, so the ground was covered only by ferns, fungi, and a thin carpet of fallen leaves and flowers.

"Listen," Jill said.

"To what?" Jim wondered.

"That's just my point," Jill answered. "I was worried that this place was going to be just crawling with bugs, birds, and critters. I don't hear anything but us."

Clay smiled but cautioned, "Wait for it, Jill. The forest is quiet at midday, but at dawn and dusk things can get pretty active."

They walked at a steady pace, making slow progress toward home and help. Clay was in the lead with the boys behind him and Jill and Tina following last.

Off to the right Tina saw something move. It was a small animal. She was curious to get a better look.

CHOICE

If Tina turns off the path to investigate, turn to page 46.

If Tina stays on the trail, turn to page 64.

The port was beautiful. Like any major shipping area, it was filled with an incredible variety of boats, people, and cargo. They came in a myriad of shapes, sizes, and conditions.

There was activity everywhere. Huge oceangoing vessels anchored out in the bay. Smaller tugs steamed about arranging the ships and steering them toward the docks. Small boats skittered everywhere like dragonflies on the water's surface.

Jim, Tina, Willy, and Nathan were in a small motor boat. Hector had decided he had to go home. They circled among the larger boats enjoying the sea breeze and the view. Each of the large ships flew a flag that showed where it came from. The kids played the "license plate game" with flags. That green one with the yellow diamond surrounding a blue globe was Brazil. That was easy to find. The red maple leaf on the white field was Canada. And of course, the stars and stripes were the U.S. There was a white cross on a red field—Denmark, and a blue cross on a white field—Finland. Several red, green, and yellow flags furled beautifully in the wind, but none of the contestants had paid enough attention in civics class to be sure what country they represented.

"Look!" Nathan pointed slightly ahead and practically straight up in the air. "That sailor is repainting the identification on their hull. That's an American ship!"

The Ringers squinted toward the sun searching for the painter. There he was . . . suspended over the side of a huge ship on a cable, swinging high over the water.

"That looks great," Jim exclaimed. "You could see everything. It looks like he could just swing free from there, like rapelling down the side of the ship."

"As long as you paid attention, it would be great," Willy said. "But, it looks to me like one false move and you could fall off that thing. I'd want to know if I was about to go high diving so I could get my nose plugged!"

The words were barely out of his mouth when something went wrong. Maybe it was the wind. Maybe something happened to the cable that was supposed to be holding the painter's tiny platform. But suddenly, he tumbled into the sea!

Nathan gunned their boat toward the scene. When they got there, Willy grabbed the emergency oar stored in the bottom of the boat and held it out to the sailor. But the sailor made no effort to be rescued. He floated, unmoving, facedown in the water.

"He must have banged his head on the way down," Tina shouted. "I think he's unconscious." Nathan and Jim reached over the side of the boat. One grabbed an arm, and the other grabbed a leg. As they pulled the limp body on board, Jill, Tina, and Willy balanced the boat.

Tina checked him out and looked up in alarm. "He's not breathing, and I don't feel a pulse!" They flipped the man over so that he was lying face up in the bottom of the boat. They propped his legs up over one of the seats, and

Tina began giving him mouth-to-mouth resuscitation. Jill got down next to her and began doing CPR.

No response.

"Don't quit girls; keep trying," Willy tried to encourage.

Suddenly, sea water began to gurgle out of the man's mouth.

"Keep going. Don't give up. If you get tired, I'll take a turn."

Just then, the sailor stirred. He began coughing hard. Color began to return to his cheeks. His lungs started working on their own. Jill and Tina set back and smiled at each other.

"Thank you, God. He's going to be OK," said Jim.

All five kids breathed a huge sigh of relief and only then noticed the boat that had pulled directly alongside of theirs.

"Thank God, but thank *you*, too," said a deep voice in English. "You kids are genuine heroes. We boarded this lifeboat as quickly as we could to rescue Jason. But if it hadn't been for you, he might have died. You saved our crewman's life!" He introduced himself as the captain of the ship.

"We need to get him back to the ship. He'll be feeling shaky for a while, and we should get him to the sick bay. Would you like to come along with us? When we get him settled, we could give you a tour."

"We'd love to," said Nathan, "but we've got to get this boat back and everybody home. I think we're out of time."

"Well, if you come back to the harbor, you will be our

honored guests. Till then, thanks again for what you did for Jason."

THE END

Turn to page 141.

36

The Ringers decided to start with the coffee plantation, so off they went.

Before long, Jill spoke up. "Hey, Hector. Look at all those fields. Are those coffee plants?"

"I can tell you're a city girl," Hector answered with a smile.

"I thought since there was so much of it growing in the area that it must be coffee," Jill explained.

"We do grow an awful lot of coffee," Hector admitted, "but that crop is sugar cane."

"Wow, do the people of Brazil eat sugar as much as they drink coffee?"

"We do like sweets, but most of the sugar cane is distilled into alcohol."

"And then you drink the alcohol?"

"Nope. The alcohol made from the sugar cane is used to fuel our cars."

"Your cars run on alcohol?"

"Most of them do. Back in 1973 Brazil recognized that we had a serious energy shortage and that if we continued to buy expensive oil from the Middle East we'd always have financial difficulties. So the government began a program to develop alcohol from sugar cane as a fuel to replace oil. At first there were lots of jokes about it. But now over one million cars in Brazil run on sugar cane alcohol. Over 75 percent of the cars sold now use alcohol rather than oil. Since it takes a ton of sugar cane to make nineteen gallons of alcohol, we need to grow a lot of sugar cane. But, it's a crop we can grow ourselves, and, unlike oil, it is a renewable resource."

"Pretty smart," Jill agreed.

The truck took a sharp turn to the left. Everybody in the back ended up jumbled on top of each other.

"Sorry, you guys. I got so wound up about the fuel situation I nearly missed our turn. If you look out the window now, you'll be able to see the coffee plantations."

"Where? All I see are rows and rows of beautiful white flower bushes. Looks like an outdoor greenhouse to me," said Willy.

"Those *are* the coffee plants. Now do you want to get out and do some walking?"

CHOICE ⇨

If the Ringers choose to get out and walk, turn to page 99.

If they choose to just drive around, turn to page 71.

Joao steered the boat with confidence. Now that the sun was out, everyone was drying off and getting hungry for lunch. Joao pointed out several plants along the route, saying they were delicious to eat, but he didn't stop and let his visitors try any.

They went down river for about half an hour. Joao docked, got out, and said, "Wait here. I'll be right back."

Joao returned to the boat carrying picnic supplies. He was full of surprises, the kids thought.

"Shall we eat right here?" Tina asked.

"No. Wait just a few minutes. I have a special picnic place picked out," said Joao with a mischievous grin.

Joao's picnic place was like a scene out of some science fiction novel. Scattered across the river's surface were lily pads. Make that *giant lily pads!* They were three feet in diameter. Joao's next suggestion made the Ringers wonder if his brain had rusted in the daily rain: "Each of you may choose a lily pad to float on while you eat your lunch."

Believe it or not, that's exactly what they did. Each sat cross-legged atop a lily pad eating a sandwich. They felt uncertain when waves set the lily pads in motion. One thing was certain, this was one meal where they couldn't keep jumping up from the table to get things!

"If your balance was excellent and you weren't afraid

of water, you could walk on these pads," Joao told them. "One thing you should appreciate about our daily rain is that it will wash off your table tops for you. Let's go. I need to make a quick stop at a friend's house, and then we'll pick some berries for dessert."

When they got to Joao's destination, Willy and Tina decided to accept his invitation to come along and meet Paulo. Jim and Jill stayed with the canoe.

What with introducing Willy and Tina to Paulo and all of their questions on the walk, the errand took longer than Joao had said.

Finally, Jill got out of the boat. She had spotted some red berries growing near the shore. She wondered if those were the ones Joao had mentioned that they would pick later. They'd be perfect for dessert.

She could almost hear her mother saying, "Don't put anything in your mouth unless you *know* it is safe to eat." But, Joao knew this area like the back of his hand, and he had said, "We'll pick some berries for dessert."

Jill rinsed out a bait bucket and began picking berries. Jim was sunning himself in the boat. When she had half a bucketful, she returned to the boat. By then, Jim had dozed off. Jill sat there looking at those delicious looking berries. She was trying to decide what to do.

 CHOICE

If Jill eats the berries, turn to page 80.

If Jill waits to eat the berries, turn to page 59.

40

The research lab turned out to be an amazing complex of many different laboratories and study areas.

Nathan continued acting as guide, talking as they walked through the door to the lab. "My mom sometimes laughs and says that if the doctor isn't too sure what is wrong with you, he calls it a virus and tells you to drink liquids and get plenty of rest. Some scientists think that the cure for every viral disease that exists can be found in the tropical forests. This research laboratory was set up in Belem back in 1954 to look for those cures. Scientists from all over the world work here. They collect animals and test their blood, trying to learn as much as they can about viruses and the animals that carry them.

"We'll find everything here from ants to zebra plants. They have made lots of discoveries over the years. Like, for example, peppers are one of the important export crops raised in this area. But a strange fungus started destroying the crop. They noticed, though, that peppers growing inside the rain forest at Belem weren't effected by the fungus. A scientist grafted the top of a field-grown pepper plant onto the bottom of a rain forest pepper plant, and the result was a farm pepper that wasn't destroyed by the fungus. That saved a lot of farmers in this area."

Nathan was about to launch into a description of the distinction between true viruses and protozoans when Jim let out a yell.

"Cuidado!"

Somehow, his tone told Jill and Willy that he was shouting a warning. He had glanced through a glass door into an open patio where there were several beehive boxes with signs around them telling people to keep away. The boxes looked solid, but they were open on the bottom so the bees could get in and out. A little boy was crouched under one of those boxes, trying to see what was in it.

While they watched in horror, the little boy stood up with his head and shoulders inside the box. Jim ran for the door. Others were coming, too. Almost immediately the boy dropped back down. Only now, from his elbows up, he was covered with bees.

Even before Jim opened the door, they could tell the little boy was screaming. He started running from the hive. The kids watched Jim catch up with him and throw him on the ground, right into a deep puddle. Then he was down on the child like he was beating him up, rolling him over and over in the mud, brushing off bees with his bare hands. In seconds, it was over. The little boy, covered with mud, was crying in his mother's arms. Jim was almost as big a mess. The boy's mother was also crying and thanking Jim. Her child had only been stung three times. Jim had actually been stung more than the boy.

As Jim came through the door, Willy said, "Man, was that ever fast thinking! How did you know what to do?"

Jim smiled a kind of painful smile. A bee had stung him on the lip. "Almost the same thing happened to me when I was a kid. My dad used the same trick to help me. The bees don't like the water or the mud. If it hadn't been for the bees, that would have really been fun!" Everyone chuckled with relief.

Several more people came by to say thanks, including the lab's beekeeper. Then Nathan announced, "Due to unexpected messing around in the mud by one of the members of this tour, we will now have to terminate our travels and get him home to clean up. I hope he has a good explanation for his mother!"

That night, they gave quite a performance for Mr. and Mrs. Whitehead, telling them how Jim had helped the little boy.

Jim was having a hard time smiling. His upper lip had swelled, and there were several painful stings on his arms. But he didn't think much about the pain. Instead, he was thinking how good it had felt to be able to help that boy. And he knew that it was because of his father's helping him that he'd been able to do so.

Actually, I'm pretty fortunate to have the dad I have, Jim said to himself. Then, with a smile, he got up to go and tell his dad how much he appreciated him.

THE END

Turn to page 141.

The Whiteheads, Jill, and Willy piled into a car and
headed for the Whiteheads' house. Willy had been
confused the first time Jim had mentioned his folks drove a
"Kombi" in Brazil. He was glad it turned out to be a
Volkswagen van they could all fit into. Since Belem is a big
city, Mr. Whitehead needed to keep his eyes on the road,
but Mrs. Whitehead turned around to face the back seat,
smiling at Willy and Jill.

"We are so pleased to meet you," she said warmly.
"Jim and Tina have written and told us so much about you.
We worried about the kids making the right kind of friends
when we sent them off to America for school. It can be
quite a transition to go from living as part of a community
of missionaries to life as an American teenager. We prayed
about it and were very thankful that they met you and the
rest of your gang. What is it you call yourselves—the
Ringers?"

"Yup, the Ringers," said Jill and Willy, almost in
unison.

"You sound like quite the group," Mr. Whitehead
piped in. "I wish it had been possible for all of you to come
visit Brazil. It would have been great having everyone, and
I think they would have enjoyed the trip. But it's a long
flight, and, unless you build up frequent flier miles for
business travel like your father did, Jill, the airfare is

expensive. We're just glad you could come along. It should be a wonderful summer. Besides, Dad still needs a few Ringers around to take care of the bell."

They all chuckled. Mr. Whitehead's father was the one who had asked the Ringers to ring the bell at church before each service. It hadn't taken the kids very long to realize it was also a great way to make sure they were at church on time.

They arrived at the plain little house where the Whiteheads lived. "I can hardly wait to see some of the places Jim and Tina have been bragging about," Willy commented. "They're convinced that Brazil is about the best place God ever made."

Mrs. Whitehead laughed. "We have the world's largest river, the world's largest tropical rain forest, and lots of other interesting things to see. In the morning you can begin your tour. But for now, let's haul these bags inside, fix you something to eat, and let you kids crawl into a hammock for some sleep. It's been a long day, and you must be tired."

A few hours later, Willy rolled over in his hammock. Thump! He landed on the floor. Sleeping in a hammock sure wasn't like sleeping in his bed at home. *Nothing here is exactly like home,* he thought as he carefully climbed back into the hammock. Instead of a soft mattress and pillow, he was sleeping on these ropes. Instead of having turkey or ham for their special "welcome" dinner, they'd had something called *pato no tucupi.* It was made of pieces of duck cooked in a rich sauce with some green herbs that had tingled all the way down. As for breakfast,

instead of a big bowl of Frosted Flakes and milk, they would be having bread and *cafe con leite,* a sweet mixture of half hot milk and half coffee.

Willy tried to settle down into his hammock, but his eyes wouldn't close. It was dark, and the whole house was quiet. He could hear the high-pitched whine of something that sounded like crickets outside the window, but other than that it was silent. Willy felt surrounded by strange things . . . and he felt alone.

Sometime during the night, it slowly dawned on Willy what was wrong. He was homesick. He'd always figured that was just for little kids who miss their mommies. But he had to admit it: he *was* homesick. He missed his mom. He missed his dad. He missed his bed. His dog. His house. His baseball and bat. His video games. The swimming pool. The church. Ice cream at the Freeze. The rest of the Ringers. Suddenly it seemed like everybody and everything he loved was at home in the States.

CHOICE

If Willy decides to rejoin the rest of the Ringers back in the United States, turn to page 61.

If Willy decides to stay in Belem and keep his homesickness to himself, turn to page 108.

If Willy decides to talk to the Whiteheads about being homesick, turn to page 72.

No doubt about it—there was something in those bushes. Something tiny. Tina started toward it carefully. She walked slowly, coming to a complete stop between each step and watching where she set each foot in order to be as silent as possible.

She got within ten feet and could see the eyes and part of the head clearly. It was a little baby pig.

She stepped into the clearing to get just a bit closer. Then she heard a yell behind her. "No! No!" Why was Jim screaming? Something must be wrong. He was yelling at the top of his voice and sounded truly alarmed.

Then Tina saw it. Coming around a large tree and toward her at full speed was a wild boar. Tina began to run as fast as she could go. The boar was snorting, running full speed. Tina scrambled through the clearing. Her heart pounded. Despite her exertion, the animal was gaining on her. Closer, ever closer.

"Jump, Tina, *jump!*" shouted her brother. She did. She hurled herself at the low branch of a tree and swung herself up. She grabbed the next branch and crawled higher. Then, once she was safely in the crotch of the tree, panting, she stopped to look below her.

As soon as the boar thought the danger had passed, she gathered her piglet and herded it safely away from the intruding humans.

Tina breathed a sigh of relief, and Clay came over to help her down from the tree. "A wild boar can weigh up to four hundred pounds," Clay said, "and its tusks can rip you wide open. You need to be cautious here." His voice was stern, but his hug was kind. "What were you thinking of?"

"I know it sounds silly, but that little pig reminded me of Wilbur in *Charlotte's Web*. I guess I need to keep my mind on the job and my feet on the path."

From then on, the group was cautious. One close call was plenty! Their trip was a long and hard one before they finally got back to civilization. When they were asked later whether they preferred to walk or fly, Willy smiled and said, "Well, I don't know which is safer, but I do know that when I'm walking I don't have to fall very far!"

THE END

Turn to page 141.

Early the next morning, Jill, Willy, and all the Whiteheads piled into the car. As they drove, Mr. Whitehead explained, "The rain forest is being cleared at the rate of two football fields every second. That's like the whole state of Pennsylvania being cleared every year.

"People come to the edge of the forest to build new roads, burn trees, work in the mines, and provide all of the support services these workers need. That's why the missionaries come here, too. There are thousands of workers who are following the forest as it is peeled back, and they need to hear the Gospel. We try to get a church established at each new outpost. It isn't always easy, but we try. It will take us several hours to reach our latest outpost. Be prepared for a dusty ride. The highway is still dirt."

When lunchtime came, they pulled into a truck stop. By then each of the Ringers could feel an added layer of dust on his or her skin. Mr. Whitehead stopped the car and said to Willy and Jill, "You are about to experience a restaurant unlike any other you've ever been in. This is a highway *churrascaria,* a special meat restaurant for travelers."

The building was quite cool inside, with tile floors. Draped over each chair was a towel. When the group was shown to their table, Mr. Whitehead said, "Before we order, we'll all take a quick shower, courtesy of the restaurant, so we'll feel fresh."

Willy's shower was already running, so he jumped right in. "Yaw! That's cold! Where's the hot water?" he yelled.

Jim laughed in the next stall as he said, "Free showers aren't usually hot, Willy!"

Cold shower or not, Willy did feel less dusty by the time he got back to the table. He had already decided that Brazilian *churrascaria*s were his favorite restaurants in the whole world. Instead of a salad bar, they had a meat bar. You could try quite a few different kinds of steaks, sausages, and other meats. Salads and vegetables were served with huge bowls of black beans and rice at the table. They had a great meal.

"Look, there's Joao," said Mr. Whitehead as they finally pulled into a small town of shacks along the highway. "He is the pastor of one of our newer churches. He's been to Bible School in Belem, but his home is actually around here." Mr. Whitehead began to whistle and wave. A gentleman waved back and crossed over to join the group.

"Good morning, Mr. Whitehead. How are you today?"

"Wonderful, Joao. You remember my son, Jim, and my daughter, Tina. These are their friends, Willy and Jill. The four of them are here for a visit."

"Pleased to see you again," said Joao. "Are you enjoying your stay?"

"It's great to be back home. But things sure are different," Jim responded. "The city is bigger than ever and getting more crowded. The highway has moved nearly 100 miles from where it was the last time we were here."

"How about you? What do you think of my country?" Joao asked Willy. Willy and Jill were both shocked that Joao spoke such good English.

"Well, sir, I guess I'd imagined a hot steamy forest with lots of vines and strange animals. I pictured small huts and natives in boats crossing the river. Belem looks pretty much like any other real city, and this station looks like a massive construction site."

"Sounds like it's time for you to see some of our rural areas," Joao answered. "Would you like to join me for a trip downriver?" He smiled when he noticed the looks on their faces and said, "You're wondering why I speak English? We all have to take it in school, and I've also had Mr. and Mrs. Whitehead helping me a lot."

"Actually, Clay Vargus is going to meet us here, and we were going to let the kids fly over the forest together," Mr. Whitehead explained. "But, I guess it's up to them what they would rather do today. What's your choice, Ringers?"

CHOICE

If the Ringers choose to travel the Amazon River, turn to page 136.

If they choose to fly over the rain forest, turn to page 93.

Jim turned to his friends and said, "I think a trip out to Hector's ranch would be great, but the day is already half over." He looked back at Hector and asked, "How about if we plan to go out there with you tomorrow for the day?"

Hector said, "I think that's a great idea. You guys look pretty busy anyway. What are those things you're handing out?"

Jill stepped up and said, "Here. Jim and Tina's parents are showing a film in the park tonight about the life of Jesus. It would be neat if you could come."

Hector and Nathan exchanged slight frowns. He smiled at Jill and said, "Well, thanks for the invitation, but I don't usually spend my evenings doing religious things."

Jill wasn't sure what to say, but Jim came to her rescue. "I've noticed, Hector, that most people think Jesus was someone important in history. Many of them don't know why, though. We show these films to help people understand Jesus better. Some of them even decide they'd like to meet him themselves."

"Hold it, Jim," said Nathan. "How can anyone meet someone who's been dead for two thousand years?"

Jim smiled and said, "Well, guys, it looks like you might have a good reason to come to the film tonight, because it answers just that question. How about it? You spend the evening with us, and we'll spend the day on your *fazenda* tomorrow."

52

"I don't know," Hector said slowly. "Maybe we'll come." Nathan looked at him in surprise, but he just said good-bye to the group, and they walked away.

If Hector and Nathan decide to show up at the film, turn to page 85.

If Hector and Nathan decide not to come to the film, turn to page 104.

The canoe continued down the river. The Ringers watched the shoreline intensely. They knew that animals like jaguars, ocelots, and giant armadillos occasionally came to the water's edge to drink. So far they'd spotted two toucans and a parrot, but nothing big or scary. (But there was still hope.)

"Get a load of that! What in the world is it?" Jim spouted, pointing at the river bank.

"You've got good eyes for a city kid," Joao admired. "Let's stop the canoe here and watch."

On the bank was an animal that looked like a guinea pig blown up to monster size. It had coarse brown hair, a tapering head, and no tail.

"That's the world's largest rodent," Joao explained. "It can weigh up to 100 pounds. The proper name is capybara, but lots of locals just say 'water pig.' Can you see how his feet are partly webbed? Capybaras love the water and are very good swimmers. They're OK for eating, too. People eat them, and jaguars really love them."

The capybara took a long drink of water and then decided to go for a swim. It paddled out toward the opposite shoreline.

Suddenly there was a whirlwind in the river. The capybara was howling, and the water's surface flashed with fish. Dozens of fish were in a feeding frenzy. Fins broke the water. Teeth snapped. Blood and bits of capybara flesh floated.

In minutes it was over. The kids were riveted to their seats. That whole animal had disappeared, and the water's surface was still and silent again.

"Piranha?" Willy finally asked.

"Piranha." Joao nodded.

"If I caught a fish like that, I'd be afraid that after he bit the bait he'd bite me, too."

"That would be a good thing to be careful of," Joao agreed. "That capybara must have had a small wound or sore that put blood in the water, and that drew the piranha. They have been known to bite off people's fingers or toes. The long piranha teeth are so sharp that natives use them to cut hair and sharpen weapons. Very few people actually get to see piranhas in action like you did. We came along at the right time."

"Guess I'll stick to trout, bass, and catfish," said Willy.

"Well, we've got catfish in the Amazon—over one thousand kinds of catfish. Full-grown catfish barely an inch long and catfish that get larger and heavier than a man. The giant horned catfish can reach four hundred pounds. We've even got fish that normally live only in salt water like sawfish and sharks."

"Maybe we can go fishing together sometime while we're here," said Willy hopefully.

"Maybe. But for now we need to head back up the river. The Whiteheads will be waiting to drive you four home for supper."

THE END

Turn to page 141.

Willy got in the line of people waiting for available
taxis, and when his turn came up, he got in. He barely got
his second foot in the cab and was still trying to shut the
door when the driver took off.

The driver turned, shrugged, and said "Eh?"

Willy tried to explain where he wanted to go. The driver
responded in broken English and seemed to be driving
confidently, so Willy relaxed. He was a little bit uneasy about
how much the ride would cost. But he had heard that public
transportation was cheap in Belem, and he knew that if worse
came to worse, he could run into his room and bring out more
cash once he was safely at the Whiteheads.

He began noticing interesting sights along the way:
the port with its boats ranging from ships to small dinghies
was back on the horizon. He remembered that once you
got outside Washington, D.C., you were in suburbs and the
houses got fancier and fancier. Here, you went from a
modern urban area to houses that got progressively
simpler. They had no air conditioners in the windows.
Some didn't even have windows. He loved the colors they
were painted. They might have seemed tacky at home, but
here the bright paint looked just right.

The taxi drove on and on. Willy had been too excited about
going to the soccer match to remember exactly how long it took
to get there, but this seemed to be taking an awful long time.

There was nothing in the scenery that looked familiar.

What if the driver had made a mistake and was lost? What if he had spotted Willy for a chump and was just taking him on a wild goose chase to run up the fare?

They traveled on in silence.

More time passed and still Willy saw nothing he recognized. The area they were driving through seemed to be quite isolated. And it also seemed to Willy that it was quite poor.

What if it wasn't a mistake? What if the driver had brought him out here on purpose. Maybe he was going to steal all of Willy's money. Maybe he was going to take Willy way out into the country and then call the Whiteheads and ask for ransom money before taking him home! Maybe he was planning to kill Willy!

Willy started to think about how to jump out of a moving vehicle, or how to jump a mugger and steal his gun, when the taxi driver spoke.

He seemed to be asking a question, but Willy didn't understand. He asked again. A third time he asked. But this time he was loud—very loud—and besides his mouth, he was talking with both hands. When Willy still didn't answer, the cabby got agitated. He talked and talked and gestured, and finally he made it clear that Willy should get out of the cab. Right there. Dead center nowhere.

Willy quickly reconsidered and knew that one thing he did *not* want to do was be abandoned on an unknown road-side. But the cabby was insistent. He talked quickly and loudly and finally got out of the driver's seat, came around, yanked open the door, and began to pull Willy out. He kept pulling until Willy let go of the door handle and fell out onto the street.

Instead of speeding off, the cabby continued to mutter at Willy shaking his head and fists.

At that moment an idea came to Willy. In his jacket pocket was the letter he was going to mail to his parents when he was downtown. He'd never mailed anything to another country before, so he'd been extra careful addressing it and had carefully copied down the Whiteheads return address in case anything went wrong.

He pulled the letter out. Tentatively he showed it to the driver. The driver pointed to the return address and then to the cab. He looked at Willy. Willy shook his head up and down as fast as he could go. The driver took the envelope and pretended to turn an imaginary steering wheel. He gave Willy a broad grin. He got back inside the cab and motioned for Willy to get back in, too.

In ten minutes they were outside the Whiteheads' door. Willy was so relieved that his legs felt like Jell-O. The driver and the Whiteheads talked for some time, but Willy went straight inside and headed for his hammock. He didn't find out until later how he and his friends got separated at the stadium . . . but that's a different adventure!

THE END

Turn to page 141.

When Tina, Willy, and Joao got back to the boat, Jill showed them the berries she had picked.

"You didn't eat any of those did you?" Joao asked as Jim woke up and stretched.

"No. I waited to share them with you guys."

"Not even a few snitches while you waited?"

"No. What's the big deal?"

"Those berries are poisonous. Eating even a few could make you sick."

"Whew, good thing I remembered Mom's advice not to eat something unless I'm sure."

Tina laughed out loud. "I thought you were going to remember the advice my mom always gives Jim: 'Young man. If you sneak one more treat before we've all had time to sit down together and say grace, I'm going to spank you!'"

Jill laughed. "Either way it's good advice to remember. It saved my neck this time."

Joao said, "Speaking of mothers, are you four ready to head back to your parents, or would you like to meet my mother? She lives just a little farther down the river. It is getting a little late, though."

60

If the Ringers head back toward the Whiteheads' home, turn to page 98.

If the Ringers decide to visit Joao's mom, turn to page 115.

Willy's mom and dad were surprised and angry when they got his phone call. The flight had cost a lot of money. The opportunity to go to another country was rare and would probably never come again. And they knew he would get over his homesickness if he stayed. They insisted he just try to get over it.

Willy came unglued. "I can't believe you're going to make me stay here!" he choked through uncontrollable sobbing. "I can't believe it! I can't believe it!" That was all Willy kept saying, over and over.

After awhile, Willy's parents decided that this was serious. Maybe this time there was nothing to do but let Willy learn his lesson the hard way. They ended the traumatic phone call with instructions for changing his flight.

Willy got home, and the first day was great. He saw his folks and played with his cat Ezra. He ate corn on the cob and burgers on the grill for supper and slept soundly in his own bed. "Ah, America," he said to himself.

Willy's contentment didn't last long. Chris was spending the summer visiting his uncle. Pete's family was on vacation. Mr. and Mrs. Whitehead were busy too. Willy and Sam sat around a lot. You can only eat so much ice cream, and with only two people, you can't even get up a decent game of Five Hundred.

62

All in all it was a pretty boring summer. Willy wished he'd stayed in Brazil.

THE END

Turn to page 141.

Jill and Tina looked at each other, both thinking the same thing: *Soccer?* They were forgetting that soccer was a much bigger deal in Brazil than in the U.S. They had no idea a soccer game could be thrilling to watch. Jim picked up on their body language.

"It's nothing like you're thinking," Jim explained. "Going to a soccer game in this country is really exciting. The excitement in the stadium is awesome!"

"OK!" said Willy.

"Sounds great!" said Jill. As they thought more about it, they were glad Jim spoke up.

CHOICE

Turn to page 131.

It seemed like they walked forever. And then they walked some more. Jill had been sure at least a hundred times that she couldn't possibly take another step. But at least ninety-nine times she'd taken another step after all.

The bugs had been bad, and the heat and humidity were awful. Now thirst was the worst. Her canteen had been empty for hours, and her lips were starting to feel crackly. In her head she kept seeing a scene from some old black and white movie where a man is crawling across the desert on his hands and knees in search of an oasis and water. Except that there was water all around them. The stagnant pools they passed looked inviting. But Clay kept reminding them that they had no handy way to purify the water. They would have to wait until nightfall when they could build a fire and boil water.

The jungle vines kept brushing Jill's face and erased the movie image for a minute or two, but then the desert man would reappear. It was like having your brain caught in a revolving door—desert becomes vines becomes desert becomes vines, and through it all there was thirst. Desert—vines—desert.

Vines. *Vines!* Now a new television image was coming to her. Tarzan swinging through the jungle. Grabbing one vine, or liana, and then another and making his way across the screen.

Jill remembered reading that lianas are strong. Some weigh more than a ton. In some parts of the jungle, so many of these vines grow that they tie the tops of the trees together. When a tree dies or is cut, lianas may keep it from falling. Foresters often have to cut a whole group of trees before the one they want will fall down.

Somewhere in Jill's imagination she saw a flickery screen of Tarzan cutting into a liana. He shared the water stored there with Boy, and both of them were refreshed enough to go on swinging through the forest.

But Jill knew you had to be sure you cut into the right kind of vine. The water stored in some lianas is poisonous!

Jill was so thirsty. Lianas were all around her. They all began to look like refreshment straws to her. She had been given one of the big knives, called a machete, to carry. She was sure it would easily slice through a vine.

CHOICE

If Jill decides to cut open a liana and drink, turn to page 78.

If Jill decides to forget about the Tarzan image and leave the lianas alone, turn to page 134.

The four stood up. They listened for Pedro in the semi-darkness. No change. They began taking baby steps toward the door. Still he stayed slumped and silent.

They stepped closer to the door and listened again. Their hearts began to pound with excitement. They were about halfway to freedom.

If it hadn't been dark, or if the smugglers had been neater housekeepers, the foursome might have made it. But they were concentrating on the distance between themselves and the door rather than on the floor. Willy kicked an old metal bucket. The sound roused Pedro. He sat up and began shaking his head.

The Ringers crouched where they were and waited. Pedro started mumbling to himself. He got up and stretched. He definitely was not asleep. This was no time to try sneaking past their guard.

CHOICE

Turn to page 26.

Dawn found the four Ringers wide awake. Between the unfamiliar surroundings and the worrying about Senhor Barros, they'd been awake most of the night. They'd come to a decision, too: when Senhor Barros arrived, they were going to disappear!

When the first humming whir of a distant airplane engine broke the quiet, all four jumped to their feet. "Quick, it's time to go!"

Jim pushed out of the back window the screen they'd loosened the night before. Tina was already standing on the boxes they'd piled up below the opening. As soon as he backed out of the way, Tina jumped through the hole and started for the stand of trees behind the hut. Willy and Jim followed her quickly. Jim twisted and fell when landing, but he covered his mouth and only groaned silently. He limped to the trees as fast as possible. Only when he got there did he take time to rub his ankle.

"Are you OK?" Willy mouthed.

"It hurts, but right now that's the least of our worries."

They huddled silently. The whir had become a full-fledged buzz. An airplane landed on the "abandoned" strip.

The kids peered from their hiding place at the men who stepped out. Willy stared wide-eyed. "I saw that guy at the airport when we landed in Belem," he whispered.

68

Senhor Barros leaned against the plane and lit a cigarette. The other men fanned out. "They should be here with the birds soon, Boss," one called back. "They knew we'd come the day of the full moon."

The Ringers heard Senhor Barros give other directions, too. "Search that plane and make sure no one is in the hut."

Moments later they heard another voice call out, "There's been somebody sleeping in the hut. Looks like they've been here recently. They went out the back window."

"Check the woods. They may still be hanging around," was the leader's order.

It didn't take long. Despite their best efforts to become invisible, the Ringers were discovered. A scruffy man grabbed Jim and grunted to the rest of them, "Get out there by Senhor Barros."

CHOICE

Turn to page 125.

They had a long drive to get to the ranch. But it wasn't one of those trips where you wonder if you will *ever* get where you are going. Off in the distance they could see a cloud of smoke. They knew that the closer they got to that smoke, the closer they were to the ranch.

Willy spoke up and said he felt like the children of Israel in the wilderness. Seeing the pillar of smoke assured him that they were going in the right direction. The others laughed, but they could tell Hector couldn't quite understand the joke.

Finally they reached the source of the smoke. Hector let them out at a large ranch house.

"What is all this smoke anyway?" Willy asked. "It's like a campfire gone berserk."

"Not a bad guess," Hector answered. "The smoke is from fires the ranchers set. In order for their cattle to eat, they need to have grazing land. The first step toward making pastures is getting rid of the forest. So, the trees are systematically burned off."

"But there's so *much* smoke!" said Willy.

"These are *big* fires. Thousands and thousands of acres of Brazilian forest are being burned. The world's population is over five and a quarter billion people. Every single one of those people is breathing every minute of every day, exhaling carbon dioxide. Lots of them are using fire to cook. All the animals everywhere are breathing in oxygen and breathing out carbon dioxide. And still ranchers' fires in the Amazon are responsible for seven percent of all the carbon dioxide released in the whole world each year.

"Would you like to go and see the cattle, or would you rather watch the burning process?" Hector said to his guests.

If the kids choose to go see the cattle, turn to page 106.

If the kids choose to see the burning, turn to page 138.

"Let's just drive around," said Willy sleepily. "I'm not into walking right now."

"Drive around?" asked the others all at once in total surprise.

"And pass up a chance to see a real-live coffee plantation up close?" asked Jill. With nods of agreement, they vetoed Willy's suggestion.

Turn to page 99.

As embarrassing as it was to be fourteen years old and homesick, there was no doubt about it: Willy was fourteen and homesick.

He wished he could just talk it over with his mom and dad. Between his dad's good advice and his mom's hugs and hot chocolate, problem-solving sessions with them eventually ended with everybody smiling and with Willy ready to face his latest challenge. But since his mom and dad were a whole continent away, Willy decided to try the next best thing: Jim and Tina's folks.

Willy clambered up out of his hammock, threw on an oversized T-shirt, and shuffled reluctantly toward the Whiteheads' room. He knocked softly. An answer came immediately. "Come on in."

What could he say? "Well, um, Mr. and Mrs. Whitehead . . . um . . . What I needed to talk with you about was, um . . . well, everything is, uh, very nice here in Belem and everything, but it is, uh, well, uh, different from home and . . . well . . . I guess what I'm trying to say is that I sure do miss my house and all the stuff that goes with it."

Whew, he'd said it! Willy felt like he'd dropped a backpack stuffed full of encyclopedias he'd been carrying for blocks. He stared intently at his own feet wondering what the Whiteheads would think.

After a moment, Mrs. Whitehead spoke. "Loneliness

can catch up with you pretty quickly in a strange new place," she began. She slipped into a robe and led Willy toward the kitchen.

On the way, Willy sighed and said, "I wish I'd stayed home." He felt a lump in his throat, like he might start crying.

Mrs. Whitehead put a snack on the table and invited Willy to sit down. *How did she know food always makes me feel a little better?* he asked himself. "I guess I wouldn't make a very good missionary," he said, smiling at her.

"Because you're lonely and homesick?" responded Mrs. Whitehead. "Missionaries have those feelings, too."

"They do?" asked Willy in surprise. "You mean you get homesick?"

Mrs. Whitehead nodded and smiled in a way that made him warm all over. "You know, Willy, it takes a lot to become a missionary. David and I came here to tell people how they could have a personal relationship with Jesus Christ. We wanted groups of these new believers to band together and form churches throughout all of Brazil.

"That was a big dream, and we worked hard to see it come true. We graduated from Bible college and then took special training beyond that in evangelism and church planting. We traveled from church to church for nearly a year raising the money and prayer support we would need. We went to language school for two years to learn to speak Portuguese. When all of that was completed, our home church had a special service called a 'commissioning,' where they prayed for us and officially sent us out as missionaries to Brazil. When we waved good-bye to our families and stepped onto the plane bound for Brazil, I was just sure that God had wonderful things in store for us here."

"Well, he did, didn't he?" asked Willy.

"Of course he did, but that didn't mean it was easy. Missionaries have feelings just like you, Willy. The first week or two that we were here were very busy. We had barrels of household goods to unpack, and we went around meeting the other missionaries who were working here. We met our Brazilian neighbors and tried out our Portuguese at the local market. We found out that two years of language school hadn't given us much help in really talking to people. That was when the homesickness started."

"*You* were homesick?" said Willy in amazement.

"Sometimes they give it a special name: 'culture shock.' My new neighbors didn't speak my language, dress like me, or eat like me. And they weren't sitting around hoping that some missionary would show up and try to change them. As far as they were concerned, their lives were going just fine. It was up to me, with God's help, to become friends with those people and eventually show them his love. That was an awfully tough time, and sometimes I even wanted to go home."

"What did you do?"

"Little by little God has helped us through. I still get lonely for my kids sometimes. Those are the times I have to trust God. I know he'll help you, too, if you ask him to. Would you like me to pray with you about that?"

"Please," said Willy with a feeling of relief.

When they'd finished praying, Mrs. Whitehead smiled and said, "Willy, when you are back home and trying to think of something more specific to pray than 'God bless the missionaries,' maybe you can remember this evening and pray about the times they get lonely."

Just knowing that people like the Whiteheads had been homesick helped Willy feel better. Knowing they would be praying for him helped a lot.

He wasn't instantly "cured," but he headed back toward his hammock certain that this was a problem he and God could handle. Sleep arrived soon after Willy cautiously crawled into his swinging bed.

In the morning Mr. Whitehead had two suggestions. "Brazil is cutting down huge swathes of rain forest to make way for farms and roads. Many people move right behind the road builders and start towns along the highways. It's a hard life. Missionaries go there to minister to those people. You can go there today and see the work. I'm also setting up a flight over the rain forest so you can see it from the air. But, if you'd rather *do* some real missionary work instead of just *see* it, you could go back to the city and help with a special project."

CHOICE

If they go to the rain forest, turn to page 48.

If they go to the city, turn to page 15.

Willy scrambled to explain to the woman that he was about to be separated from his group, so another man offered to help. Willy sighed with relief, thanked the man, and caught up with Jill. The two of them caught up with Jim and Tina in the terminal, where they were waiting with their parents.

The reunited Whitehead family was hugging and kissing and smiling like crazy. The two United States natives were a little shy about breaking into the family reunion, so they stood back a few feet and waited.

Willy was startled when Mr. Whitehead suddenly turned to him. "These must be your friends!" he said smiling. Jim introduced Willy and Jill, and Mr. and Mrs. Whitehead politely shook their hands.

"Welcome to Brazil!" said Mrs. Whitehead. "We're so glad you could come. How was the flight?"

"Fine," said the two. They wanted to say more, but they were a little too overwhelmed. Besides, nothing really interesting happened anyway.

"Stay close to us," said Mr. Whitehead. "This airport is very busy and crowded, and we don't want to lose you guys." The group started to walk to the baggage area.

Jill rolled her eyes. "We already almost lost Willy," said Jill.

"Oh?" said Mrs. Whitehead with a questioning look.

Jill was eager to explain. "Yeah, he got lost at the airport at Washington right before the flight, looking for—"

"It wasn't my fault!" Willy said defensively. "The upstairs looks just like the downstairs."

"Well, in any case," said Mr. Whitehead, "you can get lost anywhere, so just stick close to us until we get to the Kombi."

CHOICE

Turn to page 43.

Turn to page 43.

Jill trudged along the path wondering to herself. The picture of Tarzan drinking from the liana had completely eliminated the picture of the desert man. But she couldn't bring Tarzan sharply into focus. Exactly what did that liana look like? Was there any way to know for sure which lianas were drinkable and which were poisonous? Jill wondered if her teacher, Mrs. Nordstrom, had covered that in biology class when Jill was daydreaming.

Soon it was getting to be like standing on the high diving board and trying to get up the nerve to jump off: out to the edge to peer over and then back to the safe end. Or like one of those phone conversations where no one wants to hang up first, so no one ever gets off the phone until a parent yells.

Come on, Jill, she told herself, *plug your nose and take the plunge.*

She did. She cut a slit in a liana, and liquid began to ooze out. She put it just barely to her lips and felt the moistness. She stuck out the very tip of her tongue for a tiny taste. It didn't *feel* poisonous. She took a lick, like an ice cream cone. One quick swirl and then another. Finally she let the liquid fill her mouth.

It was pure water. Drinkable, refreshing, delicious.

"Hey, you guys. Try this!" Jill shouted. Jim, Willy, Tina, and Clay turned around and stared at her. After a quick

review of how she had gotten the idea from an old
television show where Tarzan saved Boy's life, everyone
joined Jill in cutting lianas and drinking their precious
contents. Clay told them he had forgotten that trick
because he had never been in a situation like this before.
He thanked Jill for her creativity but reminded them all that
they probably ought to talk about any experiments before
one person tried them.

They still faced a long walk through a hot and humid
jungle, but for the moment they had plenty of water, and
they were together. Thanks to Jill, they knew they would
survive.

THE END

Turn to page 141.

Jill popped a few of the berries into her mouth. Mmmm, delicious. She took another handful. She checked the bucket, and it still had lots of berries in it, so she enjoyed a few more.

With her stomach full, Jill settled back to wait. She took her straw hat off, leaned back, and enjoyed the sunshine on her shoulders. It made her feel warm all over.

About fifteen minutes passed, and Jill began to feel more than just warm all over. She started to feel downright feverish. Not to mention dizzy. Maybe it was just too much sun.

Just about then, Joao returned to the boat with Willy and Tina. He looked sideways at Jill. "Are you getting seasick? You don't look too well."

"Maybe I've had too much sun. I had a snack of those berries and then have been sitting here . . ."

Joao fired the boat's motor and took off without so much as the common courtesy to listen to Jill's whole sentence.

Jim woke up with a start, "Wha . . . what happened?"

They sped downriver with Joao scanning the shoreline. At a tiny private dock, Joao landed and jumped off. He ran to a tiny hut, entered it, and emerged moments later carrying a handful of leaves. These he handed to Jill with the instructions, "Chew these. Quick."

Jill wasn't used to being ordered around like that, but Joao was her host, and he looked like he meant business.

Jill hadn't even chewed long enough to turn the leaves into a smooth mush in her mouth when she started to feel nauseous. A couple of more chews and her head was over the side of the boat, and her lunch was in the river, along with lots of red berries. Again and again she vomited.

When she finally sank on the bottom of the boat, Joao lectured her. "You should know better than to eat something just because it looks good! Haven't your folks warned you that sometimes things aren't what they look like? Those berries are poisonous! Those leaves were ipecac—the source for Syrup of Ipecac most parents keep in the medicine chest. In case of accidental poisoning, they produce just the effect they gave you. Ipecac has saved hundreds of kids' lives, even though they don't exactly enjoy the process. It's much quicker and safer than trying to rush a child to the hospital to have his stomach pumped."

Jill ran a hand over her damp brow. "I'm sorry, Joao," she said weakly. "I just didn't think. And pleasant or not, thanks for the leaves. I was lucky they were so close by."

Joao smiled at her sympathetically. "The rain forest is the only place in the world where ipecac grows," he commented. "In fact, as many as one-fourth of all the prescriptions dispensed in the U.S. contain a plant-derived active ingredient that is grown only in the rain forest. That's one reason we need to protect the rain forest—if we destroy too much of it, we might eventually lose people,

82

too. Right now, though, the important thing is to get you home to rest. You'll need a while to recover."

So Joao brought Jill and the others back up the river. The Whiteheads were very glad she was all right. They drove home, tucked Jill into her hammock, and brought her fruit juices.

Jill was happy her adventure on the Amazon River was over. She promised herself to be a little less impulsive during the rest of their time in Brazil. But she didn't want to give up having adventures!

THE END

Turn to page 141.

Jim backed silently away and closed the door. "I'll tell you what we should do," he said in a lowered voice. "Hide!"

All four kids crouched on the floor. They could see each other's eyes grow big with fear, but they never said a word. They stayed that way until their muscles ached from the stillness.

Outside they could hear voices. There seemed to be a group of people wandering around the runway for a while. Someone's name was called out several times, but the kids couldn't understand it. Willy discovered a knothole just above his head in the wall, and peered through it to watch what was happening. He saw one of the men call the others over and point to Clay's footprints going into the jungle.

The Ringers stayed frozen and silent, fearful that the intruders would check out the hut next. Strange animal sounds pierced the night.

Willy frantically searched his memory to see if there were cannibals living in the rain forest.

Then it was quiet. The sounds of mosquitoes and insect wings were the only breaks in the silence.

Whoever the visitors had been, they'd slipped back into the forest. Slowly the Ringers relaxed and stood looking at one another. Now all they could do was wait until Clay came back to rescue them.

84

THE END

Turn to page 141.

T hat night, the Ringers were overjoyed to see Hector and
an obviously reluctant Nathan show up just in time for the film.
Jill and Willy couldn't get over how warm the evening was,
and how many people were out on the streets and in the park.

"Sure wish we could do something like this in the
Common back in Millersburg," said Willy. "I wonder if
people in the States would come to the park to watch a
Christian film on a summer night?"

Jim laughed and said, "That's a great idea, Willy. Let's
figure out how to do it when we get back. I'm sure my
grandfather would help us set it up. He's been doing that
kind of stuff most of his life!"

As they all watched the film, Willy was amazed at
how similar life in Jesus' time was with many of the things
he had already seen in Brazil. There were dusty roads and
simple buildings—it seemed Jesus could have walked right
out of the film onto the streets of Belem.

Hector noticed Willy shaking his head in wonder and
asked, "What's up, Willy?"

Willy told him what he had been thinking.

Hector chuckled and said, "You may be more right than
you think. Did you know that Belem is the Portuguese word
for Bethlehem? Even I know that's where Jesus was born."

Jim, who was on the other side of Willy, added,
"Yeah, sometimes it does seem like Jesus fits into life easier

86

here than in the States. Dad says he's always learning about Jesus from people in the backcountry because they often live the way Jesus lived."

By the end of the film, it was Hector's turn to shake his head in amazement. "Do you guys really believe Jesus came back to life after he was dead? I always thought that was just a story."

Willy said, "All I can tell you is that ever since I believed Jesus was alive and wanted to be a part of my life, I've been a different person. He's really inside me, helping me to do what's right." As Willy spoke, he felt a charge of excitement. *So this is what sharing Christ is all about!* he thought.

Nathan hadn't said much all evening. As soon as the movie was over, he told the others something had come up and he wouldn't be able to go with them the next day out to Hector's farm. They were sorry to see him wander off into the night like he was looking for something.

Hector quietly said, "Nathan's been having a hard time. He doesn't think he can believe in anything." He paused, then added, "But this Jesus is very interesting to me. I want to think about him. Maybe we can talk some more before you leave Brazil."

"I'd like that," said Willy.

"Maybe we'll even have a chance to talk some tomorrow when you come out to visit my *fazenda*," Hector said as he waved good-night.

CHOICE

Turn to page 104.

"**J**ose said the reason they use burn areas is to keep the fires from burning out of control," Jill said. "He's been setting forest fires for years. He'd know whether or not burn areas work. If we stay here in the burned part we should be all right." The words sounded good, but if you listened to the way Jill said them, you knew she wasn't totally confident.

"Let's just sit here and wait it out," Jim suggested.

They sat.

They waited.

They watched the storm build up.

Even though they didn't want to, they also noticed that the fire was burning closer and closer.

The wind continued to blow.

The fire grew closer.

The burn area began to grow hot from the nearby flames.

"My eyes are starting to burn like crazy," Tina complained, rubbing her fists against her eyelids again and again.

"It's getting tougher and tougher to breathe," Willy coughed.

Hector looked at them. "We need to move toward the middle of the burn area. That will be the safest place."

They got up and headed toward the center of the

clearing. Smoke filled their lungs, but they kept walking together.

They walked to what they estimated was the center of the burn area. There was some improvement, but it didn't last long. Within five minutes it was as hot there as it had been in the last spot. In another ten minutes the heat was searing, and it was all but impossible to breathe.

"Try this. I heard a fireman in school describe it once," Jill croaked. She took the scarf she'd been wearing knotted at her neck as a decoration and tied it across her face.

"You look like a cross between a bank robber and the Lone Ranger," Willy cracked.

"Maybe so," Jill agreed, "but it filters out some of the soot in the air."

Anything that could make breathing easier was worth a try. Willy took off his shirt and tore strips for Tina and Jim as well as himself. They tied them in place and continued their struggle for air. The filters helped, but the fire was spewing out hot ash.

Jim pulled out his canteen and poured water over the "mask" of each of his friends.

Then there was nothing to do but wait.

The fire swirled at the edge of the clearing. Every breath was a struggle. The kids hated to breathe because the air was thick enough to make them choke and so hot it burned their lungs. But there was no alternative to breathing! So over and over the kids gasped for air. They sat in a circle huddled together and tried to breathe. Their eyes met and offered encouragement, even when talking was impossible.

Then, amidst the crackling sound of burning leaves came a peal of thunder. Every head looked straight up and then across the circle at each other. A second roll of thunder followed the first.

The first few raindrops were easily confused with the sweat rolling off each person's face. Then the misting gave way to a full-fledged downpour. The Ringers lifted their faces to the rain and let it soak them. The water fell in thick sheets. Clouds of steam rose from the fire. Willy jumped up and down in one of the instant puddles and yelled, "This is the world's biggest sauna!"

They knew that the protection of the burn area would hold. They were safe.

"We didn't exactly come out like Shadrach, Meshach, and Abednego," Tina said as she looked at the blackened faces of her friends. "Those guys came out of the fiery furnace without even smelling like smoke. I have the feeling we are going to be smelling like smoke for days. But we did come out. Thank the Lord!"

Jill added, "And thanks, Willy, for giving us the shirt off your back!"

THE END

Turn to page 141.

How can you trust a man who breaks the law and is cruel to animals? What if Senhor Barros changed his mind about letting the kids go? What if he was lying all along and was planning to finish them off when he was done with his other business?

They *had* to think of some way to escape.

The first order of business was to do something about the leg ties. Everyone knows you can't escape while you are tied up. The Ringers had seen enough Saturday morning television that they had some ideas about how to do that. "You're supposed to flex your muscles while you're being tied up so that when you relax the ropes have some slack," Willy expounded.

"And then all you have to do is wriggle, and they will fall off," Jim finished.

Unfortunately, they'd been too surprised and too frightened when they were being tied up to think about flexing their muscles, and the wriggling business didn't work nearly as well in real life as it did on the screen.

"So much for muscle power," Tina shrugged. "I guess we're going to have to use our brain power if we're going to get out of here."

"Any bright ideas?" Jim asked.

"Not yet. But, keep alert. Something may come to us."

Soon the hollow scared feeling in the bottom of their

stomachs was joined by a growing feeling of hunger. They hadn't had anything to eat all day, and, judging by the way the building was cooling off, it was now evening.

Pedro, the smuggler who had been left behind as a guard, got up from his chair and walked over to the back corner opposite from the kids. He pulled a brown bottle from the pile of paraphernalia dumped there. Then he returned to his chair in front of the doorway. For the next hour or so he took occasional gulps from the bottle. He tipped his head all the way back to get the last drops and then started toward the back corner again. He walked slowly, like he might be feeling sleepy. He dropped the first bottle alongside the pile and took another. When that was empty he came back for a third. The Ringers could tell by the way he stumbled toward the pile what had been in the bottles.

Pedro slumped into his chair. Gradually his breathing became more and more regular. Maybe he was falling asleep.

"I've got an idea!" Tina whispered. "If there's any broken glass in that pile we could use it to cut these ropes."

"Sounds good, Sis," Jim whispered back. "If we can just skooch over there and get some, maybe we can break out of here."

"One person skooching would be the quietest," Tina said. "Here I go."

She tried to keep quiet by moving very gradually. She moved along the wall about as fast as the hour hand moves around the face of the clock. You never actually saw her moving, but eventually she was there. She flashed a huge smile and an OK sign across the back of the room. She'd found a piece of broken glass. The return trip across the wall was quicker. When she reached her friends, Jim and Willy both held out their hands, wanting to be first to be released. A few minutes of silent sawing, and they were free. They rubbed their legs and wrists while Tina cut Jill's and her own bonds.

Now they could move freely. But should they? Pedro's arms hung limp beside his body, but a gun was slung around his waist. Did they dare make a break for it?

CHOICE

If they try to escape, turn to page 66.

If they should wait until they are sure that Pedro is asleep, turn to page 26.

Mr. Whitehead gestured toward the tall man in the baseball cap who was smiling as he approached. "Kids, I'd like for you to meet Clay. He'll be taking you for a flight over the rain forest. He is a missionary pilot. He provides a terrific service for guys like me."

Mr. Whitehead smiled at the group, then continued. "Even with all the new roads being built, getting around can be pretty tricky. Some local 'roads' aren't much more than paths, and they become impassable when it rains. Some areas used to be reachable only by using the river boats, and that took days. In mountainous areas there are people who can only be reached by climbing for days. Airplanes and helicopters change those long trips into minutes. Clay is part of a whole organization of pilots that provides transportation for missionaries. They can get us where very few have walked before!"

The kids climbed over the wing strut and into the cabin of the Cessna 185 and waved good-bye to Mr. Whitehead. Willy sat next to the pilot. Jill and Jim sat in the back seat, and Tina got what's called the jump seat—a small storage area in the back of the plane.

Willy held his breath as Clay revved the engine. The propeller was turning so fast that it was invisible now. Between the droning and the shaking, he wondered if the plane could withstand much more. He felt a little silly about that, but he noticed that Jim and Tina were holding their breath, too.

The plane bumped down the dirt runway heading straight for the trees at its end. Willy was about to forget about being cool and shut his eyes tight when he felt the plane lift off the ground. The nose took a sharp turn up, and one second later the bumping from the runway was replaced with the rush of air. Looking out his window he could see the tops of the trees just beneath them. This was a lot closer and more personal than flying in a big airliner.

Clay smiled. "No matter how many times I take off, I never quite get over it. It's a thrill and an adventure every time."

Seen from above, the rain forest looked like a sea of solid green. The sea was made up of the trees that scientists call the canopy. They grow to be more than 100 feet high and act almost like an umbrella for the jungle beneath them. Willy saw a super tree, or emergent, poking up here and there.

They hadn't been in the air too long when Jim thought he smelled something hot. Clay seemed to be unusually busy. Jim knew that pilots routinely set their aircraft on auto pilot and enjoy the view with their passengers until it was time to land, but Clay was fussing with one dial after another. Who was he talking with over the radio?

A puff of smoke came from somewhere. Clay shook the transmitter in his hand and announced, "It's gone dead. The radio is out." The puff of smoke was replaced by a billowing black cloud that filled the cabin. Jim knew even before Clay opened his mouth that they were in trouble.

"We've got some kind of electrical problem. It's pretty serious. We are going to have to put down right away. There used to be a small strip a couple of minutes from here. It isn't used anymore. I'm not sure what condition it will be in, but it's our best shot. With God's help we'll make some kind of a landing and then figure out what to do from there."

The pilot shut down the engine, and they began to glide. Willy shut his eyes tight and waited for the bump of landing. The only sound was the soft whistle of the wind. No one seemed to even be breathing. The gentle motion of silent flight was pretty exciting until Willy remembered something he had heard about falling from high places—it wasn't the fall that killed you; it was the landing.

But the horrible roller coaster Willy dreaded never happened. The plane didn't threaten to tip over as it hit a huge rut or root in the runway. They did not crash into overgrown forest as the plane hurtled down a forsaken airstrip. They just landed—like a large metal bird settling in to its favorite roost.

"Praise the Lord!" Jim yelled. "We're down safe!" He thought to himself how much he had just sounded like his dad. He was glad he had been taught to thank God when God protected him from danger.

Clay joined the Ringers in thanking God, but he seemed distracted and a bit puzzled. He muttered something to himself about the airstrip being in great condition for not having been used in months.

Clay quietly began to examine the plane. Willy

remembered Mr. Whitehead mentioning that missionary pilots were trained in repairing planes as well as flying them. For a long time Clay worked with his head under the cowling. Finally he wiped his hands on his jeans and addressed the group: "We have some serious decision making to do. That smoke we saw was part of a fire that just about destroyed our electrical system. A minute or two more in the air just now, and we would have lost our hydraulic system, too. We wouldn't have been able to land. God really was watching over us! All this means we can't fly without repairs. Worse than that, it means our radio is out and we have no way of notifying anyone of our situation or location."

"So, what do we do now?" asked Willy.

"Well, we filed a flight plan, but it will be nighttime before anyone misses us. In the morning, when they can start to look, we won't be where they expect us. Finding a plane that has gone off course in Nebraska can take a week. Here, with the dense canopy, it could take a month."

He paused for a moment to let the seriousness of the situation sink in. The gang listened to his every word.

"As I see it, we have two choices. First, we can all hike out together. It will be an awfully tough trip through the jungle. The walk would take about four days, and we don't have many supplies. Otherwise, I will walk out alone and bring back help. You kids could stay here in that hut we laughingly called the terminal. I might be able to make better time walking solo, but that leaves you kids here alone. I don't know you well enough to know if you are ready to handle that. You'll have to decide for yourselves."

CHOICE

If the kids decide to hike out through the jungle, turn to page 30.

If the kids decide to stay alone in the hut, turn to page 19.

Joao turned the canoe back. The Ringers continued to watch the shoreline for exotic animals.

Long before they felt ready, Joao had them back where the river adventure had begun. They thanked him, climbed out of the canoe, and headed toward the Whiteheads' car.

But they promised themselves they would try to spend other days exploring the river.

THE END

Turn to page 141.

The gang told Hector to pull over. "We've *gotta* see this," said Jill. Hector stopped the truck.

"Those white flowers are just like the apple blossoms you see at home. They show that the tree is going to produce a crop," Hector explained.

"Or those famous Washington, D.C., cherry blossoms!" added Jill.

Hector smiled, then described how coffee is grown. "The coffee berry begins growing while the bush is still blossoming. After the tree has stopped blossoming the berry will ripen. It will change from green to yellow to red.

"Each tree yields about one and one-half pounds of berries, about enough for one pound of roasted coffee."

"Wonder if anybody here has seen Juan Valdez?" Willy chimed in.

"You've seen too many TV commercials," Hector laughed. "But a coffee plantation needs lots of workers. We don't use big machines; coffee beans have to be picked by hand. After they are picked, the berries are put through a sluice of running water. Sticks, leaves, and bad berries float to the top while good berries sink to the bottom. Every coffee berry has two beans or seeds. Each bean is covered with two skins. The skins are removed, and the beans are run through a series of fermenting and washing tanks. Next they are dried and left to cure for several weeks. Finally the fermented beans are roasted, bagged, and sold.

"Brazil is the world's number one producer of coffee. But we do more than grow coffee. We love drinking it. Here, coffee isn't just for grown-ups. Children enjoy it too. Let's go inside and have a cup."

Jill and Willy were surprised by what Hector had in mind when he said "cup." They met his parents and were ushered into the dining room where they noticed miniature cups set at each place. Willy picked his up and looked at it. It was small enough that he could wrap his hand around it and just about hide it in his palm.

"Welcome to our custom called the *cafezinho,*" said Hector's dad. "That means 'little coffee' in Portuguese. We enjoy our *cafe com leite* in the morning, but during the day, Brazilian workers often stop for a *cafezinho*. It's very strong coffee in a small cup, with lots of sugar added."

Willy had never seen coffee that black before. He watched Jim fill his cup about a third full of sugar. The woman who was serving them poured into their cups what Willy later described as molten, black lava fresh from a volcano. His own cup was so hot he couldn't drink it for quite a while. But there were plenty of tasty pastries to try while he waited.

As he sipped his drink, he thought of all the new experiences he'd be able to tell his friends and family when he got back to the States.

THE END

Turn to page 141.

"**I** think we should go see what they want," Jim said quietly. The others looked at him in surprise.

"I think you're right," Tina said after a minute. Willy and Jill nodded.

"Lead on," Willy said to Jim. Jim paused for a moment, drew a deep breath, then crouched and slowly put one foot beyond the door. Cautiously he stepped completely outside the hut, then checked over his shoulder to be sure his friends were following. The four edged toward the runway.

The mystery visitors caught sight of them. For a minute there was waving and shouting, and the Ringers wondered if they had made the right decision.

But whatever the visitors wanted, they weren't violent. They didn't intend to harm anyone.

They were waving to catch the kids' attention. They approached wearing big smiles and carrying even bigger bundles. They began an animated conversation in some unknown language. Their talking was punctuated with some kind of animal screeching that seemed to be coming from the bundles.

"Hey, I think I understand a little bit of what they are saying," Jim said in excitement.

"Well, clue the rest of us in," Tina answered.

Jim gave her one of those looks reserved for little

sisters. "They're speaking a local dialect. I learned a little bit of it when Mom and Dad were assigned to Porto Velho, back before their last furlough. I've forgotten some of it, but I'm doing my best to catch what they are saying, and I'll catch you up when I get a chance." Jim turned back to the visitors. The others watched all the pointing, shrugging, frowning, smiling, and gesturing without having any clue to what was being said.

Suddenly, the man who seemed to be the leader of the group opened one of the bundles. Inside was a rare South American parrot, with feathers of brilliant blue, yellow, green, red, and purple. That explained the screeching sounds.

What Jim couldn't figure out right away was what had caused these men to come to the airstrip with all these birds.

CHOICE ➤

If the Ringers invite the visitors to join them in the hut, turn to page 12.

If the Ringers return to the hut alone, turn to page 118.

104

Hector arrived at dawn to take the Ringers to meet his family and see their ranch. Jill, Willy, Jim, and Tina piled into Hector's pickup, and they set off.

It was a crisp beautiful morning. The scenery was incredibly lush and green. Before long the whole gang was singing silly songs (like "I've Been Workin' on the Railroad" and "Bill Grogan's Goat," complete with all the motions), camp songs, and hymns in three-part harmony. Hector didn't know many of the fun songs, but he did laugh at all the right parts, and he listened closely to some of the Christian songs the Ringers were singing.

After a while they came to a fork in the road. "What do you want to see first?" Hector asked, "The coffee plantation or the ranch and the cattle?"

 **CHOICE**

If the Ringers go to the coffee plantation, turn to page 36.

If the Ringers go to the ranch, turn to page 69.

"I vote for the church!" Jill said, raising her hand.

"Great idea," Jim responded, raising his hand in agreement. Tina and Willy followed suit, and so it was decided.

While they were finishing their drinks and getting ready to go, the Ringers started to tell Nathan about the old church in their neighborhood back home in Millersburg. It wasn't as old as the Merces church, but it was very special. That was where Willy and the Whiteheads had first gotten together and become friends. Exploring that old church had been a terrific adventure.

But the more they talked and thought about it, the more the kids decided that those adventures couldn't be topped in any other old church. They decided to visit some other places in Belem instead.

CHOICE ⇒

If they decide to go to the Ver-o-Peso Market, turn to page 22.

If they decide to go to the research laboratory, turn to page 40.

If they decide to go to the port, turn to page 32.

If you've ever been to a cattle ranch in Iowa or Nebraska, you wouldn't be impressed with what you can see in Brazil. The kids went with Hector and the ranch owner out to see his livestock. To tell the truth, they were a bit scrawny. (Naturally, the Ringers were too polite to bring this up, so they never found out that one reason cows don't gain weight well in Brazil is that the grazing land is so poor.)

Jill was such an animal lover that she just couldn't resist approaching one of the cows. She started stroking his neck like most kids would cuddle a kitten. "Oh, you're a beautiful animal," she whispered. "So strong and beautiful. I wish you could come live in my backyard."

"I wish you could come and live in my backyard," Jim mimicked.

"I wish you could come and live in my backyard," Willy chimed in with a falsetto voice.

"You boys cut it out. Leave Jill alone," Tina scolded in a playful way.

In unison the boys mocked, "You boys cut it out."

The chase was on. Tina took off after Jim and Willy, her black pigtails flying in the wind. The boys were older, but she was an excellent runner and quickly began to catch up to them. Jill stood by her adopted friend and smiled at the ruckus.

In the excitement of the race, they forgot a very basic characteristic of cow pastures. It wasn't long until they had stepped in it. Jim hit the first brown pile, and his feet slipped out from underneath him. Tina continued her pursuit until she too had stomped in a cow pie.

They slunk back to the rancher's house to clean up. They were quiet and a bit embarrassed, but they had their arms around each other's shoulders, and they were still friends.

THE END

Turn to page 141.

Willy rolled over again in the hammock. This time he remembered to be careful. It wasn't like home, but he'd manage.

Maybe he could just count sheep until he fell asleep. Or maybe, since he was in Brazil, he should count two-toed sloths, or toucans, or parrots . . .

Ninety-eight, ninety-nine, one hundred. Counting was nearly useless, no matter what he counted. Willy was still awake and still homesick.

Maybe reciting Bible verses would help. His folks taught him John 14:27: "My peace I give unto you . . . . Let not your heart be troubled, neither let it be afraid."

Leonard Whitehead had helped the Ringers learn lots of verses. Willy tried to mentally recite as many as he could.

"I can do all things through Christ who strengthens me."

"I will not fail thee nor forsake thee. Be strong and of a good courage."

"Fear not, for I am with you; be not dismayed; for I am your God: I will strengthen you; yes, I will uphold you with my right hand."

Willy knew that God was with him, but he was still homesick.

He listened to the crickets and wished he was at home. His eyes filled up with tears. He waited for morning and wondered how many more nights he'd spend like this. He decided he'd just have to live his way through his homesickness day by day.

In the morning Willy kept quiet. He ate his bread and sugary coffee and then got ready to start exploring Brazil.

Mr. Whitehead had two suggestions. "Brazil is cutting down huge swathes of rain forest to make way for farms and roads. Many people move right behind the road builders to start cities along the way. Missionaries go there to work with those people. If you'd like, you can go there today to see the work, and I'll arrange for you to take a flight over the rain forest. If you'd rather *do* some real missionary work instead of just *looking* at it, you could go back to the city and help out with a project."

CHOICE

If they go to the rain forest, turn to page 48.

If they go to the city, turn to page 15.

It was a nearly endless night.

"These ropes are cutting sores in my legs," Willy whispered.

Jim commiserated, "My legs are all pins and needles from not being able to move."

"I'd give anything even to be back in the comfort of that abandoned hut," Tina chimed in. "The floor was hard, but at least it was clean and we had blankets. We were alone, but we felt safe."

"Yeah, safe . . . ."

That was the real problem. Even if they'd had their own hammocks or their pillows and mattresses, or some magical bed from "The Princess and the Pea," no one could sleep under these conditions.

Would Senhor Barros ever return? If he did come back, would he really let them go?

After what seemed like days but was only till the wee hours of the morning, Pedro the guard slumped into a chair wedged in front of the door and began to snore. That sound was like the ticking of a time bomb. It was so regular. So peaceful. Over and over, it seemed to ask the kids, "What next, what next?"

It must have finally become morning because Pedro stopped snoring, pulled himself out of the chair, and began to stumble around. He drank his breakfast out of a dark bottle and then started rummaging around. From a cabinet that seemed mostly filled with greasy tools and cans of fresh oil, he took out a box of dried cereal. The box had been wet at least once and the lettering was smeared. He threw it at the corner with one word: "Hungry?"

"That stuff looks like it was originally served to President Lincoln," Jim said. "I wouldn't eat it on a bet."

"I thought you were the guy who could survive on nuts, berries, and grubs you scavenged in the forest," Willy replied. "You'd better choke some down. You may need all the energy you can muster before this is over. Besides, I doubt Pedro will offer you anything better. Think about John the Baptist surviving in the wilderness on locusts and wild honey. Open your mouth, shut your eyes, and chew."

Tina tried some. The cereal was slightly moldy. It had gone past crispy, on to crumbly, and then finally to chewy weeks ago. She tried to imagine the stale bits were a Denver omelet hot off the stove. That was quite a challenge even for her vivid imagination, but she knew Willy was right. They needed energy to face whatever lay ahead.

The wait continued. They thought about the possibilities. What if this? What if that? But one thing was certain. Even if Senhor Barros decided to kill them, each of his captives was ready to die. Tina, Willy, Jim, and Jill each knew Jesus personally. They had asked him to forgive their sins. They weren't anxious to die—they hoped to spend many more years on earth. But they knew that if they did die, their eternal future was secure. They huddled together and whispered encouragement to each other.

Without warning, a banging sound echoed through

112

the hangar. The door opened and was quickly shut again.

Senhor Barros was flashing a huge wad of bills. "Here's your share." He counted out a small stack and thrust them toward Pedro. "Except for those stupid kids, this was a smooth operation. I'm booked on an international flight in less than two hours. I'm taking a few months rest. Maybe we'll work some other area together again some day. Let the brats go after dark."

Then he was out the door, looking like a dapper businessman just going on a vacation.

When evening finally came, Pedro untied the Ringers, then just walked out the door and left them to their own devices. They found security personnel at the airport who helped them call the Whiteheads, and they finally returned safely home. Eventually they met with the authorities and gave them descriptions of Senhor Barros and his men. But they really couldn't do much beyond that.

From that day on they always wondered, "What ever happened to Senhor Barros? Is he still smuggling parrots?" They prayed that, somehow, God would stop him. One thing was for sure: it was an adventure they would never forget.

THE END

Turn to page 141.

Willy turned and desperately whispered to the others, "Let's get out of here!"

"What's the rush?" Jim asked.

Willy looked toward the empty chicken coops and rolled his eyes. Jim nodded, and they got on their way. They moved along between the crowded stands and the shoppers as quickly as they could without breaking into a jog and looking suspicious. They made a right turn and then a left, trying to get out of the sight of anyone who might be staring at them.

The five of them kept walking until they were well out of reach of the sound of the squawking chickens and the gentleman trying to round them up.

They sat on a curb and looked at each other.

"How did you manage that one, Willy?"

"I don't know exactly. I guess I just wasn't paying attention."

They decided it was time for a snack. They sat down to enjoy it. They peeled the fruit in silence. It was ripe and delicious, but nobody was really able to enjoy it. It stuck to their throats like peanut butter when they tried to swallow.

Tina shifted and started to speak very softly. "I think maybe you weren't the only one to goof up today, Willy. I enjoyed spending time with you, Nathan, and it was fun to see the market again, but we were supposed to be helping pass out those flyers for the film tonight. We got distracted from that and left the job for someone else to try to finish up. It was an easy mistake to not be paying attention and bump those chickens. But instead of all staying and facing the consequences together, we ran off. Guess we need some practice in facing responsibilities and meeting them. We're not as grown up yet as we think."

They all nodded their heads. Willy and Jim stood up and shook hands with Nathan. "We gotta be going. We need to meet back at the car at 3:00. Maybe we can still pass out a few flyers before then. We'll see you again another day. But I hope we'll see you at the movie tonight."

From Nathan's smile they weren't sure if he'd be there or not.

THE END

Turn to page 141.

Heading for Joao's mother's house, the canoe made its way along the river for what seemed like a long time. When Joao pulled over to the bank, it looked like he was docking in a totally undeveloped area. There was nothing to see but river bank and bush.

"Follow me," Joao said. They hiked through woods and empty fields, following a small path until they came to a clearing. From the clearing you could see a series of small huts. "Maybe this is more like the Brazil you expected to find," he said with a smile. "My family has lived off the land for generations. We earn our living tapping rubber trees and gathering nuts."

"Isn't that difficult?" Tina wondered.

"That depends on what you mean by difficult. Tapping rubber trees isn't difficult. You can learn it easily by watching your mother or father and then practicing. People with no idea what they are doing can be trained in the cutting technique in just one week. If you can't get the hang of it in one week, you'll never be a rubber tapper.

"It's a lot like making maple sugar. We make a cut in the tree bark and hang a small cup beneath it. In a few hours we come back and collect the liquid that has dripped into the cup. This liquid, which is really latex, will thicken into a gluey mass. The latex can't be sold at that stage. We boil it, wash it, and let it dry. Then we sell it. The man who purchases it from us sells it to the tire factories in the south of Brazil."

"That doesn't sound so tough," Jim commented.

"It's not. In some ways, though, it is very difficult. Henry Ford tried to create a rubber empire by growing rubber trees on farms, but when he cut the protective canopy down, the rubber trees died off. People are trying rubber farms again, and with the ability to develop hybrid trees, it may work better this time.

"But it's difficult for my family because we've never owned the land. Until now, we've lived in the forest and found what we need to survive. But now much of the forest is being sold to ranchers.

"The land quality is poor, so it takes five acres to graze a single head of cattle, then you need five different acres the next year. So ranchers continue to clear the forest. The more trees they cut and burn, the fewer there are for us to get rubber from so we can live.

"Some 'ranchers' are really land developers. They have been given or have purchased huge plots of land from the government. Then they don't use the land at all. They just wait until it goes up in value and they can sell at a profit.

"Today, there is tremendous tension between the ranchers and the squatters in my country. People like my family are trying to get the government to grant us areas of land so we can continue to live as we always have. Ranchers don't want any of the land given to squatters. It's a very difficult situation, and it often has led to bloodshed. Ranchers threaten squatters to force them to move on. If the squatters don't go, sometimes they are shot. About two hundred and fifty squatters are killed every year, and so far the police have been unable to stop the killings."

In the distance a shot rang out. The Ringers looked at each other and their host in alarm.

"I think someone is just hunting his dinner," Joao reassured them. "But we do need to get out of here. Your parents will be waiting to feed you dinner. Come and meet my mother. Later on I would love to show you more of my river."

Later that night, as the Ringers sat around talking about the day, they agreed they all were learning that life can be very hard in many places of the world. They prayed for Joao and his family.

THE END

Turn to page 141.

Before long, the visitors headed back into the forest, and Jim, Tina, Jill, and Willy returned to the hut. Tina asked Jim what he had been able to understand—if he'd figured out who those people were and what were they doing there.

"I couldn't make out all the details, but they thought that we were this Senhor Barros. He is supposed to show up here and buy those parrots from them."

"Jim, isn't that illegal?" Tina wondered.

"I think so. I'm pretty sure that parrots are animals that the government has now passed laws to protect. For years there was a steady trade of exotic animals out of the rain forest and into places where people want unusual pets. Unfortunately, the animals suffered after being captured, were often mistreated, and if they didn't die on the way, they often ended up in places that were not able to properly care for them. Besides all that, the demand for unusual pets has led to the depletion of some species. Now the government protects them from capture and export.

"But it's a hard law to enforce. There's lots of money in smuggling, and many are tempted to get involved for that reason alone. Catching poachers and smugglers isn't easy. If one suspects he's being followed, he can abandon the animals, leaving them to fend for themselves. Once the animals leave the country, they are impossible to track."

"So what can we do about it?" Willy wondered. "If it *is*

illegal, how could we stop it? I know Christians are supposed to take care of the earth and what's on it, but it sounds like a dangerous deal to me. Four kids alone in the jungle facing off against some smuggling ring. Maybe the part of God's creation we need to take good care of is ourselves!"

"I'm all for that," said Jim, "But let's not forget that God takes care of us, too. This is a golden opportunity to trust him."

If the kids choose to confront Senhor Barros in the morning, turn to page 125.

If the kids decide to hide when Barros arrives, turn to page 67.

Willy tried to wait while the throng filed out. But the crowd carried him along. He was pulled toward the exit like a cork bobbing in a river eddy. He did his very best not to panic.

As soon as the crowd had thinned enough that Willy could establish a direction of his own, he sat down. He constantly scanned the crowd looking for a familiar face. No good. He remembered his mother telling him before family outings at the zoo, the beach, or the state fair, "If anyone gets lost, stay still. We'll come looking for you." With all the self-discipline he could muster, he forced himself to stay in one place. Sooner or later they'd come looking for him. The stadium was nearly empty. Still no help in sight.

He noticed a guy waving a flag, but didn't pay much attention. But for some reason, he looked again. *Hey, wait a minute. That's not a flag that guy is waving!* Willy thought excitedly. *That's Jim waving his red jacket and trying to catch my attention!* Willy was so relieved. He jumped up and down and waved back.

They ran across aisles and met with a big bear hug. "We've been looking all over for you, Willy. What happened?" Jim asked.

Willy shuddered and answered, "I'll tell you this for sure. From now on when I have an adventure, I hope to

have some of the rest of the Ringers along. Excitement
alone is no fun!"

THE END

Turn to page 141.

Deciding to run is one thing. Knowing where to run is another.

Where do you run to get away from a fire? What if there was another fire burning toward them from over the next hill?

"We need to head toward where the rancher dropped us off. Both he and Jose would start to look for us there," Willy said.

That made sense, but it brought up a whole new problem. What if people were out looking for them? Were their potential rescuers in danger too?

"Let's move. Everybody stick together," said Hector.

Sticking together was no easy matter. Thick smoke made it difficult to keep their eyes open enough to see where the others were. The charred stubble of the burn area gave way to heavy foliage growth as they got to the area that hadn't yet been cleared. It was hard to keep track of each other and find a way through the trees.

The wind blew more smoke toward them. It filled their lungs until it was hard to run. Tina fell and scraped her leg, but there was no time for sympathy. She pulled herself up and kept struggling toward the goal.

Jim was coughing almost constantly from the smoke he'd inhaled.

The smoke and the forest made it difficult to see, so it

was almost a surprise when Willy stepped onto the road. "It's here," he tried to call to the rest, but his voice was so choked he couldn't be heard. He waved his arms. He took off his red shirt and waved that too, so the other four could see him.

As he waved, he heard the sharp blast of a Jeep's horn. Down the road came the rancher.

"Thank goodness you're all safe!" the rancher exclaimed. "Jose came to the house and told me that you were supposed to be at the edge of the burn area, but that when they saw the storm coming up and went to retrieve you, you had disappeared. We've been searching for you."

The ride home didn't seem so rough. Nobody minded the ruts and bumps. They were together, and they were safe. Besides, they'd always enjoyed those bumper car rides. And since they all reeked of smoke, they didn't mind that either.

THE END

Turn to page 141.

124

Nathan was full of ideas about what the group should do and see. He turned his cap backward, took a deep bow, and started up in a phony tour guide voice: "Ladies and gentlemen. Welcome to beautiful Belem. As you may know, Belem was founded in 1616 and is located at the mouth of the Amazon River. Some of the buildings you will see here date back to the seventeenth century. We are the nearest to the United States of any of Brazil's port cities. In addition to many other worthy tourist attractions, we have the Ver-o-Peso Market, the Merces Church (the oldest building in the city), the virus research laboratory, and the port itself. Which would you like to see first?"

If they go to the Ver-o-Peso Market, turn to page 22.

If they go to the Merces Church, turn to page 105.

If they go to the research lab, turn to page 40.

If they go to the port, turn to page 32.

"Who are you kids, and what are you doing here?" Senhor Barros demanded as soon as he saw them.

Jim spoke for the group. "I'm Jim. This is my sister, Tina, and our friends Willy and Jill. We're in Brazil visiting my parents. We were taking a tour over the rain forest, but our plane had electrical problems, and we had to land here. The pilot is hiking out to get help."

"That the plane you came in?" Barros grunted, jerking his head in the direction of the grounded Cessna.

"Yes, and we were thinking . . ." Jim began.

"You kids have made a peck of trouble for me," Barros interrupted gruffly.

The parrot hunters were now approaching the runway with their bundles.

Senhor Barros surveyed the scene and made a decision. "Throw the kids in the back," he barked. "Get the birds loaded, and let's get out of here. Somebody might show up looking for them, and that could really mess us up. We'll figure out how much they know and what to do about it after we're out of here."

Tina was about to politely explain that Clay had only been gone one day so there was no chance that he'd be back so soon, and since they knew almost nothing about Senhor Barros, he and his men might just as well leave them here and forget the groups had ever met. But one of the men shoved her toward the cargo bay. Willy and Jim were pushed in, too. By the time Jill got packed in the plane, things were getting crowded. Boxes of birds got thrown in next. Then the door slammed shut, and soon the engine roared to life.

The kids tried to find places to sit on the floor. It was filthy. Bird droppings had spilled everywhere. There was an unidentifiable rotting mass that smelled horrible in the corner of one cage. At least two birds were already dead—still beautiful but with eyes unblinking. Other birds looked very ill.

In addition to the smell and the dirt, there was the sound. The parrots screeched wildly when the plane bounced through an air pocket or dipped a wing to turn.

With the sounds of the trapped birds and the engine as cover, the four tried to figure out what to do next. They were fresh out of good ideas. Senhor Barros was definitely a crook. Was he dangerous to them as well as to the beautiful parrots? What would he do to them when they got to wherever it was they were going?

After a while, Tina noticed the plane's gradual descent. "We must be landing," she said.

"If only I could get a look outside. Maybe I could figure out where we are," Jim hoped aloud.

They never got a glimpse of the outdoors. The plane landed and taxied straight to a private hangar. The hangar door was slammed shut immediately. Kids and birds were roughly hauled from the plane into the dark hangar.

"Get those kids out of the way. Put them in the corner for now. Better tie up their hands and feet so they don't get ideas about going anywhere."

Those instructions were followed, and the Ringers were dumped in a back corner like so much garbage.

Suddenly there was a knock on the hangar door. Senhor Barros turned toward the corner where the Ringers were piled. "I've got a delivery to make. My last pickup is in the morning. We'll deliver that tomorrow noon. Pedro will watch you till sundown tomorrow. By then I'll be out of this area for good. Don't get smart. Don't pull any funny stuff, and you'll get out of this OK."

Without waiting for their response, Senhor Barros motioned to his men. He climbed into the plane. Within one minute the hangar door had opened, and he was gone.

CHOICE

If the Ringers try to escape, turn to page 90.

If the Ringers decide Barros is telling the truth, turn to page 110.

"*Help!*" Willy shouted to Nathan, Jill, Jim, Tina, and anyone else who might be willing to lend a hand. "We gotta help this guy. I ran into his stand and knocked over the cages, and now his chickens are all over."

The chase was on. If you could have just sat on top of one of the vegetable stands and watched it happen, you would have had to chuckle.

When the coops were knocked over, chickens escaped like popcorn being cooked with the popper uncovered. Bundles of white were flying in every direction.

The woman in charge of the pastry stall across the aisle was grabbing ponchos from her neighbor's display and trying to cover the baked goods before they were ruined with chicken feathers. The poncho lady didn't want anything to leave her store that hadn't been paid for, so they were playing tug of war with a poncho.

Now that he was actually faced with trying to catch one, it occurred to Willy that he didn't particularly like chickens. He chased the smallest chick to a corner and then tried to figure out how to get it back to its owner. "Here chick, chick, chick, let's go back to your cage," definitely wasn't going to cut it. Finally he scooped the chick into his baseball cap, and took off his left shoe to cover the hat so the chick couldn't escape (and so he didn't actually have to touch it).

He made his way back to the chicken stand. No one was there. The owner was chasing his valuable merchandise up and down the aisles, so Willy had to stand there and blush while shoppers stared at him. By the time Willy got rid of the chick, it had left him a nice surprise in his cap.

Nathan was crawling under tables trying to corral a chicken. He would just about catch up, and the chicken would take off again. Vendors held onto their goods to keep them from spilling while the chase went on. It continued under table after table and then back toward where it had begun.

Tina came flying around the corner. She stretched out both hands and grabbed for a chick just as it lighted on a fruit stand. She missed and fell into the stand. Melons went rolling in every direction.

Now the chicken chasers had to be careful not to fall over the melons. The scene looked like something out of a "Here's Lucy" rerun. Finally, the last chicken was captured and carried back to the local businessman.

He might very well have been angry at Willy, but he just shook his head and muttered, "Kids." His face softened, and he continued, "I got a boy just about your age at home. Some days he's so busy thinking about one thing or another that he can't walk and chew gum at the same time. Bumpin' into some stand is the sort of thing he might do. If he ever does, I sure hope he's like you and sticks around rather than slinking off like a snake. Thanks for catching my chickens. I appreciate the help. You five are good kids."

Of course, Jill and Willy couldn't understand a word, but the others filled them in as soon as they got away from there.

130

THE END

Turn to page 141.

On their way to the soccer match, Miguel told Jill and Willy about the sport. Jim and Tina took turns translating when Miguel's broken English failed.

"Baseball may be America's favorite pastime, but soccer is *the* sport in Brazil," said Miguel. "Every village has a team. Almost as soon as they can toddle, Brazilian children begin to kick a ball around and dream of careers as famous soccer stars."

The Ringers and Miguel joined a stream of excited fans approaching Belem's soccer stadium. "Be sure to stick together so nobody gets lost," Miguel warned. The stadium was nearly full by the time he led them to their seats.

Willy was wide-eyed. "This place is huge!"

"It's pretty big, but for a soccer stadium in Brazil it isn't huge," Miguel answered. "Our stadium will hold twenty to thirty thousand fans. But Brazil has the largest stadium in the world, Maracana, that will hold over 170,000 people. It is often sold out. That's down in Rio de Janeiro. I hope to visit there someday."

"You've never been to Rio?" asked Jill.

"No," said Miguel, "it's a long way there."

"Brazil is a big country, Jill," said Jim. "Most people don't realize that Brazil is actually bigger than the U.S. if you leave out Alaska."

Jill was going to ask something else, but just then the

teams came on the field and the fans cheered. That first loud cheer became a roar. Willy figured that once the first period really got underway everyone would settle down a bit. No way. The roar turned into continuous thunder.

The home team took a shot on goal. The opposing goalie leaped to his left, stretched almost totally parallel to the ground. The ball whizzed past his fingertips and into the net. The stadium exploded. Besides the screaming and foot stomping, the crowd began to wave huge flags. People even set off fireworks right there in the stands.

"Holy smoke! This could get dangerous," Willy shouted.

"Right," Miguel agreed. He leaned over and yelled something while Jim translated. "At the stadium in Maracana there is a moat nine feet wide between the spectators and the playing field. It's there to protect the players from fans who get carried away. In the stands mini-riots have been known to break out among supporters of different teams. You don't need to worry about that today. This is more like a semi-pro game. But, it goes to show you, we do love soccer."

Willy got to thinking about going to the ballpark at home: singing the National Anthem, the seventh inning stretch, and the traditional popcorn, peanuts, and ball park franks. The memory made his mouth water. "I'm going to go get something to eat," he told the others.

"I'll go with you," offered Tina.

"Let me try this one alone," Willy said. "I can see the vendor from here. I'll be right back."

Willy was never able to piece together exactly how it

happened, but when he made his way back to his seat, a stranger was sitting there. None of his friends were anywhere around. Just people who shrugged their shoulders and told him they didn't speak English.

He scanned the area—no sign of anyone he knew or anyone who had been sitting near him before.

He went back to the vendor and tried again. Still nobody familiar. He tried a third time. No luck.

Then he started just walking up and down aisles calling out for his friends. His one voice crying, "Tina, Jim, Miguel, Jill, where are you?" was drowned in an ocean of voices cheering the game.

After what seemed like an eternity to Willy, a gun went off, and the game was over. In a crash of confusion the stadium began to empty. People were pushing this way and that. Willy was pretty sure he could pick up both of his feet and the crush of people streaming for the exit would just carry him along.

If Willy decides to find a taxi and return to the Whiteheads' home, turn to page 56.

If Willy sits down and hopes the group somehow finds him, turn to page 120.

"**A**re we almost there?" Tina called to Clay. She realized that she sounded like a little kid on a long car ride, but she really wanted to know.

Clay answered her patiently. "We're not almost there. But we are nearly halfway."

"This is one huge forest," Willy remarked.

Clay smiled at him. "It sure is. The river and forest system cover almost 3 million square miles. An ambitious monkey could climb up into the jungle canopy and swing for 2,000 miles in 200 foot high trees before he'd run out of rain forest. Back in the U.S., a white pine grows less than a foot and a half a year. Here we have bamboo-like trees that grow nearly two feet a *day* till they reach their maximum height of about one hundred feet."

Willy and the others looked around in amazement as Clay continued.

"Inside this huge place there is great variety. Tropical forests cover less than 10 percent of the earth's surface, but they contain more than half the world's species. Scientists say that the jungle is so dense and teeming with life that all the biologists on earth couldn't fully describe its life forms. An acre of forest in the U.S. typically has about twenty species of trees. Here, an acre may have more than three hundred tree species. In fact, Brazil has more species of flowering plants than any other country in the world."

"I know one thing that doesn't show variety," Jim chimed in. "The weather! It drops from an average high in summer of 83 degrees to an average winter low of 80 degrees."

"That's right," Clay said smiling. "Another amazing thing is that unless things change, all that you see around you, this entire forest, will disappear." Willy and the others looked around in surprise. How could such beauty just "disappear"?

"No way!" Willy said, looking at Clay and waiting for him to say it was just a joke. But Clay shook his head sadly.

"This forest is being leveled at the rate of fifty acres a minute. The smoke from burning trees gets so thick that the airport at Porto Velho, capital of the state of Rondonia, has to be closed for days at a time. So, try to enjoy the view. This may be a difficult hike, but it's a beautiful scene. And if we don't do something to preserve it, it's a scene your grandchildren will never be able to see."

Later, after they'd reached safety and civilization again, the Ringers decided to find out more about what people outside Brazil could do to help save the rain forest. Seeing it firsthand made them realize what an important part of God's creation the rain forest is.

THE END

Turn to page 141.

As much fun as a plane ride sounded, the Ringers voted to go with Joao. So he led them to a large dugout canoe. It had been made from a tree that had been hollowed out using fire and hand tools. A small outboard motor was attached to the back. They put on life jackets and settled in for the tour.

It was obvious that Joao loved the river and knew a lot about life along it. Almost as soon as they were moving he began telling them about the river. "This is the largest river in the world. It has eleven times more water than the Mississippi. It runs for 4,087 miles—2,246 of which are in Brazil. Parts of the Amazon are so deep that scientists have never been able to measure them."

They began their journey in bright sunshine, but the weather changed quickly. One minute it was sunny. The next minute the clouds began to gather. In less than fifteen minutes they were in a regular downpour.

"We're getting drenched. Let's pull over under that tree and wait it out." Joao headed for the shelter of the tree overhanging the river, but he seemed to be suppressing a laugh as he watched Willy's and Jill's wasted efforts to keep dry. "Are you allergic to water? It rains here almost every day. Why did you think they call it the rain forest? We sometimes get three feet of rain a month."

"In a *month*?" asked Willy in shock. "That's more than

Millersburg, gets in a whole *year!*"

The rain was a steady deluge. Even with the tree protecting them, there was soon a puddle of water sloshing in the bottom of the boat. But the storm ended almost as quickly as it started, and the canoe continued down the river.

At every bend there were plants and animals that were new to the Americans, and Joao knowledgeably explained them all.

They were approaching a place where the river forked. "You're the bosses," Joao said. "Do you want to go to the left or to the right?"

If the kids choose to go left, turn to page 53.

If the kids choose to go right, turn to page 38.

"**L**et's check out the burn," Willy said, and the others nodded in agreement.

"OK. Climb into my Jeep, and I'll drive you out to where the men are working on clearing," the rancher said.

It was a bit of a squeeze to get Hector, the rancher, and all four Ringers packed into one Jeep, but since there was no roof Jill and Tina could pile on top of Jim and Willy in the back seat. "All set," they called, and the rancher took off.

What a ride! The Jeep bumped along the road— although the rutted, dirt trail they were driving on was hardly a road. Whenever they hit an especially deep hole, the entire vehicle would lurch, and the girls bounced like they might go flying right out of the Jeep. The rest of the time it was like riding in a carnival bumper car.

"I'll have to let you out here," the rancher announced. "This is as far as the road goes." He honked the horn three long blasts. One of the workers approached the Jeep.

"This is my foreman, Jose," the rancher explained. "He will show you around. He's been here for three years and knows the whole process. I'll pick you up here in two and a half hours. Then we'll go back to the house and you can sample some of my delicious beef for dinner."

Jose glanced up at the sky and then began the tour. He was proud of the work he and his men were doing. As he described the burning process, Jim and Tina took turns translating.

"Almost every day we set fire to some trees. But we don't just light whatever happens to appeal to us like some kind of Boy Scouts run amok. We burn a specific area every day. We choose the work area based partly on the weather conditions . . . if it is too windy a fire might get out of control, so we work on clearing the charred remains of previous burnings. We establish 'burn lines.' That means that we burn one area into an area that has already been burnt off. That way when the fire reaches the burn line there is no more forest for it to feed on, and it dies out."

Jose looked up at the sky again with a concerned expression on his face. "I've got to check on a burn we just started today. If you hike up just over that rise you can see the burn line we established last week. I'll catch up with you up there," Jose said as he hurried the other way.

Hector and the Ringers followed Jose's suggestion and climbed what turned out to be a pretty steep hill.

"Would'ja look at that!" Jim exclaimed. From the top of the hill they looked down on a scene of blackened tree stumps standing on a floor of soot. "Those fires sure do a whale of a job of clearing the area. This place looks completely desolate."

"I wonder if any plants or animals survive the fires?" Jill wondered.

"Let's take a look and try to find out," Tina suggested.

Hector and the others fanned out across the burn area. For about an hour they explored, occasionally calling

140

out to each other things like "Hey, come see what I found," or "Get a load of this."

Suddenly, Willy's voice screamed out, "Come here quick!" He sure didn't sound like he'd discovered an interesting animal. The rest of the Ringers ran toward him. "Look at the sky! We've been so busy we haven't noticed. The wind is really starting to blow. We're in for a storm."

The others agreed, but didn't really understand why Willy was getting so worked up. Thunder and lightning were nothing to be worried about.

"What do you think we should do?" Willy asked.

"What are you talking about?" Jill answered.

"Look at the fire!" Willy responded in frustration. "The wind is blowing it right toward us! Should we make a run for the road, or should we stay here and hope that the burn area will protect us?"

Now the rest of the gang understood why Willy had been so excited. They *did* have a major decision to make. Their lives might depend on making the right choice. They were on their own.

CHOICE

If the Ringers decide to make a run for the road, turn to page 122.

If the Ringers decide to stay in the burn area, turn to page 87.

By the time the Ringers returned to the States, they had a whole collection of stories to tell and exciting adventures they would never forget. The kids all agreed that one of the best moments was when they discovered that Hector had not only thought about Jesus, but had decided to follow Jesus with his whole life. That really made the trip worthwhile!

What do you think? Was the trip worthwhile for you? Just make sure you haven't missed any parts of this adventure, because they're all different. And be sure to read about other adventures the Ringers have enjoyed together!

The Amazon River and rain forest contain an incredible variety of animals and play an important part in the world's ecological system. Our weather and the quality of the air we breathe is affected by this fascinating part of creation. Perhaps you will be able to understand some of the news stories about the rain forest now that you have travelled there with the Ringers.

Maybe you can have your own adventure in Brazil some day!

O'Ann Steere is a Christian psychologist and college instructor. Her writing includes contributing to the *Life Application Bible*. She has two children and lives in Wheaton, Illinois.

*If you've enjoyed the **Elizabeth Gail** series,
double your fun with these delightful heroines!*

Anika Scott
Fascinating stories about an
American girl growing up in Africa.

#1 The Impossible Lisa Barnes

#2 Tianna the Terrible

#3 Anika's Mountain

#4 Ambush at Amboseli

#5 Sabrina the Schemer

Cassie Perkins
Bright, ambitious Cassie discovers God
through the challenges of growing up.

#1 No More Broken Promises

#2 A Forever Friend

#3 A Basket of Roses

#4 A Dream to Cherish

#5 The Much-Adored Sandy Shore

#6 Love Burning Bright

#7 Star Light, Star Bright

#8 The Chance of a Lifetime

#9 The Glory of Love

You can find Tyndale books at fine bookstores everywhere.
If you are unable to find these titles at your local bookstore,
you may write for order information to:

**Tyndale House Publishers
Tyndale Family Products Dept.
Box 448
Wheaton, IL 60189**

"Nonstop vampire action ... will captivate readers and leave them craving more."—Darque Reviews

Praise for the Morganville Vampires Series

Carpe Corpus

"Ms. Caine offers readers an intriguing world where vampires rule, only the strongest survive, and romance offers hope in the darkest of hours. Each character is brought to life in superb detail, with unique personality quirks and a full spectrum of emotions. *Carpe Corpus* is well described, packed with action, and impossible to set down." —Darque Reviews

"Rachel Caine has carved out a unique niche in the urban fantasy subgenre with her super young-adult Morganville Vampires. The latest thriller contains plenty of action, but as always in this saga, *Carpe Corpus* is character driven by the good, the bad, and the evil."
—*Midwest Book Review*

"The pace is brisk and a number of loose ends are tied up as one chapter on the town of Morganville closes and a new one begins." —Monsters and Critics

Lord of Misrule

"Ms. Caine uses her dazzling storytelling skills to share the darkest chapter yet ... an engrossing read."
—Darque Reviews

"Filled with delicious twists that the audience will appreciatively sink their teeth into."
—Genre Go Round Reviews

Feast of Fools

"Fast-paced and filled with action.... Fans of the series will appreciate *Feast of Fools*."
—Genre Go Round Reviews

continued ...

"Thrilling . . . a fast-moving series where there's always a surprise just around every dark corner."

—Darque Reviews

"Very entertaining . . . I could not put *Feast of Fools* down. . . . There is a level of tension in the Morganville books that keeps you on the edge of your seat; even in the background scenes you're waiting for the other shoe to drop. And it always does." —Flames Rising

"Fantastic. . . . The excitement and suspense in *Feast of Fools* is thrilling, and I was fascinated reading about the town of Morganville. I greatly look forward to reading the next book." —Fresh Fiction

Midnight Alley

"A fast-paced, page-turning read packed with wonderful characters and surprising plot twists. Rachel Caine is an engaging writer; readers will be completely absorbed in this chilling story, unable to put it down until the last page." —Flamingnet

"Weaves a web of dangerous temptation, dark deceit, and loving friendships. The nonstop vampire action and delightfully sweet relationships will captivate readers and leave them craving more." —Darque Reviews

The Dead Girls' Dance

"If you love to read about characters with whom you can get deeply involved, Rachel Caine is so far a one hundred percent sure bet to satisfy that need."

—The Eternal Night

"Throw in a mix of vamps and ghosts and it can't get any better than *Dead Girls' Dance*." —Dark Angel Reviews

THE MORGANVILLE VAMPIRES

KISS OF
DEATH

THE MORGANVILLE VAMPIRES

RACHEL CAINE

A SIGNET BOOK

SIGNET
Published by New American Library, a division of
Penguin Group (USA) Inc., 375 Hudson Street,
New York, New York 10014, USA
Penguin Group (Canada), 90 Eglinton Avenue East, Suite 700, Toronto,
Ontario M4P 2Y3, Canada (a division of Pearson Penguin Canada Inc.)
Penguin Books Ltd., 80 Strand, London WC2R 0RL, England
Penguin Ireland, 25 St. Stephen's Green, Dublin 2,
Ireland (a division of Penguin Books Ltd.)
Penguin Group (Australia), 250 Camberwell Road, Camberwell, Victoria 3124,
Australia (a division of Pearson Australia Group Pty. Ltd.)
Penguin Books India Pvt. Ltd., 11 Community Centre, Panchsheel Park,
New Delhi - 110 017, India
Penguin Group (NZ), 67 Apollo Drive, Rosedale, North Shore 0632,
New Zealand (a division of Pearson New Zealand Ltd.)
Penguin Books (South Africa) (Pty.) Ltd., 24 Sturdee Avenue,
Rosebank, Johannesburg 2196, South Africa

Penguin Books Ltd., Registered Offices:
80 Strand, London WC2R 0RL, England

First published by Signet, an imprint of New American Library,
a division of Penguin Group (USA) Inc.

First Printing, May 2010
10 9 8 7 6 5 4 3 2 1

To the wonderful people in Des Moines, Carroll, Fort Dodge, Rockwell City, and Clive for making me welcome in the great state of Iowa!
To my wonderful friends at Legacy Books (Dallas), the Mystery Bookstore (LA), Murder by the Book (Houston), and Borders Express (Exton, PA) for all your support and enthusiasm. See you soon, I hope!

Acknowledgments

Far too many awesome people have made it possible for this book to be in your hands today, but I must send extraspecial thanks to my Sunday Night pals (Pat, Jackie, Bill, Heidi, J.T., and Joanne), who make even the worst weeks bearable. Also, Joe Bonamassa, Lucienne Diver, Anne Sowards, Jim Suhler, Felicia Day, Jim Conrad, and M. Conrad—all of whom make my days a little brighter. Bless.

Introduction

WELCOME TO MORGANVILLE. YOU'LL NEVER WANT TO LEAVE.

So, you're new to Morganville. Welcome, new resident! There are only a few important rules you need to know to feel comfortable in our quiet little town:

- Obey the speed limits.
- Don't litter.
- Whatever you do, don't get on the bad side of the vampires.

Yeah, we said vampires. Deal with it.

As a human newcomer, you'll need to find yourself a vampire Protector—someone willing to sign a contract to keep you and yours safe from harm (especially from the other vampires). In return, you'll pay taxes . . . just like in any other town. Of course, in most other towns those taxes don't get collected by the Bloodmobile.

Oh, and if you decide *not* to get a Protector, you can do that, too . . . but you'd better learn how to run fast, stay out of the shadows, and build a network of friends who can help you. Try contacting the residents of the Glass House—Michael, Eve, Shane, and Claire. They know their way around, even if they always end up in the middle of the trouble somehow.

Welcome to Morganville. You'll never want to leave.

And even if you do . . . well, you can't.

Sorry about that.

1

The way the Glass House worked, on a practical level, was that there was a schedule for the stuff that had to be done—cooking, cleaning, fixing things, laundry. Technically, they were all on every housemate's list. In practice, though, what happened was this: the boys (Michael and Shane) bribed the girls (Eve and Claire) to do the laundry, and the girls bribed the boys to fix things.

Claire glared at her new iPod—which was actually really nice—and put it on shuffle as she looked at the mess she'd made of her latest laundry effort. And there was the problem: she loved the hot pink iPod, which had been a *heck* of a good bribe, and she really didn't deserve it, because the laundry was . . . also *pink*—which would have been almost fine if it had been a load full of girls' underwear or something.

But not so much with guy clothes; she could not even imagine what kind of screaming that was going to bring.

"Yeah." She sighed, staring at the very definitely pink piles of shirts, socks, and underwear. "Not going to be a good afternoon." It was amazing what one—*one*—stupid red sock could do. She'd already tried running it all through the washer again, hoping the problem would just go away. No such luck.

The basement of the Glass House was big, dark, and

creepy, which wasn't really such a surprise. Most basements were, and this was *Morganville*. Morganville went in for dark and creepy the way Las Vegas went in for neon. Apart from the area Claire was in, with a battered washer and dryer, a table that had once been painted some kind of industrial green, and some shelves filled with unidentifiable junk, the rest of the basement was dim and quiet. Hence the iPod, which pumped cheery music through the headphones and made the creepy retreat a little less creepy.

Creepy, she could fight.

Pink underwear ... apparently not.

She had the music cranked up so high that she failed to hear steps coming down the stairs. In fact, she had no clue she wasn't completely alone until she felt a hand touch her shoulder and hot breath against her neck.

She reacted as any sensible person living in a town full of vampires would. She screamed. The shriek echoed off the brick and concrete, and Claire whirled, clapped her hands over her mouth, and backed away from Eve, who was collapsing in laughter. The Goth look usually didn't go well with hysterical giggles, unless they were *evil* giggles, but somehow Eve managed to pull it off.

Claire ripped the headphones out of her ears and gasped. "You—you—"

"Oh, spit it out already," Eve managed to say. "*Bitch.* I am. I know. That was evil. But, oh my God, funny."

"Bitch," Claire said, late and not at all meaning it. "You scared me."

"Kind of the point," Eve said, and got herself under control. Her mascara was a little smeared, but Claire supposed that was all part of the Goth thing, anyway. "So, what's up, pup?"

"Trouble," Claire replied with a sigh. Her heart was still pounding from the scare, but she was determined not to let it show. She pointed at the laundry on the table.

Eve's eyes went wide, and her black-painted lips parted in horrified fascination. "That's not trouble; that's *fail.* Tell me that isn't all the whites. Like, Michael's and Shane's, too."

"All the whites," Claire said, and held up the guilty red sock. "Yours?"

"Oh, damn." Eve snatched it out of Claire's fingers and shook the sock like a floppy rattle. "Bad sock! Bad! You are *never* going anywhere fun ever again!"

"I'm serious. They're going to kill me."

"They'll never get the chance. *I'm* going to kill you. Do I look to you like someone who rocks pastel?"

Well, that was a definite point. "Sorry," Claire said. "Seriously. I tried washing them again, without the sock, but—"

Eve shook her head, reached down to the lowest level of the shelf, and pulled out a bottle of bleach, which she thumped down on the table next to the laundry. "You bleach; I'll supervise, because I'm not taking the chance of getting a drop on this outfit, 'k? It's new."

The outfit in question was hot pink—it matched Claire's new iPod, actually—with (of course) black horizontally striped tights, a black pleated miniskirt, and a blazing magenta top with a skull all blinged out in crystal on it. Eve had done up her dyed black hair in a messy pile on top of her head, with stray bits sticking up in all directions.

She looked creepy/adorable.

As Claire reloaded the laundry, with a shot of bleach, Eve climbed up on the dryer and kicked her feet idly. "So, you heard the news, right?"

"What news?" Claire asked. "Do I do hot? Is hot good?"

"Hot is good," Eve confirmed. "Michael got another call from that music producer guy. You know, the one from Dallas? The important one, with the daughter at school here. He wants to set Michael up with some club

dates in Dallas and a couple of days at a recording studio. I think he's serious."

Eve was trying to sound excited about it, but Claire could follow the road signs. Sign one (shaped like an Exit sign): Michael Glass was Eve's serious, longtime crush/boyfriend. Sign two (DANGER, CURVES): Michael Glass was hot, talented, and sweet. Sign three (yellow, CAUTION): Michael Glass was a vampire, which made everything a million times more complicated. Sign four (flashing red): Michael had begun acting more like a vampire than the boy Eve loved, and they'd already had some pretty spectacular fights about it—so bad, in fact, that Claire was not sure Eve wasn't thinking about breaking up with him.

All of which led to sign five (STOP).

"You think he'll go?" Claire asked, and concentrated on setting the right temperature on the washer. The smell of the detergent and bleach was kind of pleasant, like really sharp flowers, the kind that would cut you if you tried to pick them. "To Dallas, I mean?"

"I guess." Eve sounded even less enthusiastic. "I mean, it's good for him, right? He can't just hang around playing at coffee shops in Jugular, Texas. He needs to . . ." Her voice faded out, and she looked down at her lap with a focus Claire thought the skirt really didn't deserve. "He needs to be out there."

"Hey," Claire said, and as the washer began chugging away, washing away the stains, she put her hands on Eve's knees. The kicking stopped, but Eve didn't look up. "Are you guys breaking up?"

Eve still didn't look up. "I cry all the time," she said. "I hate this. I don't *want* to lose him. But it's like he just keeps getting farther and farther away, you know? And I don't know how he feels. What he feels. *If* he feels. It's awful."

Claire swallowed hard. "I think he still loves you."

Now she got Eve to look at her—big, vulnerable dark

eyes rimmed by all the black. "Really? Because . . . I just . . ." Eve took a deep breath and shook her head. "I don't want to get dumped. It's going to hurt so bad, and I'm so scared he'll find somebody else. Somebody, you know, better."

"Well, *that's* not going to happen," Claire said. "Not ever."

"Easy for you to say. You haven't seen how the girls throw themselves at him after shows."

"Yeah, you'd *never* do that."

Eve looked up sharply, smiled a little, then looked back down. "Yeah, okay, whatever. But it's different when he's *my* Michael and *they're* the ones who are all, you know . . . Anyway, he's just always so *nice* to them."

Claire jumped up next to her on the dryer and kicked her feet in rhythm with Eve's. "He has to be nice, right? That's his job, kind of. And we were talking about whether you guys were breaking up. Are you?"

"I . . . don't know. It's weird right now. It hurts, and I want the hurt to be over, one way or another, you know?" Eve's shoulders rose and fell in a shrug that somehow managed to be depressed at the same time. "Besides, now he's running off to Dallas. They won't let me go, if he does. I'm just, you know. *Human.*"

"You've got one of the cool frat pins. Nobody would stop you." The cool frat pins were a gift from Amelie, the town's Founder, one of the most frighteningly quiet vampires Claire had ever met, and Claire's boss, technically. They worked like the bracelets most people in town wore, the ones that identified individuals or families as being Protected by a specific vampire, only these were better. . . . People who wore *these* pins didn't have to give blood or take orders. They weren't *owned.*

As far as Claire knew, there were fewer than ten people in all of Morganville who had this kind of status, and it meant freedom—in theory—from a lot of the scarier elements of town.

This was all because they'd gotten in over their heads, had to fight their way out of it, and done some good for Amelie in the process. It was heroism by accident, in Claire's opinion, but she definitely wasn't turning down the pin or what the pin represented.

"If they decide Michael can go, I'll still have to file an application for temporary leave," Eve said. "So would you, or Shane, if you wanted to tag along. And they could turn us down. They probably would."

"Why?"

"Because they're mostly asshats? Not to mention *bloodsucking vampire* asshats, which doesn't exactly make them fair from the beginning."

Claire could see her point, actually, which was depressing. The air filled with the smells of laundry, which was homey and didn't go too well with depressing. Claire remembered her iPod, which was still blaring away at her headphones, and clicked it off. They sat in silence for a while, and then Eve said, "I wish the dryer were running, because *man*, I could use a good . . . tumble dry."

Claire burst out laughing and, after a second, Eve joined her, and it was all okay.

Even in the dark. Even in the basement.

In the end, the laundry was only a *little* pink.

Dinner was taco night, and it was Claire's turn for that, too, which somehow seemed wrong, but she'd switched with Michael when she'd been staying late at the university library, so she was stuck with Chore Day. Not that she minded making tacos; she liked it, actually.

Shane blew in the door just as she was chopping the last of the onions, which was typical Shane timing; five minutes earlier, and she'd have made him do the chopping. Instead, he arrived just as she was wiping tears away from her stinging eyes. Perfect.

He didn't care that her eyes were red, apparently, be-

cause he kicked the kitchen door shut, slammed the dead bolt with a gesture so smooth it looked automatic, set a bag on the counter, and leaned over to kiss her. It was one of those hi-I'm-home kisses, not one of his really good ones, but it still made Claire's heart flutter a little bit in her chest. Shane looked ... like Shane, she guessed, which was fine with her. Tall, broad, he had sun-streaked slacker hair and a heartbreaker's smile. He was wearing a Killers T-shirt that smelled like barbecue, from his job.

"Hey!" she protested—not very sincerely—and waved the knife she'd been using to chop onions. "I'm armed!"

"Yeah, but you're not very dangerous," he said, and kissed her again, lightly. "You taste like tacos."

"You taste like barbecue."

"And that's a win-win!" He grinned at her, reached over, and rattled the paper bag he'd set on the counter. "How about some brisket tacos?"

"That is so wrong, you know. Brisket does not go in tacos."

"Twisted, yet delicious. I say yes."

Claire sighed and dumped the chopped onions into a bowl. "Hand me the brisket." Secretly, she liked brisket tacos; she just liked giving him a hard time more.

"You know," Claire said as she got the barbecue out of the bag, "you really ought to talk to Michael."

"About what?"

"What do you think? About what's going on with him and Eve!"

"Oh *hell* no. Guys don't talk about that crap."

"You're serious."

"Really."

"What do you talk about?"

Shane looked at her as if she were insane. "You know. Stuff. We're not *girls.* We don't talk about our *feelings.* I mean, not to other guys."

Claire rolled her eyes and said, "Fine, be emotionally stunted losers; I don't care."

"Good. Thanks. I'll do that." The door opened, and Michael shuffled in, rocking the worst bed head Claire had ever seen him with. "Whoa. Dude, you look like crap. You getting enough iron in your diet?"

"Screw you, and thanks. I just woke up. What's your excuse?"

"I work for a living, man. Unlike the nightwalking dead."

Michael went straight past them and from the refrigerator took a sports bottle, which he stuck in the microwave for fifteen seconds. Claire was grateful the smell of the onions, brisket, and taco meat covered the smell of what was in the bottle. Well, they all knew what it was, but if she pretended *really hard*, it didn't have to be quite as obvious.

Michael drank from his sports bottle, then wandered over to look at what they were doing. "Cool, tacos. How long?"

"Depends on whether or not she lets me do the chopping," Shane said. "Five minutes, maybe?"

The doorbell rang. "I'll get it!" Eve yelled, and there was something in her voice that really didn't sound quite right. More . . . desperate than eager, as if she wanted to stop them from getting to it first. Claire glanced over at Shane, and he raised his eyebrows.

"Uh-oh," he said. "Either she's finally dumping you, Mikey, and her new boy's coming for dinner, or—"

It was the *or*, of course. After a short delay, Eve opened the swinging door just wide enough to stick her face inside. She tried for a smile. It almost worked. "Uh—so I invited someone to dinner,"

"Nice time to tell us," Shane said.

"Shut up. You've got enough food for the Fifth Armored Division *and* all of us. We can fill one more plate." But she was having trouble keeping eye contact, and as Claire watched, Eve bit her lip and looked away completely.

"Crap," Michael said. "I'm not going to like this, am I? Who is it?"

Eve silently opened the door the rest of the way. Behind her, standing with his hands stuffed in the pockets of his jeans jacket, head down, was her brother, Jason Rosser.

Jason looked—different, Claire thought. For one thing, he usually looked strung out and dirty and violent, and now he looked almost sober, and he was definitely on speaking terms with showers. Still skinny, and she couldn't say much for the baggy clothes he was wearing, but he looked . . . better than she'd ever seen him.

And even so, something inside her flinched, hard, at the sight of him. Jason was associated with several of her worst, scariest memories, and even if he hadn't actually *hurt* her, he hadn't helped her, either—or any of the girls who'd been hurt, or killed. Jason was a bad, bad kid. He'd been an accomplice to at least three murders and to an attack on Claire.

And neither Shane nor Michael had forgotten any of that.

"Get him out of here," Shane said in a low, dangerous-sounding tone. "Now."

"It's Michael's house," Eve said, without looking at any of them directly. "Michael?"

"Wait a second—it's *our* house! I live here, too!" Shane shot back. "You don't get to drag his low-life ass in here and act as if nothing happened with him!"

"He's my *brother*! And he's trying, Shane. *God*, you can be such a—"

"It's okay," Claire said. Her hands were shaking, and she felt cold, but she also saw Jason lift his head, and for a second their eyes met. It was like a physical shock, and she wasn't sure what she saw, or what he saw, but neither one of them could hold it for long. "It's just dinner. It's not a big deal."

Shane turned toward her, eyes wide, and put his hands on her shoulders. "Claire, he *hurt you*. Hell, he hurt *me*, too! Jason is not some stray mutt you can take in and feed, okay? He's psycho. And *she* knows it better than anybody." He glared at Eve, who frowned but didn't glare back as she normally would have. "You expect us all to just play nice with him now that he figures out the bad guys aren't winning, so he cranks out a quick apology? Because it's not happening. It's just not."

"Yeah, I figured it would go this way. Sorry I bothered you," Jason said. His voice sounded faint and rusty, and he turned and walked away, toward the front door and out of their line of sight. Eve went after him, and she must have tried to stop him, because Claire heard his soft voice say, "No, he's not wrong. I've got no right to be here. I did bad things, sis. This was a mistake."

Of all of them, only Michael hadn't spoken—hadn't moved, in fact. He was staring at the swinging door as it swayed back and forth, and finally he took a deep breath, set down his sports bottle, and went out into the hallway.

Claire smacked at Shane's arm. "What the hell was that, macho man? You have to come to my rescue all the time, even when nobody's trying to hurt me?"

He seemed honestly surprised. "I was just—"

"I know what you were *just* doing. You don't speak for me!"

"I wasn't trying to—"

"Yes, you were. Look, I know Jason's no saint, but he got himself together, and he stuck with Eve when all of us were—out of commission, when Bishop was in charge. He protected her."

"And he let his crazy buddy Dan grab you and almost kill you, and he didn't do anything!"

"He did," Claire said flatly. "He left me to find help. I know because Richard Morrell told me later. Jason went to the cops and tried to tell them. They didn't be-

lieve him or they'd have gotten help to me a lot earlier." Earlier would have meant a lot less terror and pain and despair. It wasn't Jason's fault that they'd figured him for crazy.

Shane was thrown, a little, but he came back swinging. "Yeah, well, what about those other girls? He didn't help *them*, did he? I'm not friending up somebody like that."

"Nobody said you had to," Claire shot back. "Jason's done his time in jail. Sitting at the same table isn't like swearing eternal brotherhood."

He opened his mouth, closed it, and then said, very tightly, "I just wanted to make sure he didn't have a chance to hurt you again."

"Unless he uses a taco as a deadly weapon, he hasn't got much of a shot. Having you, Michael, and Eve here is about the best protection I could want. Anyway, would you rather have him where you can see him, or where you *can't*?"

Some of the fire faded out of his eyes. "Oh. Yeah, okay." He still looked uncomfortable, though. "You do crazy crap, you know. And it's contagious."

"I know." She put her hand on his cheek, and got a very small smile in return. "Thanks for wanting to keep me safe. But don't overdo it, okay?"

Shane made a sound of frustration deep in his throat, but he didn't argue.

The kitchen door swung open again. It was Michael, looking fully awake and very calm, as if bracing for a fight. "I talked to him," he said. "He's sincere enough. But if you don't want him here, Shane—"

"I damn sure don't," Shane said, then glanced at Claire and continued. "But if she's willing to give it a shot, I will."

Michael blinked, then raised his eyebrows. "Huh," he said. "The universe explodes, hell freezes, and Shane does something reasonable."

Shane silently offered him the finger. Michael grinned and backed out of the kitchen again.

Claire handed Shane the biggest knife they had. "Chop brisket," she said. "Take out your frustrations."

The brisket didn't stand a chance.

Jason didn't say much at dinner. In fact, he was almost completely silent, though he ate four tacos as if he'd been starving for a month, and when Eve brought out ice cream for dessert, he ate a double helping of that, too.

Shane was right. The brisket *was* delicious in the tacos.

Eve, compensating for her brother, chattered like a magpie on crack the whole time—about dumb-asses at the coffee shop where she worked, Common Grounds; about Oliver, her vampire boss, who was a full-time jerk, as far as Claire was concerned, although apparently he was a surprisingly fair supervisor; gossip about people in town. Michael contributed some juicy stuff about the vampire side of town (Claire, for one, had never considered that vampires could fall in and out of love just like regular people—well, vampires other than Michael, and maybe Amelie.) Shane finally loosened up on his glares and brought up some embarrassing stories from Michael's and Eve's pasts. If there were embarrassing stories he knew about Jason, he didn't get into telling them.

It started out deeply uncomfortable, but by the time the ice cream bowls were empty, it felt kind of—normal. Not great—there was still a cautious tension around the table—but there was guarded acceptance.

Jason finally said, "Thanks for the food." They all stopped talking and looked at him, and he kept his own gaze down on the empty dessert bowl. "Shane's right. I got no right to think I can just show up here and expect you not to hate my guts. You should."

"Damn straight," Shane muttered. Claire and Eve both glared at him. "What? Just sayin'."

Jason didn't seem to mind. "I needed to come and tell you that I'm sorry. It's been—things got weird, man. Real weird. And I got real screwed up, in all kinds of ways. Until that thing happened with Claire . . . Look, I never meant—she wasn't part of it. That was all on him." *Him* meant the other guy, the one none of them mentioned, ever. Claire felt her palms sweating and wiped them against her jeans. Her mouth felt dry. "But I'm guilty of other stuff, and I confessed to all of it to the cops, and I did time for it. I never killed anybody, though. I just— wanted to be somebody who got respect."

Michael said, "That's how you think you get respect around here? As a killer?"

Jason looked up, and it was eerie, seeing eyes exactly like Eve's in such a different face, simmering with anger. "Yeah," he said. "I did. I still do. And I don't need a frigging *vampire* to set me straight about that, either. In Morganville, when you're not one of the sheep, and you're not one of the wolves, you'd better be one mean-ass junkyard dog."

Claire glanced over at Shane and was surprised to see that he wasn't hopping on the angry train. In fact, he was looking at Jason as if he understood what he was saying. Maybe he did. Maybe it was a guy thing.

Nobody spoke, and finally Jason said, "So anyway, I just wanted to say thanks for helping get me out of jail. I'd be dead by now if you hadn't. I won't forget." He scraped his chair back and stood up. "Thanks for the tacos. Dinner was real good. I haven't—I haven't sat at a table with people for a really long time."

Then, without making eye contact with any of them, he walked away, down the hall. Eve jumped up and ran after him, but before she got to him, he was out the front door and slamming it behind him. She opened it and looked out, but didn't follow. "Jason!" she called,

but without any real hope he'd come back. Then, finally, hopelessly, she called again, "Be careful!"

She slowly closed the door again, locked it, and came back to flop in her chair at the dinner table, staring at the remains of their taco feast.

"Hey," Shane said. "Eve."

She looked up.

"It took guts for him to come here and try to apologize. I respect that."

She looked surprised, and for a second she smiled. "Thanks. I know Jason's never going to be . . . well, a good guy in any kind of way, but he's—I can't just turn my back on him. He needs somebody to keep him from going off the rails."

Michael took a drink from his sports bottle. "He's the train," he said. "You're on the tracks. Think about what's going to happen, Eve."

Her smile faded. "What are you saying?"

"I'm saying that your brother is a junkie and one sick dude even if he's feeling sentimental right now. That's probably not really his fault, but he's trouble, and now we sat down with him and he apologized and it's all done, okay? He's not coming back. He's not family. Not in this house."

"But—"

When Claire had first met Michael Glass, he'd been cold and kind of harsh to her, and now that Michael came out again.

At Eve.

"Eve, we're not going to argue about it," Michael said flatly, and he looked like an angry, angry angel, the smiting kind. "House rules. You don't bring that kind of trouble in the door."

"Oh, *please*, Michael, don't even think about pulling that crap. If that's the rule, are you throwing Claire out now? Because I'm betting she is the most trouble that ever walked in here on two feet. You and Shane

drag your own hassles in all the time. But I don't get to have my own brother over for dinner?" Eve's voice was shaking, she was so angry now, and she was trying not to cry, but Claire could see the tears welling up in her dark eyes. "Come on! You're not my dad!"

"No, I'm your landlord," he said. "Bringing Jason in here puts everybody at risk. He's going to go back to the dark side on us, if he ever left in the first place. I'm just trying to keep things sane around here."

"Then try talking to me instead of just ordering me around!" Eve shoved dishes off onto the floor, spilling the remains of tacos everywhere, and dashed for the stairs.

Michael got there first, easily; he moved in a blur, vampire speed, and blocked her access. Eve came to a skidding halt, pale even underneath her rice-powder makeup. "So you're proving your point by going all vamp on me?" she said. "Even if Jason was still here, you'd be the most dangerous thing in the room and you know it!"

"I *know*," Michael said. "Eve. What do you *want*? I'm trying, okay? I sat down with Jason. I'm just saying once was enough. Why am I the bad guy?"

Shane muttered, loud enough for only Claire to hear, "Good question, bro." She hissed at him to be quiet. This was private, and she was feeling bad for both Eve and Michael, having witnesses to all this. It was bad enough to be fighting and worse to have Shane making snarky comments from the sidelines.

"I don't know, Michael. Why *are* you the bad guy?" Eve shot back. "Maybe because you're acting as if you own the world!"

"You're being a brat."

"A *what*?"

"You're going to dump crap all over the floor and walk away? What else do you call it?"

Eve looked so shocked, it was as if he'd hit her. Claire winced in sympathy. "It's okay; we'll do it," Claire said,

and started picking up plates and piling them up. "It's not a big deal." Shane was still staring at their friends as if they were some kind of sideshow exhibit; she kicked him in the shin and shoved plates at him. "Kitchen," she said. "Go."

He raised his eyebrows, but he went. She began cleaning up the mess on the floor. In Shane's absence, it felt as if things changed, as if the balance shifted again. Claire kept herself small, quiet, and invisible as she worked at scraping up the spilled food into a pile with napkins.

"Eve," Michael said. He wasn't angry anymore, Claire realized. His voice had gone soft and quiet. She glanced up and saw that Eve was silently crying now, tears dragging dirty trails of mascara down her cheeks, but she didn't look away from him. "Eve, what is it? This isn't about Jason. What?"

She threw herself into him, wrapping her arms around him. Even with vampire reflexes, Michael was surprised enough to rock backward, but he recovered in just a second, holding her, stroking her back with one hand. Eve put her head down on his shoulder and cried like a lost little girl. "I don't want to lose you," she finally snuffled. "God, I really don't. Please. Please don't go."

"Go?" Michael sounded honestly baffled. "What? Where would I go?"

"Anywhere. With anyone. Don't— I love you, Michael. I really do."

He sighed and held her even more tightly. "I'm not going anywhere with anyone else," he said. "I swear. And I love you, too. Okay?"

"You mean it?"

"Yeah, I mean it." He seemed almost surprised and let out a slow breath as he hugged her tighter. "I mean it, Eve. I always have, even when you didn't believe it."

Eve dabbed at her running mascara, hiccuping little breaths, and then looked past Michael to Claire, who was getting all the mess put onto one plate for disposal.

Eve looked stricken. "Oh God," she said. "I'm sorry. I didn't mean— Here, let me. I'll get it."

And she pulled free of Michael and got down on her hands and knees to clean up the rest.

And Michael got down there with her. Claire backed through the kitchen door with a load of stuff, and as it swung closed, she saw Michael lean over and kiss Eve. It looked sweet and hot and absolutely real.

"Well?" Shane asked. "World War Fifteen over out there, or what?"

"I think so," she said, and hip-bumped him out of the way at the sink to dump her armload of plates. "You're washing, right?"

"I'll play you for it."

"What?"

"Best high score wins?"

That was the same basic thing as doing it herself now and saving herself the humiliation, Claire thought. "No bet," she said. "Wash, dish boy."

He flicked suds at her. She shrieked and laughed and flipped more at him. They splashed water. It felt . . . breathlessly good, when Shane finally captured her in his soapy hands, pulled her close to his wet T-shirt, and kissed her.

"And that's World War *Sixteen*," he said. "Officially over."

"I'm still not playing Dead Rising with you."

"You're no fun."

She kissed him, long and sweet and slow, and whispered, "You sure?"

"Well, I'm certainly changing my mind," Shane said, straight-faced, at least until he licked his lips. His pupils were large and dark and completely fixed on hers, and she felt as if gravity had reversed, as if she could fall up into his eyes and just keep on going.

"Dishes," he reminded her. "Me dish boy. And I can't believe I just said that, because that was lame."

She kissed him again, lightly this time. "That's for later," she said. "By the way? You look really hot with suds all over you."

The kitchen door opened, and Eve walked in, dumped a plateful of trash in the can, and practically danced her way over to the sink. She still had smeared mascara, and her tears weren't even dry, but she was smiling, and there was a dreamy, distant look in her eyes.

"Hey," Shane said. "How about you? Want to play Dead Rising?"

"Sure," Eve said. "Fine. Absolutely."

She wandered out. Shane blinked. "That was not what I expected."

"She's floating," Claire said. "What's wrong with that?"

"Nothing. But she didn't even insult me. That's just *wrong*. It disturbs me."

"I'm taking advantage of all this calm," Claire said. "Study time."

"Bring it downstairs," Shane said. "I need a cheering section, because she is going to *suck* at zombie killing tonight. Just way too happy."

Claire laughed, but she dashed upstairs and grabbed her book bag, which promptly ripped right down the seam, spilling about twenty pounds' worth of texts, supplies, and junk all over the wooden floor. "Great," she said with a sigh. "Just great." She gathered up what she needed in an untidy armload and headed back downstairs.

She was halfway down the stairs when someone knocked at the front door. They all stopped what they were doing—Michael, in the act of picking up his guitar; Shane and Eve, taking seats on the couch with game controllers. "Expecting anybody else?" Shane asked Eve. "Is your distant cousin Jack the Ripper dropping in for coffee?"

"Screw you, Collins."

"Finally, the world is back to normal. Still not up to

the usual Rosser Olympic-level insult standards, there, sunshine. Never mind. I'll get it."

Michael didn't say anything, but he put down the guitar and followed Shane to the end of the hall, watching. Claire descended the rest of the steps quickly, trying to keep her pile of stuff from tottering over, and dumped it on the dining table before hurrying over to Michael's side.

Shane checked the peephole, stepped back, and said, "Uh oh."

"What?"

"Trouble?"

Michael crossed the distance in a flash, looked out, and bared his teeth—*all* his teeth, including the vampiry ones, which didn't exactly bode well. Claire sucked in a deep breath. Damn stupid book bag, picking a bad time to break; usually, she'd have brought all the stuff down, but she'd left her antivamp supplies upstairs in the ruined bag's pocket.

"It's Morley," Michael said. "I'd better go out and talk to him. Shane, stay here with them."

"Word of advice—stop telling me to stay with the girls," Shane said, "or I will seriously bust you in the mouth one of these days. Seriously. I could break one of those shiny fangs."

"Today?"

"Ah . . . probably not."

"Then shut up." Michael opened the door just wide enough to slide out, looked back, and said, "Lock it."

Shane nodded, and as soon as the wood thumped closed, he shot all the bolts and glued his eye to the peephole.

Claire and Eve, by common silent decision, dashed to the living room window, which gave them an angled view of the porch—not perfect, but better than nothing.

"Oh no," Eve whispered.

Michael was standing in a wash of moonlight, facing

not just one vampire, but *three*. Morley—a ragged, rough vampire who rocked the homeless look, although Claire knew he actually did have a home—was standing there, with two of his crew. He had quite a number of them, disaffected vampire youth, although *youth* was a relative term when you talked about vampires. It was mostly a matter of status, not just age; the have-nots, or the ones feeling squeezed by those who had power over them.

They also had a human with them.

Jason.

And he wasn't there voluntarily, as far as Claire could tell. One of the vampires had a hand around his arm in what looked like a friendly grip but was probably bone-crushing hard.

"Jase," Eve whispered. "Oh God. I *told* you to be careful!"

Shane left the door, came into the living room, and dragged a black canvas bag out from under a chair. He unzipped it and took out a small crossbow, cranked it back, and loaded it with an arrow. He tossed silver-coated stakes to Claire and Eve, then joined them at the window. "So," he said, "your brother's already said he was a vampire wannabe. Does he need rescuing, or is this his idea of a really great date?"

"Don't be an asshole," Eve said, and gripped the stake so hard her whole hand turned paler than normal. "They wouldn't turn him, anyway. They'll just drain him." It was a lot of work for a vampire to turn a human, and from what Claire had seen, they didn't seem all that eager to go through it themselves. It hurt. And it took something out of them. The only one she'd ever seen take any real pleasure out if had been Mr. Bishop, Amelie's vile, old vampire father. She'd seen him turn Shane's father, and that had been—horrible. *Really* horrible.

This was why Shane, however he felt about Jason Rosser, was loading up a crossbow, and was more than prepared to use it.

"What's Michael doing?"

"Talking sense," Shane said. "It's always his A game. For him, it usually works. Me, I'm usually Plan B, all the time."

"B for brute force?" Eve said. "Yep, that's you."

Shane slotted the arrow in place and raised the window sash. He kicked out the screen on the other side and aimed the crossbow right at Morley.

Morley, who was dressed in clothes that seemed pieced together out of rags, except for one brand-new Hawaiian shirt in disgustingly bright shades of neon, looked straight at the window, smiled, and tipped his head just a little in acknowledgment.

"Just so we're clear, bloodsucker," Shane said.

"Can he hear you?"

"He hears every word. Hey, Morley? I will put this right between your ribs, you got me?"

Once again, Morley nodded, and the smile stayed in place.

"You sure that's a good idea?" Eve whispered. "Threatening him, I mean?"

"Why not? Morley speaks fluent threat."

It went on for a while, all the talking; Shane never took his eyes off Morley. Claire kept her hand on him, somehow feeling as if that were helping—helping them both—and finally Morley made some polite little bow to Michael, then waved at the other vampire, who was holding Jason.

The vampire let go. Jason stumbled backward, then took off at top speed, running flat out down the street. The vampires watched him. Nobody followed.

Eve breathed a slow sigh of relief and leaned against the wall.

Shane didn't move. He still had the crossbow aimed at Morley's chest.

"Emergency's over," Eve said. "Stand down, soldier."

"Go open the door. I stand down when Michael's back

inside." Shane smiled, all teeth. Not quite as menacing as a vampire smile, but it got the point across. Eve nodded and ran to the door. Once it was open, Michael—still looking cool and calm—backed in, said good night, and shut the door. Claire heard him shooting the locks, and still Shane kept his aim steady until Morley, touching a finger to his brow, turned and walked off into the dark with his two followers.

Claire slammed down the window, locked it, and Shane let out his breath in a slow sigh, removing the arrow from the bow. "Nothing like a little after-dinner terrification," he said, and gave Claire a quick kiss. "Mmmm, you still taste like brisket tacos."

She would have called him a jerk, but she was shaking, and she was too short of breath, anyway. He was already down the hall by the time she pulled in enough air, and she used it to follow him. Michael was standing beside Eve, an arm tight around her waist.

"So?" Shane asked. "What's Morley hanging around for? Waiting for us to get ripe?"

"You know what he was here for," Michael said. "We haven't gotten his people passes to leave town yet, which is what you promised him in return for not killing you three when he had the chance. He's getting impatient, and since you three are on the hook as his own personal blood donors, I think we need to get serious about making that happen."

"He wouldn't dare."

"No? Can't say that I agree with you. Morley isn't afraid of much that I can tell, including Amelie, Oliver, or a wooden arrow in the heart." Michael nodded at Shane. "Still. Thanks. Nice."

"Brute force. It's what I do."

"Just keep it aimed the right way."

Shane looked as innocent as Shane ever could and put his hand over his heart. "I would never. Unless you

flash fang at me again, or ever tell me to stay with the girls. Except for that."

"Cool. Let's go shoot some undead things on the TV, then."

"Loser."

"Not if I win."

"Like *that* ever happens."

2

The next day, Claire had classes at Texas Prairie University, which was always a mixture of fascinating and annoying; fascinating, because she'd managed to finagle her way into a lot of advanced classes she really didn't have the prerequisites for, and annoying because those not in the know about Morganville in general—which was most of the students at the school—treated her like a kid. Those who didn't, and knew the score about the vampires and the town of Morganville itself, mostly avoided her. It occurred to her, the second time somebody tried to buy coffee for her but not make eye contact, that some people in town still looked at her as *important*—as in Monica Morrell–level important.

This seriously pissed off Monica, Queen Bee of the Morganville Under-Thirty set. Still, Claire had come a long way from the clueless early-admission freshman she'd been last year. When Monica tried to bully her—which was virtually certain to happen at least a couple of times every week—the outcome wasn't usually in Monica's favor, or always in Claire's, either. But still, a draw was better than a beat-down, in Claire's view. Everybody was left standing.

Claire's first stop was at the campus student store, where she bought a new backpack—sturdy, not too flashy, with lots of pockets inside and out. She ducked

into the next bathroom she found to transfer the contents of her taped-together book bag to the new one, and almost threw the old one away ... but it had a lot of sentimental value, somehow. Ripped, scuffed, stained with all kinds of things she didn't want to remember, but it had come with her to Morganville, and somehow she felt that throwing it away would be throwing away her chance of ever getting out of here.

Crazy, but she couldn't help it.

In the end, she stuffed the rolled-up old backpack into a pocket of the new one, hefted the weight, and jogged across campus to make her first class of the day.

Three uneventful (and mostly boring) hours later, she ran into Monica Morrell, who was sitting on the steps of the Language Arts building, sunglasses on, leaning back on her elbows and watching people go by. One of her lipstick mafia girls was with her—Jennifer—but there was no sign of the other one, Gina. As always, Monica looked expensive and perfect—Daddy's estate must be holding up well no matter what the economy dudes were saying on TV—and Jennifer looked as though she shopped the cheap knockoffs of what Monica bought for full price. But they both looked good, and about every thirty seconds some college boy stopped to talk to them, and almost always got shot down in flames. Some of them took it okay. Some of them looked as if they were one more rejection from ending up on a twenty-four-hour channel as breaking news.

Claire was heading up the steps, ignoring them, when Jennifer called out brightly, "Hey, Claire! Good morning!"

That was creepy enough to stop Claire right in her tracks. She looked over, and Jennifer was *waving*.

So was *Monica*.

This, from the two girls who'd punched and kicked her, thrown her down a flight of stairs, abducted her at least twice, threatened her with knives, tried to set

her house on fire . . . yeah. Claire didn't really feel like redefining the relationship on their new buddy-buddy terms.

She just gave the two of them a long look, and kept on up the stairs, trying to focus on what it was she was supposed to remember today about early American literature. Nathaniel Hawthorne? So last week . . .

"Hey!" Monica grabbed her two steps from the top, yanking on the strap of her new book bag to drag her to a halt. "Talking to you, bitch!"

That was more like it. Claire glanced down at Monica's hand and raised her eyebrows. Monica let go.

"I figured it couldn't be me," she said. "Since you were acting so nice and all. Had to be some other Claire."

"I just thought since the two of us are more or less stuck with each other, we might as well try to be friendly, that's all. You didn't have to act as if I stole your boyfriend or something." Monica smiled slowly and pulled her sunglasses down to stare over the top. Her big, lovely blue eyes were full of shallow glee. "Speaking of that, how *is* Shane? Getting bored with the after-school special yet?"

"Wow, that's one of your better insults. You're almost up to junior high level. Keep working on it," Claire said. "Ask Shane yourself if you want to know how he's doing. I'm sure he'd be glad to tell you." Colorfully. "What do you want?"

"Who says I want something?"

"Because you're like a lion. You don't bother to get up unless you're getting something out of it."

Monica smiled even wider. "Hmmm, harsh, but accurate. Why work harder than you have to? Anyway, I hear you and your friends made a deal that's getting you into trouble. Something with that skanky homeless Brit vamp—what's his name? Mordred?"

"Mordred is from the King Arthur stories. It's Morley."

"Whatever. I just wanted to tell you that I can take care of it for you." Her smile revealed teeth, even and white. "For a price."

"Yeah, I didn't see that coming," Claire said with a sigh. "How are *you* going to take care of it, exactly?"

"I can get him the passes out of town he wants. From my brother."

Claire rolled her eyes and adjusted her book bag a little more comfortably on her shoulder. "Meaning what? You're going to forge his signature on a bunch of photocopies that will get everybody thrown in jail except you? No thanks. Not interested." Claire had no doubt that whatever Monica was offering, it wasn't real; she'd already talked to Monica's brother, Mayor Richard Morrell, several times about this and gotten nowhere. But Monica liked to pretend she had "access"—with full air quotes. "If that's all, I've got class."

"Not quite," Monica said, and the smile vanished. "I want the answers to the final exam in Lit 220. Get them."

"You're kidding."

"Do I look like I'm kidding? Get them, or—well, you know what kind of *or* there is, right?" Monica pushed the sunglasses back up. "Get them to me by Friday or you're fried, special needs."

Claire shook her head and took the last two steps, walked to her class, dumped her bag at her lecture hall seat, and sat down to think things over.

By the time class began, she had a plan—a warm, fuzzy plan.

Some days, it was absolutely worth getting out of bed.

When Claire got home, the sun was slipping fast toward the horizon. It was too early for most vampires to be out—not that they burst into flames that easily; most of the older ones were sort of flame-retardant—but she

kept a sharp lookout, anyway. Instead of going straight
to the Glass House, she turned at the cross street and
went a few more blocks. It was like déjà vu because her
parents' house looked almost exactly like the Glass
House; a little less faded, maybe. The trim had been
painted a nice dark green, and there were fewer bushes
around the windows, different porch furniture, and a
couple of wind chimes; Claire's mom loved wind chimes,
especially the big, long ones that rang those deep bell
sounds.

As Claire climbed the steps to the porch, a gust blew
by her, sounding the bells in a chorus. She glanced up
at the sky and saw clouds scudding by fast. The weather
was changing. Rain, maybe. It already felt cooler.

She didn't knock, just used her key and went right
in, dumping her backpack in the entry hall. "Hey, I'm
home!" she yelled, and locked the door behind her.
"Mom?"

"Kitchen," came the faint yell back. Claire went down
the hall—same as in the Glass House, but Mom had
covered this version with photos, framed ones of their
family. Claire winced at her junior high and high school
photos; they were unspeakably geeky, but she couldn't
convince Mom to take them down. *Someday, you'll
be glad I have them*, Mom always said. Claire couldn't
imagine that would ever be true.

The living room was, again, disorientingly familiar;
instead of the mismatched, comfortable furniture of the
Glass House, the stuff from Claire's childhood occupied
the same space, from the old sofa to her dad's favorite leather chair. The smells coming from the kitchen
were familiar, too: Mom was making stuffed bell peppers. Claire fortified herself, because she couldn't stand
stuffed bell peppers, but she almost always ate the filling
out of them, just to be nice.

"Why couldn't it be tacos?" She sighed, just to her-

self, and then pushed open the door to the kitchen. "Hi, Mom, I'm—"

She stopped dead in her tracks, eyes wide, because *Myrnin* was sitting at her mother's kitchen table. Myrnin the vampire. Myrnin her boss. *Crazy* mad scientist Myrnin. He had a mug of something that had *better* not be blood in front of him, and he was almost dressed like a sane person—he had on frayed blue jeans, a blue silk shirt, and some kind of elaborate tapestry vest over it. He wore flip-flops for shoes, of course, because he seemed to really love those. His hair was long around his shoulders, black and glossy and full of waves, and his big, dark eyes followed Claire's mother as she busied herself at the stove.

Mom was dressed the way Mom usually dressed, which was way more formal than people Claire's era would ever think was appropriate for lounging around the house. A nice pair of dress pants, a boring shirt, mid-heeled shoes. She was even wearing jewelry—bracelet and earrings, at least.

"Good evening, Claire," Myrnin said, and transferred his attention over to her. "Your mother's been very kind to me while I waited for you to get home."

Mom turned, and there was a false brightness to her smile. Myrnin made her nervous, although Myrnin was obviously making a real effort to be normal. "Honey, how was school?" She kissed Claire on the cheek, and Claire tried not to squirm as her mom rubbed at the lipstick mark left on her skin. At least she didn't use spit.

"School was great," Claire said, which completed the obligatory school conversation. She got a Coke from the fridge, popped the top, and settled in across the table from Myrnin, who calmly sipped from his coffee cup. "What are you doing here?"

"Claire!" her mother said, sounding a little scandalized. "He's a guest!"

"No, he's my boss, and bosses don't drop in on my parents without an invitation. What are you doing here?"

"Dropping in on your parents without an invitation," Myrnin said. "I thought it would be good to get to know them better. I've been telling them how satisfied I am with the work you've been doing. Your research is some of the best I've ever seen."

He really *was* on his best behavior. That didn't even sound a little crazy; overdone, maybe, but not crazy.

"I'm off today," Claire pointed out. Myrnin nodded and rested his chin on his hand. He had a nice smile, when he chose to use it, as he did now, mostly directed at Claire's mother, who brought over a coffeepot and refilled his cup.

Oh, good. Not anything red being served, then.

"Absolutely. I know you had a full class schedule today," he said. "This is a purely social call. I wanted to reassure your parents that all was going well for you." He looked down into his coffee. "And that what happened before would never happen again."

What happened before was code for the bite marks on her neck. The wounds were healed, but there was a scar, and as she thought about it, her hand went up and covered the scar, on its own. She forced it back down. Her parents didn't have any idea that Myrnin was responsible for that; they'd been told that it had been some other random vamp, and that Myrnin had helped save her. It was partly true, anyway. Myrnin *had* helped save her. He'd just also been the one to bite her.

Not that it had really been his fault. He'd been hurt, and desperate, and she'd just been there. At least he'd stopped himself in time.

She certainly hadn't been able to stop him.

"Thanks," she said. She couldn't really be mad at him, not for any of it. It would have been easier if she could have. "Are you staying for dinner?"

"Me? Delicious as it smells, I fear I'm not one for bell peppers," he said, and stood up with one of those graceful moves vampires seemed so good at pulling off. They moved like humans, but *better*. "I'd better take my leave, Mrs. Danvers. Thank you so much for your hospitality, and the delicious coffee. Please tell your husband I thank him as well."

"That's it?" Claire asked, mystified. "You came to talk to my parents, and now you're leaving?"

"Yes," he said, perfectly at ease, and perfectly weird. "And to drop this off for you, from Amelie." He patted his vest pockets, and came up with a cream-colored envelope, which he handed over to her. It was heavy, expensive paper, and it was stamped on the back with the Founder's Seal. It was unopened. "I'll see you tomorrow, Claire. Don't forget the donuts."

"I won't," she said, all her attention on the envelope in her hands. Myrnin said something else to her mother, and then the kitchen door opened and closed, and he was gone.

"He has such beautiful manners," her mother said, locking the back door. "I'm glad you work for someone so—civilized."

The scar on Claire's neck throbbed a little. She thought of all the times she'd seen Myrnin go off the rails—the times he'd curled up weeping in a corner; the times he'd threatened her; the times he'd raved like a lunatic for hours on end; the times he'd begged her to put her out of his misery.

The time he'd actually given her samples of his own brain—in a Tupperware container.

"Civilized," she repeated softly. "Yeah. He's great." He was; that was the awful thing. He was great until he was horrible.

Kind of like the world in general.

Claire slit open the envelope with a kitchen knife,

slipped out the heavy folded paper inside, and read the beautiful, looped handwriting—Amelie's, without a doubt.

> *In accordance with recent requests, I hereby am providing you with passes to exit and return to Morganville. You must present these to the checkpoints at the edge of town. Please provide them to your party and give them the same instructions. There are no exceptions to this rule.*
>
> *Coordinate with Oliver to arrange your exit time.*

Claire's breath left her in a rush. Morley's passes! Perfect timing, too; she didn't know how much longer any of them could keep Morley and his people from losing patience, and coming to take it out in blood. They wanted out of Morganville.

She could give it to them.

She realized immediately, however, as she took the passes out of the envelope, that there weren't *nearly* enough. Morley's people would need about thirty passes in total. Instead, there were only four in the envelope.

The names read *Michael Glass*, *Eve Rosser*, *Shane Collins*, and *Claire Danvers*.

What the hell was going on?

Claire pulled out her cell phone and hit SPEED DIAL. It rang, and rang, but there was no answer. She hung up and tried another number.

"Oliver," said the voice on the other end.

"Um, hi, it's Claire? Is—is Amelie there with you?"

"No."

"Wait, wait, don't hang up! You're on the town council—I just got a letter that has some passes in it, but it's not enough for—"

"We turned down Morley's request for emigration out of Morganville," Oliver said. He had a low, even

tone to his voice, but Claire felt herself go cold anyway. "He has a philosophy that is too dangerous to those of us who wish to remain . . . What's the phrase? Under the radar."

"But—we made a deal. Me, Shane, Eve, and Michael. We said we'd get them passes."

"I'm aware of your deal. What is your question?"

"It's just—Morley said he'd kill us. If we didn't get the passes for him. We told you that."

Oliver was silent for a long second, then said, "What part of *I'm aware* did you not comprehend, Claire? You and your friends have passes out of Morganville. As it happens, Michael requested leave to travel to Dallas for his recording and concert session. We've decided to allow that, under the condition that all of you travel together. With escort."

"Escort?" Claire asked. "You mean, like police?" She was thinking of Sheriff Hannah Moses, who would be good company in addition to a bad-ass bodyguard; she'd liked Hannah from the moment she'd met her, and she thought Hannah liked her, too, as much as a tough ex-soldier could like a skinny, geeky girl half her age.

"No," Oliver said, "I don't mean police." And he hung up. Claire stared at the screen for a moment, then folded the phone closed and slipped it back in her pocket. She looked down at the passes, the envelope, the letter.

Amelie had decided to really piss off Morley, but at least she'd also decided to get Claire and her friends out of town.

With an escort.

Somehow, Claire knew it wouldn't be as simple as just picking a responsible adult to go with them.

"Go get your father," her mom said, and began setting dishes on the table. "He's upstairs on the computer. Tell him dinner's ready."

Claire gathered up everything and put it in her backpack before heading upstairs. Another wave of same-

but-not-quite washed over her; her mother and father had reserved the same room for her here that she had over in the Glass House, though the two were nothing alike. *Home*—in name, anyway—had her frilly white bed and furniture, stuff she'd gotten when she was ten. Pink curtains. Her room at the Glass House was completely different—dark woods, dark fabrics. Adult.

Dad's computer room would have been Shane's bedroom in the other house, which woke all kinds of thoughts and memories that really weren't appropriate right now and caused her face to heat up as she poked her head in the room and quickly said, "Dad, dinner's ready! Help me eat the stuffed bell peppers before I gag and die?"

Her father looked up from the computer screen with a surprised, guilty jerk, and quickly shut down what he was doing. Claire blinked. *Dad?* Her dad was . . . normal. Boringly normal. Not an activist, not a freak, not somebody who had to hide what he was doing on the computer from his own daughter. "Tell me you weren't looking at porn," she said.

"Claire!"

"Well, sorry, but you did the guilty dance. Most people I know, that means porn."

Her dad pulled in a deep breath, closed his eyes, and said, "I was playing a game."

That made her feel oh-so-much better. Until he said, "It's one of those online multiplayer games."

"Yeah? Which one? One of the fantasy ones?"

He looked mortally embarrassed now. "Not—not really."

"Then what?"

In answer, he brought up the screen. On it was a night scene, a castle, a graveyard—typical horror fare, at least if you were from the 1950s.

A character appeared on the screen—pale, tall, dressed in a Dracula cape and tuxedo.

With fangs.

Her mouth dropped open, and she stared at her father, her normal, boring father. "You're playing a *vampire* game?"

"It's called Castlemoor. I'm not just playing it. I get paid to be there, to watch what people are doing online."

"You—get paid—to play a vampire? By *who*?"

Her father sat back in his chair, and he slowly shook his head. "That's my business, Claire."

"Is it Amelie? Oliver?"

"Claire." This time, his voice had the parental ring of authority. "Enough. It's a job, and I get paid well enough to do it. We both know it's the best thing I can find, with all my restrictions. The doctors don't want me exerting myself too much."

Her dad wasn't well, and hadn't been for a while now. He was frail, fragile, and she worried about him more and more. About her mother, too. Mom looked frayed around the edges, with a kind of suppressed panic in her eyes.

"You'll be okay?" Claire said. Somehow she made it a question, although she didn't mean to. "Did they find anything else?"

"No, honey, everything's fine. I just need time to get stronger."

He was lying to her, but she could tell that he didn't want her to pursue it. She wanted to; she wanted to yell and scream and demand to know what was going on.

But instead, she swallowed and said, "Playing a vampire online. That's a pretty wild career move, Dad."

"Beats unemployment. So, stuffed bell peppers, huh? I know how much you love those." Claire made a gagging sound. Her dad reached over and ruffled her dark hair. "Why don't you just tell her you don't like them?"

"I did. I do. It's a mom thing. She just keeps telling me I *used* to like them."

"Yeah," he agreed. "That's a mom thing."

* * *

Dinner passed the way it normally did, with Claire picking out edible parts of the bell pepper and her mother holding forth about whatever she was doing for the week. Claire contributed when direct questions came her way; otherwise, she just stayed out of it. She always knew what Mom was going to say, anyway. And she knew Dad wouldn't say much, if anything.

What he *did* say was, "Why don't you bring Shane over some night for dinner?"

It was as if time stopped. Her mother froze, fork halfway to her mouth; Claire froze, too, but unfortunately she was in the process of gulping down a mouthful of Coke at the time, which meant coughing and sputtering, watering eyes, the whole embarrassing bit.

"Honey, I'm sure Shane's very busy," her mother said, recovering. "Right, Claire?"

"I'd like to talk to him," her father said, and right now there wasn't any warm-and-fuzzy daddy vibe. It was more PARENT, in big, flashing red letters. "Soon."

"Uh—okay, I'll see if— Okay." Claire frantically cut up a piece of stuffed bell pepper and ate it, bell pepper and all. She nearly choked again, but she managed to get it down. "Hey, I might be taking a trip."

"What kind of a trip?"

"To Dallas. With my friends."

"We'll see," Dad said, which meant *no*, of course. "I'd need to talk to Shane first."

Oh God, now they were bargaining. Or she was being blackmailed. Sometimes it was hard to tell the difference. Claire mumbled that she'd try, or something like that, choked down another bite of food that no longer tasted even a *little* good, and jumped up to clear her plate. "Claire!" her mother called after her as she dashed into the kitchen. "You're not running off tonight, are you? I was hoping we could spend some time with you!"

"You just did," Claire muttered as she rinsed the

plate and put it in the dishwasher. She raised her voice and yelled back, "Can't, Mom! I've got to study! All my books are over at the Glass House!"

"Well, you're not walking over there in the dark," Mom said. "Obviously."

"I told you, I've got a pin from Amelie! They're not going to bother me!"

Her dad opened the door of the kitchen. "And what about just garden-variety humans? You think that little pin protects you from everything that could hurt you?"

"Dad—"

"I worry about you, Claire. You take these risks, and I don't know why. I don't know why you think it's okay."

She bit her lip. There was something in his voice, a kind of weary disappointment that cut her to the core and nearly brought tears to her eyes. She loved him, but he could be so *clueless.*

"I didn't say I'd walk, Dad," she said. "I make mistakes, sure, but I'm not *stupid.*"

She took out her cell phone, dialed a number, and turned her back on her father. When Eve answered with a bright, chirping, "Hit me!" Claire said, "Can you come get me? At my house?"

"Claire," her father said.

She turned to look at him. "Dad, I really have to study."

"I know," he said. "I'll drive you home." He said it with a funny little smile, sad and resigned. And it wasn't until she smiled that she realized what he'd really said.

Home. The Glass House.

"It's hard for us to let go," he said. "You know that, right?"

She did. She hesitated for a second, then said into the phone, "Never mind, Eve. Sorry. Dad's bringing me."

Then she hugged her father, and he hugged her back, hard, and kissed her gently on the forehead. "I love you, sweetie."

"I know. I love you, too."

"But not enough to eat more stuffed bell peppers and play Jenga with your folks."

"No more bell peppers, but I'd completely play Jenga," she said. "One game?"

He hugged her even harder. "I'll get the game."

Three games of Jenga later, Claire was tired, happy, and a little bit sad. She'd seen her mom laugh, and her dad look happy, and that was good, but there'd been something odd about it, too. She felt like a visitor, as if she didn't fit here anymore, the way she once had. They were her family, but seen from the outside. She had too many experiences now that didn't include them.

"Claire," her dad said as he drove her home through the darkened streets of Morganville. It was quiet out, only a few cars moving about. Two of them were white police cruisers. At least three other cars they passed had heavy tinting, too heavy for humans to see through. "Your mom had a talk with me, and I'm not going to insist you keep on living at home with us. If you want to live with your friends, you can."

"Really?" She sat up straight, looking at him. "You mean it?"

"I don't see how it makes much difference. You're seventeen, and a more independent seventeen than I ever was. You've got a job and responsibilities beyond anything I can really understand. It doesn't make much sense for us to keep trying to treat you like a sheltered little girl." He hesitated, then went on. "And I sound like the worst dad in the world, don't I?"

"No," she said. "No, you don't. You sound like—like you understand."

He sighed. "Your mother thinks if we just put more restrictions on you, things would get back to normal. You'd go back to being the same little girl she knew. But they won't, and you won't. I know that."

He sounded a little sad about it, and she remembered

how she'd felt at the house—a little out of place, as if she were a visitor in their lives. Her life was splitting off on its own.

It was such a strange feeling.

"But about Shane—," her father continued.

"Dad!"

"I know you don't want to hear it, but I'm going to say it anyway. I'm not saying Shane is a bad guy—I'm sure he's not, at heart—but you really need to think about your future. What you want to do with your life. Don't get in too deep, too fast. You understand what I'm saying?"

"You married Mom when you were nineteen."

He sighed. "I knew you'd bring that up."

"Well? It's okay for you to make decisions before twenty, but not me?"

"Short answer? Yes. And we both know that if I really wanted to, I could make Shane's life a living hell. Dads can do that."

"You wouldn't!"

"No, I won't, because I do think he really loves you, and he really wants to protect you. But what Shane may not get at that age is that he could be the worst thing in the world for you. He could completely derail you. Just—keep your head, okay? You're a smart girl. Don't let your hormones run your life."

He pulled the car to a stop at the Glass House, behind Eve's big monster of a car. There were lights blazing in the windows—warmth and friendship and another life, *her* life; one her parents could only watch from the outside.

She turned to her father and saw him watching her with that same sad, quiet expression. He moved a strand of hair back from her face. "My little girl," he said, and shook his head. "I expect you for dinner soon."

"Okay," she said, and kissed him quickly. "Bye, Daddy. I love you."

He smiled, and she quickly got out of the car and ran up the cracked walk, jumped up the steps to the porch, and waved at him from the front door as she got out her keys. Even so, he waited, watching until she'd actually opened the door, stepped in, and closed it. Only then did she hear the engine rev as his car pulled out.

Michael was playing in the living room. *Loud.* That wasn't normal at all for him, and as Claire came around the corner, she found Eve and Shane sitting on the floor, watching the show. Michael had set up an amplifier, and he was playing his electric guitar, which he rarely did at home, and *damn.* That was impressive stuff. She sank down next to Shane and leaned against him, and he put his arm around her. The music was like a physical wall pushing over her, and after the first few seconds of fighting it, Claire finally let herself go; she was pulled away on the roaring tide of notes as Michael played. She had no idea what the song was, but it was fast, loud, and amazing.

When it was over, her ears were left ringing, but she didn't care. Along with Shane and Eve, she clapped and whooped and whistled, and Michael gravely took a bow as he shut down the amp and unplugged. Shane got up and high-fived, then low-fived him. "Nothing but net, man. How do you do that?"

"No idea, really," Michael said. "Hey, Claire. How are the folks?"

"Okay," she said. "My dad says I can officially move back in." Not that she'd ever really moved out.

"I knew we'd wear them down," Eve said. "After all, we really are amazingly cool." And now it was Eve's turn for the high five with Shane. "For a bunch of misfit geeks, slackers, and losers."

"Which one are you?" Shane asked. She flipped him off. "Oh, right. Loser. Thanks for reminding me."

Claire dug in her backpack and came out with the passes Myrnin had delivered. "Uh—I got these today. Somebody want to fill me in?"

Michael, at vampire speed, crossed the distance and snatched the paper out of her hand. He spread out the individual passes and stared at them with a blank, shocked expression. "But—I didn't think—"

"Apparently, somebody agreed," Claire said. "Eve?"

Eve frowned. "What? What is it?"

"Passes," Michael said. "To leave town, to go to Dallas. To do the demo."

"For you?"

"For all of us." Michael looked up and slowly smiled. "You know what this means?"

Shane threw back his head and let out a loud wolf howl. "Road trip!" he yelled! "Yes!"

Michael put his arms around Eve, and she melted against him, her pale-painted face against his chest, hands around his waist. Claire saw her dark eyes flutter closed, and a kind of peaceful happiness came over Eve's face—and then her eyes snapped open. "Wait," she said. "I've never—I mean—outside? Of Morganville? To *Dallas*? You can't be serious. Michael?"

He held up a pass with her name on it. "It's signed. Official."

"They're letting us *leave town*? Are they *insane*? Because once I hit the shops in Dallas, I don't think I'm ever coming home." Eve made a face. "And I can't believe I just thought of Morganville as *home*. How much of a saddie am I?"

"Eight out of ten," Shane said. "But we do have to come back, right?"

"Right," Michael said. "Well, *I* have to come back. I've got nowhere else to go. You guys . . ."

"Stop," Eve said, and put a hand over his mouth to enforce the order. "Just stop there. Please."

He looked down at her, and their eyes locked. He took her hand away from his mouth, and then lifted the backs of her fingers to his lips for a long, slow kiss. It was just about the sexiest thing Claire had ever seen,

full of sweetness and love and longing. From the expression on Eve's face, it was just about the sexiest thing *she'd* ever seen, too. "We'll talk about it on the road," Michael said. "The passes are good for a week. I'll make some calls and see when they need me in the studio there."

Eve nodded. Claire doubted she could put any words together, right at that moment.

"Hey," Shane said, and tapped Claire on the nose. "Snap out of it."

"What? What!"

"Seriously. You've got this chick flick hit-by-the-romance-hammer look. Stop it."

"Ass."

He shrugged. "I'm not one of those romantic guys," he said. "Hey, date Michael if you want that."

"No, don't," Eve said dreamily. "Mine."

"And there goes my blood sugar level," Shane said. "It's getting late, Claire has school tomorrow, I've got a long day of chopping fine barbecue—"

"I think we'll stay down here," Michael said. He and Eve still hadn't blinked or looked away from each other.

"I am *really* not sticking around for that." Shane took Claire's hand in his. "Upstairs?"

She nodded, hitched her bag on her other shoulder, and followed him up. Shane opened the door of his room, turned, and lifted her hand up to his lips. He didn't *quite* kiss it. His dark eyes were wicked with laughter.

"Ass," she said again, more severely. "You couldn't be romantic if your life depended on it."

"You know what's lucky? Most bad guys don't ask you to be romantic on command, so that probably won't matter."

"Only girlfriends do that."

"Well, they *can* qualify as supervillains. But only if

they have a secret underground base. Wait—you've got a mad scientist for a boss, and a lab—"

"Park it," she said, and smacked his arm. "Are you going to kiss me good night, or what?"

"Romantic on command. See?"

"Fine," Claire said, and this time she actually *did* feel a little annoyed. "Then don't. Good night."

She pulled away from him and walked away the few steps to her own room, opened the door, slammed it, and flopped on her bed without bothering to turn on the lights. After a few seconds she remembered that in Morganville that was never a smart choice, and switched on the bedside Tiffany lamp. Rich colored light threw patterns on the wood, the walls, her skin.

No monsters were hiding in the shadows. She was too tired to check under the bed or in the closet.

"Ass," she said again, and put her pillow over her face to scream her frustration into it. "Shane Collins is an ass!"

She stopped at the sound of a soft knock on the door. She put the pillow aside and waited, listening.

The knock came again.

"You're an *ass*," she yelled.

"I know," came Shane's voice through the door. "Let me make it up to you?"

"As if you can."

"Try me."

She sighed, slid off the bed, and went to open up.

Shane was standing there, of course. He came inside, closed the door behind him, and said, "Sit down."

"What are you doing?"

"Just sit down."

She did, perching on the edge of the bed and already frowning. There was something really different in the way he was acting now—the flip side of how he'd been just a few moments ago, teasing and teen-boy.

This seemed much more . . . adult.

"When you were in the hospital, after Dan . . . well, you know." He shrugged. "You were kind of drugged up. I'm not sure what you remember."

She didn't remember all that much, really. A boy had abducted her and hurt her pretty badly. She'd lost a lot of blood, and they'd given her something for the nightmares. She remembered everybody coming to see her— Mom, Dad, Eve, Michael, Shane. Even Myrnin. Even Amelie and Oliver.

Shane . . . he'd stayed with her. He'd said . . .

She couldn't really remember what he'd said.

"Anyway," Shane said, "I told you this was for later. I guess it's kind of later, so, anyway."

He took out a small velvet box from his pocket, and Claire's heart just . . . stopped. She thought she might faint. The top of her head felt very hot, and the rest of her felt very cold, and all she could look at was the box in his hand.

He wasn't. He *couldn't.*

Was he?

Shane was looking at the box, too. He turned it in his fingers restlessly. "It's not what you think," he said. "It's not—look, it's a ring, but I don't want you to think—" He opened the box and showed her what was inside.

It was a beautiful little ring, silver, with a red stone in the shape of a heart, and hands holding it on either side. "It's a claddagh ring," he said. "It belonged to my sister, Alyssa. My mom gave it to her. It was in Alyssa's locker at school when she—when the house burned." When Alyssa died. When Shane's life completely collapsed around him.

Tears burned in Claire's eyes. The ring glittered, silver and red, and she couldn't look at Shane's face. She thought that might destroy her. "It's beautiful," she whispered. "But you're not asking—"

"No, Claire." He suddenly sank to his knees, as if the

strength had just gone out of him. "I suck, I know, but I can't do something like that, not yet. I'm . . . Look, family doesn't mean to me what it means to you. Mine fell apart. My sister, my mom—and I can't even think about my dad. But I love you, Claire. That's what this means. That I love you. Okay?"

She looked up at him then, and felt tears break free to run hot down her cheeks. "I love you, too," she said. "I can't take the ring. It means—it means too much to you. It's all you have left of them."

"That's why it's better if you have it," he said, and held out the box, cupped in one hand. "Because you can make it a better memory. I can barely look at this thing without seeing the past. I don't want to see the past anymore. I want to see the future." He didn't blink, and she felt the breath leave her body. "You're the future, Claire."

Her head felt light and empty, her whole body hot and cold, shaking and strong.

She reached out and took the velvet box. She pulled the ring out and looked at it. "It's beautiful," she said. "Are you sure—"

"Yes. I'm sure."

He took the ring from her and tried it on her right hand. It fit perfectly on the third finger.

Then he lifted her hand to his lips and kissed it, and it was *definitely* better than Michael had done it, *definitely* sexier, and Claire dropped to her knees with him; then he was kissing her, his mouth hot and hungry, and they fell back together to the throw rug next to the bed, and stayed there, locked in each other's arms, until the chill finally drove them up to the bed.

3

Of all the mornings Claire didn't want to get up, the next one was the worst. She woke up warm and drowsy, cuddled like a spoon against Shane, their hands clasped even in sleep. She felt *great*. Better than any day, ever, in her whole life.

In the still hush of early morning, she tried to freeze the moment, the sound of his soft, steady breathing, the feel of him relaxed and solid next to her.

I want this, she thought. *Every day. For life. Forever.*

And then her alarm clock went off, shrieking.

Claire flailed and slapped at it, then succeeded in knocking it to the floor. She dived for it and finally got it switched off, feeling like a complete fool that she'd ever left it on in the first place. She twisted around and saw Shane had opened his eyes, but hadn't otherwise moved. He looked drowsy and sweet and lazy, hair mussed, and she leaned back down to kiss him, sweet and slow.

His arms went around her, and it felt so natural, so perfect, that she felt that glow again, that feeling of absolute *rightness*.

"Hey," he said. "You're cute when you're panicked."

"Just when I'm panicked?"

"Ouch. Yeah, that didn't come out as absolutely complimentary as I'd planned. And you hang around Eve *way* too much." His fingers drew lazy circles on her back,

which felt like trails of sunlight. "What's the plan for today? Because I'm in favor of nothing but this."

She *so* wanted that, too. But there was a reason her alarm had gone off. "I have class," she said with a sigh.

"Skip it." He kissed her bare shoulder.

"I—you've got work! Remember? Sharp pointy knives and beef to chop?"

"Fun as that is, this is better."

Well, his arguments were persuasive. *Really* persuasive. For about another thirty minutes, and then Claire forced herself to get up, grab the shower before Shane could get to it, and try to get her mind off the fact that he was lying in her bed.

And he still was when she came back in to grab her backpack. His hands were behind his head, and he looked ridiculously satisfied with the world—and with himself.

She smacked his bare foot, which was sticking out from under the sheet. "Get up, Lord of the Barbecue."

"Ha. Don't have to yet. You're the one who had the bad idea to sign up for seven a.m. classes. Me, I go to work at a sensible hour."

"Well, you're not lying around in my bed all day, so get up. I don't trust you alone in here."

His smile was wicked and really, really dangerous. "Probably a good idea," he said. "Not that you can exactly trust me in here when you're with me."

Oh, she was *not* going to climb back in bed with him. She was *not*. She had things to do. After gulping in a few deep breaths, she leaned over, gave him a quick kiss, avoided his grabby hands, and dashed to the door. "Out of my bed," she said. "I mean it."

He yawned. She grinned and shut the door on her way out.

Downstairs, the coffeepot was already brewing, and Michael was sitting at the table, a laptop computer open in front of him. She was a little surprised; Michael wasn't

really the computer type. He had one, and she supposed he had e-mail and stuff, but he wasn't always on it or anything. Not like most people their age. (Not like her, honestly.)

He looked up at her, then down at the screen, and then back up, to stare at her as if he'd never seen her before.

"What?" she asked. "Don't tell me some of Kim's skanky home video made YouTube." That was something she really didn't ever want to think about again. Kim and her little sneaky spying habits. Kim and her plans to make herself a star with all her hidden video cameras recording every aspect of life in Morganville.

Yeah, that hadn't gone so well for Kim, in the end.

He shook his head and went back to the computer. "I've been checking about the studio, the recording session, you know? They're serious, Claire. They want me in there on Thursday."

"Really?" She grabbed a cup of coffee and slid into a chair across from him, then doctored up her drink with milk and sugar. "So we have to leave Thursday morning?"

"No, I'm thinking we leave tonight. Just in case. And besides, it gives us some time to get used to Dallas, and I don't want to travel during the day." Right. Vampires. Road trip. Sunlight. Probably not the best idea.

"We can't take your car, can we? I mean, the tinting's not legal outside of Morganville."

"Yeah. Which is another reason for night driving. I figure we can take Eve's car. It's roomy and it's got a big trunk, in case."

In case they got caught in the sun, he meant. Claire tapped her fingers on the coffee cup, thinking. "What about supplies?" she said. "You know."

"I'll stop at the blood bank and pick up a cooler," he said. "To go."

"Seriously? They do that?"

"You'd be surprised. We can even put Cokes in there, too."

That didn't seem too sanitary, somehow. Claire tried not to think about it. "How long are we going to be gone?"

"If we leave tonight and I do the demo on Thursday during the day, we could be back on Friday night. Or Saturday, depending on what kind of stuff you guys want to do. I'm easy."

That made Claire remember something. "Uh—you know we're going to have an escort, right?"

"Escort?" Michael frowned. "What kind of escort?" Claire mimed fangs. Michael rolled his eyes. "Perfect. Who?"

"No idea. All I know is Amelie's letter said we had to clear our departure time with Oliver."

Michael kept on frowning. He reached for his cell phone and dialed as he sipped more coffee. "It's Michael," he said. "I hear we have to clear leaving town with you. We're planning on going tonight, around dusk."

His face went entirely blank as he listened to whatever Oliver said on the other end. Michael didn't say anything at all.

Finally, he put the coffee cup down and said, "Do we have a choice?" Pause. "I didn't think so. We'll meet you there."

He hung up, carefully laid the cell phone down on the table next to his coffee, and sank back in his chair, eyes closed. He looked—indescribable, Claire decided. It was as if there were so many things inside him fighting to come out that he couldn't decide which one to let off the leash first.

"What?" she finally asked, half afraid to even try.

Eyes still shut, Michael said, "We've got an escort, all right."

"Who?"

"Oliver."

Claire set down her own coffee cup with a thump that slopped brown liquid over the rim. *"What?"*

"I know."

"We have to be trapped in a car with *Oliver*?"

"I *know*."

"So much for the fun. Fun all gone."

He sighed and finally opened his eyes. She knew that look; she remembered it from when she'd first met him. Bitter and guarded. Hurt. Trapped. Then, he'd been a ghost, unable to leave this house, caught between human and vampire.

Now he was just as trapped, only instead of the house, his boundaries were the town limits. He'd felt, for the last few hours, as if he could break free, be someone else.

Oliver had just taken that away from him.

"I'm sorry," Claire said. He shut the computer, unplugged it, and stood up. He didn't meet her eyes again.

"Be ready at six," he said. "Tell Shane. I'll tell Eve."

She nodded. He kept his head down as he walked toward the kitchen door. When he got there, he stopped for a few seconds without turning back to look at her. "Thanks," he said. "Sucks, you know?"

"I know."

Michael laughed bitterly. "Shane would have said, *And so do you.*"

"I'm not Shane."

"Yeah." He still didn't turn around. "I'm glad you're happy with him. He's a good guy, you know."

"Michael—"

He was already gone by the time she said his name, just the swinging door left behind. There was no sense chasing him. He wanted to brood in private.

She called Shane to tell him what time they were leaving, but *not* about Oliver. Frankly, she didn't want to have that grief just yet. She went on to class. After her early ones, she had a two-hour break, which meant she had things to do, so she could leave town with a clear conscience.

And besides, she'd been looking forward to this since she'd first thought of it.

First step—she walked the few blocks from campus to Common Grounds, Oliver's coffee shop, and ordered up a mocha. He was behind the bar—a tall older man, with hippie hair and a tie-dyed T-shirt under his coffee-stained apron. When he was serving customers, you'd never know he was a vampire, much less one of the meanest she'd ever met.

Mocha in hand, Claire texted Monica's cell. *Meet me at Common Grounds ASAP.*

She got back an immediate *Btr B good.*

Oh, it would be.

Claire sipped and waited, and Monica eventually rolled up in her hot red convertible; no Gina and Jennifer this time. Monica seemed to be getting out more and more without her backup singers, which was interesting. Claire supposed even they were getting tired of providing constant on-demand validation.

Monica blew in the front door of the shop in a dress that was too short for her, but showed off her long tanned legs; the swirl of wind *almost* made it illegal. She shoved her expensive sunglasses up on top of her glossy black hair and scanned the room. The sneer that twisted her full lips was probably mostly reflex.

After putting in her coffee order, Monica slipped into a chair across from Claire. "Well?" she said, and dropped her tiny purse on the table. "Like I said, this had better be good."

When Oliver brought over Monica's coffee, Claire said, "Would you mind staying for a minute?"

"What?"

"As a moderator." Oliver was a broker of deals in Morganville. Common Grounds was a key place where humans and vampires could meet, mingle in safety, and reach all kinds of agreements that Oliver would witness and enforce.

Pretty rarely between humans, though.

Oliver shrugged and sat down between the two girls. "All right. Make it quick."

Monica already looked thunderously angry, so Claire spoke first. "Monica made a deal with me for test answers. I want you to witness me handing them over."

Oliver's eyebrows twitched up, and the look on his face was bitterly amused. "You're asking me to witness a schoolyard transaction for cheating. How ... quaint."

Claire didn't wait. She pushed over a thumb drive toward Monica. "There's an electronic file on there," she said. "It's password protected. If you can figure out the password, you can have the answers."

Monica's mouth dropped open. *"What?"*

"You said I had to give them to you. I did. That's what I wanted Oliver to see. Now you have them, so we're done. No comebacks. Right?"

"You put them under a *password*?"

"One you can guess," Claire said. "If you did the homework. Or can read fast."

"You little *bitch*." Monica's hand flashed out—not for the thumb drive, but for Claire's arm. She crushed it to the table, her nails digging in deep enough to draw blood. "I told you, I'll fry your ass."

"With you, I know that's not an empty threat," Claire said. "Alyssa Collins is proof of that."

Monica went very still, and something flickered across her eyes—shock? Maybe even regret and guilt. "I'm not taking this thing. You give me the answers without the password."

Oliver cleared his throat. "Did you specify how she had to give you the answers?"

"No," Claire said. "She just said I had to. I did. Hey, this is the nicest way I could have done it. I could have given it to her in Latin or something."

"Let go of her," Oliver said mildly. When Monica didn't, his tone turned icy. "Let. *Go.*"

She pulled her hand back and folded her arms over her chest, glaring at Claire, her jaw set hard. "This isn't over."

"It is," Oliver said. "Not her fault you made a poor definition of what it was you wanted from her. She satisfied all requirements. She's even given you a reasonable chance of discovering the password. Take it and walk away, Monica."

"This isn't over," Monica repeated, ignoring him. When she reached for the thumb drive, Oliver's pale, strong hand slapped down over it, and over her fingers, holding her in place. Monica yelped. It must have hurt.

"Look at me," he said. Monica blinked and focused on his face, and Claire saw her pupils widen. Her lips parted a little. "Monica Morrell, you are my responsibility. You owe me respect, and you owe me obedience. And you *will* leave Claire Danvers alone. If you have cause to attack her, you will tell me first. *I* will decide whether or not you can take action. And you do *not* have my permission. Not for this." He let go. Monica yanked her hand back and cradled it against her chest. "Now, take your business and your coffee elsewhere. Both of you."

Monica reached out and snatched up the small memory stick. As she did, Claire said, "The thumb drive cost me ten bucks." Monica's glare reached nuclear levels, but since Oliver was still sitting there, she dug in her tiny purse, found a crumpled ten-dollar bill, and flung it over the table to Claire. She smoothed it out, smiled, and put it in her pocket.

"If you're quite finished," Oliver said. "Leave. Monica, go first. I won't have you doing anything messy. I'm not your maid."

Monica sent him a look that was definitely *not* a glare; it was much more scared than angry. She picked up her purse, the coffee, and stalked to the door. She didn't look back as she piled into her convertible and burned rubber pulling out.

"One of these days," Oliver said, still looking toward the street, "you're going to be too clever for your own good, Claire. You do realize that."

She did, actually. But sometimes, it was just impossible to do anything else.

"I guess you're coming with us tonight?"

Oliver turned his head to look at her this time, and there was something so cold and distant in his eyes that she shivered. "Did you hear me when I told you to leave? I don't like being used to settle your problems."

She swallowed, picked up her stuff, and left.

The afternoon was spent with Myrnin at his freaky mad-scientist lab, which was actually much nicer after the renovations he'd done: new equipment; computers; nice bookcases; decent lighting instead of crazy turn-of-last-century things that emitted sparks when you tried to turn them off or on.

Still, no matter how nice the decor, Myrnin was never less than half crazy. He was under pressure from Amelie, Claire knew; with the death—could computers die?—of Ada, the town's master computer; he was struggling to figure out a way to make a replacement, but *without* putting a human brain into it, which Claire strongly discouraged, seeing how well that had worked out with Ada, and the fact that Claire herself was almost certainly the next candidate.

"Computers," Myrnin said, then shoved the laptop she'd put out for him aside and glared at it as if it had personally insulted him. "The technology is entirely idiotic. Who built this? Baboons?"

"It works fine," Claire said, and took command of the computer to bring up the interface she'd designed. "All you have to do is explain to me how Ada was connected into the portal and security systems, and I can build some kind of connector. You can run it right from this screen. See?" She'd even gotten an art student at the school to design the interface in a steampunky kind

of way, which she thought would make him feel more at home. Myrnin continued to frown at it, but in a less aggressive way. "Try it. Just touch the screen."

He reached out with one fingertip and pressed the screen over the icon of the shield. The security screen came up, all rusted iron and ornamental gears. He made a humming sound in the back of his throat and pressed again. "And this would control the programming."

"Yeah, it's GUI—a graphic user interface."

"And this program would be able to detect vampires and humans, and treat them differently?"

"Yeah. We just use heat-sensing technology. Vampires have a lower body temperature. It's easy to tell the difference."

"Can it be cheated?"

Claire shrugged. "Anything can be cheated. But it's pretty good."

"And the memory alteration?"

That was a problem—a big problem. "I don't think you can actually do that with a computer. I mean, isn't that some kind of vampire mind thing?" Because Ada had, in fact, been a vampire. And the machine that Myrnin had built to keep her brain alive had somehow allowed her to broadcast that vampire power on a wide field. Claire didn't really understand it, but she knew it worked—*had* worked.

"That's a rather large failure. What's this?" Myrnin tapped an icon that had a radar screen icon. Nothing happened.

"That's an early-warning system, to monitor approaches to town. In case."

"In case what?"

"In case someone like Mr. Bishop decides to visit again."

Myrnin smiled and leaned back in his chair, folding his hands in his lap. "There is no one like Mr. Bishop," he said. "Thank the most holy. And this is excellent work,

Claire, but it doesn't solve our fundamental problem. The difference engine needs programming to allow for removal of dangerous memories. I know of no other way to achieve what we need than to interface it with a biological database."

"A brain."

"Well, if you want to be technical."

Claire sighed. "I am *not* getting you a brain, because I am not that kind of lab assistant, Dr. Frankenstein. Can we go through the map again?"

The map was a giant flowchart that stretched the length of the lab, on giant notepads. She had painstakingly mapped out every single *if*, *then*, and *and/or* that Myrnin had been able to describe.

It was huge. Really huge. And she wasn't at all sure it could be done, period—except that he had done it, once, to Ada.

She just wanted to take the icky brain part out of the equation.

"It's so much easier," Myrnin insisted as they walked the row of pages. "The brain is capable of processing a staggering number of calculations per second, *and* is capable of incorporating variables and factors that a mere computer cannot. It's the finest example of a calculating machine ever developed. We're fools not to use it."

"Well, you're not putting my brain into a machine. Ever."

"I wouldn't." Myrnin picked a piece of lint from his shiny vest. "Unless it was the only answer, of course. Or, of course, unless you weren't using it anymore."

"*Never.* Promise."

He shrugged. "I promise." But not in any way that mattered, Claire thought. Myrnin's promises were kind of—flexible. "You're leaving town the rest of the week?"

"Yeah, we're leaving tonight. You'll be okay?"

"Why wouldn't I?" He clasped his hands behind him and paced back and forth, staring at the charts. He was wearing shorts today, and flip-flops, of course—like some homeless surfer from the waist down, some Edwardian lord from the waist up. It was strange, and ridiculously Myrnin. "I'm not an infant, Claire. I don't need you to take care of me. Believe me."

She didn't, really. Yes, he was old. Yes, he was a vampire. Yes, he was crazy/smart—but the crazy part was always as strong as, or stronger than, the smart part. Even now.

"You're not going to do anything stupid, are you?" she asked him. He turned and looked at her, and looked utterly innocent.

"Why in the world would I do that?" he asked. "Have a good time, Claire. The work will still be here when you return."

She shut down the laptop and closed the lid, packing it up to put it away. As she did, he finally nodded at the machine. "That's not bad," he said. "As a start."

"Thanks." She was a little surprised. Myrnin didn't often give out random compliments. "Are you feeling okay?"

"Certainly. Why wouldn't I be?"

There was just something off about his mood. From visiting her parents to the way he was restlessly prowling the lab—he just wasn't his usual, unsettlingly manic self. He was a *different* manic self.

"I wish I were going with you," he finally said. "There. I've said it. You may mock me at your will."

"Really? But—we're just going for Michael, really." That wasn't true. It was a chance to get out of Morganville, experience life out in the real world. And she knew it would be amazing to feel free again, even for a little while. "Couldn't you go if you wanted?"

He sat down in his leather wing chair, put on his spec-

tacles, and opened a book from a pile next to it. "Could I?" he asked. "If Amelie didn't wish me to leave? Not very likely."

She'd never considered that Myrnin, of all people, could be just as trapped in Morganville as everybody else. He seemed so . . . in control, somehow, at the same time he was wildly *out* of control. But she could see that of everyone in town, Amelie would trust Myrnin the least in terms of actually exiting the town limits. He had too much knowledge, too much insanity brewing around in that head of his.

As careful as Amelie was, she'd never take the risk. No, Myrnin, of everybody in Morganville, would be the next to last to leave, right before Amelie herself. He was her—pet? No, that wasn't right. Her *asset*.

It had never really occurred to Claire that he might not altogether like that.

"Sorry," she said softly. He waved at her, a shooing motion that left her feeling a little lost. She genuinely liked Myrnin, even though she was always intensely aware, these days, of the limits of that friendship—and of the dangers. "Call me if you—"

"Why? So you'll come running back to Morganville?" He shook his head. "Not likely. And not necessary. Just go, Claire. I'll be here."

There was a grim sound to that she didn't like, but it was getting late. Michael had said to be ready at six, and she needed to pack for the trip.

When she looked back, Myrnin had given up the pretense of reading and was just staring off into the distance. There was something horribly sad about his expression, and she almost turned back. . . .

But she didn't.

4

The Glass House was chaos when Claire opened the door. Mostly that was Eve and Shane, fighting stereo wars and yelling at each other upstairs. Eve was favoring Korn; Shane was fighting back by blasting "Macarena" at the limit of the boom box knob. There was no sign of Michael, but his guitars were cased and sitting in the living room, along with a duffel bag and a rolling cooler that looked like it could hold any normal drinks. Claire just wasn't sure what it *did* hold, and she didn't open it to find out.

She dropped her backpack, which she figured she'd take anyway, and jogged upstairs. Eve was standing in a pile of clothes, an open suitcase on the bed, holding two identical-looking shirts and frowning at them. Terminal fashion indecision. Claire dashed in, tapped her right hand, and Eve gave her a grateful grin and tossed the shirt into the suitcase. The music was so loud, conversation was impossible.

As she passed Shane's door, she saw him sprawled on his bed. He had a duffel bag, like Michael's but brown instead of blue. He looked bored, but he brightened up when he saw her.

"Seriously?" she yelled. "'The Macarena'?"

"It's war," he yelled back. "I had to bring out the heavy artillery. Next up, Barry Manilow!"

Claire hit the POWER button on the stereo, leaving Korn thundering victoriously through the house. After a second or two, Eve turned it down. "See how easy that was?" Claire said.

"What, giving up? Giving up is *always* easy. It's the peace that follows that sucks." Shane slithered off the bed and followed her as she headed for her room. "How was it?"

"What?"

"Everything."

"You know." She shrugged. "Normal." Yeah. She'd manipulated the second most powerful vampire in town into taking her side against a psycho bitch-queen sorority girl. She'd talked rationally about putting people's brains into computers. This was a normal day. No wonder she was screwed up. "How was yours?"

"Brisket. Chopping block. Cleaver. It's all good. You packed yet?"

"Did you just see me walk in?"

"Oh. Yeah. Guess not, then."

He parked himself on her bed, flopped out again as she opened up her one battered suitcase and began filling it. That wasn't tough; unlike Eve, she wasn't a clothes fanatic. She had a couple of decent shirts, a bunch of not-so-great ones, and some jeans. She put in her one skirt, along with the shoes that matched it, and the fishnet tights. Shane watched, hands laced behind his head.

"You're not going to try to tell me what to take?" she asked. "Because I figured that was why you followed me."

"Do I look crazy? I followed you because your bed is more comfortable." His smile widened. "Wanna see?"

"Not right now."

"Last chance before we hit the road."

"Stop it!"

"Stop what?"

"Looking so . . ." She couldn't think of a word. He

looked just as ridiculously hot to her now as he had this morning, when it had been so tough to leave. And that was a good thing. "I've got to get stuff out of the bathroom."

"Good luck. I think Eve took everything already except the aftershave."

Actually, Eve hadn't; it was just that Claire didn't have a whole lot. Shampoo and conditioner, all in one bottle. A little makeup bag. A razor. She didn't really need a blow-dryer, but if she did, Eve would have packed one—or two. From the size of the suitcase, Eve was planning to take everything she'd ever owned.

Back in the bedroom, Claire almost shut her suitcase, then stopped and frowned. "What did you take?" she asked. "For, you know, protection?"

Shane lifted himself up on his elbows. "What, like, uh, *protection*?"

"No!" She felt her face flush, which was pretty ridiculous, considering what they'd done this morning. "I mean, against any vampire things that might happen. You know."

"Stakes in the bottom of the duffel bag," he said. "Brought some extra silver nitrate in bottles, too. We should be okay. It's not as if there's a big vampire problem where we're going."

Maybe not, but living in Morganville had made it a reflex. Claire couldn't honestly imagine *not* planning for it, and she hadn't been raised here, in the hothouse. She was surprised Shane seemed so . . . calm.

But then, Shane had been outside of Morganville, for two years. And they hadn't been a good two years, either, but at least he knew something about what it was going to be like; more than Michael and Eve, anyway.

Claire dug in her underwear drawer, came up with four silver-coated stakes, and dumped them in on top of her clothes. Just in case. Shane gave her a thumbs-up in approval. She slammed the bag shut and locked it,

then wrestled it off the bed. It was heavier than she'd expected, and it wasn't one with wheels and a handle. Shane, unasked, slid off the bed and took it from her. He lifted it as if it were the weight of a bag of feathers, went into his room, grabbed his duffel, and headed toward the stairs. As he passed Eve's room he looked in, shook his head, and yelled, "You are totally on your own for that one!"

Claire saw why, as she looked in. Eve had closed the suitcase and somehow gotten it to the floor, but it was the size of a trunk.

At least it had wheels.

Michael was downstairs when Shane and Claire came down; Shane thumped their bags down and said, "You'd better wrangle your girlfriend's bag, man. I would, but I don't want to spend the entire trip in traction."

Michael grinned and zoomed upstairs. He came down carrying the suitcase as if it were nothing. Claire noticed it was new and shiny, and had hand-applied death's-head stickers and biohazard marks. Yeah, that was definitely Eve's. Oh, and it was black. Of course.

"Snacks!" Eve yelped, and dashed into the kitchen. She came back with a bag full of things. "Road food. Trust me. Totally necessary. Oh, and drinks—we need drinks." She caught sight of the cooler. "Okay, not you, Michael. The rest of us."

They were loading the second cooler with non-blood-related drink items when the doorbell rang. Claire opened it to find Oliver standing on the doorstep. The sun was still up, but he was wearing a hat and a long black coat, which didn't in any way make him less sinister. His hair was tied back and must have been tucked up under his hat. She wondered if it was flammable, like the rest of him. Age had made him flame-retardant, but he'd still suffer out in the sun, and eventually burst into flames, if he couldn't get out of it.

He came in without waiting for an invitation. "Yeah,

welcome." Claire sighed and shut the door. "We're getting stuff together. Uh, is that all you brought?" It was one bag, smaller even than Michael's or Shane's.

Oliver didn't bother to answer her. He walked past, into the living room, and straight for Michael. Eve and Shane, who were bickering over the placement of the Cokes versus the bottled iced coffees, fell silent, and Claire joined them.

"You're surely not taking all this," Oliver said, looking at the pile of stuff on the floor. It was, Claire had to admit, a lot—mainly because Eve's suitcase was the size of Rhode Island, but they'd all contributed. "Is there room?"

"I have a major trunk," Eve said. "It'll fit."

Oliver shook his head. "I hate traveling with amateurs," he said. "Very well. Get the car loaded. Michael and I will wait inside until the sun is down."

He acted as if he were the boss, which was annoying, but the truth was, he *was* the boss. Amelie had assigned him as escort, and that meant he could boss them around all he wanted. Heaven, for Oliver. Hell, for everybody else.

Claire shrugged silently, then picked up her suitcase and backpack and led the way.

Packing the car was hilariously awful, because trying to get Eve's suitcase wedged in was a drama nobody needed. It finally worked, and everything else fit in, including the guitars and the coolers. It left the three of them sweaty, annoyed, and exhausted, but by the time they'd worked it all out, the sun was safely down.

Nobody tried to call shotgun. Oliver took the front seat, Michael got in the driver's seat, and Eve, Claire, and Shane took the back. It wasn't even all that crowded.

"Passes," Oliver said, and held out his hand. Michael handed them over, and Oliver examined them as if he didn't know they'd already been cleared to leave town. "Very well. Proceed."

"Tunes!" Eve said. "We need—"

"No music," Oliver said. "I will not be subjected to what you consider *tunes*."

"FYI, I know it's a disguise, but you even suck at being a hippie," Eve muttered. "At least like the Beatles or something."

"No."

"It's going to be a really long trip," Shane said, and put his arm around both Claire and Eve, since he was in the middle. "But at least I've got all the babes. Backseat, for the win."

"Shut up," Michael said.

"Come back here and make me, *Dad*."

Michael and Shane exchanged rude gestures, and then Michael started up the car and pulled away from the curb. Eve squirmed in her seat and clapped her hands.

Oliver turned and glared at her. He took off his black hat and set it on the dashboard, next to Eve's nodding skeletal figurine. "Enough of that," he said. "It's bad enough I have to be trapped in a car with you children. You'll do your best not to *act* like children."

"Oliver," Michael said, "back off. It's our first time out of town. Let us enjoy it a little."

"The first time for some of you," Oliver said, and looked out the window as the houses of Lot Street began to roll by, one after another. "For some of us, this is not quite as life-changing an event."

That was kind of true, but still, Claire felt Eve's excitement was contagious. Michael was smiling. Shane was enjoying being the dude in the backseat. And she was . . . leaving Morganville behind, at least for a little while.

At the town limits, Claire watched the WELCOME TO MORGANVILLE sign approach. This side said PLEASE DON'T LEAVE US SO SOON!

They rocketed past it doing at least seventy, maybe

eighty miles an hour. Beyond the sign sat a police cruiser—one of Hannah Moses's crew. Claire felt her breath rush out, but the cop behind the wheel just waved them on, and Michael didn't even slow down.

Morganville, in the rearview mirror.

Just like that.

It shouldn't have been so easy, Claire thought. After all that, all the fighting and the terror and the threats.

They just . . . drove away.

Michael switched on the radio and found a scratchy rock 'n' roll station, and although Oliver kept glaring, he turned it up, and before long they were all singing "Born to Be Wild," out of tune and at the top of their lungs. Oliver didn't, but he didn't pitch an übervamp fit, either. Claire was almost certain that once or twice, she saw his lips moving with the lyrics.

The sunset was glorious, spilling colors all over the sky in shades of orange and red and gold, fading into indigo blue. Claire rolled down the window and smelled the cool, crisp air, flavored with dust and sage. Outside of Morganville there was scrub desert, and a lot of it. Nothing to see for miles except flat, empty land, and the two-lane blacktop road stretching into the distance, straight as an arrow.

"We have to do some jogging around on farm roads," Michael said, once the song was over and the music shifted to something not as karaoke worthy. "Should be on the interstate in about two hours or so."

"You're sure you know where you're going?" Shane asked. "Because I don't want to wake up in the Gulf of Mexico or something."

Michael ignored that, and Claire slowly settled into her seat, feeling relaxed and light. They'd *left*. They'd actually *left Morganville*. She could feel the same suppressed thrill and relief in Shane, and, on his other side, from Eve, whose dark eyes just glowed with excitement. She'd been dreaming of this her whole life, Claire re-

alized. Maybe not being trapped in a car with Oliver, or that Michael would be a vampire, but leaving town with Michael had always been one of Eve's top-ten fantasies.

And here they were, more or less, anyway, which just went to show you that your top-ten fantasies might turn out to be completely different experiences than you'd ever thought.

"We're out," Eve said, almost to herself. "We're out, we're out, we're *out*."

"You'll go back," Oliver said, and turned his head to stare out the side window. "You all go back, eventually."

"Even for a vampire, you're a ray of sunshine," Shane said. "So, we should probably talk about what we're going to do in Dallas."

"Everything!" Eve said, instantly. "Everything, everything, everything. And then everything else."

"Whoa, hit the brakes, girl. We've got, what, a hundred bucks between the two of us? I'm pretty sure the all-inclusive everything party package costs more."

"Oh." Eve looked surprised, as if she hadn't even thought about money at all. Knowing Eve, she likely hadn't. "Well, we have to at least go to some of the good clubs, right? And shopping? Oh, and they have some really good movie theaters."

"Movies?" Michael repeated, looking in the rearview mirror. "Seriously? Eve."

"What? *Stadium seating*, Michael. *Digital*. With three-D and everything."

"You're going to waste your first trip outside of Morganville inside a movie theater?"

"No, well, I—*stadium seating!* Okay, okay, fine. Museums. Concerts. Culture. Better?"

Shane just shook his head. "Not really. Where's the fun, Eve?"

"That *is* fun!"

Oliver sighed and let his head fall against the window glass with a soft thump. "One of you is going to be left to walk to Dallas if you don't *shut up.*"

"Wow. Who got up on the wrong side of the coffin this evening?" Eve shot back. "Well? You're the expert. Where would you go?"

Oliver straightened up and looked back at her. "Excuse me?"

"I'm asking your opinion. You probably know where the best places are to go."

"I—" Oliver seemed at a loss for words, which was pretty funny; Claire couldn't imagine the last time that had happened to him. Probably not in the last couple of centuries, she guessed. "You're asking for my recommendations. Of things to do in Dallas."

"Yep."

He stared at Eve for a long, silent, chilly moment, then turned back, face forward. "I doubt our tastes have anything in common. You're too young for the bars, and too old for the playgrounds. I know nothing of what you'd like." Then, after a second's pause, he continued. "Perhaps the malls."

"Malls!" Eve almost shrieked it, then clapped both hands over her mouth. "Oh my God, I forgot about the malls. With actual stores. Can we go to the mall?"

"Which one?"

"There's more than one! Okay, uh—one with a Hot Topic store."

Oliver was—from Claire's point of view—almost *smiling.* "I believe that could be arranged."

"Great." Shane sighed, and let his head drop back against the seat. "The mall. Just what I always wanted."

Claire reached up and threaded her fingers through his. "We can do other stuff." When he glanced over at her, and she realized that everybody *else* was looking

at her, too, she colored and added, "Cultural stuff. You know. Bookstores. Museums. There's a cool science museum I'd like to see."

"Is there not a video game store in this entire town?"

"Let's just get there first," Michael said.

That was good advice, Claire thought as the last colors faded from the sky and night took over. That was *really* good advice.

She dozed a little bit, but she woke up when the car jerked violently, veered, and she heard the tires squeal. She was still trying to understand what had happened when Oliver snapped, "Pull over."

"What?" Michael, in the glow of the dashboard, looked like a ghost, his eyes wide and his face tense.

"You've never driven outside of Morganville. I have. Pull over. Vampire reflexes will put you into an accident, not save you from one. Humans can't react in the same way you can. It takes practice to drive safely around them on the open road."

So Michael must have tried to dodge a car. Wow. Somehow, Claire had never considered that vampire reflexes could be a downside. Michael must have felt spooked enough to agree with Oliver, because he pulled the car off to the shoulder, gravel crunching under the tires, and got out. He and Oliver changed places. Oliver checked the car's mirrors with the ease of long practice, eased the car back on the road, and the whole thing settled into a steady, rolling rhythm. Claire looked over at the other two in the backseat. Eve had her headphones on and her eyes closed. Shane was sound asleep. It was . . . peaceful, she supposed. She looked out at the night. There was a quarter moon, so it wasn't all that bright out, but the silver light gilded sand and spiky plants. Everything in the wash of the car's headlights was vivid; everything else was just shadows and smoke.

It was like space travel, she decided. Every once in a

while you could see an isolated house, far out in the middle of nowhere, with its lights blazing against the night. But mostly, they were out here alone.

Oliver took a turn off the two-lane highway, heading for the interstate, she supposed. She didn't ask—not until they passed a road sign that had an arrow pointing to Dallas.

The arrow pointed left. They headed straight on.

"Hey," she said. "Hey, Oliver? I think you missed your turn."

"I don't need advice," Oliver said.

"But the sign—"

"We have a stop to make," he said. "It won't take long."

"Wait, what? What stop?" It was news to Michael, apparently. That didn't ease the sudden anxiety in Claire's chest. "What's this about, Oliver?"

"Be still, all of you. It's none of your affair."

"Our car," Michael pointed out. "And we're in it. So it looks like it *is* our affair. Now, where are you taking us, and why?"

Shane woke up, probably sensing the tension in Michael's voice. He blinked twice, swiped at his face, and leaned forward. "Something wrong?"

"Yeah," Michael said. "We're getting hijacked."

Shane sat up slowly, and Claire could feel the tension coiling in him.

"Easy, all of you," Oliver said. "This is a directive from Amelie. There's a small issue I need to address. It won't take long."

Eve, who'd removed one earphone, gave a jaw-cracking yawn. "I could stretch my legs," she said. "Also, bathroom would be good."

"What kind of small issue?" Shane asked. He was still tense, watchful, and not buying Oliver's no-big-deal attitude. Oliver's cold eyes fixed on him in the rearview mirror.

"Nothing of consequence to you," he said. "And this isn't a debate. Shut up, all of you."

"Mikey?"

Michael gazed at Oliver for a long few seconds before he finally said, "No, it's okay. A short stop would do us all good, probably."

"Depending on where," Shane said, but shrugged and sat back. "I'm cool if you are."

Michael nodded. "We cool, Oliver?"

"I told you, it's not a debate."

"Four of us, one of you. Maybe it could be."

"Only if you want to answer to Amelie in the end."

Michael said nothing. They drove on through the inky night, surrounded by a bubble of backwashed headlights, and finally a faded sign glowed green in the distance. Claire blinked and squinted at it.

"'Durram, Texas,'" she read. "Is that where we're going?"

"More importantly, does it have an all-night truck stop?" Eve groaned. "Because I was serious about that bathroom thing. Really."

"Your bladder must be the size of a peanut," Shane said. "I think I see a sign up there."

He did, and it was a truck stop—not big, not very clean, but open. It was crowded, too—six big rigs in the lot, and quite a few pickup trucks. Oliver took the exit and pulled off into the truck stop, edging the car to a halt at a gas pump. "Top off the tank," he told Michael. "Then park it and wait for me inside. I'll be back."

"Wait, when?"

"When I'm done. I'm sure you can find something to occupy yourselves." And then the driver's side door opened, and Oliver walked away. As soon as he was outside of the wash of the harsh overhead lights, he vanished.

"We could just leave," Shane pointed out. "Fill up and drive off."

"And you think that's a good plan?"

"Actually? Not really. But it's a *funny* plan."

"Funny as in getting us killed. Some more than others, I might add."

"Fine, rub the resurrection in our faces. But seriously. Why are we doing this? We ditch Oliver; we never have to go back to Morganville. Think about it."

Claire licked her lips and said, softly, "Not all of us can walk away, Shane. My parents are there. Eve's mom and brother. We can't just pick up and leave, not unless we want something bad to happen to them."

He looked actually ashamed of himself, as if he'd really forgotten that. "I didn't mean—" He gave a heavy sigh. "Yeah, okay. I see your point."

"Added to that, I'm Amelie's blood now," Michael said. "She can find me if she wants me. If you want to include me in the great escape, I'm like a giant GPS tracking chip of woe."

"Whoa."

"Exactly."

Eve said, plaintively, "Bathroom?"

And that closed the discussion of running away.

At least, for the moment.

The Texas Star Truck Stop was worse on the inside than the outside.

As Claire pushed open the door—with Shane trying to open it for her—a tinny bell rang, and when she looked up, Claire found herself being stared at—a lot.

"Wow," Shane murmured, close behind her as he entered the store. "Meth central."

She knew what he meant. This was a scary bunch of people. The youngest person in the place, apart from them, was a pinched, too-tanned skinny woman of about thirty wearing a skimpy top and cut-off shorts. She had tattoos—a lot of them. Everybody else was older, bigger, meaner, and uncomfortably fixed on the newcomers.

And then Eve stepped in, in all her Goth glory, bouncing from one Doc Marten–booted foot to the other. "Bathroom?" she asked the big, bearded man behind the counter. He frowned at her, then reached down and came up with a key attached to a big metal bar. "Thank you!" Eve seized the key and dashed off down the dark hall marked as RESTROOMS; Claire wasn't sure she'd have the guts, no matter how much she had to pee. That did *not* look safe, never mind clean.

Michael stepped in last, and took it all in with one quick, comprehensive look. He raised his eyebrows at Shane, who shrugged. "Yeah," he said. "I know. Fun, huh?"

"Let's get a table," Michael said. "Order something." Under the theory, Claire guessed, that if they spent money, the locals would like them better.

Somehow, she didn't think that was going to work. Her gaze fell on signs posted around the store: YOU DRAW YOUR GUN, WE DRAW FASTER. GUN CONTROL MEANS HITTING WHAT YOU AIM AT. NO TRESPASSING—VIOLATORS WILL BE SHOT; SURVIVORS WILL BE SHOT AGAIN.

"I don't think I'm going to be hungry," she said, but Michael was right. This really was their only option, other than sitting outside in the car. "Maybe something to drink. They have Coke, right?"

"Claire, people in Botswana have Coke. I'm pretty sure Up the Road Apiece, Texas, has Coke."

By the time they'd gotten seated at one of the grungy plastic booths, still being stared at by the locals, Eve finally joined them. She looked more relaxed, bouncy, and more—well, Eve. "Better," she announced, as she slipped into place next to Michael. "Mmm, *much* better now."

He put his arm around her and smiled. It was cute. Claire found herself smiling, too, and snuggled up against Shane. "How was the bathroom?"

Eve shuddered. "We shall never speak of it again."

"I was afraid of that."

"You want a menu?"

"Absolutely. They might have ice cream."

The last thing bouncy, happy Eve needed was a sugar rush, but ice cream did sound good. . . . Claire looked around for a waitress and found one leaning against the cracked counter, whispering to the man on the other side. They were both staring straight at Claire and her friends, and their expressions weren't exactly friendly.

"Uh, guys? Maybe ixnay on the ice cream-ay. How about we wait in the car?" she asked.

"And miss *ice cream*? Hella don't think so," Eve said. She waved at the waitress and smiled. Claire winced. "Oh, relax, CB. I'm a people person."

"In Morganville!"

"Same thing," Eve said. She kept on smiling, but it started getting a little strained as the waitress continued to stare but didn't acknowledge the wave. Eve raised her voice. "Hi? I'd like to order something? Helloooooooo?"

The waitress and the guy behind the counter seemed frozen in place, glaring, but then they were blocked out by someone stepping into Claire's line of sight—more than one someone, in fact. There were three men, all big and puffy, and with really unpleasant expressions.

Shane, who'd been slumped lazily next to her, straightened up.

"Don't y'all got no manners where you come from?" the first one asked. "You wait your turn. Sherry don't like being yelled at."

Eve blinked, then said, "I wasn't—"

"Where you from?" he interrupted her. The men formed a redneck wall between the table and the rest of the room, pinning the four of them in place. Shane and Michael exchanged a look, and Michael took his arm away from Eve's shoulders.

"We're on our way to Dallas," Eve said, just as cheerfully as if the situation hadn't gone from inhospitable to

ominous. "Michael's a musician. He's going to record a CD."

The three men laughed. It wasn't a nice sound, and it was one Claire recognized all too well—it was deeper in register, but it was the same laugh Monica Morrell and her friends liked to give when stalking their prey. It wasn't amusement. It was a weird sort of aggression— laughing *at* you, not *with* you; sharing a secret.

"Musician, huh? You in one of those *boy* bands?" The second man—shorter, squattier, wearing a dirty orange ball cap and a stained University of Texas sweatshirt with the arms cut off. "We just love our *boy* bands out here."

"I ever meet those damn Jonas Brothers in person, I'll give 'em what for," the third man said. He seemed angrier than the others, eyes like black little holes in a stiff, tight face. "My kid can't shut up about 'em."

"I know what you mean," Eve said with a kind of fake sweetness that made Claire wince, again. "Nobody's really been worth listening to since New Kids on the Block, am I right?"

"What?" He fixed those dead, dark eyes on her.

"Wow, not a New Kids on the Block fan, either. I'm shocked. Okay, I'm thinking not Marilyn Manson, then. . . . Jessica Simpson? Or . . ." Eve's voice faded out, because Michael's hand had closed over her arm. She looked over at him, and he shook his head. "Right. Shutting up now. Sorry."

"What do you want?" Michael asked the men.

"Your little freak vampire girlfriend needs to learn how to keep her mouth shut."

"Who you calling *little*?" Eve demanded.

Shane sighed. "Wrong on so many levels. Eve. *Shut up.*"

She glared at him but made a little key-and-lock motion at her lips, folded her arms, and sat back.

Michael had locked gazes with the third man, the an-

gry one, and they were staring it out. It went on for a while, and then Michael said, "Why don't you just let me and my friends have our ice cream, and then we'll get back in our car and leave? We don't want a problem."

"Oh, you don't, you whiny little bitch?" The angry man shoved the other two aside and slapped his palms flat against the table to loom over Claire and her friends. "Why'd you come in here, then?"

Eve said, in a very small voice, "Ice cream?"

"Told you to shut the hell up." And he tried to hit her with a backhanded smack.

Tried because Michael leaned forward in a flare of motion, and had hold of the man's wrist in a flicker of time so fast Claire didn't even see it. Neither did the angry man, who looked just kind of confused by being unable to move his hand, then put it all together and looked at Michael.

"Don't," Michael said. It was soft, and it was a warning, through and through. "You try to hurt her again and I'll pull your arm off."

He wasn't kidding, but the problem was, *none* of them was kidding. While he was holding the angry one, the guy in the orange cap reached in his pocket, flicked open a big, shiny knife, and grabbed Eve by the hair. She squeaked, raised her chin, and tried to kick him. He was good at avoiding her. It looked as if he'd had practice. "Let Berle go," Orange Cap said. "Or I'll do a hell of a lot worse than slap this one. I can get me real creative."

Shane was cursing softly under his breath, and Claire knew why; he was stuck in the corner, she was in front of him, and there was no way he could be effective in helping Michael out from that angle. He had to just sit there—something he wasn't very good at doing. Claire stayed very still, too, but she looked Orange Cap in the eyes and said, "Sir?" She said it respectfully, as her mom had taught her. "Sir, please don't hurt my friend. She didn't mean anything."

"We don't like smart-mouthed freaks around here," he said. "We got our ways."

"Yes sir. We understand now. We were just trying to have a little fun. We won't be any trouble, I promise. Please let my friend go." She kept her tone calm, sweet, reasonable—all the things she'd learned to do when Myrnin was running off his rails.

Orange Cap blinked, and she thought he was seeing her for the first time. "You need better friends, little girl," he said. "Shouldn't be running around with a bunch of freaks. If you was my daughter—" But he'd lost his edge, and he let go of Eve's hair and wiped his hand on his greasy jeans as he folded up his knife. "You get on up out of here. Right now. You let Berle go, and we'll let this pass. Nobody gets hurt."

"We're going," Claire said instantly, and grabbed Shane's hand. Michael let go of the angry guy, Berle, who snatched his arm back and rubbed at his wrist as if it hurt. It probably did. Claire could see white marks where Michael had held him. That was restraint, for Michael; he probably could have broken the bone without much effort. "Sir?" She spoke again to Orange Cap, treating him like the man in charge, and he nodded and clapped his friends on the shoulders.

They all stepped back.

Claire slipped out of the booth and squeezed by the men, practically dragging Shane with her. Eve and Michael followed. They walked away from the table, into the store, and Claire pushed open the door and led them all outside, into the harsh white light near the gas pumps and the car.

She looked back at the store. The three men, the people working the restaurant, and practically everyone else were looking out the windows at them.

Claire turned on Eve first. "Are you *crazy*?" she demanded. "Just couldn't shut up, could you? And *you*!" She pointed at Michael. "You're not in Morganville any-

more, Michael. Back there you were a big dog. Out here, you're what *we* were back *there*. Vulnerable. So you need to stop thinking that people owe you respect just because you're a vampire."

He looked stunned. "That's not what I—"

"It was," she said, interrupting him. "You acted like a vamp, Michael. Like any vamp getting back-talked by a human. You could have gotten us hurt. You could have gotten Eve killed!"

Michael looked at Shane, who lifted his shoulders in a tiny, apologetic shrug. "She's not wrong, bro."

"That's not what it was," Michael insisted. "I was just trying to—look, Eve started it."

"Hey! That thump you heard was me under the bus, there!"

Shane shrugged again. "And now Michael's not wrong. Hey, I like this game. I don't have to be the wrong one for once in my life."

"Shut up, Shane," Eve snapped. "What about you, Miss *Oh, sir, please let my friends go; I'm such a delicate little flower*? What a crock of shit, Claire!"

"Oh, so now you're mad because I got you out of it?" Claire felt her cheeks flaming, and she was literally shaking now with anger and distress. "You started it, Eve! I was just trying to keep you from getting killed! Sorry you didn't like how I pulled that off!"

"You just—can't you stand up for yourself?"

"Hey," Shane said softly, and touched Eve's arm. She whirled toward him, fists clenched, but Shane held up both hands in clear surrender. "She stood up for *you*. Might want to consider that before you go calling Claire a coward. She's never been that."

"Oh, *sure*, you take her side!"

"It's not a side," Shane said. "And if it is, you ought to be on it, too."

Michael had been watching, calming down (or at least shutting down), and now he reached out and put

his hands on Eve's shoulders. She tensed, then relaxed, closed her eyes, and blew out an impatient breath. "Right," she said. "You're going to tell me I can't be upset about nearly getting my face cut off."

"No," Michael said. "But don't take it out on Claire. It's not her fault."

"It's mine."

"Well . . ." He sighed. "Kind of mine, too. Share?"

Eve turned to face him. "I like my blame. I keep it close like a warm, furry blanket."

"Let go," he said, and kissed her lightly. "You're taking my side of the blame blanket."

"Fine. You can have half." Eve was calmer now, and relaxed into Michael's embrace. "Damn. That *was* stupid, wasn't it? We nearly got killed over ice cream."

"Another thing I don't want on my tombstone," Shane said.

"You have others?" Claire asked.

He held up one finger. "I thought it wasn't loaded," Shane said. Second finger. "Hand me a match so I can check the gas tank." Third finger. "Killed over ice cream. Basically, any death that requires me to be stupid first."

Michael shook his head. "So what's on your good list?"

"Oh, you know. Hero stuff that gets me rerun on CNN. Like, I died saving a busload of supermodels." Claire smacked his arm. "Ow! *Saving* them! What did you think I meant?"

"So," Claire said, taking the high ground, "what now? I mean, I guess ice cream is kind of off the table, unless you're okay with random violence as a topping."

"Got to be something else in town," Michael said. "Unless you just want to sit here and take up a gas pump until Oliver gets his act together."

"He told us to wait here."

"Yeah, well, I'm with Michael on this one," Shane said. "Not really into doing what Oliver wants, you

know? And this is supposed to be our trip, not his. He's just along for the ride. Personally, I like moving the car. Even if we're not leaving him behind."

"You really *do* have a death wish."

"You'll save me." He kissed Claire on the nose. "Mikey, you're driving."

5

Durram, Texas, was a small town. Like, *really* small. Smaller than Morganville. There were about six blocks to it, not really in a square; more like a messy oval. The Dairy Queen was closed and dark; so was the Sonic. There was some kind of bar, but Michael quickly vetoed that suggestion (from Shane, of course); if they'd gotten into trouble asking for ice cream, asking for a beer would be certain doom.

Claire couldn't fault his logic, and besides, none of them was actually bar-legal age, anyway. Though she somehow doubted the folks in Durram really cared so much. They didn't seem like the overly law-abiding types. Cruising the streets seemed like a big, fat waste of time; there weren't any other cars on the streets, really, and not even many lights on in the houses. It seemed like a really boring, shut-up town.

Shades of Morganville, though in Morganville at least you had a good *reason* to avoid being out after dark.

"Hey! There!" Eve bounced in the front seat, pointing, and Claire squinted. There was a tiny, dim sign in a window, a few lights were on, and the sign *might* have said something about ice cream. "I knew no self-respecting small Texas town would shut down ice cream service at night."

"That makes no sense."

"Shut up, Shane. How can you not want ice cream? What is wrong with you?"

"I guess I was born without the ice cream gene. Thank God."

Michael pulled the car to a stop in front of the lonely little ice cream parlor. When he switched off the engine, the oppressive silence closed in; except for street signs creaking in the wind, there was hardly a sound at all in downtown Durram, Texas.

Eve didn't seem to care. She practically flung herself out of the car, heading for the door. Michael followed, leaving Claire and Shane behind in the backseat.

"This isn't going at all how I'd thought," Claire said with a sigh. He laced their fingers together and raised hers to his lips.

"How'd you think it would go?"

"I don't know. Saner?"

"You *have* been paying attention this last year, right? Because saner isn't even in our playbook." He nodded toward the ice cream parlor. "So? You want something?"

"Yes." She made no move to get out of the car.

"Then what—oh." He didn't sound upset about it. He'd been telling the truth, Claire thought. He really didn't have the ice cream gene.

But he *did* have the kissing gene and didn't need that much of a hint to start using it to both their advantages. He leaned forward, and at first it was a light, teasing brush of their lips, then soft, damp pressure, then more. He had such wonderful lips. They made her ignite inside, and it felt like gravity increased, all on its own, dragging her back sideways on the big bench seat; pulling him with her.

Things might have really gone somewhere, except all of a sudden there was a loud metallic knock on the window, and a light shined in, focusing on the back of Shane's head and in Claire's eyes. She yelped and flailed,

shoved Shane away, and he scrambled to get himself together, too.

Standing outside of the car was a man in a tan shirt, tan pants, a big Texas hat.... It took a second for Claire's panicked brain to catch up as her eyes fastened on the shiny star pinned to his shirt front.

Oh. Oh, *crap.*

Local sheriff.

He tapped on the window again with the end of a big, intimidating flashlight, then blinded them again with the business end. Claire squinted and cranked down the window. She licked her lips nervously, and tasted Shane. Inappropriate!

"Let's see some ID," the man said. He didn't sound like the Welcome Wagon. Claire searched around for her backpack and pulled out her wallet, handing it over with trembling hands. Shane passed over his own driver's license. "You're seventeen?" The sheriff focused the beam on Claire. She nodded. He shifted the light to Shane. "Eighteen?"

"Yes sir. Something wrong?"

"Don't know, son. You think there's something wrong about taking advantage of a girl who's under eighteen on a public street?"

"He wasn't—"

"Sure looked that way to me, miss. Out of the car, both of you. This your car?"

"No sir," Shane said. He sounded subdued now. Reality was setting in. Claire realized they'd just made the same mistake that Michael had—they'd acted as if they were home in Morganville, where people knew them. Here, they were a couple of troublemaking teenagers—one underage—making out in the back of a car.

"You got any drugs?"

"No sir," Shane repeated, and Claire echoed him. Her lips, which had felt so warm and lovely just a minute ago, now felt cold and numb. *This can't be happening. How*

could we be this stupid? She remembered Shane's list of ways not to die. Maybe this ought to be number four.

"You mind if I search the car, then?"

"I—" Claire looked at Shane, and he looked back at her, his eyes suddenly very wide. Claire continued. "It's not our car, sir. It's our friend's."

"Well, where's your friend?"

"In there." Claire's throat was tight and dry, and she was holding Shane's hand now in a death grip. *If he searches the car, he'll open the coolers. If he opens the cooler and finds Michael's blood . . .*

She pointed to the ice cream shop door. The sheriff looked at it, then back at her, then at Shane. He nodded, switched off his flashlight, and said, "Don't you go nowhere."

Through all of that, Claire had only a blurry impression of him as a person—not too young, not too old, not too fat or thin or tall or short—just average. But as he walked away, his belt jingling with handcuffs and keys and his gun strapped down at his side, she felt cold and short of breath, the way she had when she'd faced down Mr. Bishop, the scariest vampire of all.

They were in trouble—*big* trouble.

"Fast," Shane said, as soon as the door started to close behind the sheriff. He yanked open the door, grabbed Michael's cooler, and looked around wildly for someplace to put it. "Go to the door. Cover me."

Claire nodded and walked up to the door, looking in the grimy glass, blocking any view past her of the street. She made little blinders out of her hands as if it were hard to see in. It wasn't. The sheriff had walked straight up to Michael and Eve, who were still standing at the counter of the ice cream shop. Eve had an ice cream cone in her hand, fluorescent mint green, but from the look on her face, she'd forgotten all about it.

Claire glanced back. Shane was gone. When she looked back into the store, the sheriff was still talking to

Michael, Michael was answering, and Eve had a terrified look in her eyes.

Claire nearly screamed when someone touched her shoulder, and jumped back. It was Shane, of course. "I put it in the alley, behind a trash can. Covered it with a stack of newspaper," he said. "Best I could do."

The sheriff had finished his conversation, and he, Eve, and Michael were heading for the door. Claire and Shane backed up to the car. Claire leaned against him and felt his heartbeat thudding hard. He looked calm. He wasn't.

Eve didn't even *look* calm. She looked, well, distressed. "But we didn't *do* anything!" she was saying, as they came outside. "Sir, please—"

"Got a report of trouble up at the Quik-E-Stop," the sheriff said. "People fitting your description threatening folks. And to be honest, you kind of stand out around here."

"But we didn't—" Eve bit her lip on blurting that out, because in fact they had. Michael had, for sure. "We didn't mean anything. We just wanted to get some ice cream, that's all."

Hers was starting to leak in thin green streams. Eve, startled, looked down and licked the melted stuff off her fingers.

"Better eat that before it's all over you," the cop said, sounding relaxed and almost human this time. "Do I have your permission to search your vehicle, ma'am?"

"I—" Eve's eyes fixed on Shane, behind the sheriff, who was giving a thumbs-up. "I guess so."

He seemed surprised; maybe even a little disappointed. "Sit down over there, on the curb. All of you."

They did. Eve had trouble doing it gracefully in the poofy black skirt she was wearing, but once she was down, she started wolfing down her ice cream. Halfway through, she stopped and pounded her forehead with an open palm. "Ow, ow, ow!"

"Ice cream headache?" Claire asked.

"No, I'm just wondering how the hell we could be so *bad* at this," Eve said. "All we were supposed to do was drive to Dallas. It shouldn't be this hard, right?"

"Oliver made us stop."

"I know, but if we can't stay out of trouble on our own—"

"That *was* an ice cream headache, right? Not an aneurysm?"

"That's where things explode in your brain? Probably that last thing." Eve sighed and bit into the cone part of her dessert. "I'm tired. Are you tired?"

Michael wasn't saying anything. He was staring at the car, and the cop searching it—going through bags, purses, glove box, even under the seats. He finally glanced over at Shane. "What about the weapons?"

Shane's mouth opened, then closed.

"Uh—"

Right at that moment, the cop opened Claire's suitcase and pulled out a sharp silver stake. He held it up. "What's this?"

None of them answered for a few seconds; then Eve said, "It's for the costumes. See, we're going to this convention? And I'm playing the vampire, and they're playing the vampire hunters? It's really cool."

That almost sounded real.

"This thing's sharp."

"The rubber ones looked really fake. There's a prize, you know? For authenticity?"

He gave her a long look, then dropped it back into Claire's bag, rummaged around, then closed it. He left the suitcases and bags outside the car, scattered around, and after checking in the wheel wells and in the spare tire section, he finally shook his head. "All right," he said. "I'm going to let you all go, but you need to go right now."

"What?"

"I need to see your taillights disappearing over the town limits. And I'm going to follow to make sure you get there nice and safe."

Oh *crap*. "What about Oliver?" Claire whispered.

"Well, we can't exactly give him as an excuse," Eve whispered back fiercely. She ate the last bit of ice cream cone and smiled at the cop. "We're ready, sir! Just let us get loaded up."

Michael grabbed Shane, and they had an urgent conversation, bent over Eve's giant suitcase. Eve leaped up, tripped over a random bag, and went down with a yelp that turned into a howl.

The sheriff, proving he wasn't a total jerk, immediately came to bend over her and see if she was okay.

This gave Michael enough vampire-speed time to retrieve the cooler from the alley, put it back in the car, and be innocently reaching for the next bag before the sheriff helped flailing, clumsy Eve up to her feet.

"Sorry," Eve said breathlessly, and gave Michael a trembling little smile and wave. "I'm okay. Just bruised a little."

"That's it," Shane said. "No more ice cream for you."

They finished loading things in the car, and Claire took a last look at the deserted streets, the flickering, distant, dim lights. There was no sign of Oliver; none at all.

"Well?" the sheriff said. "Let's go."

"Yes sir." Eve slid into the driver's side, closed her eyes for a second, then fumbled for her keys and started the car. Michael took the passenger seat in front, and Claire and Shane climbed in the back.

The sheriff, true to his word, got in his cruiser, parked across the street, and turned on the red and blue flashers; no siren, though.

"Thanks," Michael said, and sent Eve a quick smile. "Good job with the tripping. It gave me time to get the blood."

"Wish I'd meant it, then." She put the car in reverse. "And could we please have another word for blood, outside of Morganville? Something like, oh, I don't know. Chocolate? Red velvet cake?"

"Why is it always sugar with you?" Shane asked.

"Shut up, Collins. This one was all on you, you know."

He shrugged and put his arm around Claire's shoulders. "Yeah, I know. Sorry."

"What are we going to do?" Claire asked. "About Oliver?"

Nobody had an answer.

The sheriff's cruiser let loose a shocking little *whoop* of siren, just to let them know he meant business. Eve swallowed, put the car in reverse, and backed the sedan onto the street. "Guess we'll figure it out as we go," she said. "Anybody got his cell number?"

"I do," Michael and Claire said, simultaneously, and exchanged guilty looks. Michael took out his phone and texted something as Eve drove—staying well under the speed limit, which Claire thought was very smart—and as they passed a sign announcing the town limit, the sheriff's car coasted to a stop. The lights were still flashing.

"Keep going?" Eve asked. She kept looking in the rearview mirror. "Guys? Decision?"

"Keep going," Shane said, leaning forward. "We can't get back as long as he's watching. If we're going back at all. Which I don't vote for, by the way."

"Better idea," Michael said, and pointed up ahead, on the left side of the narrow, very dark road. "There's a motel. We check in, wait for Oliver to join us. We're going to have to sit the day out somewhere, anyway."

"*There?*" Eve sounded appalled, and Claire could see why. It wasn't exactly the Ritz. It wasn't even as good as that motel in the movie *Psycho*. It was a little, straight line of cinder-block rooms with a neon sign, a sagging porch, and one big security light for the parking lot.

And the parking lot was empty.

"You can't be serious," Eve said. "Guys. People get *eaten* in places like this. At the very least, we get locked in a room and terrible, evil things get done to us and put on the Internet. I've seen the movies."

"Eve," Michael said, "horror movies are not documentaries."

"And yet, I really think a serial killer owns this place. No. Not going to—"

Michael's phone buzzed. He flipped it open and read the text. "Oliver says to stop here. He'll join us in about another hour."

"You are *kidding.*"

"Hey, you're the one who had to have the ice cream. Look what kind of trouble we got ourselves into. At least this way we're safe in a room with a door that locks. And the sign says they have HBO."

"That stands for Horrible Bloody Ohmygod," Eve said. "Which is the way they kill you. When you think you're safe."

"Eve!" Claire was starting to get creeped out, too. Eve put her hands up, briefly, then back down to the wheel.

"Fine," she said. "Don't say I didn't warn you, while we're all screaming and crying. And I'm sleeping in my clothes. With a stake in both hands."

"It's probably not run by vampires."

"First, you wanna bet?" Eve hit the brakes and put the car in park. "Second, sharp pointy things tend to work on everything else, too. Including cannibals running creepy motels."

They sat in silence as the engine ticked and cooled, and finally Shane cleared his throat. "Right. So, we're going in?"

"We could stay in the car."

"Yeah, that's safe."

"At least we can see them coming. And also run."

Claire sighed and got out of the car, walked into the

small office, and hit the bell on the counter. It seemed really, really loud. She heard doors slamming behind her—Shane, Michael, and Eve finally bailing out. The office was actually nicer than the outside of the building, with carpet that was kind of new, comfortable chairs, even a flat-screen TV playing on the wall with the sound turned off. The place smelled like . . . warm vanilla.

Out of the back room came an older lady with graying hair tied back in a ponytail. Claire couldn't imagine anyone looking *less* like a serial killer, actually—she looked like a classic grandma, even down to the small, round glasses. She was wiping her hands on a dish towel and was wearing an apron over blue jeans and a checked shirt. "Help you, honey?" she asked, and put the towel down. She looked a little nervous as the others came in behind her. "Y'all need a room?"

"Yes ma'am," Claire said softly. Michael and Shane were doing their best to look like nice boys, and Eve was, well, Eve. Smiling. "Maybe two, if they're not too expensive?"

"Oh, they're not expensive," the lady said, and shook her head. "Ain't exactly the Hilton, you know. Thirty-five dollars a night, comes with breakfast in the morning. I make biscuits and sausage gravy, and there's coffee. Some cereal. Ain't fancy, but it's good food."

Michael stepped up, signed the book, and counted out cash. She read the register upside down. "Glass? You from around here?"

"No ma'am," he said. "We're just passing through. Heading for Dallas."

"What the hell possessed you to come all the way out here?" she asked. "Never mind; glad you did. Fresh sheets and towels in the rooms, soaps, some complimentary shampoo. You need anything, you just call. You kids have a good night. Oh, and no hell-raising. We may be outside of town, but I know the sheriff personally. He'll make a special trip."

"Why does everybody think we're so insane?" Eve asked, and rolled her eyes. "Honestly, we're *nice*. Not everybody our age rolls with anarchy."

"You would, if anarchy offered free ice cream," Michael said. He accepted the two keys and smiled. "Thank you, ma'am—"

"Name's Linda," the lady interrupted. "Ma'am was my mother. Though I guess I'm old enough now to be ma'am to you folks, more's the pity. You go on. Let me finish up my baking. You stop back later. I'll have fresh chocolate chip cookies."

Eve's mouth dropped open. Even Michael looked impressed. "Uh—thanks," he said, and they retreated out to the parking lot, staring at one another. "She's making cookies."

"Yeah," Shane said. "Terrifying. So, how are we doing this thing?"

"Girls get their own room," Eve said, and plucked one of the keys out of Michael's hand. "Oh, come on, don't give me that face. You know that's the right thing to do."

"Yeah, I know," Michael said. "Looks like they're right next door to each other."

They were, rooms one and two, with a connecting door between. Inside, the rooms—like Linda's office—were really pretty nice. Claire checked out the bathroom; it was nicer than the one at home—and cleaner. "Hey, Eve?" she called, sticking her head around the door. "Should I be terrified now, or later?"

"Shut up," Eve said, and flopped on one of the two beds, crossing her feet at the ankles as she reached for the remote on the TV. "Okay, it's not Motel Hell. I admit it. But it could have been. . . . Hey, check it out—there's a *Saw* marathon on HBO!"

Great. Just what they needed. Claire rolled her eyes, went out to the car, and helped the boys unload the stuff they needed—which was, actually, pretty much every-

thing by the time they finished. Eve remained loftily above it all, flipping channels and searching for the most comfortable pillow.

Shane dragged her suitcase into the room and dumped it on the floor beside her bed. "Hey, Dark Princess? Here's your crap. Also, bite me."

"Wait, here's your tip—" She flipped him off, without taking her eyes off the TV. "Nice to know we can still be just the same even outside of Morganville, right?"

He laughed. "Right." He looked at Claire, who leaned her own suitcase against the wall and looked around. "So I guess this is good night?"

"Guess so," she said. "Um, unless you guys want to watch movies?"

"I'll bring the chips."

Two hours later, they were lying on the beds, propped up, groaning and wincing and yelling stuff at the screen. The sound was turned up loud, and what with all the screaming and chain saws and such, it took a few seconds for the sound *outside* the room to filter through to any of them. Michael heard it first, of course, and nearly levitated off the bed to cross the room and pull back the curtains. Eve scrambled to mute the TV. "What? What is it?"

Out in the parking lot, Claire could now hear hoots, drunken laughter, and the crash of metal. She and Shane bounced off the bed, too, and Eve came last.

"Hey!" she screamed, and Claire winced at the rage in her voice. "Hey, you assholes, that's my *car*!"

It was the three jerks from the truck stop, only about a case of beer more stupid, which really didn't seem possible, in theory. But they were going after Eve's car with a great big sledgehammer and two baseball bats. The glass in the front window shattered at a blow from the sledgehammer, which was swung by Angry Dude. Orange Cap swung a baseball bat and added another deep

dent to the already horribly damaged hood. The last guy knocked off the side mirror, sending it to left field with one hard blow.

Orange Cap blew Eve a gap-toothed kiss, reached in his back pocket, and pulled out a glass bottle filled with something that looked faintly pink, like lemonade. . . .

"Gas," Michael said. "I have to stop them."

"You'll get your ass killed," Shane said, and flung himself in the way. "No way. This ain't Morganville, and if you end up in a jail cell, you'll *die*. Understand?"

"But my *car*!" Eve moaned. "No no no . . ."

Orange Cap poured gas all over the seats inside, then tossed in a match.

Eve's car went up like a school bonfire at homecoming. Eve shrieked again and tried to lunge past Shane, too. He backed up to block the door and dodged a slap from her. "Claire! Little help?" he yelped, as Eve actually connected. Claire grabbed her friend's arms and pulled her backward. It wasn't easy. Eve was bigger, stronger, and more than a little crazy just now.

"Let go!" Eve yelled.

"No! Calm down. It's too late. There's nothing you can do!"

"I can kick their asses!"

Michael had already come to the same conclusion as Shane, and as Eve broke free from Claire, he got in her way and wrapped his arms around her, bringing her to a fast stop. "No," he said, "no, you can't." His eyes were shimmering red with fury, and he blinked and took deep breaths until he was himself again, blue-eyed Michael, under control—barely.

The three men in the parking lot whooped and hollered as Eve's car burned, then scrambled for their big pickup truck as the motel's office door slammed open.

Grandma Linda stood there, looking like the wrath of God in an apron. She had a shotgun, which she pointed at an angle at the sky and fired. The blast was shockingly

loud. "Get lost, you morons!" she yelled at the retreating three men. "Next time I see your taillights I'll give you a special buckshot kiss!"

She racked another shell, but she didn't need to reload; the truck was already peeling out, spitting gravel from tire treads as it flew out of the parking lot, did a quick, drunken U-turn, and headed back inside Durram's town limits.

Grandma Linda shouldered the shotgun, frowned at the burning car, and went back into the office. She returned with a fire extinguisher, and put the blaze out with five quick blasts of white foam.

Shane opened the door and got immediately mowed down by Eve, who blew past him, with Michael right behind. Shane and Claire followed last. Claire felt physically sick. The car was utterly *trashed*. Even with the fire put out, the windows were shattered, the bodywork dented and twisted, the headlights broken, tires flat, and the seats were burned down to the springs in several places.

She'd seen better wrecks at the junkyard.

"Those three ain't got the sense God gave a virus," Linda said. "I'll call the sheriff, get him out here to write up a complaint. I'm sorry, honey."

Eve was crying, violent little jerks of sobs that came with shudders as she stared at the wreckage of the car she'd loved. Claire put her arm around her, and Eve turned and buried her face in Claire's shoulder. "Why?" she cried, full of rage and confusion now. "Why did they follow us? Why'd they do that?"

"We scared them," Michael said. "Scared people do stupid things. Drunk, scared bullies do even stupider things."

Linda nodded. "You got that right, son. It's a damn shame, though. Hate to see something like this happen to nice kids just minding their own business. People like that, they just got to pick on somebody, and everybody

around here's had enough of 'em. Guess they figured you for the new toys."

"They figured wrong," Michael said. His eyes glittered briefly red, then faded back to blue. "But we've got problems. What are we going to do for a car?"

"Just be glad we got our stuff out of it," Shane said, and Michael, knowing what he was getting at, looked briefly sick, then nodded. "Eve and I will do some shopping tomorrow. See what we can get in town."

Eve sniffled and wiped at her eyes, which made a mess of her mascara. "I don't have the money for a new car."

"We'll find a way," Shane said, as if it made sense and happened to him on a regular basis. Claire guessed, with his history, it probably had. "Come on, moping around out here isn't fixing anything. Might as well go in for the night. We're not going anywhere."

Linda sighed. "Hate to see this kind of thing happen," she said again. "Damn fools. You wait here a second."

She went back into the office, carrying the fire extinguisher, and came back out with a small ceramic bowl full of . . .

"Cookies," Shane said, and accepted it from her. "Thanks, Linda."

"Least I can do." She kicked a rock, frowning, and shook her head. "Damn fools. I'll sit up the rest of the night, make sure they don't come back here."

Somehow, Claire didn't think they'd take the chance. Linda had looked pretty serious with that shotgun.

The joys of the movie party were over, but the cookies were warm, fresh, and delicious. Eve's tears dried up and left a feverish anger in their place. She took a long shower to burn it off, and when she came out of the bathroom, wreathed in steam, she looked small and vulnerable, stripped of all her Goth armor.

Claire hugged her and gave her a cookie. Eve

munched it and hugged her black silk kimono around herself as she climbed onto the bed. "Boys gone?" she asked.

"Yeah, they're gone," Claire said. "Mind if I—?"

"No, go ahead. I'll just sit here and watch my car smoke." Eve stared moodily at the curtains, which were closed, thankfully.

Claire shook her head, grabbed her stuff, and went in to take her own bath. She did it at light speed, half convinced that Eve would find some way to get herself in trouble while she was gone, but when she emerged pink and damp and glowing from the hot water, Eve was exactly where she'd left her, flipping channels on the TV.

"This is the worst road trip *ever*," Eve said. "And I missed the end of the movie."

"Jigsaw always wins. You know that."

There was a soft sound at the motel room door. Something like a scratching sound; then a thud. Eve came bolt upright in bed. "What the hell was that? Because I'm thinking serial killer!"

"It's Shane, trying to freak you out. Or maybe it's those guys again," Claire said. "Shhh." She went to the curtains and peeked out, carefully. The light was dim in front of the door, but she saw someone slumped against the wall. Alone. "Just one guy—I can't really see him."

"So the serial killer option's still on the table? New rule. The door doesn't open."

They both jumped as a fist thudded once on the door. "Let me in," Oliver's voice commanded. "Now."

"Oh," Eve said. "In that case, new rule. Also, technically, he *is* a serial killer, right?"

Claire didn't really want to think too much about that one, because she was afraid Eve might have a point on that.

She slipped back the locks and opened the door, and Oliver came into the room. He made it two steps before his knees gave out on him, and he fell.

"Don't touch him!" Claire said as Eve slipped off the bed to approach him. She could see cuts and blood on him. "Get Michael. Hurry."

That wasn't a problem; Michael and Shane were already opening their own door, and the four of them were standing together when Oliver rolled over on his side, then to his back, staring upward.

He looked bad—pale, with open wounds on his face and hands. His clothes were cut, too, and there was blood soaked into them. He didn't speak. Michael dashed back into his room and came back with the cooler. He knelt next to Oliver and looked over his shoulder at the three of them. "You guys need to leave. Go next door. Now. Hurry."

Shane grabbed the two girls and steered them out, closing the door behind him and leaving Michael alone with Oliver.

Claire tried to turn around.

"No, you don't," Shane said, and shepherded them into his room. "You know better. If he needs blood, let him get it from the cooler. Not from the tap."

"What happened to him?" Eve asked the logical, scary question, which Claire had been at some level trying not to face. "That's *Oliver*. Badass walking. And somebody did that to him. How? Why?"

"I think that's what we have to ask him," Shane said. "Providing he's not having a serious craving for midnight snacks."

"Damn," Eve said. "Speaking of that, I left the cookies. I could use another cookie right now. How screwed are we, anyway?"

"Given the car and whatever trouble Oliver stirred up? Pretty well screwed. But hey. That's normal, right?"

"Right now, I wish it really, really wasn't."

They sat around playing poker until Michael came back, with Oliver behind him. He was upright and walk-

ing, though he looked as if he'd put his clothes through a shredder.

He didn't look happy. Not that Oliver ever really looked happy when he wasn't playing the hippie role, but this seemed unhappy, plus.

"We need to leave," he said. "Quickly."

"Well, that's a problem," Shane said, "seeing how our transpo out there is not exactly lightproof anymore, even if we didn't mind sitting on half-burned seats." Not even the trunk, anymore, thanks to the sledgehammer's work. "Plus, we've got t-minus two hours to sunrise. Not happening, anyway."

Michael said, "Oliver, it's time to tell us why we came here in the first place. And what happened to you."

"It's none of your business," Oliver said.

"Excuse me, but since you dragged us into it with you, I'd say it *is* our business now."

"Did my business destroy your car? No, that was your own idiocy. I say again, you don't need to know, and I don't need to tell you. Leave it." He sounded almost himself, but subdued, and he sat down on the edge of the bed as if standing tired him—not like Oliver.

"Are you okay?" Claire asked. He looked up and met her eyes, and for a second she saw something terrible in him: fear—overwhelming, tired, ancient fear. It shocked her. She hadn't thought Oliver could really be afraid of anything, ever.

"Yes," he said, "I'm all right. Wounds heal. What won't is what will happen if we remain trapped here. We can't wait for rescue from Morganville. We must get on our way before the next nightfall."

"Or?" Claire asked.

"Or worse will happen. To all of us." He looked . . . haunted. And very tired. "I need to rest. Find a car."

"Ah—we're not exactly rolling in cash."

Without a word, Oliver took out a wallet from his

pants, grimaced at the scratches and tears in the leather, and opened it to reveal a bunch of crisp green bills.

Hundreds.

He handed over the entire stack. "I have more," he said. "Take that. It should be enough to buy something serviceable. Make sure it's got sufficient trunk space."

After a second's hesitation, Eve's fingers closed around the money. "Oliver? Seriously, are you okay?"

"I will be," he said. "Michael, do you suppose there is another room in this motel I can occupy until we are ready to leave?"

"I'll get one," Michael said. He slipped out the door and was gone in seconds, heading for the office. Oliver closed his eyes and leaned back against the headboard. He looked so utterly miserable that Claire, without thinking, reached out and, just being kind, put her hand on his arm.

"Claire," Oliver said softly, without opening his eyes, "did I give you permission to touch me?"

She removed her hand—quickly.

"Just—leave me alone. I'm not myself at the moment."

Actually, he was pretty much like he always was, as far as Claire could tell, but she let it go.

Eve was fanning out the money, counting it. Her eyes were getting wider the higher she went. "Jeez," she whispered. "I could buy a genuine pimped-out land yacht with this. Wow. I had no idea running a coffee shop was this good a job."

"It's not," Shane said. "He probably has piles of gold sitting under his couch cushions. He's had a long time to get rich, Eve."

"And time enough to lose everything, once or twice," Oliver said. "If you want to be technical. I have been rich. I am currently . . . not as poor as I once was. But not as wealthy, either. The curse of human wars and politics.

It's difficult to keep what you have, especially if you are always an outsider."

Claire had never really thought about how vampires got the money they had; she supposed it wouldn't have been easy, really. She remembered all the TV news shows she'd seen, with people running for their lives from war zones, carrying whatever they could.

Oliver would have been one of those people, once upon a time. Amelie, too. And Myrnin. Probably more than once. But they'd come through it.

They were survivors.

"What happened out there?" Claire asked, not really expecting him to answer.

He didn't disappoint her.

6

Once Oliver had his own room—room three, of course—at the motel, Claire, Eve, and Shane set out lightproofing the rooms Michael and Oliver would be staying in during the day. That wasn't so hard; the blackout curtains in the windows were pretty good, and a little duct tape around the edges made sure the room stayed dim—that and a DO NOT DISTURB sign on each knob.

"Dead bolt and chain," Shane told Michael as the three of them left the room. Dawn was starting to pink up on the eastern horizon. "I'll call when we're at the door again, on your cell. Don't open for anybody else."

"Did you tell that to Oliver?"

"Do I look stupid? Let him figure out his own crap, man."

Michael shook his head. "Be careful out there. I don't like sending the three of you out by yourselves."

"Linda's riding shotgun with us," Eve said. "Literally. With an actual, you know, *shotgun.*"

"Actually, Linda's driving us. We said we'd buy her breakfast and haul some heavy stuff for her at the store. Kind of a good deal, plus I think everybody likes her. Nobody's going to come after us while she's with us."

It might have been wishful thinking, but Michael seemed a little relieved by it, and he knocked fists with

Shane as they closed the door. They heard the bolts click home.

"Well," Eve said, "it's the start of a beautiful day in which I have had no sleep, had my car burned, and can't wear makeup, which is just so great."

The no-makeup thing was Shane's idea, and Claire had to admit, it was a good one. Eve was, by far, the most recognizable of their little group, but without the rice powder, thick black eyeliner, and funky-colored lipsticks, she looked like a different person. Claire had lent her a less-than-Gothy shirt, although Eve had insisted on purple. With that and plain blue jeans, Eve looked almost . . . normal. She'd even pulled her hair back in a single ponytail at the back.

Not a skull in sight, although her boots still looked a little intimidating.

"Think of it as operating in disguise," Shane said. "In a hostile war zone."

"Easy for you to say. All you had to do was throw on a camo T-shirt and find a ball cap. If we can find you some chewing tobacco, you're gold."

"I'm not in disguise," Claire said.

Eve snorted. "Honey, you *live* in disguise. Which is lucky for us. Come on, maybe Linda's still got some cookies left."

"For breakfast?"

"I never said I was the Nutrition Nazi."

Linda was up—yawning and tired, but awake—when they opened up the office door. She was sipping black coffee, and when Eve said good morning, Linda waved at the plate of cookies on the counter. Eve looked relieved. "Ah—could I have some coffee, too?"

"Right there on the pot. Pour yourself a big one. It's already a long day." Linda had put on another shirt—still checked, but different colors—but otherwise, she looked pretty much the same. "So, you kids get any sleep at all?"

"Not much," Shane mumbled around a mouthful of cookie as Eve poured a chunky white mugful of coffee. He held out his hand in a silent demand for her to get him some, too. She rolled her eyes, put the pot back on the burner, and walked past him to the cookie tray. "Hence, Miss Attitude."

"The attitude comes from *someone* not even wanting to fetch his own coffee."

Shane shrugged and got his own, as Eve raided the cookie tray and Claire nibbled on part of one, too. She supposed she ought to feel more tired. She probably would, later, but right now, she felt—excited? Maybe nervous was a better term for it. "So," she ventured, "where do you go to buy a car here?"

"In Durram?" Linda shook her head. "Couple of used places, that's all. Any new cars, we go to the city for them. Not that there's many new cars round here these days. Durram used to be an oil town, back in the boom days, pumped a lot of crude out of the ground, but when it folded, it hit the ground hard. People been leaving ever since. It never was huge, but what you see now ain't more than half what it was fifty years ago, and even then a lot of those buildings are closed up."

"Why do you stay?" Shane asked, and sipped his coffee. Linda shrugged.

"Where else I got to go? My husband's buried here; came back dead from the war in Iraq, that first one. My family's here, such as they are, including Ernie, my grandson. Ernie runs one of the car lots, which is why I figure we can find you what you want at a good deal this early in the morning." She grinned. "If an old woman can't make her own grandson get out of bed before dawn to do her a favor, there's no point in living. Just let me finish my coffee and we'll be on our way."

She drank it fast, faster than Shane and Eve could gulp their own, and in about five minutes the four of them were piling into the bench seat of Linda's pickup

truck, with more rust than paint on the outside, and sagging seats on the inside. Claire sat on Shane's lap, which wasn't at all a bad thing from her perspective. From the way he held her in place, she didn't think he objected, either. Linda started up the truck with a wheezing rattle of metal, and the engine roared as she tore out of the gravel parking lot and onto the narrow two-lane road heading toward Durram.

"Huh," she said as they passed the town limits sign, barely readable from shotgun blasts. "Usually there's a deputy out here in the mornings. Guess somebody overslept. Probably Tom. Tom likes those late nights at the bar, sometimes; he's gonna catch hell for blowing it again."

"You mean fired?"

"Fired? Not in Durram. You don't get fired in Durram; you get embarrassed." Linda drove a couple of blocks, past some empty shops and one empty gas station, then took a right turn and then a left. "Here it is."

The sign said HURLEY MOTORS, and it was about a million years old. Somebody had hit it with buckshot, too, once upon a time, but from the rust, it had been a while ago—maybe before Claire was born; maybe before her *mother* was born. There was a small, sad collection of old cars parked in front of a small cinder-block building, which looked like it might have been built by the same guy who'd built Linda's motel.

Come to think of it, it probably had.

The cinder blocks were painted a pale blue with dark red trim on the roof and windows, but the whole thing had faded to a kind of pale gray over time. As Linda stopped the truck with a squeal of brakes, the front door of the shack opened, and a young man stepped out and waved.

"Oooh, cute," Eve whispered to Claire. Claire nodded. He was older, maybe twenty or so, but he had a nice face. And a great smile, like his grandma.

"Oh, he *is* cute!" Shane said in a fake girly voice. "Gee, maybe we can ask him out!"

"Shut *up*, you weasel. Claire, hit him!"

"Pretend I did," Claire said. "Look, he's bleeding."

Shane snorted. "Not. Okay, out of the truck before this gets silly."

Linda, ignoring them, had already gotten out on the driver's side and was walking toward her grandson. As they hugged, Claire scrambled down from Shane's lap to the pavement. He hopped down beside her, and then Eve slithered out as well. "Wow," she said, surveying the cars on the lot. "This is just—"

"Sad."

"I was going more for horrifying, but yeah, that works, too. Okay, can we agree on nothing in a minivan, please?"

"Yep," Shane said. "I'm down with it."

They wandered around the lot. It didn't take long before they'd looked at everything parked in front, and from Eve's expression, Claire could tell there wasn't a single thing she'd be caught dead driving—or, more accurately, caught *with* the dead, driving. "This *sucks*," Eve said. "The only thing that has decent trunk space is *pink*." And not just a little pink, either; it looked like a pink factory had thrown up all over it.

Linda's grandson wandered over, trailed by her. He caught the last bit of Eve's complaint, and shook his head. "You don't want that thing, anyway," he said. "Used to belong to Janie Hearst. She drove it fifteen thousand miles without an oil change. She thinks she's the Paris Hilton of Durram. Hi, I'm Ernie Dawson. Heard you're looking for a car. Sorry about what happened to yours. Those fools are a menace—have been since I was a kid. Glad nobody was hurt."

"Yeah, well, we just want to get the heck out of town," Eve said. "It was my car. It was a really nice old classic Caddy, you know? Black, with fins? I was hoping maybe

somebody could tow it in, fix it up, and I could pick it up later on, maybe in a couple of weeks?"

Ernie nodded. He had greenish eyes, a color that stood out against his suntanned skin; his hair was brown, and wavy, and got in his face a lot. Claire liked him instinctively, but then she remembered the *last* cute stranger she'd liked. That hadn't turned out so well. In fact, that had turned out very, very badly, with her blood getting drained out of her body.

So she didn't smile back at Ernie—much.

"I think I can set that up," he said. "Earle Weeks down at the repair shop can probably work some magic on it, but you'd have to leave him a pretty good deposit. He'll have to order in parts."

"Hey, if you can make me a good deal on a decent car that isn't *pink*, I'm all good here."

"Well, what you see is pretty much what you get, except—" He gazed at Eve for a few long seconds, then shook his head. "Nah, you won't be interested in that."

"In what?"

"Something that I keep out back. Nobody around here will buy it. I've been trying to make a trade with a company out of Dallas to get it off my hands. But since you said big classic Caddy—"

Eve jumped in place a little. "Sweet! Let's see it!"

"I'm just warning you, you won't like it."

"Is it pink?"

"No. Definitely not pink. But"—Ernie shrugged—"okay, sure. Follow me."

"This ought to be good," Shane said, and reached into his pocket for a cookie he'd hidden there. He broke it in half and offered it to Claire.

"Can't wait," she said, and wolfed it down, because Linda was world-class with the cookies. "I can't believe I'm eating cookies for breakfast."

"I can't believe we're stuck in Durram, Texas, with

a burned-out car, two vamps, and the cookies are this *good*."

And . . . he had a point.

Eve had a look on her face as if she'd just found the Holy Grail, or whatever the Gothic equivalent of that might be. She stared, eyes gone wide and shiny, lips parted, and the glee in her face was oddly contagious. "It's for sale?" she asked. She was trying to play it cool, Claire thought, although she was blowing it by a mile. "How much?"

Ernie wasn't fooled even a little bit. He rubbed his lips with his thumb, staring at Eve, and then at the car. "Well," he said thoughtfully, "I guess I could go to three thousand. 'Cause you're a friend of Grandma's."

Linda said, "Don't you go cheating this gal. I know for a fact you paid Matt down at the funeral parlor seven hundred dollars for the damn thing, and it's been sitting for six months gathering dust. You ought to let her have it for a thousand, tops."

"Gran!"

"Don't *Gran* me. Be nice. Where else in this town are you going to sell a hearse?"

"Well," he said, "I've been working on making it more of a party bus."

It was *gigantic*. It was gleaming black, with silver trim and silver curlicues on the same, and faded white curtains in the windows at the back. Grandma Linda was right—it was covered in desert dust, but underneath it looked sharp—*really* sharp.

"Party bus?" Eve said.

"Yeah, take a look."

Ernie opened the back door, the part where the casket would have gone . . . and there was a floor in there, with lush black carpet, not metal runners or clamps as there would have usually been for coffins. He'd built in low-riding seats down both sides, two on each side, facing each other.

"I put in the cup holders," he said. "I was going for the fold-down DVD screen, but I ran out of money."

Eve, as though in a trance, reached in her pocket and pulled out the cash. She counted out three thousand dollars and passed it over to Ernie.

"Don't you want to drive it first?" he asked.

"Does it run?"

"Yeah, pretty well."

"Does it have air-conditioning?"

"Of course. Front and back."

"Keys." She held out her hand. Ernie held up one finger, ran back to the shack, and returned with a set dangling from one finger. He handed them to her with a smile.

Eve opened the front door and started up the hearse. It caught with a cough, then settled into a nice, even purr.

Eve stroked the steering wheel, and then she *hugged* it—literally. "Mine," she said. "Mine, mine, mine."

"Okay, this is starting to seriously creep me out," Shane said. "Can we move past the obsessive weird love and into the actually driving it part?"

"You guys go on and take it out for a spin," Ernie said. "I'll get the paperwork ready for you to sign. Be about fifteen minutes."

"Shotgun!" Shane said, one second before Claire. He winked at her. "And you get the Dead Guy Seat."

"Funny."

"Wait until there are actual dead guys sitting back there."

It wasn't safe to say that, not in front of Ernie and Linda; after a second, Claire saw Shane realize that. He blinked and said, "Well, maybe not. But it would be funny."

"Hilarious," Claire agreed, and went around to the back. Getting in was a bit of a challenge, but once she was sitting down, it felt kind of like what she imagined a limo would be. She looked around for a seat belt and

found one, then strapped herself in. No sense dying in a car crash in a hearse. That seemed a little too tragically ironic even for Eve. "Hey, there really *are* cup holders."

"Fate," Eve said with a sigh.

"I'm not sure fate had to burn up your car to get the point across," Shane said, buckling his own seat belt.

"No, not that. The hearse. I'm going to name it Fate."

Shane stared at Eve for a long, long few seconds, then slowly shook his head. "Have you considered medication, or—"

She flipped him off.

"Ah. Back to normal. Excellent."

Eve pulled the hearse around carefully, getting used to the size of the thing. "It probably gets crap gas mileage," she said. "But *damn.* It's so *dark!*"

Claire moved aside the white curtains to look out the back window as they drove past the front of the used car lot. Linda and Ernie were standing in front of the shack, waving, so she waved back. "I'm probably the first person to wave from back here," she said. "That's weird."

"No, that is *awesome.* Awesome in the deliciously creepy sense. Okay, here we go, hold on. . . ." Eve hit the gas, and the hearse leaped forward. Shane braced himself against the dash. "Wow. Nice. I thought it might only go, you know, funeral speed or something."

"You're not seriously naming this thing."

"I am. Fate."

"At least call it Intimidator. Something cool."

"My car," Eve said, and smiled. "My rules. You can go buy the pink one if you want."

He shuddered and shut up.

Eve made the block without incident, and pulled the hearse back into the car lot about five minutes later, bumping it carefully up the drive and parking in front of the shack. As she switched the key off, she sighed and wiggled in the big leather seat in satisfaction. "This is the *best road trip ever.*"

Shane bailed out. Claire scrambled to slide out the back and found him waiting for her, grabbing her around the waist and helping her out. He didn't let go immediately, either. That was nice, and she felt herself sway toward him, as if the world had tilted his direction. "I guess we'd better go in and make sure she doesn't pay him even more money," Shane said, "because you know she would, for this thing."

"She's a giver," Claire agreed. "Also, maybe Linda's got more of those cookies."

"That's a good point."

Inside, they found Eve already signing the papers. Her driver's license and proof of insurance were already on the table, and as Ernie said hello to the two of them, he gathered up her information and made a copy at the back of the office. It was small, and crowded, and pretty dusty. It looked as though Ernie was the only one who worked here, at least most of the time. Linda was leaning against the wall, staring out at the car lot through the big glass window. She looked pensive.

"Is there something wrong?" Claire asked her. Linda glanced at her, then shook her head.

"Probably nothing," she said. "I just wonder why the sheriff hasn't been around yet. He's usually circling the town pretty regular, and he hasn't been here yet. Deputy wasn't at the sign, either. Strange."

Ernie filled out the title and handed it over, along with the paperwork and Eve's driver's license and insurance. Eve juggled all the paper to shake hands with him, and he gave her a smile that was definitely flirting. "Thanks," he said. "You staying in town long?"

"Oh—ah, no, I'm—we're heading out. To Dallas. With my boyfriend." Eve said it without too much emphasis, which was good; Claire didn't think Ernie was a bad person or anything. And Eve was cute, even when she hadn't made an effort to dress herself up Goth-style.

Ernie winced. "Should've seen that coming," he said. "Well, enjoy the new ride, Eve. And don't be a stranger."

"No stranger than I am already," she promised, straight-faced, and then they went out to admire the big black hearse again.

Linda moved straight past them to her own truck. "Hey," Shane called. "How about breakfast? We were going to buy—"

"No need," she said, and climbed into the cab. Through the open window she said, "I'm going to go see the sheriff, see if I can find out what the heck's going on today. If I don't see you kids before you go, have a safe trip. And thanks for livening up my week. Hell, my whole month, come to that."

"No, thank *you*," Shane said. "Your motel is great."

She gave him a tight, quiet smile. "Always thought so," she said. "Good-bye, now."

She took off in a spray of gravel, raising plumes of dust as she skidded back onto the road. Ernie, who'd come out with them, sighed. "My grandma, the race car driver," he said. "Have a good trip, now."

They said their thanks, got into the hearse, and headed back to the motel.

They never got there. As they passed the town limits sign, and the road rose up a little in a mini-hill, Claire caught sight of flashing red and blue lights up ahead. "Uh oh," she said. Eve hit the brakes, and she and Shane exchanged a look. "That's the motel, right? They're at the motel."

"Looks that way," Shane said. "This is not good."

"Ya think?" Eve chewed her lip. "Call Michael."

"Maybe they're—"

"What, hanging out there looking for somebody else? Call him, Shane!"

Shane dialed the number of Michael's cell phone, listened for a second, then closed his phone. "Busy," he said. "We need to get in there."

"And do *what*, exactly?"

"I don't know! You want your boyfriend dragged out to french fry in the sun?"

Eve didn't answer that. She drummed her fingers on the steering wheel, looking agonized, and then said, "I'll apologize later, then."

She hit the gas, and the hearse picked up momentum coming down the hill. It zipped past the motel, doing way past the speed limit.

One of the police cars—there were two in the parking lot—backed out and raced after them. Eve didn't slow down. She hit the gas.

"Eve, what the hell are you doing? We can't outrun them in a *hearse*, in the middle of the desert!"

"I'm not trying to," she shot back. "Claire, look out the back. Tell me if the other car joins in."

It took a few seconds, but then Claire saw another flare of red and blue flashers behind them. "They're both following," she called back. "And how is this good, exactly?"

"Text Michael," Eve told Shane. "Tell him the coast is clear and to get his butt out of there."

"What about Oliver?"

"Michael's too much of a Boy Scout not to tell him, too. Don't worry about that."

Shane texted fast. "It's still kind of sunny out, you know."

"Oliver's older," Claire said. "He can stay out in the sun a lot longer than Michael. Maybe he can lead the police away, or something."

"That's up to them," Eve said. "I just need to keep driving as long as I can before we give up. The more we piss these guys off, the more chance Michael and Oliver have of getting away."

It turned out, as the police cars cranked it up, that Eve's hearse really wasn't made for car-chase speeds. They were overtaken in about another mile, and boxed up in another two.

Eve, surrendering, eased off the gas and hit the brakes to slow down and pull over.

"Okay, here's the deal," Shane said. "Keep your hands up, and play nice. You panicked, that's all. We were telling you to pull over, but you locked up. Got it?"

"It's not going to help."

"It will if you play the ditz. Better sell it, Eve. We're in enough trouble already."

The rest of it went straight out of the reality-TV-show playbook. The police ordered them out of the car, and before she knew it, Claire was being thrown up against the back of the hearse and searched. It felt humiliating, and she heard Eve crying—whether that was acting or not remained to be seen; Eve cried over smaller things. Shane was answering questions in a quiet, calm voice, but then, he'd spent a lot of time getting hassled by the Morganville police. For Claire, it was kind of a new experience, and not at all a good one. She had the deputy, she supposed; he was a tall, skinny guy whose uniform didn't fit very well, and he seemed nervous, especially when he put handcuffs on her.

"Hey," Shane called as his own hands were secured behind his back. "Hey, please don't hurt her. It wasn't her fault!"

"Nobody's hurting anybody," said the sheriff from the night before. "Okay, let's just calm down. Now, let's have some names. You?" He pointed at Claire.

"Claire Danvers," she said. Oh *man*, there went any chance at all of ever getting into MIT. She was going to have a mug shot that got pasted all over Facebook. People were going to mock her. It would be high school all over again, times a million.

"Address?"

She gave him the address in Morganville, on Lot Street. She didn't know what the others would have done; maybe she ought to have lied, made something up. But she didn't dare. Like Shane had said—they were in enough trouble already.

Eve gave her name in a trembling, small voice, and

then Shane finished things up. They both gave the Glass House address.

"So, you're all, what, sharing a house?" the sheriff asked. "Where's the blond kid from last night?"

"I—" Eve bit her lip and closed her eyes. "We had a fight. A big one. He—he left."

"Left how? Seeing as the car you came in is still smoking in the parking lot back there, and it ain't going anywhere. There's no bus coming through here, young lady."

"He hitched a ride," Eve said. "With a truck. I don't know which one. I just heard it on the road."

"A truck," the sheriff repeated. "Uh huh. And he wouldn't be back there in Linda's place with the door all locked up, then."

"No sir."

That, Claire reflected, might be almost true, because if Eve's gamble had paid off, Michael and Oliver weren't there any longer. Where they *were* was another story.

"Well, we're waiting for Linda to get back; then we'll open up those doors and see what's going on. Sound okay to you?"

"Yes sir," Eve said. "Why the handcuffs?"

"You three are a bunch of desperate characters, way I see it," the sheriff said. "I find you causing trouble last night, get a report your car's been trashed by the very same boys who say you threatened them, and next thing you know, I've got one man dead and two men missing this morning. The dead one got found in his pickup truck just about a mile up the road from your motel."

"I—" Eve stopped, frozen. "Sorry, what?"

"Murder," the sheriff repeated, slowly and precisely. "And you were the last ones to see them alive."

7

For a long, long moment, nobody moved, and then Shane said, "You don't think we killed—"

"Let's just stop right there, son. I don't want to be making any mistakes about how we do this." The sheriff cleared his throat and recited something about rights and remaining silent. Claire couldn't make sense out of it. She felt sick and horribly faint.

She was being *arrested.*

She was being arrested *for murder.*

Eve's crying was uncontrollable now, but Claire couldn't help her. She couldn't help herself.

Shane stayed uncharacteristically silent as they loaded him into the back of the squad car, then put Claire and Eve in with him. The sheriff leaned in before he closed the door to look at them. He almost looked kind now. That didn't make Claire feel any less sick.

"I'm going to have the deputy drive your, ah, vehicle back into town," he said. "Can't leave it out here. Might get stolen, and you folks already lost one car in Durram. Don't want it happening again."

He slammed the door on them. Claire felt Eve flinch all over at the boom of solid metal.

"Deep breaths," Shane said softly. "Eve. Sack up. You can't go to pieces like this. Not now."

The sheriff got in the front, on the other side of a wire mesh screen. He put on his seat belt, looked in the rearview mirror, and said, "No talking."

Then they drove back to the motel, where Linda's truck had just pulled in. She looked pale and worried, but she didn't betray much of anything at the sight of her three former guests in the back of a squad car. She listened to the sheriff, nodded, and went into the office to get master keys.

She opened up all three rooms they'd rented. Shane let out a sigh of relief even before the sheriff went in to look around. "They're gone," he said. "They got out. Somehow."

"How can you be sure?"

"Because Michael's smarter than me, and he'd have found a way. Ow, Eve, stop squirming. Not like there's a lot of room in here!"

"Sorry," Eve said. She sniffled uncomfortably. Her eyes were red and puffy, and so was her nose, and in general she looked pretty miserable. Claire bumped shoulders with her gently.

"Hey," she said. "It'll be okay. We didn't do this."

"Yeah, they never put innocent people on death row in Texas," Eve said. "Don't kid yourself. We're in big trouble. *Big* trouble. Like, not-even-Amelie-can-get-us-out-of-it trouble."

Her eyes started to tear up again. Claire repeated the shoulder bump. "Don't. We'll be okay. We'll figure this out."

Sniffle. "You're just Little Miss Optimist, aren't you? Do you come with accessories, like a glass half full and lemons to make into lemonade, too?"

"I'm not an optimist," Claire said. "I just know us."

"Damn straight," Shane said. "Look, they'll separate us at the station. Don't say anything about anything. Just watch and listen, okay? No matter what they say, just stay quiet."

"I've seen cop shows," Eve said, offended. "I'm not stupid, you know."

Shane leaned forward and looked across her at Claire. "Okay, Eve's going to spill her guts the first time they look at her harshly. What about you?"

"Quiet as a mouse," Claire said. Her heart was pounding, and she wasn't sure she could keep that promise, but then again, she'd kept secrets from Mr. Bishop.

This wasn't nearly as bad.

Was it?

The sheriff's station in Durram, Texas, was basically two rooms, if you didn't count the bathroom; there was a small open area with a couple of desks and computers, some cork boards on the walls full of notices and pictures, and behind that, a door with iron bars. But first, before they got to the iron bar part, Claire and Shane were seated on a wooden bench—it was a lot like a church pew, only with big bolts drilled into it on either side—and cuffed to the bench; too far apart, for Claire's comfort. She really ached to be held by him right now.

"Hey, sir? Could I use the bathroom?" Shane asked.

"Not until you're processed."

"I'm not kidding. I really need to go. Please? Or would you rather clean it up?"

The deputy stared at him, harassed and doubtful, and Shane did a convincing squirm that Claire wasn't absolutely sure was fake. The deputy finally sighed and unhooked him to escort him to the small bathroom off the main room.

Eve, meanwhile, had been taken straight to the sheriff's desk, where he offered her a big box of tissues and a glass of water.

Claire was wondering what the heck to do, when she saw a flash of a face in the window of the station, behind the sheriff's back. A tall, lean figure in a long black coat, hat, and gloves.

Oliver. Dressed for the sun. Out and moving, getting an assessment of where they were and what had happened. He saw her watching him and gave her a quick nod that told her nothing at all, not even, *Don't worry.* Then he vanished.

Her phone gave out an ultrasonic ringtone. She blinked and looked around, but neither the sheriff nor the deputy had noticed it at all. Eve had, but after that first involuntary glance, she kept her back turned and stared off into space, Kleenex crumpled in both hands.

Claire squirmed and managed to get her phone out of her pocket without attracting attention.

She had a text message, from Michael. It read, *We'll get you guys out of there soon. Meanwhile, stay quiet.*

It was pretty much the same advice Shane had given. She wanted to believe it, but her insides were still shaking. She was *definitely* not meant to be a career criminal.

Right. She should just sit here, then, and—think of something else. Like science. Some people recited baseball scores to distract themselves; Claire liked to go through the entire periodic table of elements, and once she'd finished with that, she started on all of the alchemical symbols and properties Myrnin had taught her. That helped. It made her remember that there was something out there beyond this room, this moment, and that there were people out there who might actually care if she didn't come back.

Shane came back from the toilet and was cuffed in place again. He edged over a little closer to her and leaned forward, elbows on his thighs, head hanging down so his hair covered his face.

"There's a window in the bathroom," he said. "Not very big, but you could get out of it. Doesn't open, though. You'd have to break it out, and that would be noisy."

Claire coughed and covered her mouth. "I'm not breaking out of jail! Are you crazy?"

"Well, it was a thought. I mean, seemed like a good idea at the time." Shane sat back up and looked at her, forehead crinkling in a frown. "I just don't want you here. It's not—" He shook his head. "It's just not right. Me and Eve, well, yeah, she piled into it head-on, and I'm always in trouble. But you . . ."

"I'm okay." She reached out and put her palm against his cheek, feeling the slightly rough stubble there. It made her steadier. It made her want to be somewhere else, like in the motel room, with the door closed. "I'm not going anywhere without you."

"I am *such* a bad influence on you."

"Trying to get me to stage a jailbreak? Yeah. You really are."

"Well, at least you didn't do it. There's that."

The deputy got up from his desk and came to unlock Shane from the bench. "Let's have a talk, Mr. Collins," he said.

"Oh, let's," Shane said, with totally fake enthusiasm. He winked at Claire, which made her smile for a second, until she remembered there really was something tragic here—one man dead; two missing. Granted, they hadn't been the nicest people, but still . . .

She realized, with a grim, cold, drenched feeling down her spine, that she had no idea what Oliver had been doing when those men were being killed.

No idea at all.

The sheriff kept them talking for hours, then locked them in the cell in the back. Shane went in one cell; Eve and Claire together in the other. All of their stuff was taken away, of course, including cell phones. Claire had erased the text messages, but she figured it was only a matter of time before the sheriff got them, anyway. And then he'd know for sure that Michael was out there, a fugitive from justice.

That sounded romantic, but probably wasn't, espe-

cially since he was a vampire caught without shelter in the daytime.

She hoped he and Oliver had remembered to take the cooler of blood with them. They might really need it, especially if they got burned.

And here I am, worrying about a couple of vampires who can take care of themselves, she thought. *I ought to be worrying a lot more about what's going to happen when they call my parents.* They would—and that would make it just about a million times worse.

"Hey," Shane said from the other side of the bars. "Trade you cigarettes for a chocolate bar."

"Funny," Eve said. She was almost back to her old un-Gothed self again, though there were still red splotches on her cheeks and around her eyes. "How come you're always behind bars, troublemaker?"

"Look who's talking. I didn't try to outrun the cops in a hearse."

"That hearse had horsepower." Eve got that moony look in her eyes again. "I love that hearse."

"Yeah, well, I hope it loves you back, because otherwise, that's just sad. And a little sick." Shane drummed his fingers on the bars. "This isn't so bad. At least I've got better company this time around." And he wasn't scheduled to be turned into a vampire, or burned alive, but that kind of went without saying. "And they even have toilet paper."

"Oh, I *really* didn't need to hear that, Collins." Eve sighed and paced around the cell again, hugging herself tight. "It tells me way too much about your past."

Claire leaned into the bars. Shane leaned in from the other side, and their fingers brushed, then intertwined. "Hey," he said. "So, this is familiar."

"Not for me," she said. "I'm usually *outside* the bars."

"You're doing fine."

Claire smiled at him, then drew in a quick, shaking

breath. "I have to tell you something," she said. "It's important."

Shane's fingers tightened on hers, and his index finger stroked gently over the silver claddagh ring, with its bright stone. "I know."

"No, you don't. I saw Oliver," she whispered, quickly and as softly as she could. Clearly, that was not what Shane was expecting to hear, and she watched him go through a whole list of reactions before he finally settled on annoyed.

"Great," he said. "When?"

"Outside the windows while they were talking to you," Claire said.

"Was he barbecued?"

"No, he was wearing a big coat and hat. I don't guess he was any too excited about being out in the daytime, though."

"I guess barbecued was too much to hope for." Shane fell silent as he thought about it, then finally shook his head. "They'll wait for dark," he said. "They'll have to, whatever they plan to do; Michael's just too vulnerable out there in the day. I wish we knew what they were doing."

"I'm pretty sure they're thinking the same thing about us," Claire said. "Since they probably have no idea what happened. As far as they know, this hassle is all about Eve's bad driving."

"Hey, I heard that!" Eve said.

Shane smiled, but it was brief, and his dark brown eyes never left Claire's. "I don't like this," he said. "I don't like seeing you two in here."

"Yeah, well, welcome to my world," Claire said. "I haven't enjoyed it much seeing you behind bars, either." She laughed sadly. "This was supposed to be a fun little trip, remember? We should be in Dallas by now."

"My dad used to say that life's a journey, but somebody screwed up and lost the map."

Claire wasn't sure she wanted to think about his father right now. Frank Collins wasn't the kind of ghost she wanted drifting around between them, especially since being in jail—again—probably made Shane think a lot about his dad. Not that Frank was a ghost. Unfortunately. He'd been a terrible, abusive father, and now he was a vampire, and she couldn't really imagine that it had improved him all that much.

Even if he had saved her life once.

"As long as we're together," she said. "That's what matters."

"Speaking of that," Shane said, "we could be together and headed anywhere when we get out of this, you know. I'm just putting that on the table."

He was talking about not going back; about leaving Morganville. She'd been contemplating it, and she knew he had, too. "I—I can't, Shane. My parents . . ."

He bent his head closer and dropped his voice to a whisper. "Do you really think they want you to be there? Risking your life, every day? Don't you think they want you out, and safe?"

"I can't, Shane. I just can't. I'm sorry."

Shane was silent a moment, then let out a long breath. "I bet I could convince you if I could get through these bars. . . ."

"You'd get arrested all over again."

"Well, you're just that tempting. Jailbait." He kissed her fingers, which made her shiver all over; his lips lingered warm on her skin, reminding her of what it felt like to be alone with him, in that timeless, special silence. "Not a lot we can do until—" He stopped, then, frowning, looked over at the barred door that led into the sheriff's office. "Did you hear that?"

"What?" Even as she asked it, Claire heard the growl of an engine outside—a big one. It had to be some kind of truck, maybe, but not just a pickup—a big delivery van, or an eighteen wheeler. The brakes sighed, and the

roar of the engine cut out. "I guess they're getting some sort of delivery, maybe?"

Maybe, but somehow, Claire didn't think so. She had a bad feeling. From the way Shane was staring at the jail door—which wasn't telling them anything—he was feeling the same thing.

And then in the outer office, glass crashed, someone yelled, and Claire heard laughter.

Then more crashing. More yelling.

Shane let go of her. "Claire, Eve—get to the back of the cell." When they hesitated, he snapped, "Just go!"

They did it, not that there was anywhere in particular to go, or to hide. They sat together on one of the two small cots, close together, watching the jail door to see what would come through.

What came through wasn't Oliver. It wasn't even Michael.

It was Morley, the vampire from Morganville, in all his homeless-bum glory. He was dressed in layers of threadbare clothes, and he had a large, floppy black hat on his head over his straggly graying hair.

He looked at the bars on the jail cell door, sneered, and snapped the whole thing off its hinges with a heave. He tossed the iron aside as if it weighed next to nothing.

Morley stepped through the open space, surveyed the three of them, and swept off his hat in a low, mocking bow. He was good at the bowing thing. Claire supposed he'd probably had a lot of practice. He seemed old enough to have lived in a time when bowing well got you somewhere.

"Like lobsters in a tank," he said. "I know we agreed you'd give up your blood to me, but really, this is just too *easy.*"

He smiled.

With fangs.

Claire got up and walked toward the bars. She didn't like letting Morley—or any vampire—see she was afraid

of him; from working with Myrnin in his crazy days—
crazier?—she'd realized that showing fear was an invitation to them. One they found really hard to resist.

"What are you doing here?" she asked. Because for
a confusing few seconds, she thought that maybe Oliver
had teamed up with Morley to rescue them. But that
was flat-out impossible. The idea of Oliver and Morley
ever being able to have a civilized conversation, much
less actually work together, was completely ridiculous.
"You're not supposed to leave Morganville!"

"Ah, yes. Amelie's rules." He said that last word with
a lot of relish, and there was a muddy red flare in his
eyes to match. "Poor, dear Amelie is operating at a dis-
advantage these days. Rumors said she was unable to
keep the boundaries of the town in quite the same condition they had been. I decided to test the theory, and
behold. I am *free.*"

That was really, really not a good thing. Claire didn't
know a whole lot about Morley, but she knew he tended
more to the bad-old-days model of vampire—take what
you want, when you want, and don't care about the
consequences. The opposite of how Amelie—and even
Oliver—ran things. To Morley, people were just blood
bags that could talk—and sometimes outrun him, which
only made it more exciting.

"They'll come after you," Claire said. "Amelie's people. You know that."

"And I look forward to seeing how that turns out
for her." Morley paced back and forth in front of the
bars, humming a song Claire didn't recognize. In the net
of his wild hair, his eyes glittered with a kind of silvery
light. They expressed not exactly hunger, but more like
amusement. "You look cramped in there, my friends.
Shall I get you out?"

"Actually, it's pretty roomy," Shane said. "I'm feeling
better about it all the time."

"Perhaps . . ." Morley turned. "Ah, you're playing

the gentleman, I see. Of course, by all means. Ladies first."

"No!" Shane lunged at the bars. Morley had his eyes fixed on Eve and Claire now, and Claire thought, with a sinking sensation, that putting on a brave face wasn't going to get her very far—not with him. "Changed my mind. Sure. I'll go first."

Morley shook his finger gently in Shane's direction, but without taking those shining eyes off the girls. "No, you had your chance. And I despise those who think themselves *gentlemen* in any case. You're not making friends that way."

"No!" Shane yelled, and slammed his hand into the bars, which rattled uneasily. "Over here, you ratty flea-bag! Come and get it!"

"Fleas suck blood," Morley said mildly. "Quite the cousin of the vampire, those clever little creatures, so why should I find that insulting? You really must find more interesting ways to bait me, boy. Tell me my beard would better stuff a butcher's cushion. Or that I have more hair than wit. Live up to your heritage, I beg you."

Shane had no idea what to say to that. Claire cleared her throat. "Like . . . you're . . . an inhuman wretch, void and empty from any dram of mercy?" She hated Shakespeare. But she'd had to memorize lines back in high school for a production of *The Merchant of Venice*.

And it had finally paid off, from the surprise in Morley's face. He actually took a step back.

"It speaks!" he said. "And in lilting, glorious words. Though I am not so partial to the Bard, myself. He was a pitiful man to drink with, always dashing off to scribble away in the dark. Writers. Such a boring lot."

"What are you *doing* here? Because I know you didn't come to get us," Claire said. She advanced and wrapped her hands around the bars, as though she wasn't at all afraid of him. She hoped he couldn't hear her heartbeat, but she knew he could. "We're not important enough."

"Well, that's certainly true. You're entirely incidental. Actually, we're in search of a town. Something small, remote, easily controllable. This seemed a good possibility, but it's rather too large for our purposes."

We. Morley hadn't just slipped out of Morganville alone. Claire remembered the big, throbbing engine outside. Might be a big truck. Might be a bus. Either way, it would probably hold a lot of vampires—like the ones Morley had applied to be allowed to leave Morganville with in the first place.

Oh, this just got better and better.

"You can't just move in here," Claire said, trying to sound reasonable, as if that would do any good. She let go of the bars and backed away as Morley took a step toward her again. "People live here."

"Indeed, I'm not planning on it. Too much trouble to subdue such a large population. However, we're in need of supplies, and this town's quite well stocked. Couldn't be better." Morley suddenly lunged forward, grabbed the bars of their cell, and *ripped the door off*—just like that, with a shriek of iron and sharp snapping sounds.

Eve, behind Claire, screamed, and then the sound went muffled, as if she'd covered her mouth.

Claire didn't move. There didn't seem to be much point. Shane was yelling something, and for some odd reason the place on her neck hurt, the place where Myrnin had bitten her, where there was still a nasty scar.

Morley stood there for a moment, hands on both sides of the doorway, and then stepped inside. He *glided,* like a tiger. And his eyes turned red, the irises lighting up the glittering color of blood.

"Get down!" somebody yelled from behind him, and Claire hit the floor, not daring to hesitate even for a second. There was a loud roar that it took her a second to identify as gunfire, and Morley staggered and went down to one knee.

The sheriff looked dazed, and there was blood on the side of his head, but he held his gun very steady. "Get down, mister," he said. "Don't make me shoot you again."

Morley slowly toppled forward, face-forward, on the floor. The sheriff breathed a sigh of relief and gestured for Eve and Claire to come out. Claire did, jumping over Morley's outstretched hand and expecting that any second, any second at all, he'd reach up and grab her, just like in the movies.

He didn't. Eve hesitated for a few seconds, then jumped for it, clearing Morley by at least a couple of feet, straight up. The sheriff grabbed them and hustled them off to the side, then unlocked Shane's cell. "Out," he said. "Help me get him inside."

"It won't do any good to lock him up," Shane said. "He already ripped off two of your doors. You want him to go for three?"

The sheriff had clearly been trying not to think about that. "What the hell are these people?" he snarled. "Some kind of damn monsters?"

"Some kind of," Shane said. He'd put his hands on Claire, and now he wrapped his arms around her, and after a second, included Eve in the hug, too. "Thanks. I know you don't believe us, but we're not the bad guys here."

"I'm starting to think you might be right about that."

"What gave you your first clue? The fangs, or the door ripping?" Shane didn't wait for an answer. "He's not dead. He's playing with you."

"What?"

"You can't kill him with that thing," Eve said. "Can't even slow him down, really."

The sheriff whirled to stare at Morley, who was still facedown on the floor. He aimed his gun at the body again and kept it there.

Morley didn't move.

"No, he's down," the sheriff said, and walked over to press fingers to Morley's dirty neck. He yanked his hand away quickly, stumbling back. "He's cold."

Morley laughed, rolled over, and sat up, doing his very best risen-from-the-grave imitation. It helped that he was filthy and looked kind of crazy scary.

The sheriff backed away, far away, all the way to the wall, then aimed his gun at Morley and pulled the trigger, again.

Morley brushed his clothes lightly, dismissing the bullet even before the echoes from the shockingly loud gunshot stopped ringing in Claire's ears. "Please," he said, and practically levitated to his feet. He reached out and took the sheriff's gun from him, then tossed it in the corner of the cell where Eve and Claire had been kept. "I hate loud noises. Unless it's screaming. Screaming's all right. Let me demonstrate."

He reached out and grabbed the sheriff around the neck.

Something pale and very fast flashed through the doorway, and suddenly another vampire was there—Patience Goldman, with her slender hand wrapped around Morley's wrist. She was a dark-haired young woman, pretty, with big dark eyes and skin that would have probably been olive had she still been alive. It added a honey undertone to her pallor.

"No," Patience said. Claire had met her—and the entire Goldman family—more than once. She liked them, actually. For vampires, they had real concern for other people—as demonstrated by Patience's trying to keep Morley from killing the sheriff. "There's no need for this."

Morley looked offended, and shoved her back with his free hand. "Do *not* lay hands on me, woman! This is none of your concern."

"We came to—get supplies," Patience said. She seemed uncomfortable with that, and Claire immedi-

ately realized that *supplies* was code for *people*—to eat. "We have what we need. Let's go. The longer we delay, the more attention we attract. It's unnecessary risk!"

Patience and Jacob, her brother, had been hanging out with Morley for a while, and they'd wanted to break out of Morganville, and their parents' restrictions— Theo Goldman was a good guy, but kind of strict, as far as his family went, or at least that had been Claire's impression. Claire could easily believe that Morley had convinced Patience and Jacob to come along, since he was leaving, anyway, but she also didn't believe they'd go along with killing people.

Not unnecessarily, anyway. Vampires in general were a little shaky on the details of morality in that area—a hazard of being top predator, Claire guessed.

"Hmmm," Morley said, and turned his gaze back to the sheriff. "She does have a point. Fortunately for you." He released the man, who slammed back against the wall, looking sick and shaky. "Stay. If you move, speak, or in any way irritate me, I'll snap your neck."

The sheriff froze in place, clearly taking it all very seriously. Claire didn't really blame him. She remembered her first encounter with vampires, her first realization that the world wasn't the neatly ordered place she'd always been told it was. It could really mess up your head.

In fact, she wasn't entirely sure hers had ever recovered, come to think of it.

She was just starting to relax when Morley reached out and grabbed her and Eve by the arms. When Shane yelled a protest, Morley squeezed, and Claire felt agony shoot in a white bolt up her arm. Yeah, that was *almost* broken.

"Don't cause a fuss, boy, or I'll be forced to shatter bones," Morley said. "The girls come with us. If you want to run, you may. I won't stop you."

Like Shane would. Or even *could*, being Shane. He

fixed Morley with a bleak, grim stare and said, "You take them, I'm coming, too."

"How gentlemanly of you," Morley said, smiling. "I believe I already told you how I feel about *gentlemen*. But suit yourself."

He hustled Claire and Eve out into the open room that was the police bullpen. Desks had been shoved around, papers littered the floor, and Deputy Tom was lying half hidden behind one of the chairs. Claire was glad she couldn't really see him. She hoped he was just . . . knocked out.

Somehow, though, she really didn't think so.

Shane followed behind Morley. Patience walked next to him, but she didn't try to touch him—which was probably smart, given the fiery look in Shane's eyes. His muscles were tight, his hands bunched into fists, and the only thing holding him back from punching Morley was the certain knowledge that it would be Claire and Eve who'd get hurt.

Morley shoved open the glass outer door with a booted foot, and glanced up at the blazing sun. "Quickly, if you please," he said, and dragged Eve and Claire across the open ground at a stumbling run to an idling bus.

It was an old passenger bus, with darkened windows, and the next thing she knew, Claire was being shoved up the steep, narrow steps ahead of Morley, with Eve being dragged along behind him. It was dark inside, with only a few overhead reading lights on to show her the interior. There were worn, fraying velvet seats, and in almost every one sat a vampire, at least in the front two-thirds of the bus.

In the back were mostly humans—tied up, gagged, and looking desperate. There were no Morganville residents, at least that Claire could spot offhand, but she saw two immediately familiar faces—Orange Cap and Angry Guy, from the diner, who'd trashed Eve's car. The sheriff had said they'd disappeared; she'd assumed

they were dead, like their friend who'd been left with his pickup truck.

Morley had grabbed them. Claire thought that the other one, the one who'd died, had been more of an accident than deliberate murder, although maybe he'd done something to make Morley angry, too. There was no way to tell, really.

The two bullies weren't looking quite so in control now. Their eyes were wide, their noses were running, and they kept wrestling against the ties that held them in place.

"Friends of yours?" Morley asked, seeing her expression. "I'll see if I can seat you in the same section. Aisle or window?" He shoved Eve into a seat next to a window, across from Orange Cap, and then slung Claire into the empty chair beside her, on the aisle. Then he turned to Shane.

Shane sat down silently in the chair in front of Claire. Patience, watching this, bit her lip and shook her head, but when Morley snapped the orders, she broke out some plastic cable ties and fastened Claire and Eve to the seats, then turned to Shane.

"I'm sorry for this," she said softly. "You should have gone. Gotten help. I would have made sure no harm came to them."

"I don't trust their lives to anybody but me," he said. "No offense."

"None taken," Patience said with a sigh. "But Morley will require you to provide blood. He's promised not to drain any of our captives, but I'm sure you understand his temper. Resistance would not be wise."

Shane shuddered and looked away. He didn't like giving blood, even at the Bloodmobile or the blood bank, and that was a lot more removed from having a vampire taking it, no matter whether they used medical equipment or went the old-fashioned way. Claire wasn't too

cool with it herself, and she knew Eve well enough to know she'd fight it, hard.

"Let us go," Claire blurted. Morley had wandered away toward the front of the bus now, talking to someone else, and Patience was leaning over her, checking her bonds, which were very tight. "Patience, please. You know this isn't right. Just let us go."

"I can't do that."

"But—"

"I *can't*," Patience said, with soft but unyielding emphasis. "Please don't ask again."

She straightened and walked away without another glance, leaving them in the back, pinned like the other UnHappy Meals. At least she hadn't gagged them. Claire supposed she would, if they started screaming. *Note to self: don't scream.* Good advice.

Shane twisted around in his seat to peer at her over the top of the seat. "Hey," he whispered. "You okay?"

"I'm fine. Eve?"

Eve was fuming, her cheeks bright, her eyes hot with fury. "Fine," she snapped, biting off the word and leaving a sharp, broken silence. After a second, she softened a little. "Pissed off. *Really* pissed off. What kind of stupid trip is this? So far, I've been assaulted, insulted, arrested, and now I'm tied to a chair by a bunch of vampires in case they crave a little O negative at lunch. And my boyfriend is out there somewhere, dodging sunbeams. This *sucks*!"

"Ah—" Claire didn't quite know how to answer that. She looked at Shane, who shrugged. "He'll be okay."

"I know," Eve said with a sigh. "I'm just—I need him right now, you know? Shane was all gallant and came with you. I feel . . . abandoned, that's all."

"You're not abandoned," Shane said. "Dude, don't bag on Michael. It's a whole different problem when you're flammable."

Eve turned her face away, toward the window, and said, "I know. I'm just—Gah, seriously, I *hate* being help-less! We have to do something," she said. "We have to get out of this."

But, as Morley dropped into the driver's seat of the bus, slammed the doors closed, and put the beast in gear, Claire wasn't at all sure what options they really had. Morley wasn't interested in bargains, and they had nothing to trade, anyway. No way they could threaten him, not even with Amelie; he'd already given Amelie the finger on his way out of Morganville, and he clearly wasn't worried about her coming after him—or, if so, what would happen when she did. Claire didn't have anything else in her bag of tricks; nothing at all.

"Wait it out," Shane said, as though he knew what she was thinking—and he probably did, actually. He was starting to get really good at that. "Just wait and watch. Something will happen. We just need to be ready to move when it does."

"Fantastic," Eve muttered sourly. "Waiting. My favor-ite. Next to skinny-dipping in acid and having vampires *suck my blood*."

"Sorry," Shane said to Claire.

"For what?"

"That you're sitting next to Little Miss Sunshine. It's not going to be a fun trip."

He was right about that. It wasn't.

8

Eve mostly sat in silence, but she was just crackling with anger. Claire could feel it coming off her like static electricity. She wasn't cooling off anytime soon, either; Claire thought she was being angry to keep from being scared, which wasn't a bad choice. Being scared under these circumstances wasn't going to get them anywhere. It certainly hadn't helped Orange Cap and Angry Guy much, or the five other people Claire could spot who were bound and gagged, waiting for a vamp to get hungry.

She saw it happen once, but in the medically approved way; Jacob Goldman—Patience's vampire brother, and under other circumstances kind of an okay guy—had fixed somebody up with a tourniquet and drawn out about ten tubes of blood from one of the men sitting two rows up. He was good at it. Theo, his dad and a doctor, had probably taught him how to do it. She supposed there was one advantage to having a vampire draw your blood—he wasn't likely to miss a vein and have to try again.

Jacob looked unhappy about what he was doing, and at the end, even patted his victim on the shoulder in a gentle, reassuring way. Claire half expected him to hand over a lollipop—although since the man was gagged, that probably wouldn't make much sense.

"Not happening," Eve whispered next to her. "No, not happening. This cannot be *happening*. Where the hell is Oliver? Isn't he supposed to be our chaperone?"

Claire didn't know and couldn't begin to reassure Eve, because there was a creeping sense of doom coming over her, too. Michael wasn't showing up, and neither was Oliver, and that had to be bad. It just had to be, somehow. Oliver, at least, could stand the sun; she'd seen him outside the jail before Morley had made his dramatic entrance. So why wasn't he stepping in?

Because you're not important, Claire's little, traitorous voice whispered. *Because you're just human. Fast food on legs.*

No, that wasn't true. Even Oliver had treated them—well, not exactly *nicely*, but he had developed a kind of basic respect for them. Maybe, in Eve's case, even a little liking.

He wouldn't just stand by and watch things happen.

Unless he thought he couldn't win, the little voice responded, and ugh, the little voice was way too logical for Claire to argue with. Oliver wasn't the self-sacrificing type, except maybe—*maybe*—where it applied to Amelie—and only in little glimpses.

But Michael was, and Michael would have shown up unless something had stopped him.

Or someone.

Claire cleared her throat. "Jacob? Can I ask you something?"

Jacob slipped the blood vials into a pocket of his jacket and came back down the aisle of the bus. He swayed gracefully with the motion of the road, not even bothering to check his balance against the tops of the seats, the way a human probably would have. He crouched down next to Claire, bringing them to eye level.

"I'm so sorry," he said immediately. "This was not what we'd planned. We never intended to do it this way, but we couldn't get to either the blood bank or the

Bloodmobile—they were both well guarded. We had to choose—leave without supplies, or . . ."

"Or pick them up at the convenience store?" Claire tried to keep the judgy tone out of her voice, but it was hard. "That's not what I wanted to talk about."

Jacob nodded, waiting.

"Have you seen Michael?"

Jacob's eyes widened. "No," he said, and he was an even worse liar than Claire expected. "No, did he come with you?"

"Jacob, you know he did." Claire said it softly, and hoped that Eve couldn't hear what she was saying. "Did something happen to him?"

Jacob stared at her for a few long, sick seconds, then said, "I don't know."

He stood up and walked away. Claire bit her tongue on an almost-overpowering urge to yell something after him; it probably would have just gotten her gagged, anyway.

Shane was turned in his seat, as much as his bonds would allow, and he was staring at her. He knew, too.

Claire risked a glance over at Eve, but she was staring out the window. Not crying, not anymore. She just looked . . . distant, as if she'd removed herself from everything happening around her.

Shane was right. There was nothing to be done now except wait.

Claire was bad at it, but she spent the time trying to think through the problem. What would Myrnin do? Probably invent some device made out of fingernails and coat threads that would cut through plastic handcuffs. Then again, Myrnin would be cheerfully chugging down the blood, so maybe he was not such a good example to follow. Sam. What would Michael's grandfather have done? Still a vampire, but he'd never have gone along with this stuff. He'd have stood up for people. He had his whole life, both as a human and a vampire.

And he'd have never been handcuffed to a seat, genius, Claire's little voice reminded her. *How about Hannah Moses?* That was a good suggestion, for once. Claire couldn't imagine how Hannah, who'd been a big-time soldier, would have gotten out of this, but it probably would have involved a concealed knife—which, of course, Claire didn't have.

The steady throb of the road was hypnotic, and since the windows were blacked out, there wasn't much to see out there except some passing shadows. The vampires were mostly whispering among themselves, and she could feel their suppressed excitement. It was strange, but the vampires seemed to feel they'd been prisoners in Morganville, too—mostly prisoners of its strict rules of conduct, but Claire knew they hadn't been allowed out of town freely any more than the human residents.

It was odd that the *vampires* would now be feeling that same freedom that she, Eve, Michael, and Shane had felt leaving the town borders. It seemed . . . wrong.

"Eve?" Claire tried bumping Eve's shoulder with her own. She did it often enough to finally pull Eve out of her staring trance and get her attention. "Hey. How you doing?"

"Fantastic," Eve said. "Adventure of a lifetime." She dropped her head back against the seat's built-in pillow and closed her eyes. "Wake me for the massacre, okay? Don't want to miss it."

Claire had no idea what to say to that, so she just settled her own head back, closing her eyes, too. The road hiss became a kind of white noise in her head, and then . . .

She was asleep.

When she woke up, the bus was pulling to a stop. Claire flinched, tried to lift her arms, and immediately was reminded that plastic handcuffs *hurt* as they cut into her skin. She took a deep breath and relaxed, deliberately,

looking around. Eve was awake, too, her dark eyes narrow and glittering in the dimness. In the row ahead, Claire could see the back of Shane's head as he tried to make sense of whatever was outside the window.

"Where are we?" Claire asked. Shane's head shook.

"No idea," he said. "Can't really see a whole lot. It looks like maybe some little town, but I can't tell."

"They don't need more, uh, supplies. No empty seats."

"That's what I was thinking," Shane said. There was nothing in his voice, but Claire knew he was feeling just as worried as she was about this development.

Morley brought the bus to a stop with a hiss of air brakes and a lurch, then opened the door and descended the steps. It was still daylight out there; the light spilling in from the opened accordion doors was milky white and intense.

None of the other vampires tried to follow. They just waited. Morley came back, stood at the front of the bus, and grinned. "Brothers and sisters," he said, "I have stopped for gas. Feel free to snack while I attend to the fuel."

"Oh no," Eve whispered. "No no *no*."

Claire tried to get her hands free, again. The plastic handcuffs cut deep, almost drawing blood, and she had to stop; the smell of blood wouldn't be a good thing, just now.

The vampires were turning to look at those in the back of the bus, and their eyes were glowing.

Patience and Jacob Goldman weren't among them. They were closer to the back, and they had their heads bent together, whispering. Patience seemed upset at something Jacob was saying, but he was insistent, and as the first vampire got up to get his snack, Jacob suddenly flashed out of his seat and stood in the way.

The vampire was a woman, nobody Claire had ever met; she looked older, and not very nice. She also didn't

like Jacob's getting in her face, and she said something in a language Claire didn't recognize. Jacob must have, because he spouted something right back.

Patience finally got out of her seat and stood nearby, clearly backing him up.

Jacob reached into his pocket and handed over two blood vials. He switched to English to say, "This will hold you for now. There's no need for anyone to be killed, and you know what will happen if we allow feeding in here. Take it and sit down."

"Who do you think you are, *Amelie*?" The woman bared her fangs in a mocking laugh. "I left Morganville to escape these stupid rules. Give me what I want, or I'll take it."

"The rules are not stupid," Patience said. "The rules are sensible. If you want to alert humans to our presence and restart the bad old times, the times when we ran for our lives, owned nothing, *were* nothing—then wait until we have reached our destination. You can go off on your own and do what you will. But while Jacob and I are here, you *will not* feed directly from these people. I will not see them dead because you can't control yourself."

She sounded absolutely sure about what she was doing, and very matter-of-fact, as if only an idiot would argue with her. The other vampire frowned, thought about it, and then made a sound of frustration. She grabbed two vials from Jacob's outstretched hand. "I'll expect more," she snapped. "You'd better start draining them. You have a lot of mouths to feed."

Jacob ignored her. "Who else? I can give out four more...."

Four more vampires got up and accepted the vials. Jacob took out his medical kit and handed it to Patience. "I'll stay here," he said. "Draw the blood."

"Yeah, don't make any of them short!" one of the other vampires called, and there was a ripple of laughter.

"Enough," Jacob said, and there was a hint of relaxed

humor in his voice. "You'll all get what you want. Just not now. And not here."

He looked over his shoulder at Patience, who was strapping a tourniquet around the first human she'd found—a woman, this time. There was a little resistance, but not much, and Patience proved herself to be just as good at drawing blood as her brother. She filled ten more vials, which she handed over to Jacob for distribution as she moved on to the next donor.

So it went, even after Morley came back inside after fueling up the bus. He saw what was going on, and shook his head. "You can take the vampire out of Morganville . . . ," he said, and left the rest unsaid as he dropped into the driver's seat. "Right, young ones, bloodbath later. First, we drive."

Claire half hoped that the vamps would be done with lunch before Patience worked her way back to her row, but no such luck. However, she turned left, and started with Angry Guy, whose bug eyes and muffled shrieks seemed to make no impression on her at all. She did the blood draw quickly and easily, pocketed the vials, and moved on to Orange Cap, who'd lost his cap now and was crying wet, messy tears. His nose was dripping, too.

When Patience was finished tapping him, she turned to Claire. She looked at her for a long moment, then said, "I will not take your blood. Nor that of your friends. Not yet."

Next to Claire, Eve let out a little sigh of relief. Shane, who'd been sitting tensely in the row ahead, relaxed as well.

Claire didn't. "Why?"

"Because—we owe you a favor, I think. Let this be payment." She started to move on to the next row.

"Wait," Claire said. Patience's dark, strange eyes returned to her face. "They're going to kill us all. You don't want that, you and Jacob."

"Jacob and I are outnumbered," Patience said softly.

"I am sorry, but there is little we can do more than we are doing now. Forgive me."

"There has to be something—" Claire bit her lip. Eve was paying attention now, and Shane, although Claire was trying to keep the whole conversation to a whisper. "Can't you maybe let us loose? We promise, we won't tell Morley."

"Child, you have no idea what you're saying," Patience said, a little sadly. "He'll catch you, and then Morley will find out what he wants to find out. He has no reason not to rip this information from you, and it would be suspicious enough that I haven't drawn blood. He already thinks Jacob and I are too weak. You put us at risk, as well as yourselves."

"So what's our choice?" Eve hissed, leaning over as far as she could. "Getting fanged to death? No, thank you. Pass. If I'd wanted that kind of gruesome, horrible horror-movie ending, I could have stood on a street corner in Morganville and saved myself the trouble!"

Patience looked even more uncomfortable. "I can't help you," she said again. "I'm sorry."

That was her final answer, apparently. Claire watched her continue on with her blood work, apparently satisfied that she'd done her good deed for the day.

"We're screwed," Shane said, in a matter-of-fact voice, and turned back, face forward. "Still want to go back to Morganville? Because every day is pretty much just like this, one way or another."

Eve sighed, slumped against the window, and looked as if she was close, again, to bursting into tears. She didn't. Claire almost wished she would. It wasn't like Eve, all this nervous anger. It made *her* nervous, and the last thing she needed right now was more to raise her pulse rate.

"Michael will find us," Eve said. "They'll come for us."

Claire wished she felt that sure about it.

*   *   *

Patience and Jacob distributed all of the collected blood, two vials per vampire, and gave the rest to Morley, who chugged it back like shots at happy hour. It was disgusting, watching all the vampires having their snack; Claire's stomach turned, and she found it was easier staring down at her feet than actually paying attention.

Some of the blood donors had actually passed out, though whether that was just sleep, low blood pressure, or panic, Claire wasn't sure. It was quieter, at least. Morley kept driving, and it seemed like hours before he slowed the bus again. He didn't stop, just geared down and beckoned to a vampire sitting behind him. The vampire nodded, pointed to three others, and gestured for them to follow.

"What's going on?" Shane asked. "Can you tell?"

"No," Claire said, and then gasped as Morley opened the bus doors. The bus was still rolling along at maybe thirty-five or forty miles an hour. The four vampires up front put on coats, hats, gloves—sunny-day wear—and lined up on the stairs.

One by one, they bailed out.

"What the hell?" Shane twisted around awkwardly to the limit of his ability. "Eve, can you see anything? What's going on?"

"I can't—wait, I think—" Eve squinted, leaned her head against the window, and finally continued. "I think they're going after something behind us. A car, maybe."

Four vampires had just bailed out of a moving bus, in broad daylight, to attack a car that was behind them. Following them?

Claire gasped as an electric shock zipped up her spine. Michael. Oliver. It had to be! They'd figured it out. They were right behind them.

Yeah, her tragic, pessimistic little voice said in her head. *They're right behind us, and four vampires are about to drag them out of the car and leave them to fry.*

"Can you see—" Claire's voice was shaking now. Eve didn't answer. "Eve!"

"I'm trying!" Eve snapped. "It's all just shadows out there, okay? I can barely tell there's a car! Oh no . . ."

"What?" She and Shane blurted it out together, leaning toward Eve as if somehow they could make things out any better.

"The car," Eve said. "I think—I think it crashed. It's not behind us now." She sounded dull again; defeated. "It's gone."

"Dammit," Shane said. "Probably was some farmer driving to market. Didn't have anything to do with all this crap."

"Doesn't matter now," Eve whispered. "They're not coming now."

She began to cry, producing wrenching sobs that made her whole body vibrate, and banged her forehead against the window glass—hard. Claire instinctively tried to reach out for her, and came up against her restraints, again. "Hey," she said, trying hard to sound compassionate and soothing. Her heart just ached for Eve, who sounded so . . . lost. "Eve, please don't. Please don't do that. It's going to be okay; it's all—"

"No, it's not!" Eve screamed, and turned toward Claire in a tearful fury. "It's not okay! Michael! Michael!"

She started thrashing against her restraints. Shane tried to calm her down, too, but Eve wasn't listening anymore—not to anybody.

Patience came and, with a sad but determined look at Claire, leaned over and gave Eve a quick injection in her shoulder. It was so fast Claire couldn't react to try to stop her, and Eve stopped thrashing to say, in blank surprise, "Ow!"

Then her eyes rolled back in her head, and she went completely limp in her chair, her head tilting toward the window, wild strands of hair covering her face.

"What did you do?" Claire demanded, and tried not to scream it. She'd just seen what screaming got you.

"She'll sleep," Patience said. "She's not injured. It's better this way. She could hurt herself, otherwise."

"Yeah, can't have that," Shane said bitterly. "Gotta save that for you guys. What was that, with the vamps getting off the bus?"

Patience put the cap back on the needle she'd used to inject Eve and put it in her pocket. "Someone was following," she said. "They're not now. That's all you need to know." The bus changed its pitch again, air brakes sighing, and slowed to a relative crawl. The doors banged open again, and two vampires got on, wearing hats and gloves and long coats against the sun.

One of them was smoking, even with all the protective gear.

The other one, a little taller and thinner, grabbed Morley by the neck, dragged him out of the driver's seat, and tossed him right out the door.

"Go!" he shouted, and stripped off his hat.

The tall one was Oliver.

Michael—who was the incoming vampire trailing wisps of smoke—raced down the aisle, slammed into Patience and Jacob, and knocked them out of the way. Nobody else had time to stand up, although a few vampires lunged and caught pieces of his coat as he ran toward the back of the bus. Oliver was right behind him, and as they reached the rows where the humans were, Oliver turned and snarled at the other vampires, who were starting to get to their feet. They were hampered by close quarters, but there were a lot of them.

Jacob bounded up, gave Oliver a second's dark look, and then jumped up on top of the headrest of the seat next to him, crouching like a bird of prey. Patience did the same on Oliver's other side.

"No," she said flatly, as the vampires started to move toward them. "Stay where you are."

Michael reached them and snapped Claire's bonds first. It took him a precious few seconds, because the plastic was tougher than he'd thought, and he had to try not to hurt her. As soon as she was free, he leaned over Eve and pushed out the side window with one powerful punch. Metal bent and shrieked, glass shattered, and the whole window assembly fell out onto the road.

Light streamed in, pure and white-hot, and hit him full in the face. Michael jerked back into the shadows with a choked cry. Claire had a blurred impression of burns, but he didn't give her time to worry about him. "Out!" he yelled, and grabbed her by the waist to boost her toward the window. The inch of skin exposed between his coat and gloves sizzled like frying bacon. Claire grabbed hold of the jagged edge of the window and looked down. The bus was still rolling, and it was picking up speed as it started down the hill. "Claire, jump!"

She didn't really have a choice.

Claire jumped, hit the hard pavement with a stunning thump, and rolled. She managed to protect her head and curled up in a ball on the white-hot surface.

The bus kept on rolling. She could hear screaming—and fighting. Another window broke, next to Shane.

"Come on," Claire whispered, and clambered to her feet. She hurt all over, and her ankle felt as if she'd sprained it, but that didn't matter right now.

She watched the bus.

Nobody came out the window.

Claire started to run after the bus—limped after it—and had to stop when her ankle folded under her after a dozen steps. "Shane!" she screamed. "Shane, come on! Get out!"

Her attention was completely fixed on the bus, but she had good survival instincts, thanks to Morganville's harsh training; she sensed a shadow behind her, and dropped just in time.

Morley. He was baking in the blazing day—not siz-

zling like Michael, but definitely turning toxic-sunburn red. And he was angry. His hand blurred through space where she'd been, and if she'd been in the way, he would have broken her neck. She rolled and stumbled back to her feet, felt the left one give way again, and hopped backward.

Morley gave her a feral, awful grin. "Nobody leaves the tour," he said. "Especially not you, little girl. Amelie wants you back. I'm certain of that. You're my insurance. No fair limping off on your own."

He reached for her, and out of the corner of her eye, Claire saw a black shape hurl itself from the shattered bus window and streak toward them. At first she thought it was Michael, but no—Oliver.

He hit Morley like a brick wall and threw him fifty feet down the road in a rolling, slapping mess. Then, after an irritated look at her hopping on one foot, he scooped Claire up in his arms, then turned back to shout, "Michael, leave it! Get out!"

A car was roaring over the hill behind them—a police car, with half the light gear ripped off and dangling, and holes punched in the doors and windows. It had clawlike scrapes in the hood.

It didn't slow down for Morley, who scrambled to his feet and dived out of the way as the cruiser rocketed past. It screeched to a sliding halt, crossways in the road, and the driver threw the passenger door open, then the back. Oliver tossed Claire into the back of the car, left the door open, and raced back to the bus. He leaped up, clinging to the open window, reached in, and grabbed something—a handful of black coat—and dragged.

Michael toppled out the window and fell heavily on the road. Oliver dropped down, cat-steady, and reached down to pull Michael to his feet. He took off his own hat and jammed it down on Michael's bare blond head, stripped off his own long black coat, and flung it over him as additional protection.

Michael fought to get free, but as Claire flailed and struggled to sit up, Oliver dragged her friend all the way to the police car, shoved him in the back door, and slammed it, hard, penning Michael inside. The handles didn't work, of course. Michael landed half on top of her, heavy and smelling like burning hair, but he quickly rolled up and tried to smash out the window glass—which, Claire realized with a shock, was painted over black—spray painted. Only the driver's side part of the front window was left unaltered.

Oliver got in the front, turned, and drove a fist through the metal grating that separated the back of the squad car from the front. He peeled back the metal, grabbed Michael's arm, and said, "You can't help them by dying. You tried. We'll try again. This isn't over."

"Eve's still in there! I can't leave her there!" Michael yelled, and yanked free.

Oliver, with a weary, impatient sigh, grabbed him by the neck this time, and pinned him back against the stained vinyl seat. "Listen to me," he said, and peeled back more of the grate so their eyes could meet, and hold. "Michael, I swear to you that we will not abandon your friends. But you must stop this nonsense. It's doing nothing to help them, and everything to destroy your usefulness to me and everyone you love. Do you understand?"

Michael was still tense, ready to fight, but Oliver held him there, staring him down, until Michael finally let go of Oliver's arm and held up both hands in surrender. His whole body slumped. Defeated.

Still, Oliver didn't let go. "Drive," he told the man behind the wheel. "Follow the bus. Morley's already back on board. He'll keep driving, but we should hang back out of sight."

"I can't follow it if I can't see it!" the driver protested, and Claire knew that voice, but it didn't sound like the sheriff from Durram, or even his deputy. It sounded . . .

No way.

Claire leaned forward and peered through her half of the grate, which was still in place. "Jason?" Jason Rosser? Eve's brother? "What the hell are you doing here?"

"Oliver needed some support that wouldn't combust," Jason said. "Besides, that's my sister in there, right?"

Eve. Eve was still in the bus—that was why Michael was fighting so hard. Claire felt strangely behind the curve right now; maybe she'd banged her head harder than she'd thought. It ached on the right side. She was starting to feel a whole lot of aches, as the adrenaline started to recede a little.

Shane. Shane was still on the bus, too. Why was he still on the bus?

"Jason. Use this to track them," Oliver said, and pulled something out of the glove compartment of the cruiser. It looked like a GPS navigation device. "It's been keyed to follow the bus."

"You bugged the bus?"

"I bugged your sister. I slipped a cell phone into her pocket during the confusion. Hopefully she'll have an opportunity to use it."

He handed the device over to Jason, who stuck it up on the dashboard, angled so he could see the colored road-map display. "Nice," he said. "Hey, if you could unlock the shotgun, that would be good, too."

"No," Oliver said flatly. "The last thing I trust you with is a firearm. Just drive."

Claire was having trouble focusing, she realized. "You gave Eve a phone?"

"I put it in her pocket," Oliver said. "Unless they search her again, I doubt they'll find it. There were plenty of distractions."

"What about Shane? Is he okay?"

"I don't know." Oliver kept staring at Michael. "Was he?"

"I got one of his hands free," Michael said. "I could

have gotten them both out. You just had to give me one more—"

"One more second and you'd have been pulled to pieces, which would have done me no good at all," Oliver said. "Patience and Jacob were stepping aside. They know a lost cause when they see one, and you couldn't have gotten Eve and Shane both out in any case. It's better to leave them together, where they can protect each other. Now, are you going to behave yourself? Or do I need to prove to you, again, who is master here?"

Michael didn't answer, but he dropped his hands to his sides.

Oliver let him go. "How do you feel?"

Michael let out a brittle little laugh. "What, you're concerned?" He looked bad, Claire realized, even in the dim light bouncing in from Jason's side of the front window. He was burned red, his face swollen.

"Not really," Oliver said. "I'm concerned you'll be a liability. Which is almost certainly going to be the case, if you continue to act like some lovesick boy instead of a thinking man. Are we understood? If you want to save your fragile little friends, you must be a great deal smarter about when you risk your own safety."

It was hard to tell what the expression on Michael's swollen face was, but there was no mistaking the flash of hate in his eyes. Claire swallowed, hard. Michael took a deep breath and turned toward her. "You're okay?" he asked, and stripped off his gloves. His hands were pale, but just above the line where the gloves had been were vivid black and red burns. He gently touched her face, turning it to one side, then the other. "You're going to have some action-star bruises, tough girl." But she knew what he was looking for, really.

"No fang marks," she said. "Well, none that weren't already there, from before, you know. Look, not even any needle marks."

"Needle marks?"

"Patience and Jacob, they insisted that all blood get drawn with a needle. I think they were trying to sort of ration it out."

"They were trying to keep you alive," Oliver said, turning back to face the front. "That many vampires in an enclosed space, a feeding frenzy would be inevitable. None of you would have survived it, especially not restrained as you were."

As Eve and Shane still were. Claire felt sick. She also felt horribly, horribly guilty. "Why me?" she asked. "Why save me, not Eve? Or Shane?"

"You were the closest," Michael said. "And—you're the youngest. Eve and Shane would both kick my ass if I tried to save them ahead of you." But he looked sickly guilty, too, and she knew he was thinking, just as she was, of Eve. "I heard her screaming for me. That was why we—why we decided to go in."

"It was that or listen to his yowling the rest of the drive," Oliver said. "I've never been in love, and more and more, I'm glad I haven't. It seems to make you foolish, as well as very tiresome."

Jason snorted; it might have been a choked laugh. "Yeah, you got that right."

Oliver smacked Jason in the back of the head. "I don't need your agreement. Drive."

Claire tried to pull her head back together. "Wh-what are we going to do?" she asked. "Just follow them? What if—what if something happens on the bus? Are we just going to sit here?"

"Yes," Oliver said. "Because going back now, we've lost the element of surprise, and Morley will be ready for us. In fact, he may try to engineer a provocation, to force us to do something stupid. We follow them until they stop. Once they're off the bus, we have a much better chance."

Jason said, "What about, you know, ramming the bus? Out here in the sun, they can't really chase us down on foot. Not for long."

"Ramming a bus will simply yield us a car that will no longer drive, and will not ensure the bus is disabled," Oliver said. "It would take something larger. Much larger. In any case, it's not prudent. Too much risk of damage to your delicate little humans on board."

"But—"

"Oh, just shut up and follow," Oliver snapped. "I am tired of debate. There will be no more."

Claire knew a door slamming when she heard it. She twisted around a little and pulled up the pant leg over her left ankle. It was puffy and starting to bruise. Yep. That was sprained. "Do we have any first aid stuff in here?"

Oliver dug out a box and passed it through the torn grate on Michael's side. She found some of that rubberized wrapping bandage stuff, and tried to do it herself, but Michael took it away from her, removed her shoe and sock, and wrapped it for her without saying a word.

"Thanks," she said softly. It felt better, once that was done, although there was still a dull red ache that flared up every time she moved. "Is there anything—"

"I'm healing," Michael said. He put the medical kit down and let his head fall back against the seat. "Man. This has not been the trip I planned."

"Really?" Oliver's voice was dry. "It's exactly what I expected. Sadly."

9

They drove for what seemed like a very long time, but according to the clock built into the cruiser's dashboard, it was only a couple of hours. The bus kept taking crazy back-road turns, as if they were searching for something. Finally, though, the dot stopped moving. "What is that?" Jason asked, and tapped the screen. It magnified. "Is that a town?" Claire couldn't see through the grate, other than a dot on a map. "It's tiny, if it is. Smaller than that last place where you got yourselves jacked."

"No other roads in," Oliver said, looking at the display. "They'll see us coming in any case. The land is as flat as a griddle. And just as hot."

"Yeah, who ever decided to locate Vampireville in Texas, anyway? Whose good idea was that?" Jason asked.

"Amelie's," Oliver said. "And none of your business why she chose it. It'll do us no good to wait until dark—they will only have sharper senses with which to detect us. Better to strike in the day, if we can. Unfortunately, my army consists of one unreliable criminal, one girl with a disability, and one incredibly foolish young vampire with a tanning issue. I am not confident."

"We don't have a choice," Claire said. "We have to go. Eve and Shane—"

"I am more concerned with what Morley is doing," Oliver interrupted. "He's defying Amelie. Defying *me*. I can't allow that to go unanswered."

It boiled down to the same thing, luckily—they didn't have a choice, and Oliver had to help. He thought about it in silence for a few minutes as the cruiser continued on its path to the dot on the map, then nodded sharply. "All right," he said. "We go in. Now. But when we do, you must be fast, and you must be ruthless. Michael, since you're so hell-bent on saving the girl and your friend, that will be your mission. Claire, Jason, you will stay with me. I may require someone to act as distraction."

"He means bait," Michael said. "You're not using Claire."

"She's a wounded deer," Oliver said. "She's perfect."

"*You're not using Claire*. And that's not optional. I don't care if you think you're the boss; you're not using her." Michael sounded utterly, completely dedicated to that proposition, and Oliver, after a second's frozen silence, nodded.

"Very well. I'll use the criminal. He's serviceable, I suppose."

Jason cleared his throat. "Do I get the shotgun if you're staking me out for bait?"

"No," Oliver said. "Not ever."

Claire was struck by a random thought, which was proof her brain was finally shaking off the effects of bailing out of the bus at speed. "Hey," she said. "It takes hours to get here from Morganville. How did Jason—"

"Jason says shut up," Eve's brother snapped. "It's none of your business, okay? Let's just say I was in the neighborhood."

Oliver said nothing. That meant that either Jason had tried to get out of Morganville and managed to get himself caught, by Oliver—or he'd been on Oliver's business errands. Either way, there was some kind of relationship there that Claire was sure hadn't been in force a month

ago. In fact, Oliver had been pretty definitely on the "Let's execute the jerk" team. So why was Jason suddenly part of his crew—and a trusted part, if Jason had gotten some kind of permission to leave Morganville?

Claire figured she would probably never know. Jason was angrily not talking; Oliver was never Mr. Great Communicator even when he was in a good mood, and this wasn't one.

He looked angry, focused, and very, very dangerous.

"Take us in," Oliver said. "You all know what's required. Do it. Get allies from Morley's people if you can, by whatever means you can. Intimidate if you can't persuade. Don't allow yourself to be surrounded. Arm your friends, destroy your enemies, and whatever the cost, *win.* Are we understood? I will take care of Morley."

Michael nodded. His face was healing faster than Claire had expected, but she guessed it wouldn't last, not if they were going out in the daylight again. She wondered how much he could really take, before the pain and damage got too much and just overwhelmed him.

She hoped she wouldn't have to find out.

Jason drove way too fast, gunning the engine to race-car levels, chasing dust devils down the road, and grinning like the maniac he was, from Claire's glimpses of his expression. He looked more than ready for a fight. She'd never exactly seen him like this, and it was more than a little frightening.

Next to her, Michael was closed off, focused on controlling the pain he had to be feeling, and the worry. Oliver probably didn't feel anything. He'd sneer at the idea of being worried.

Claire wanted to throw up, but she was determined to hang on and be as strong as she could. She rooted through the first aid box and found a couple of extra-strength pain relievers, not that they would help much. She also asked Michael, quietly, if he had any kind of weapon he could give her.

He silently dug a silver-coated stake out of his pocket and handed it to her. It had a wicked-sharp tip, enough to slice as well as stab, and it felt cold and solid in her hand as she gripped it hard enough to leave sweat prints on the shiny surface. "Last resort," he told her. "Don't get close enough to need it, okay?"

"Okay," she agreed, and tried for a smile. She thought she actually managed to pull one off. "Does it hurt? Never mind; stupid question. Of course it hurts. I'm sorry."

His pale hand, with its vivid red burns at the wrist, gripped hers tightly for a few seconds. "You're a good person, Claire. You know that, right?"

"So are you."

"Technically not really a person anymore, as Shane likes to remind me."

"Shane can be an idiot."

"But a good friend."

"That, too." She sighed. "We have to get them back, Michael. We have to."

"And we will," he said. "I promise."

He might have said more, but just then the car's acceleration slowed. Jason eased off the gas and said, "Okay, we're here. Looks like about three blocks' worth of town, if that. Maybe thirty buildings total? What's the plan?"

"Find the bus," Oliver said. "They won't have gone far."

"Why not?"

"Because Morley is a lazy sod, and he won't want to put himself out. Look for the biggest building, and you'll likely find the bus parked right in front of it."

Sure enough, as Jason turned the sharp corner into town—if you could call it a town; it was more like a random collection of buildings—the bus was immediately and obviously parked right in front of what looked like a miniature version of the Morganville Courthouse—sort of Gothic, with towers and peaked roofs, and con-

structed of gray stone blocks. It looked about twenty years out from any kind of maintenance work; the iron fence around the place was leaning, rusted through, and the grass inside was ragged and overgrown.

The sign said BLACKE TOWNSHIP CIVIC HALL AND COURTS. In front of the entrance sat some kind of civic monument—a big, not very good greenish bronze statue of an old man wearing an antique suit, looking very self-satisfied. The plaque at his feet, visible even from the street, said HIRAM WALLACE BLACKE. Hiram hadn't fared too well. There were dents in his bronze form, and the whole thing leaned a little to the left, as though built on unsteady ground. Another few inches, and the whole thing was going to do a faceplant of Hiram into the overgrown grass.

The bus looked deserted. The doors were wide-open. There was no sign of Morley, his people, or anybody else.

"How do you blow this screen up? Oh yeah, I see," Jason said. "Okay, the phone is inside the building. That's where they've got Eve, anyway."

"You know what to do. Michael, when you find your friends, bring them back here if you can. If you can't, find a defensible position and hold it, and wait for me."

"What are you going to do?"

"Find Morley," Oliver said. "And explain to him why it is a terrible idea to make me come after him. This will be over quickly. Morley's not a brave man, and he'll order his people to comply. The only risk is that something could happen before I find him and . . . convince him."

The way he said that last part made Claire shiver. Oliver was capable of a lot of things, and some of them were really not very civilized. She'd seen some of it. It still woke her up at night, heart pounding.

But right now, at least he was pointed in the right direction. Kind of like a cannon.

"Go," Oliver said. He didn't yell it, and there wasn't

any special emphasis to it, but Claire heard the absolute flat command in the word. He flung open his door, opened Michael's side in the back, and then he was moving toward the door, walking, not running, moving with deliberate speed, as if he had all the time in the world, and couldn't be stopped by anything or anyone. Jason scrambled out and scurried to keep up. He forgot to open Claire's side, but that was okay; Michael zipped around in less than two seconds, opened it, and flung Oliver's extra coat over his head to give himself extra protection from the fierce afternoon sun. "Check the bus!" he ordered.

"Wait, where are you—"

Too late. Michael was gone, racing at an angle across the overgrown grass, heading for the leaning shadow of the building. He got there and slammed his back against the stone, bent over and shaking, and finally stripped off the coat and shattered one of the windows that led into the courthouse.

It was odd, Claire thought, that there wasn't a single person coming out of the buildings to see what was going on—not even out of the Civic Hall and Courts. There wasn't a soul anywhere in sight. Blacke couldn't have very many people in it, but it must have at least a hundred or so.

They couldn't *all* be completely clueless, especially if Morley had been his usual obnoxious self.

Claire lurched for the bus, hobbled up the steps, and found the whole thing deserted. None of the prisoners were still in their seats, and the floor was littered with cut plastic ties in the back.

She left the bus at a limping run, crossed to the broken window—Michael hadn't waited—and groaned when she realized it was almost head-high for her. With no time to complain about it, she jumped, grabbed the sill, and ignored the cuts she got from the broken glass. Michael had swept away most of it; what was left was irritating, that was

all. Her arms trembled with the strain, but she managed to lift herself up, get the toes of her right foot into one of the cracks in the stone, and boost up onto the window's broad ledge. From there it was easy enough to swing her legs in, but it was a longer drop to the floor than she'd thought, and she hit too hard. Her left ankle let out a fiery burst of pain, and she paused to brace herself against the cold stone wall, panting and waiting for the agony to subside.

She was in some kind of office, but it hadn't been used in recent years; the desks looked like something left over from the turn of the century, but these weren't antiques; they were junk. The wood was rotten, drawers were cracked and hanging loose, and in some cases the legs had actually broken off.

She surprised a mouse in one of the broken drawers, and nearly screamed as it zipped across the dirty floor in her path. *Deep breaths. Come on, keep it together; they need you. Shane needs you.*

Claire pulled the heavy silver-coated stake out of her pocket and held it in her left hand as she opened the door with her right, ready to attack if she had to . . . but the hallway was empty.

She could hear running footsteps, though. Noise upstairs. That didn't mean there weren't bad guys down here, however. Thanks to a thorough education in Morganville—Survival 101—she *always* assumed there were bad guys around every corner.

There was a lot of chaos going on upstairs—furniture crashing, thumping, running feet. People yelled—Claire tried not to think of it as screaming—and it sounded like that might be where Oliver had chosen to go after Morley.

But where was Michael?

Claire opened another door and found an office, with a desk and a computer and an old cup of molding coffee sitting on top of some papers. Nobody there. She tried the next door—same result, only no coffee.

In the third one, she found a woman slumped in the corner. She was unconscious, not dead, thankfully, as Claire discovered on checking her pulse, which proved to be strong. Claire moved the woman into a more comfortable position, rolled over on her side; recovery position, it was called. Shane had taught it to her—he was good at first aid.

The woman was older, kind of heavy, and she looked tired and pale.

Pale.

Claire checked her neck on both sides, but found nothing. Then she checked the woman's wrists and found a slowly bleeding wound, and not a neat one, either. Claire shuddered, breathed in a few times to steady herself, and then looked around for something to use to tie up the wound. There was a scarf on the woman's desk; Claire carefully wrapped it around her wrist and tied it tight, and checked the woman again. She was still unconscious, but didn't seem to be in any trouble.

"It'll be okay," Claire promised, and went on. The thing that was worrying her now was that while she certainly wouldn't put it past Morley and his crew to be snacking on random people, this hadn't just happened. The blood streaking the woman's hand had been mostly dried and flaking off, the wound had been half healed, and Morley's party bus had only just arrived in town.

That didn't sound right at all.

Out in the hall, the fight was still going on upstairs, and as Claire carefully edged toward the stairs, trying to get a look, there was a sudden thump-rattle-crash, and a body came flying into view, hit the wall, and tumbled down the big, scarred wooden steps to sprawl at her feet.

It was a vampire.

It was *not* one of Morley's vampires. She'd gotten a look at every one of them on the bus, and they'd all been typical Morganville folks. None of them had looked

Shane's age, or been wearing a bloodstained, tattered old football jersey that smelled like dead feet even from twenty yards away.

This was *not* a Morganville vampire.

This was something else.

And it rolled up, bared terrifying lengths of fangs, and came after her with a roar full of fury, hunger, and delight.

10

Claire yelped, backed up, and got the stake level just in time to bury it in his chest. His momentum drove him onto the silver-coated wood, and pushed her into the wall behind her with a bruising slam. Her head hit the bricks, and she felt a hot yellow burst of pain, but she was more concerned by his bloody red eyes, crazy with rage, and those sharp, sharp fangs. . . .

Then he slumped against her; she shoved, and he toppled off her and down to the floor with a crash, hands thumping out to either side. Man, he really *stank*, as if he hadn't bathed or washed his clothes in a year. And he smelled like old blood, which was sick.

His eyes were open, staring at the ceiling, but Claire knew he wasn't dead—not yet. The silver in the stake was hurting him, and the stake itself was keeping him immobilized for now. Whether or not the silver would kill him was a question of how old he was, but somehow she didn't think he was one of the ancient ones, like Amelie and Oliver and Morley. He was more like some bully who'd turned vamp a few years back, if that.

The silver was burning him. She saw black around the wound now.

He tried to kill me. She swallowed hard, her hand tentatively touching the stake, then dropping away. *I should let him die.*

Except she really needed that stake. Without it, she was unarmed. And she knew—because Michael had told her—that getting staked was painful. Getting staked with *silver* was agony.

Claire reached for the stake to pull it out. She'd just grabbed hold when a voice behind her said, in a rich, rolling English accent, "You don't want to be doing that."

Morley. He must have come down the stairs while she was otherwise occupied. He was bloody, clothes ripped even worse than they had been before, and he had open scratches across his pale face that were healing even as Claire turned to stare at him.

She tightened her grip on the stake and yanked it free as she rose out of her crouch, turning to fully face him.

Morley sighed. "Do any of you fools actually ever *listen*? I said *don't* do that!"

"He's hurt," Claire said. "He's not getting up any time soon."

"Wrong," Morley said. "He's not getting up at all. But then, he doesn't really have to."

She felt something cold brush her aching ankle, then wrap hard around it. The teen vamp had grabbed her and was pulling himself toward her.

Morley reached out, grabbed the stake from her hand, and stabbed the vampire again, with easily three times the strength Claire had used. She heard the crunch as the stake pushed through bones and into the wooden floor beneath.

The boy, no older than Shane, went limp again. His skin started to smolder from the silver.

"You can't—," she began, and Morley turned on her, his face hard.

"It might have dawned on you by now that I *can*," he snapped. "It might also have occurred to you that this boy is not one of my little flock. Doesn't that make you at all alarmed, Claire?"

"I—"

"It should," he said, "because apart from those vampires gathered in Morganville, there shouldn't *be* more. Amelie, whatever you think of her, is a thorough sort. Those who didn't agree to participate in her social experiment in Morganville were put down. There *are* no vampires still walking that I don't know." He nudged the boy with one worn boot. "But I don't know him, or his pack of jackals who just ate my supplies!"

"Pack?" Claire looked up, startled, at another thump and crash from upstairs. Morley ignored her and dashed for the stairs, racing in a blur. There was screaming up there. "Hey, wait! Ate your—*supplies*—you don't mean—"

Morley got to the top of the stairs and disappeared before she could manage another word. "My friends?" she finished lamely, and then blinked, because two seconds after Morley had crossed out of sight, Michael emerged from the shadows up there, with Shane beside him.

Michael was carrying Eve, who still seemed unconscious.

They came down the stairs fast, and Claire didn't like the tense worry she saw on Michael's face—or on Shane's. "We have to go," Michael said. "Now. Right now."

"What about Oliver? And Jason?"

"No time," Michael said. "Move it, Claire."

"My stake—"

"I'll make you a shiny new one," Shane promised. He sounded short of breath, and he grabbed her hand and towed her at a fast limp after Michael, who was heading down the hall for the broken window where they'd entered. "You all right?"

"Sure," she said, and controlled a wince as she came down wrong, again, on her ankle. But in the great scheme of things, yeah, she was all right—more all right than the

people upstairs, from what Morley had said. "What is going on up there?"

"Morley's having a very bad day," Michael said. "Tell you later. Right now, we need to get out of here before—"

"Too late," Shane said, in a flat, quiet voice, and the four of them stopped in the middle of the hall as two vampires glided out of the shadows at either end, blocking them in. One was a shuffling, twisted old man with crazy eyes and drifting white hair. The other was a young man, wearing a football jersey—teammate of the vamp Claire had already staked, she guessed. This one was broader than Shane, and taller. Like the old man, he looked . . . weird; crazy, even for a vampire.

"Give," the old man said in a rusty, strange voice. "Give."

"Holy crap, that's creepy," Shane said. "Okay, plans? Anybody?"

"In here." Michael slammed his foot against the door on the opposite side of the hall and blew it back on the hinges with a splintering crash. Shane hustled Claire ahead of him into the room, and Michael jumped in after, slamming the door in the faces of the two vampires and shoving his back against it. "Barricade!"

"On it!" Shane said, and nodded for Claire to grab the other end of a heavy wooden desk, which they slid across the floor to block the door as Michael, with Eve in his arms, jumped effortlessly up onto the desk's top and then lightly down as it slid past. "Think that'll hold?"

"Hell no," Michael said. "Did you *see* that guy?" Eve stirred in his arms, murmuring, and he looked down at her, his face going still with concern. As she restlessly turned her head, Claire saw a matted spot in her hair— blood, almost invisible against the black.

"What happened?" Claire blurted.

Michael shook his head. "I don't know," he said.

"She got on Morley's bad side," Shane said. "He back-handed her into a wall. She hit her head on the corner. I thought—" He went quiet for a second. "Scared the shit out of me. But she's okay, right?"

"I don't know," Michael said.

"Well, use your superpowers or something!"

"I'm a *vampire*, idiot. I don't have X-ray vision."

"Some supernatural monster you are," Shane said. "Remind me to trade you in for a werewolf, bro. Probably be more useful right now."

Claire ignored the two of them and moved to the other side of the room. There was a window, but as she unlocked it and threw up the sash—which didn't want to move, and was caked with dust and old, dead bugs—she discovered that the grime had disguised a thick set of iron bars on the other side. "Michael," she said, "can you break these?"

"Maybe. Here." Michael handed Eve over to Shane, who balanced her with a lot more difficulty. He looked at the bars, which were in full, blazing sunlight. "That—could be a problem."

He was still wearing his leather coat, but his gloves were ripped—it looked as if somebody had shredded them with claws. Pale strips of skin showed through on the backs of his hands.

Shane, who was leaning against the desk that blocked the door, was almost knocked over as the vampires on the other side slammed into the barrier, sliding the desk nearly a foot before Shane dug in his feet and shoved back. The desk slid toward the door, inch by slow inch, until he'd jammed it hard against the old vampire's grabbing hands caught in the doorway. "Decide quick!" he yelled. "We're running out of time!"

Michael took a deep breath, grabbed one of the ancient, dusty drapes on the side of the window, and yanked it down. He wrapped it over both hands, then grabbed the bars. Even then, the sleeves on his coat rode

up, and Claire saw the strips of reddened skin, already
burned from before, start to smoke and turn black. Michael shook with effort, but the sun was too much for
him. He let go of the bars and stumbled backward, panting, eyes gone red and wild. "Dammit!" he yelled, and
tried kicking the bars. That worked better; his booted
feet and jeans protected him better, and the first kick
landed solidly, bending the bars and rattling the bolts.

He didn't have time for another one, because the
vampires on the other side of the door hit it again, sliding the desk halfway into the room and sending Shane
stumbling into Claire. Michael whirled in time to face
the first vamp in, which was the younger one in the
ragged football jersey.

Michael was fast, but his multiple exposures to the
sun had slowed him down, and the other vamp hit first
and hard in a blocking tackle, and Michael was thrown
all the way into the back wall. He shook it off and rolled
back to his feet just as the bloodsucking jock reached
out for Claire.

Michael wrapped a fist in the back of the boy's jersey
and yanked him off his feet, throwing him down with a
bang flat on his back. He planted a knee on the guy's
chest, holding him down, but that wasn't a permanent
solution, and as Claire watched, the other vampire, the
twisted old man, shuffled into the room, grinning with
one side of his mouth. He looked even more dead than
most vampires, and there was something familiar about
the disorganized way he was moving, something—

She didn't have time to think about it, because the
old man jumped at them like some creepy hunting spi-
der, hands outstretched and hooked into claws. Shane
dived one way, burdened by Eve; Claire dived the other.
That put Shane and Eve closer to the door, and with a
tormented look back, Shane ducked out.

"Claire, go!" Michael said. "Run!"

"I can't run," she said, very reasonably. Hobbling

wasn't really an option; either one of these vamps could take her down in seconds. One slow, sliding step at a time, she backed away from the approaching old vampire, heading for the window.

He didn't seem to get her plan until he'd followed her into the sunlight and begun to burn. Even then, it seemed to take a few seconds to really sink in that he was in trouble. He kept coming in that awkward crab walk even as his clay white skin turned pink, then red, then began to smoke.

Then, finally, he howled and ducked away into the shadows.

Claire, pressed up against the windowsill and bathed by the hot sun, breathed a sigh of relief. Briefly.

"Smart," Michael said. He stayed where he was, holding Vamp Boy down, and watching the older vampire shuffle around and stalk Claire. "Stay where you are. He may try to grab you and pull you out of the sun. If I let this one go—"

"I know," Claire said. "I've got it." She didn't, really, but what choice did she have? She looked around frantically for something, anything, to use, and blinked. "Can you throw that over here?" she asked, and pointed. Michael looked around and picked up something off the floor, frowning.

"This?"

"Throw it!"

He did, and Claire snatched it out of the air just as the older vampire made his run at her, howling.

Claire buried the pencil in his chest. She got lucky, sliding it between his ribs just as Myrnin had taught her to do in his occasional, completely random self-defense classes, and the older vamp's eyes went wide and he fell at her feet, in the sun. Claire rolled him out of the way, but she left the pencil in his chest.

"You've *got* to be kidding," Michael said, and shook his head. "That is just embarrassing."

"Have you noticed something about them?" Claire asked, shaking now that the surge of adrenaline was passing. The vampire Michael was leaning on swiped at him, but Michael easily avoided the blow.

"These guys? They're not too smart."

"They're sick," she said. "I recognize the way the older one moved. Notice that they're not really talking? They can't. They've been broken down to basic levels. Hunt and kill. Like the worst-off vampires in Morganville when I got there."

Michael clearly hadn't thought of that. His whole body language changed, and for a second Claire thought he was going to get up and move away from the other vampire, but sense won out over fear, and he stayed put. Michael had never gotten sick from the disease the rest of the vampires had carried; as the youngest, he'd never had the chance. But he'd seen what it had done to some of the others in Morganville. He'd seen the creatures they'd become, confined for their own protection in cells in an isolated prison.

"It's okay," she said. "You've had the shot, Michael. I don't think you can get it now."

She hoped that was true, anyway. If this was some new strain of the disease, then that was worse. Lots worse, especially if—as she suspected, from the condition of these two vampires, and the one she'd staked in the hall—they were actually getting sicker a lot faster than the typical Morganville vampire had.

Shane came pelting into the room, almost tripped over the pencil-staked vampire, and looked around, lost. "Uh—what happened?"

"Where's Eve?"

"I left her next door," he said. "She's okay."

"You *left* her?" Michael snapped. "Oh, you'd better tell me you didn't just say that."

"She's fine, Mike. She's awake, kind of. I left her with a letter opener, hiding under a desk. She's safer than any

of us right now." Shane looked down at the staked vamp at his feet. "Claire?"

"Yes?"

"You staked a vampire with a number two pencil."

"I didn't actually check the number."

"Have I told you lately how freaking awesome you are?"

She tried to smile, but her heart was fluttering in her chest now, and not in a good way. "Compliments later. We really need to get out of here and get to the car. Any ideas?"

"Find another pencil and I'll pin this one down, too," Michael said.

"You know how weird that sounds, right?" Shane said. "Right, never mind. Number two pencil, coming up. Why do I feel like we're taking a test?"

"Claire." Michael looked past Shane, at her. "Go to Eve. Make sure she's okay."

Claire nodded and hobbled out the door, across the hall. The door was shut but not locked, and she pushed it open . . .

Only to have to duck an awkward lunge from Eve, who was standing up, clinging to a chair and holding a glittering silver letter opener in one deathly tight-gripped hand. Eve yelped and opened her fingers to drop the knife when she saw what she'd almost done, and fell into Claire's arms with a sob of relief. "You're okay, you're okay," Eve whispered, and hugged her with feverish, shaking strength. "God, so sorry. I thought you were one of the creeps."

"Not today," Claire said, and winced at the blood trickling down the side of Eve's face. "That must hurt."

"Not so much now." Eve's eyes looked kind of vague and unfocused, but she was staying on her feet. That had to be a good sign. "I thought—I thought I saw Michael. But then Shane was here, and—"

"Michael's here," Claire said. "He was carrying you,

but he had to fight. He's coming, Eve. I told you he would."

Eve squeezed her eyes shut for a moment, breathing deep. "Okay," she said then, and her voice sounded stronger. "Okay. We'll be okay."

From the other room, Claire heard the sound of metal bending, and then a loud *clang.* "Yo!" It was Shane's voice, ringing off stone and wood. "Girls, the party's over. We are *leaving*!"

"Come on," Claire said, and put her arm under Eve's shoulders to keep her upright. "Time to go."

"Where's Jason?" Eve almost sounded in focus now, and on just the wrong topic. "We have to find him!"

"He's with Oliver," Claire said. "We'll find him. First, we have to make sure we stay alive, okay? Very important."

The two of them staggered together across the hall into the room where two vampires were lying on the floor, pinned by pencils, and Michael and Shane were standing at the window. The bars were broken out. Michael was sensibly off to the side, away from the sun, and he'd draped one of the thick, dusty curtains over his shoulders. Claire supposed he was going to use it to cover his head.

But neither he nor Shane was moving.

"What?" Claire asked, and as she came to the window and looked out, she realized what the problem was.

The police car was on fire.

And so was the bus, with big, crackling, very public flames.

And nobody, *nobody* had come out to gawk. No police had come running. Not even the volunteer fire department.

Blacke was a dead town—literally.

"We are screwed," Shane said, very matter-of-factly. "Plan B?"

"There isn't one," Michael said.

"You know, I kind of saw that one coming," Eve said. "Even with a concussion."

They stood there for a moment, watching the car and bus burn, and for a few seconds nobody said anything. Then Michael said, "Morley didn't do that. Morley isn't that stupid."

"It damn sure wasn't Oliver," Shane added. "So what the hell is going on around here?"

"You should tell us. You were riding with Morley; we just got here."

"Yeah, funny thing, getting tied up and hustled around by hungry vampires made me not notice the little things. All I know is that we got into the building, Morley was making some speech, and next thing I knew, one of Morley's crew was yelling that we were being attacked. I grabbed Eve and tried to get her under cover, but she got clocked by Morley when she got between him and some guy he was fighting. She hit her head." Shane paused and glanced at Michael. "What's your excuse?"

"I lost track a while ago," Michael said. "Right about the time Oliver detoured us into Crazytown for no good reason. Unless this is what he was looking for all along."

"What, a town full of sick vampires?" When Claire said it, suddenly it made sense. "He *was*. He knew they were here. Somewhere, anyway. He was looking for them!"

"He thought they were in Durram," Michael agreed. "That's why he went off in the middle of the night searching. But if they ever were there, they moved on, to here. Smaller town. Easier to control, before they got too sick to care."

"But these dudes are not exactly historical," Shane said, and nodded toward the kid in the football jersey. "That's not some vintage outfit he's wearing; he can't

have been vamped more than a few months ago, a year at the most. So how did he—"

"Bishop!" Claire interrupted. "Bishop was looking for Amelie. And he was making new vampires all the time, just making them and leaving them." She shuddered. "He must have come through here, or someplace close." Bishop was Amelie's father—both physically, and in a vampire sense, apparently. And in neither sense was he going to win a Father of the Year award. Or get a humanitarian plaque, either. He'd snacked on necks, and this was what he'd left behind him.

Scary, and disgusting.

"If Oliver was looking for them, he must have some kind of plan," Eve said. She was leaning against the wall now, holding one hand to her must-be-aching head, and she still looked kind of vague and unfocused. "Find him. He'll know what to do."

"He might have had a plan, but that was before Morley and his merry bunch of idiots crashed into it," Shane said. "Now we're in the middle of a three-sided vampire war. Which would be an awesome video game, but I'm really not interested in playing for real. I like my reset buttons."

"Then we have to find another car," Michael said. "One that runs."

"No, man, *I* have to find another car," Shane said. "And black out the windows. And get it back here so you don't combust strolling around town shopping for one. So here's an idea: *You* take care of the girls; *I'll* get the wheels."

"Did you just tell me to stay with the girls?" Michael said, and grinned. Shane did, too.

"Yeah," he said. "In your *face*, man. How does it feel?"

They tapped fists. Eve sighed. "You are both *morons* and we're all going to die, and my head hurts like crazy," she said. "Can we please just get out of here? Please?"

Michael went to her and put his arms around her, and Claire heard her let out a little, sad sob as she melted against him. "Shhh," he whispered. "It's okay, baby."

"So not," Eve said, but she'd lost her edge. "And where the hell were you while I was getting dragged along on the party bus, nearly getting fanged?"

"Racing after you," he said. "Jumping onto the bus? Breaking out windows? Almost rescuing you?"

"Oh yeah," Eve said. "But I was unconscious for all that part, so I couldn't really appreciate how brave you were. This is all right, though. Being with you."

Shane exchanged a look with Claire, made a gagging sound, and got her to laugh. Then he took her hand, held it for a second, then lifted it to his lips. His mouth felt so warm, so soft, that she felt every muscle in her body shiver at the touch. His thumb brushed over the claddagh ring, their secret little promise.

"Wait for me," he said. "Any requests on the kind of car?"

"Something with armor?" she said. "Oooh, and headrest DVD. Bonus for surround sound."

"Rocket launchers," Michael said.

"One hot yellow Hummer with optional mass destruction package, coming up." Shane squeezed her fingers lightly, one more time, then ducked out the window. Claire watched him drop to the grass, roll to his feet, and take off at an angle through the afternoon glare.

The glare, she realized, was at a lower level than before.

It was late afternoon, and the sun was heading west, fast.

"Nightfall," she said. Michael stepped up near her, out of range of the sun still flooding the window. "We don't have too long before it gets dark, right?"

"Right," he said. "But if we stay here in this building, I think we're going to have even less time. There are a

lot of these . . . other vampires. And they're not exactly shy."

He grabbed the two fallen vampires and dragged them out into the hallway, where he dumped them next to the one still decorated with Claire's silver stake—that one was definitely dead now, burned by the silver. She tried not to look too closely.

Michael barricaded the doors again and sat Eve down in a somewhat-secure chair, in the corner. "Stay," he told her. "Rest." He ripped down the other half of the dusty, thick curtain and wrapped it around Eve; one of those cute romantic gestures that was a little spoiled by her bout of uncontrollable sneezing as a gray cloud floated up around her face.

Claire stayed by the window, staring out. Not that it would help; even if she saw Shane, even if she saw he needed help, what was she going to do? Nothing, because she was human, slow, and had a torn-up ankle on top of all that.

But somehow, it was important that she stand there and watch for him, as though it were some agreement they'd made, and if she didn't keep it, something bad would happen.

Superstition. *Well, I'm standing in some kind of pseudo-Gothic castle thingy with a bunch of vampires fighting in the halls. Maybe superstition just makes sense.*

"Did you see Jason?" Eve was asking Michael. "Was he okay?"

Michael acted as if he didn't hear her. He came to join Claire at the window, although just to the dark side of the sunlight. "Anything?"

"Nothing yet," she said. "Did you see him? Jason?"

"Not really."

"That's not really an answer, is it?"

Michael shot her a look. Whatever he was about to say was interrupted by a thump from overhead—a hard

one, followed by what sounded like scratching. Lots of scratching, like very sharp claws. Maybe knives.

Like something was digging *down* through the floorboards from the second floor.

"Okay, that's not a good sound," Eve said. "Michael?"

He was standing very still, staring upward, his face marble white in the shadows.

Dust filtered down from the ceiling. Pieces of old plaster rained down in flakes, like snow. Claire backed away from the window, away from that *sound*—all the way back to the heavy desk blocking the door leading into the room.

Suddenly the door shoved against her, as someone *outside* the room hit the door with a shocking crash and howled. More scraping, this time at the wooden door. Michael lunged forward and slammed the desk back in place and held it there as the door shook under the force of the battering. "Dammit," he hissed. "Where is he?"

Overhead, something snapped with a dry crack— boards, being broken and peeled away, ripped free, and tossed aside.

They were digging through.

Eve stood up, bracing herself on the wall, and kicked loose the leg of a rickety smaller table lying near her chair. It broke loose with a splintered end, not as sharp as a spear, but not as blunt as a club, either. She gripped it in both hands, dividing her attention between the ceiling, which was now snowing plaster like a blizzard, and Michael, who was struggling to hold the desk in place as a barricade at the door.

We're going to die here, Claire thought. It came to her with terrifying clarity, as if she'd already seen the future through an open window in time. Eve would be lying there, her eyes wide and empty, and Michael would die trying to protect her. Her own body would be a small, broken mess near the window, where Shane would find it. . . .

No.

The thought of Shane's finding her, more than just the dying itself, made Claire refuse to accept it. He'd seen enough; suffered enough. Adding this on top of it— no. She wouldn't do it to him.

"We have to live," she said out loud. It sounded half crazy. Michael glanced at her, and Eve outright stared.

"Well, duh," Eve said. "And *I'm* the one who got clocked today."

The ceiling gave way with a low groan of wood and a flood of plaster and debris, and three bodies, covered in blood where they weren't white with plaster dust, dropped through the opening. They looked like monsters, and as the taller one turned to Claire and she caught the glint of fangs, she screamed.

The scream lasted for about a heartbeat, and then recognition flooded in—and relief. "Oliver?" Great. She was relieved to see *Oliver.* The world was officially topsy-turvy, cats were living with dogs, and life as she knew it was probably over.

Oliver looked . . . well, like a monster—like a monster who'd fought his way out of hell, inch by inch, actually, and, weirdly, loved every minute of it. He grinned at Claire, all wickedly pointy fangs, and whirled toward Eve as she lunged at him with the business end of her broken stick. He took it away from her with contemptuous ease and shoved her into Michael, who had checked himself before attacking, but was clearly just as stunned as Claire felt.

"At ease, soldiers," Oliver said, and it was almost a laugh. Next to him, Morley slapped white dust from his clothes, raising a choking cloud that made Claire's eyes water as she coughed. "I think we're still allies. At least for now."

"Like Russia and England during the Second World War," Morley agreed, then looked thoughtful. "Or was that the first? So difficult to remember these things. In

any case, enemies with a common worse foe. We can kill each other later."

The third person in the group was Jason, who looked just as bad as the other two, and not nearly as fine with it. He was shaking, visibly shaking, and there were rough bandages wrapped around his left wrist and hand that were soaked through with blood.

Eve finally, belatedly, recognized her brother, and reached out to grab him into a hug. Jason stayed frozen for a moment, then patted her on the back, awkwardly. "I'm okay," he said. That was a lie, Claire thought, but a brave one. "You've got blood on your face."

"Hit my head," Eve said.

"Oh, so, no damage, then," Jason said, which was *such* a brother thing to say that Claire smiled. "Seriously, that looks bad, Eve."

"No broken bones. My head hurts, and I feel dizzy. I'll live. What the hell happened to you?"

"Don't ask," Jason said, and stepped away. "Need some help, man?"

Michael had grabbed hold of the desk and shoved it back against the door again, and he was now struggling to keep it in place. "Sure," he said. Not that Jason's muscle power was going to work any miracles, Claire thought; he was stringy and strong, but not vamp-strong.

"Let them in," Morley said, and finished redistributing dust from his clothes to the rest of them with a final slap. "It's my people. Unless you don't trust us?"

"Now, why wouldn't we?" Eve said sweetly, and turned to Michael. "Don't you dare!"

"You'd rather leave them out there to be torn apart?" Morley asked, without any particular emphasis, as though it didn't really matter to him one way or the other. "I would have thought someone with so much compassion would be less judgmental."

"Excuse me, but *you tied us to seats.* And *put needles*

in our arms. And *drank our blood.* So no, I'm not really seeing any reason to get all trusty with you!"

Morley shrugged. "Then let them die. I'm sure you'll have no problem listening to their screams."

Someone was, in fact, shouting on the other side of the door now, not so much battering on it as knocking. "Michael! Michael, it's Jacob Goldman! Open the door! They're coming!"

Michael exchanged a quick look with Claire, then Eve, then Oliver. Oliver nodded briskly.

Michael grabbed the desk and pulled it backward, nearly knocking Jason to the ground in the process. "Hey!" Jason protested. "A little warning next time, man!"

"Shut up." Michael shoved him back as the door pushed open from the outside, and vampires started flooding into the room.

Morley's people. They, like Morley, hadn't come through this unharmed; every one of them, including Jacob and Patience Goldman, looked as if they'd fought for their lives. A few were wounded, and Claire knew from experience that it took a lot to hurt a vampire, even temporarily.

Jacob was cradling his right arm, which was covered in blood. Patience was supporting him from the other side. Even Eve looked a little concerned at the sight of his ice white face and blind-looking eyes. He seemed to be in serious pain.

Patience settled him against the wall and crouched next to him as Morley and Oliver, with Michael's help, engineered some kind of barrier for the door when the last of Morley's people were crammed into the small room.

There weren't nearly so many as before.

"What happened?" Claire asked Patience. The vampire girl looked up at her, and there was a shadow of fear in her face that turned Claire cold inside.

"They wouldn't stop," Patience said. "They came for our prisoners. They wouldn't—we couldn't make them stop. Even when we destroyed one, two came out of the shadows. It was—we couldn't *stop* them." She looked down at Jacob, who had closed his eyes. He looked dead—more dead than most vamps. "Jacob almost had his arm torn off trying to protect them. But we couldn't help."

She sounded shocked, and deeply distressed. Claire put a hand on her shoulder, and Patience shuddered.

"You're okay," Claire said. "We're okay."

"No, we're not," she said. "Not at all. These are not vampires, Claire. They are animals—vicious beasts. And we—we are just as much prey for them as you are."

"Right," Morley said, raising his voice over the rising babble of conversation. "Everybody, shut it! Now, we can't stay here—"

"The bus is burning," someone said from near the window. Morley seemed to pause, obviously not expecting that, but he moved past it at light speed.

"Then we don't use the bus, clot-for-brains. We find another way out of this accursed graveyard of a town."

"In the sunlight?" Jacob asked. His voice was soft and thready with pain. "Not all of us will survive for long, and those who do will suffer. You know that."

"Your choice—go and burn; stay and be torn apart." Morley shrugged. "For my part, burns heal. I'm not sure that my disconnected pieces would, and I'd prefer not to find out."

"Something's coming," a voice called from the window. "A truck. A delivery van!"

Claire shoved through the crowd of vampires, ignoring the cold touch of skin and the hisses of annoyance, and managed to get a clear space right in front of the window, where a solid couple of feet were still bathed in sunlight. Eve had already claimed it, but she let Claire squeeze in beside her.

The van was a big yellow thing, some kind of bread truck, with a boxy, windowless back. As Claire watched, it jumped the curb and bounced up onto the lawn, charged forward, and knocked down the leaning iron fence around the Civic Hall. It missed the statue of what's-his-name, the town's patron saint, but the vibrations caused the whole thing to wobble uncertainly, and as Claire watched, it toppled over that last couple of inches, and gravity took over, slamming the smug statue's face into the grass once and for all.

Thankfully, not in the way of the van.

The van reversed, turned, and then backed up fast toward the window. It stopped a few feet away, and Shane hopped down from the driver's side. He ran to the window and grinned at Eve and Claire.

His grin faded fast as his eyes adjusted to the shadows, and he saw all the vampires in the room. "What—"

"Morley's people," Claire said. "I guess we're all in this together right now."

"I'm . . . not loving that."

"I know. But we all need to get out of here."

Shane shook his head, shaggy hair sticking in damp points to his face, but he turned and opened up the back doors of the van. Inside, there wasn't much space, but there was enough to hold all the vamps—maybe. "I'll take as many as can fit," he said. "But seriously, once they're out of here, all bets are off."

"Agreed," Morley said, and stepped forward into the sun. If it bothered him, it was only to make him narrow his eyes a little. He grabbed the frame of the window and, with one hard pull, ripped it right out of the stone and tossed it out into the overgrown grass. "Right, youngest first. Go, now."

There was a hesitation, until Morley gave a low-decibel growl, and then vampires started stepping up, quickly throwing themselves out into the sunlight and moving fast to the sheltering darkness of the van. In

only a few seconds it was just her, Michael, Jason, Eve, Morley, and Oliver, with Shane standing outside the window.

"I said *youngest first*," Morley said, glowering at Michael. Michael raised pale eyebrows at him. "Idiot."

"I stay with my friends."

"Then it would appear you get to tan with them, as there's no more room in the back."

"No," Oliver said. "Michael goes in the back. You and I ride outside."

Morley let out a black bark of a laugh. *"Outside?"*

"I'm sure you're familiar with the concept." Oliver, without even looking at him, grabbed Michael by the shoulder and almost threw him across the open space to the back of the van. Michael crashed into the small open space left and was pulled inside by Patience Goldman, who looked anxious, almost frightened. Shane slammed the back doors of the truck and ran to the front. "Right. Move it, ladies."

Jason didn't wait for girls first; he jumped out and went. Oliver boosted Eve up to the window, and she ran for the cab of the truck, where Jason was already climbing inside. Claire followed, avoiding any help from Oliver, and as she pulled herself up on the truck's mounting step, she saw Oliver and Morley jump out of the building and flatten themselves on top of the truck, in full sun, arms and legs spread wide for balance. She banged the door shut behind her and squeezed in next to Eve, with Jason on the other side next to Shane.

"We couldn't have done this boy/girl?" Shane complained, and started up the car. "Back off, freak!" That last was for Jason, who was pushing too close for Shane's comfort, evidently. Claire tried wiggling closer to the passenger door, but the cab wasn't made for four, no matter how relatively skinny they might be. And Shane wasn't small.

"Just drive, smart-ass," Jason snapped. Shane looked

like he was considering hitting him. "Unless you want the two on top baked golden brown."

"*Crap*," Shane spat, and glared at the steering wheel as if it had personally offended him. He put the truck in gear, ground the gears, and got it roaring through the grass. It bumped hard over the curb, sending Claire into the dashboard, and she flailed to regain her balance as the truck slewed back and forth, got traction, and roared off down the street.

"Where the hell are you going?" Jason yelled.

"Your sister gets to talk. You don't."

"Fine," Eve said. "Where the hell are you going, Shane?"

"The library," he said. "I promised I'd bring the truck back."

Claire blinked, looking over at him, and Eve, wide-eyed, shook her head.

"You know it's desperate," she said. "Shane is going to the *library*."

And in spite of everything, that was actually funny.

11

The library was about a block down, on the left. They passed a lot of empty, blank buildings, broken windows, destruction that seemed like the aftermath of a good looting. It didn't seem recent, though.

The library's windows were all intact, and there were people patrolling outside it—the first living people Claire had seen in Blacke, actually. She counted four of them, armed with shotguns and crossbows.

"My kind of library," Shane said. "What with all the weapons and everything. I tried to boost the truck, and they finally let me have it, but I had to bring it back. This looks like the place to be. At least we can find out what the hell is going on, maybe get a bus or something."

The guards outside the library were certainly paying attention. The guys with shotguns tracked the truck as it approached, and they looked really serious about firing, too. Claire cleared her throat. "Uh, Shane—?"

"I see it," he said. He slowed the truck to a crawl. "So, I'm guessing, *Hi, we're friendly strangers with a bunch of vampires in your bread truck* probably isn't the way to go here." He put the truck in reverse. "Guess this wasn't as good an idea as it looked at a distance."

"Maybe we should—"

Whatever Eve was about to suggest became useless, because two police cruisers, carrying *more* armed bub-

bas, came screaming out of alleys on either side of the library building and blocked Shane's exit. Shane hit the brakes. In seconds, Claire's door was yanked open, and a huge man with a shotgun glared at her, grabbed her, and dragged her out onto the hot pavement. He pressed fingers to her throat for a second, then yelled, "Live one!"

"This one, too!" yelled his buddy, who was pulling a fighting, screaming Eve out of the cab. "Watch it, girl!"

"*You* watch it, you pervert! Hands!"

"Hey, leave her alone!" That was Jason, flinging himself out after Eve, looking every bit the feverish little maniac Claire remembered from the first time she'd seen him. Maybe a little cleaner. Maybe.

He must have moved too fast for the armed guard's comfort, because he got hit in the guts with the stock of the shotgun, and collapsed to the street. Eve screamed his name, and got picked up and bodily carried into the library, along with Claire. "No!" Claire screamed, and looked back at the truck. Shane was getting wrestled out of the driver's side, and Jason was being dragged to his feet.

This was *not* going well. And where the *hell* were Oliver and Morley? They weren't on top of the van anymore. . . .

Oliver dropped from the overhanging roof of the library and drop-kicked the bubba holding Claire. He shoved Claire out of the way as the one holding Eve aimed a crossbow and fired; Oliver snatched the arrow right out of the air and snapped the thick shaft with a twist of his fingers, grinning. "Let the girl go," he said. "I've played this game with many better than you. And they all died, friend."

He was looking pink from exposure to the sun, but not burned. Not yet. Uncomfortable, maybe. The guard's eyes darted around, looking for support, and found it in the form of two more cowboy-hatted men racing to the rescue.

With shotguns.

Claire threw herself forward, throwing her arms wide. Eve let out a warning cry, but Claire stepped in front of Oliver as the shotguns came up. "Wait!" she yelled. "Just wait a second! He's with us!"

The shotguns focused on *her*.

Oh, crap.

"You're running with the bloodsuckers?" one of them said in a soft, dangerous voice. "Little girl like you?"

"He's not like—like those things at the courthouse," she said. She put her hands up in the surrender position and took a step toward them. "We're not supposed to be here. We just want to leave, okay? All of us. We want out of town."

"Well, you ain't leaving town," the guy holding Eve said. "You or any of your fanged little friends. We're not letting this thing spread any farther. Blacke is under quarantine."

The heavy library doors opened, and a small, gray-haired woman stepped out. She didn't look much like a leader—Claire wouldn't have picked her out of a crowd at first glance—but immediately, everybody looked toward her, and Claire felt the gravity of the scene shift in her direction.

"Charley?" the woman asked. "Why are you pointing a shotgun at this pretty little girl? I heard somebody say she was a live one."

"She's with them!"

"There are no collaborators, Charley. You know that. Either she's infected, or she's not. There's no in-between. Now lower your gun, please." The woman's pleasant voice took on a steely undertone. "Lower it. Now."

"That one behind her, *he's* infected," Charley said. "Guaranteed."

"Actually," Oliver said, "in the sense you mean it, I'm not infected. Not in the way you're thinking."

The older woman, without so much as a pause, un-

slung a strap from her shoulder, loaded a crossbow bolt, and fired it right into Oliver's chest.

He toppled over and hit the ground with a heavy thud. Claire screamed and ran to his side. When she reached for the bolt to pull it out, the woman grabbed her arm and pulled her back, struggling. She shoved Claire at one of her guards, who held her securely. "You know what to do," she said to another one of them, nodding toward Oliver. "Let's get these kids inside. I don't want them to see this."

"No, you don't understand!" Claire shouted. "You can't—"

"I understand that he's a vampire, and for whatever twisted reason, you want to protect him," the woman said. "Now be quiet. You're not in any danger here."

Claire thought about all the vampires locked in the back of the truck. *Michael.*

She couldn't tell them about that. If they were going to kill Oliver, just like that, she couldn't imagine what they might do to a whole, confined load of vampires. It'd probably be way too easy. The sun was sliding steadily toward the horizon. Maybe, when it was blocked by the eastern buildings and there was enough shadow, they could get out of the truck and scatter.

The woman looked at her sharply. "You seem to be thinking very hard," she said. "About what?"

"Nothing," Claire said.

"I see. What's your name?" When Claire didn't answer, the woman sighed. "All right. I'm Mrs. Grant. I'm the librarian. I'm what passes for authority in Blacke these days, since all our peace officers and elected officials are dead. Now, let's be friendly. I've told you my name. What's yours?"

"Claire," she said.

"And where are you from, Claire?"

Claire looked her right in the eyes and said, "None of your business."

Mrs. Grant's graying eyebrows hitched up, but under them, her faded green eyes didn't seem surprised. "All right. Let's get you and your friends inside, and you can tell me why you thought that vampire was someone you ought to be caring about."

Claire looked back over her shoulder as she was pushed/pulled along. Oliver was being carried away, limp as a bag of laundry.

And there was nothing she could do about it.

The inside of the library was cool and dark, lit mostly by the natural sunlight trickling in the windows, although there were some camp-style fluorescent and LED lanterns scattered around, and even some old-fashioned oil lamps on the tables. The Blacke library was larger than Claire would have expected, with rows and rows of books, and lots of rooms off to the sides. In the middle was a kind of command center, with a small desk, a laptop computer, and some kind of small pedal-powered generator. Ranked on the shelves nearby were weapons, including a pile of silver chains—jewelry, Claire guessed, ransacked from all over town. There were a lot of first aid supplies, too.

Inside the library there were about twenty or thirty people; it was hard to see, because they were scattered around on cots between the aisles of books. Claire heard a small voice, then someone crying; it sounded like a little kid, maybe four or five. "What is this?" she asked, looking around. Mrs. Grant led her over to a long reading table and pulled out a chair for her.

"This is what's left of our town," she said. "The survivors. We're a tough bunch, I'll tell you that."

"But"—Claire licked her lips and settled into the seat—"what *happened* here?"

Mrs. Grant waited while the others—Eve, Shane, and Jason—were deposited in chairs around the table, with varying degrees of gentleness. Shane was furious, and he looked as if he were seriously thinking of grabbing a fist-

ful of weapons from the racks. Mrs. Grant evidently saw that, because she pointed at two of her burly cowboy guards and had them stand behind Shane, blocking him in at the table.

"Blacke's never been what you might call a cross-roads," Mrs. Grant said. "Most folks living here were born here. Their families have been here forever; we don't see new people real often out here." That was, in fact, pretty much like Morganville, minus the attraction of Texas Prairie University. It was pretty much like every other small town in the area, too. Claire nodded. "One night, we got us some visitors. An old man in a suit, and his niece and nephew. Foreign people. French, maybe."

Claire looked at Eve and Shane. Eve mouthed *Bishop.* Confirmation for what they already had guessed— Mr. Bishop had hit Blacke on his way through to Morganville.

And he'd had fun.

"They stayed at the Iron Lily Inn," Mrs. Grant continued. "It's the closest thing we've got to a hotel. Or had, anyway. Mrs. Gonzalez owned it. She made the best apple pie in the world, too." She slowly shook her head. "Next morning, Mrs. Gonzalez was missing; never showed up at the school—she worked in the office up there. Sheriff John went around to the hotel and found her dead. No sign of those . . . people."

That couldn't be the whole story, Claire thought; she knew how vampires were made, and if Mrs. Gonzalez had been drained to death, she wouldn't have come back. So she just waited. Mrs. Grant seemed to want to take her time, and Claire was trying hard not to think about what might be happening outside, with Oliver. Morley had run off, she supposed. And she had no idea what would happen to the vampires still in the back of the truck.

"We thought the murder of Mrs. Gonzalez was the end of it—shocking, first serious trouble this town had

seen in close to thirty years, but still, the end. And then the next night Miss Hanover just vanished from her store—gas station, right up the street. Best we can tell, those two women were the first victims. We know the three strangers left town that night; somebody saw them driving that big, black car of theirs like a bat out of hell. Didn't matter. They left *this* behind."

Mrs. Grant looked down at her hands, which were spread out on the table in front of her. Strong and scarred, they suggested she hadn't always been a librarian. "It started slow. People started disappearing, maybe one every few weeks. Disappearing, or dying. Then it got bad, fast, just—in days, it all of a sudden seemed like half the town was gone. Sheriff John didn't call for help soon enough. Next thing we knew, we saw *them* for the first time, in force. Terrible things, Claire. Terrible things happened. And we had to do terrible things to survive."

"Why didn't you just—," Eve began to ask, but was interrupted as Mrs. Grant's head came up sharply.

"Leave?" she snapped. "Don't you think we tried? Phones were out, landlines and cells. Internet went down with the power the first day; they ripped the power station apart while they were still thinking. We sent everybody we could out of town on the school buses. They never made it. Some kind of trap on the road, blew out all the tires. Some made it back here. Most didn't."

It was like some horror movie come to life. Claire had thought Morganville was bad, but *this*—this was beyond bad.

"I'm sorry," she whispered. "But why stay here? Why don't you just—try again?"

"You know how many people used to be in Blacke?" Mrs. Grant asked. "One hundred seventy-two. What you see here in this building is what's left. What's left still breathing, anyway. You think we can just walk away? These were our friends, our families. And if we leave, what happens? How far does this spread?" Mrs. Grant's

eyes hardened until they were like cold green ice. "It stops here. It has to stop here. Now, you explain to me how you're traveling around with one of *them*."

"What's more important is that Oliver wasn't—like those people you're talking about. They're sick. He's not."

Mrs. Grant let out a sharp laugh. "He's *dead*. That's as sick as it gets, Claire from nowhere."

"Look," Shane said, leaning forward and putting his elbows on the table, "I'm not saying the vampires aren't the essence of freaky; they are. But they're not *like* this. Not—normally. They can be—"

"And how do the four of you know anything at all about vampires?" Mrs. Grant asked. None of them answered, and her eyes narrowed. "There are more out there. More of them. Even if we finish here, there are more."

"Not like these!" Claire said again, desperately. "You have to believe me; they're not all—"

"Not all bad," said Morley, who stepped out of the shadows of one of the racks of books, looking terrifying and bloody and as unreassuring as possible. "No, we're not. Although some of us are no doubt better than others."

And *Oliver* appeared on top of the bookcase, looking down. In his long black coat, he looked very tall, very strong, and even more intimidating than Morley. More came out of the shadows, too. Claire spotted Patience and Jacob, near the edges of the group.

And Michael, golden Michael, who smiled at Eve as though it would all be all right, somehow.

Mrs. Grant came out of her chair and lunged for the weapons.

Shane slammed his chair backward, throwing the two guards behind him off balance. That was all the time Oliver needed to jump from the bookcase to the table, then to the floor, and take the guns out of their hands.

He didn't hurt them. He didn't have to.

Morley did that way-too-fast vampire thing and was suddenly at the weapons rack ahead of Mrs. Grant, baring his fangs and grinning. He made a little finger-wagging gesture, and she skidded to a stop and backed off, breathing fast. Scared to death, of course, and Claire didn't blame her.

Michael, meanwhile, was already at Eve's side. She threw her arms around his neck. "How did you get out?" she asked, her voice muffled against his shirt. He rubbed her back gently and rested his chin against her hair.

"The building across the way casts a pretty big shadow," he said. "We bailed as soon as we could. From there it wasn't hard. They thought they had everybody they needed to worry about."

"You didn't—"

"No," Michael said. "We didn't hurt anybody. Patience made sure of that."

The townspeople of Blacke—all twenty or thirty of them—were gathering together in a tight block now, with their kids safely in the center. They looked about to make their last stand. Not one of them, Claire realized, thought they were going to live through this.

"Hey," she said to Mrs. Grant. "Please. Don't be afraid. We're not going to hurt you."

Morley laughed. "We're not?"

"No, we're not," Oliver said, and piled the weapons on the table. "Shane, get the silver."

"Can I keep some?"

Oliver smiled grimly. "If it makes you happy."

"You have no idea."

"Distribute the chains to everyone else. Make sure they're wearing silver at their necks and wrists. It'll help protect them, should some of us, *Morley*, suffer a lapse of character." He checked each shotgun for shells, and tossed them to specific individual vampires, who snatched them out of the air with lazy accuracy. "Right.

I'm afraid Mrs. Grant is quite right; we can't allow this infection—and it *is* an infection—to spread any farther than it has already. We must hunt down and dose everyone who's contracted the disease, or destroy them. That's as much for our kind as yours, you see."

"*Dose* them?" Mrs. Grant blurted. "What are you—"

Patience Goldman opened up a small black satchel—her father's doctor bag, Claire realized—and inside were dozens of vials of liquid, as well as some bottles of red crystals. Claire herself had helped develop those; the liquid contained a cure for the bloodborne disease that Bishop had spread here, or at least she hoped it did. The crystals would help restore people's sanity, temporarily. It worked best doing the crystals, then giving the shot. It had for the far-gone vampires in Morganville.

"They can be saved," Oliver said. "Your family and friends can be restored to sanity, we believe. But they can't be restored to human. You understand? What's done is done on that score. But you can have them back, if you can adjust to that small difference."

"This is insane," one of the guards said, a little wildly. His crossbow was now in the hands of one of Morley's vampires, a little guy with a lined, twisted face and a limp. "We have to fight! Lillian—"

"We're not here to fight you," Oliver said. "And we're not here to save you. *I* am here to stop the spread of this infection by any means necessary, which, as I see it, aligns with your goals. My other friends," he said, putting some irony into that last word, "are just passing through your fine town. None of us have any reason to want to harm you."

"You're *vampires*," Mrs. Grant said blankly.

"Well, obviously. Yes." Oliver snapped another fully loaded shotgun closed and tossed it through the air.

To Mrs. Grant.

"Any questions?" he asked.

She opened her mouth, closed it, and looked around.

There were a lot of vampires—just about as many as there were humans. And none of them were making threatening moves. Shane walked around, handing out silver chairs to people, smiling his best I'm-a-nice-guy smile. Even Jason seemed to be doing his best to be non-threatening, which wasn't exactly easy for him.

"Then let's sit down," Oliver said, and pulled out a chair at the table. "I, for one, have had a very hard day."

12

Night fell as tensions gradually eased; the people of Blacke never quite got comfortable, but they loosened up enough to put on some stew in the library's small kitchen, which had a miniature stove that ran on gas. Apparently, the gas was still flowing, even though the electricity was out. As the light faded outside the windows, Mrs. Grant and three of her burly cowboy-hatted guards—Claire guessed the cowboy hats were a kind of uniform—made the rounds to barricade the doors and windows.

Morley joined them, and after a long, uncomfortable moment, Mrs. Grant decided to ignore his presence. The guards didn't. Their knuckles were white on their weapons.

"May I assist?" he asked, and put his hands behind his back. "I promise not to eat anyone."

"Very funny," Mrs. Grant said. Morley gave her a grave look.

"I wasn't joking, dear lady," he said. "I do promise. And I never make a promise I don't intend to keep. You should feel quite secure."

"Well, I'm sorry, I don't," she said. "You're just—"

"Too overwhelmingly dashing and attractive?" Morley grinned. "A common problem women face with me.

It'll pass. You seem like the no-nonsense sort. I like that."

Claire smiled at the look on Mrs. Grant's face, reflected in the white LED light of the lantern she was holding. "You are really—odd," the older woman said, as if she couldn't quite believe she was even having the conversation.

Morley put his hand over his heart and bowed from the waist, a gesture that somehow reminded Claire of Myrnin. It reminded her she missed him, too, which was just *wrong*. She should not be missing Morganville, or anyone in it. Especially not the crazy boss vampire who'd put fang marks in her neck that would never, ever go away. She was doomed to high-necked shirts because of him.

But she *did* miss him. She even missed Amelie's dry, cool sense of power and stability. She wondered if this was a kind of vacation for Amelie, too, not worrying about Oliver, or Claire, or Eve, or any of them.

Probably. She couldn't imagine Amelie was losing any sleep over them—presuming she slept, which Claire really wasn't sure was the case, anyway.

"Hey." Shane's hip nudged her chair, and he bent over, putting his mouth very close to her ear. "What are you doing?"

"Thinking."

"Stop."

"Stop thinking?"

"You're doing way too much of it. It'll make you go blind."

She laughed and turned her face toward his. "I think you're thinking of something else."

"I'm *definitely* thinking of something else," he said, and bent over to kiss her. It was a long, sweet, slow kiss, full of gentle strokes of his tongue over her lips, which parted for him even though she was *sure* she hadn't exactly told them to do that. Warmth swept over her, mak-

ing her oddly shivery, and she grabbed the neck of his shirt when he tried to pull away and kissed him some more.

When she let go, neither of them moved far. Shane sat down in the chair next to her, but scooted it over and leaned in so they were as close together as possible. There weren't many lights here in the corner, where Claire had retreated to eat her cup of stew and think, and it felt wildly romantic sitting together by candlelight. Shane's skin looked golden in the glow, his eyes dark, with only a hint of shimmering amber when the light hit them just right. His chin was a little dark and rough, and she felt it with her palm, then smiled.

"You need a shave," she said.

"I thought you liked me scruffy."

"Scruffy is for good dogs and bad rockers."

"Oh yeah? And which am I, again?" He was *so close* to her, and in this little bubble of candlelight it felt as if everything happening around them, all the craziness, all the bad things, was taking place a world away. There was something about Shane that just made it all okay, for as long as she was with him, for as long as he was looking at her with that wonderful, fascinated glow in his eyes.

He moved a little strand of hair back from her face. "Some road trip, eh?"

"I've had worse," Claire said. His expression was priceless. "No, really. I have. I went on a trip with my parents all the way to Canada once. A week in the car, with my folks, having educational experiences. I thought I'd go nuts."

"I thought you liked educational experiences."

"Bet *you* could teach me a few things."

He kissed her again, hungrily, and there was such focus in him that it took her breath away. She wanted— yeah, she knew what she wanted. She knew what *he* wanted, too. And she knew it wasn't going to happen, not here, not tonight—too bad, because if she got killed

before getting some privacy with Shane again, she was going to be *really* upset with Oliver.

Somebody coughed out in the shadows, at the edges of their candle, and Shane sat back. Claire licked her damp lips, tasting him all over again, and struggled to try to focus on something else, such as whoever was interrupting them. "What?" That came out a little harsh.

"Sorry." That was Jason, and he didn't sound sorry at all. He sounded kind of amused. "If you want to go on with the porn show, please. I'll wait."

"Shut up," Shane growled.

"You know, we could get into this make-me-no-you-make-me kind of thing, but I think we have better things to do," Jason said. "I'm not talking to you, anyway. I need Claire."

She needed a lot of things, all from Shane, and she couldn't think of a blessed thing right now that she needed from Jason Rosser. It made her voice go even colder. "Why?"

He rolled his eyes, just like his sister, which was creepy. She didn't even like to think they came from the same gene pool, much less shared things she thought were cute and funny in Eve. "Because Oliver wants you, and what Oliver wants, Oliver gets, right? So get your sweet little butt up already."

"Hey," Shane said, and stood up. "I'm not telling you again, Jase. Stop."

"What, because I said she had a sweet little butt? You don't think she does? Hard to believe, since you spend so much time staring at it."

Shane's hands closed into fists, and Claire remembered Jason on the street in the dark outside Common Grounds, coming after them—after her and Eve, specifically, at least that was what he'd said to Shane.

Shane didn't forget.

"You and me, man, one of these days, we're going to

finish this," he said softly. "Until that day, you stay the hell away from my girl. You understand?"

"Big tough guy," Jason said, and laughed. "Yeah, I understand. Personally, she's too skinny for me, anyway."

He walked off, and Claire saw a tremor go through Shane, something she figured was an impulse to slam into Jason and knock him flat, and then pound him.

But Shane didn't move. He let out a slow breath and turned back to face her. "That guy," he said, "is not normal; I don't care what Eve says. And I don't like him around you."

"I can take care of myself."

"Yeah, I know." He forced a smile. "It's just that—" This time, he shrugged and let it go. "Oliver, huh?"

"I guess." Claire picked up the candle and headed through the stacks for the unofficial—or official?—command desk, where Oliver was now sitting, talking to a couple of vampires whose faces glowed blue-white in the light of the fluorescent lamp.

"About time," Oliver said. "I need you to see if you can get a message out on this thing." He nodded to the computer, which sat there dead and unresponsive.

"There's no electricity."

"They've been trying to use this," he said, and pointed toward the pedal generator. "They tell me it should work, but there's some problem with the computer. Fix it."

"Just like that."

"Yes," Oliver said. "Just like that. Whine about it quietly, to yourself."

She seethed, but Shane just shrugged and looked at the pedal generator, which was sort of like an exercise bike. "This thing could be a real workout," he said. "Tell you what: I'll pedal; you do the magic. Sound fair?"

She liked that he was willing to help. Their fingers intertwined, and he kissed her again, lightly.

"Sounds fair," she agreed.

She turned the laptop over and took a look at it. Nothing obviously wrong jumped out—nothing cracked or broken, anyway. Shane climbed on the seat and started turning the pedals—which must have been harder than it seemed, because even *he* seemed to be working at it. The resistance built up energy, which translated into electricity, which went into a power strip with some kind of backup battery built into it. Immediately, the battery began beeping and flickering a red light. "Right, that's working," Claire said. "It'll probably take a while to recharge the backup, though."

"How much time are we talking?" Shane asked.

She grinned. "Slacker."

"Well, yeah, obviously."

In a few moments, the computer's power light finally came on, and she booted up and started looking into the computer problem. It took her thirty minutes of diagnostics before she located the problem and got the operating system booted up.

Shane, poor thing, kept pedaling. He stopped wasting his breath with quips after a while. When the power strip's battery finally clicked over to green, he stopped, gasping for breath, slumped over the handlebars. "Okay," he panted, "let's not screw it up, shall we? Because I do not want to do that again. Next time, get a vamp. They don't need to breathe."

Claire looked over at Oliver, who was ignoring them and jotting down notes on a map of Blacke.

But he was smiling a little.

"It's booting up," she said, watching the lines scroll by. "Here goes. . . ."

The Windows tones sounded, and it felt like everybody in the library jumped. Mrs. Grant and Morley abandoned their security sweep and came back to stand by Claire's elbow as the operating system load finished, and the desktop finally appeared. She let it finish, then double-clicked the Internet icon.

"Four oh four." She sighed.

"What?" Morley peered over her shoulder. "What does that mean?"

"Page not found," she said. "It's a four oh four error. Let me try something else." She tried for Google. Then Wikipedia. Then Twitter. Nothing. "The ISP must be down. There's no Internet service."

"What about e-mail? It is e-mail, yes?" Morley asked, leaning even closer. "E-mail is a kind of electronic letter. It travels through the air." He seemed very smug that he knew that.

"Well, not exactly, and would you please either *back off* or go find a shower? Thanks. And to send e-mail you have to have Internet service. So that doesn't work."

"I pedaled for nothing," Shane said mournfully. "That deeply bites."

"Does anyone else think it's too quiet?" Oliver asked, and looked up from the map.

There was a moment of silence, and then Mrs. Grant said, "Sometimes they don't come at us for a few hours. But they always come. Every night. We're all there is for them."

Oliver nodded, stood up, and gestured to Morley. The two vampires stalked off into the dark, talking in tones too quiet for human ears to catch at all.

Mrs. Grant stared after them, eyes narrowed. "They'll turn on us," she said. "Sooner or later, your vampires will turn on us. Count on it."

"We're still alive," Claire said, and pointed to herself, Shane, Jason, and Eve. Eve was sitting a few feet away, curled in Michael's arms. "And we've been at this a whole lot longer than you."

"Then you're deluded," Mrs. Grant said. "How can you possibly trust these—*people*?" She acted as if that wasn't the word she wanted to use.

"Because they gave you back your guns," Claire said. "And because they could have killed you in the first

couple of minutes if they'd really wanted to. I know it's hard. It's hard for all of us, sometimes. But right now, you need to believe what they're telling you."

Mrs. Grant frowned at her. "And when exactly do I *stop* believing them?"

Claire smiled. "We'll let you know."

There weren't a lot of kids in the library, but there were a few—seven total, according to Claire's count, ranging from babies who were still being bottle-fed to a couple of trying-to-be-adult kids of maybe twelve. Nobody was too close to Claire's own age, though. She was kind of glad; it would have been just too creepy to see the kind of blank fear in their faces that she saw in the younger kids. Too much like seeing herself, in the beginning of her Morganville experience.

She wound up thinking about the kids because Eve had brought over a lantern, gotten them in a circle, and started reading to them. It was something familiar, from the few words Claire could hear; it finally clicked in. Eve was reading *Where the Wild Things Are.* All the kids, even the ones who would probably have said they were too old for it, were sitting quietly, listening, with the fear easing away from their expressions.

"She's got the touch, doesn't she?" That was Michael, standing behind Claire. He was watching Eve read, too. "With kids." There was something quietly sad in his voice.

"Yeah, I guess." Claire glanced over at him, then away. "Everything okay?"

"Why wouldn't it be? Just another day for us Morganville brats." Now the *smile* was quietly sad, too. "I wish I could take her away from all this. Make it all—different."

"But you can't."

"No. I can't. Because I am who I am, and she is who she is. And that's it." He lifted his shoulders in a shrug

so small it almost didn't even qualify. "She keeps asking me where we're going."

"Yeah," another voice said. It was Shane, pulling up a chair beside Claire. "Girls do that. They've always got to be taking the relationship somewhere."

"That's not true!"

"It is," he said. "I get it; somebody's got to be looking ahead. But it makes guys think they're—"

"Closed in," Michael said.

"Trapped," Shane added.

"Idiots," Claire finished. "Okay, I didn't really mean that. But jeez, guys. It's just a question."

"Yeah?" Michael's blue eyes were steady on Eve, watching her read, watching her smile, watching how she was with the kids clustered around her. "Is it?"

Claire didn't answer. Suddenly, *she* was the one who felt closed in. Trapped. And she understood why Michael was feeling so . . . strange.

He was watching Eve with kids, and he was never going to have kids with Eve. At least, she didn't *think* vampires could. . . . She'd never really asked. But she was pretty sure she was right about that one. He looked like someone seeing the future, and not liking his place in it one bit.

"Hey," Shane said, and nudged Claire's shoulder. "You noticed what's going on?"

She blinked as she realized that Shane wasn't figuring out Michael—that he hadn't even really noticed all the personal stuff at all. He was, instead, looking out into the shadows, where there had been vampires patrolling at the edges.

"What?" she asked. She couldn't see anyone.

"They're gone."

"What?"

"The vampires. As in, no longer in the building. Unless there's a big line for the bathroom, all of a sudden. Even Jason's gone."

"No way." Claire slid off her chair and went to the desk. There was no sign of Oliver, or Morley. The map of Blacke was still spread out on the table, anchored with weights on the corners, marked in colored pencils with things she didn't understand. She grabbed the lantern and went to the library doors, where Jacob Goldman had been standing.

He wasn't there.

"See?" Shane said. "They've bailed. All of them."

"That's impossible. Why would they just leave us?"

"You have to ask?" Shane shook his head. "Claire, sometimes I think your head's not really in the survival game. Think: why would they leave us? Because they can. Because as much as you want to believe the best about everybody, they're not the good guys."

"No," she blurted. "No, they wouldn't. *Oliver* wouldn't."

"The hell he wouldn't. Oliver is a rock-solid bastard, and you know it. If he added up the numbers and it looked like it might benefit him by adding even a second or two to his life, he'd be out of here, making up some sad story. It's how he survives, Claire." Shane hesitated for a second, then plunged on. "And maybe this is a good thing. Maybe if he's taken off, we should, too. Just—run. Get as far away, as fast as we can."

"What are you saying?"

"I'm saying . . . ," he began with a sigh. "I'm saying we're out of Morganville. And Oliver is all that's stopping us from heading anywhere in the world, other than there."

She really didn't want to believe that Oliver was gone. She wanted to believe that Oliver was, like Amelie, someone who took his word seriously, who, once having granted his protection, wouldn't just walk away because the going got tough.

But she really, really couldn't be sure. She never was, with Oliver. She had absolutely no doubts about Morley;

he was all vampire, all the time. He'd smile at you one minute and rip out your throat the next, and wouldn't see any contradiction in that at all.

He was right, though. Oliver *was* all that stood between them and a life out in the world; a life free of Morganville.

Except for the people they'd leave behind.

She glanced back at Eve, surrounded by the kids in a circle of light, and at Michael, watching her from the shadows with so much longing and pain in his face.

And it hit her.

"Michael," she blurted. "Whatever Oliver might do to us, he can't leave Michael behind to die. He *can't*. Amelie would kill him."

No doubt about that. Amelie had deeply loved Sam, Michael's grandfather, and when she'd turned Michael into a vampire, she'd considered him family—*her* family. If Oliver planned to throw them to the infected wolves, he was going to have to figure out how to do it *and* somehow save Michael, without letting Michael know what had happened to the rest of them.

Michael must have heard her say his name, because he looked over at her. Shane crooked a finger at him. Michael nodded and walked over.

He was much more observant than Claire was, because before he ever reached them, Michael looked around and said, "Where are they?"

"Thought maybe you knew," Shane said. "They being your fellow fanged ones. Isn't there some kind of flock instinct?"

"Bite me, blood bank. No, they didn't tell me anything." Michael frowned. "Stay here. I'm going to check the rest of the building. Be right back."

He was gone in a whisper of air, hardly making any sound at all, and Claire shivered and leaned against Shane's solid, very human warmth. His arms went around her, and he touched his lips lightly to the back of

her neck. "How can you smell this good after the kind of crappy day we've had?"

"I sweat perfume. Like all girls."

He laughed and squeezed her. He smelled good, too—more *male*, somehow, a little grungy and edgy and sweaty, and although she loved soap and water and shampoo, sometimes this was better—wilder.

Michael was back in—true to his word—just a few minutes, and he didn't look at all happy. "I found Patience," he said. "She and Jacob are guarding the doors from the outside. Oliver went out to do a patrol."

"And everybody else?" Claire asked.

"Morley took everybody else to go after the enemy. He said he wasn't going to wait for them to come to us. At least, that's what he said he was doing. For all Patience knows, Morley may be trying to find another truck or bus and get his people out of town."

"Did Oliver know about this?"

Michael shook his head. "He's got no idea, although he might now, if he spotted them outside. Don't know how he'd stop them on his own, though."

Claire didn't, either, but it was *Oliver*. He'd figure out something, and it probably wouldn't be pretty.

"How long until dawn?"

"A couple of hours," Michael said. He looked over at Eve, who had finished up the story and was hugging kids who were on their way to their beds. "Mrs. Grant said they always come during the night. That means they'll be coming soon, if Morley's people didn't screw up their whole day. And we'd better be ready."

When there had been a bunch of vampires running around on *their* side, Claire hadn't felt too worried, but now she was. And looking at Michael, at Shane, she knew they were, too.

"So let's hat up, guys," Shane said. "Nobody gets fanged tonight. New rule."

He and Michael did a fast high-low five, and went for the weapons.

Claire got Eve and updated her; then they joined the boys to get their vampire-repelling act together. Mrs. Grant had been dozing in an armchair, shotgun across her lap, but she woke up as soon as the four of them started raiding the weapons pile on the table. Claire was impressed; for an old lady, she woke up fast, and the first thing she did was look for trouble. When she didn't find any immediately, she looked at the four of them and said, "Are they coming?"

"Probably," Michael said, and picked up a couple of wooden stakes, leaving the silver-coated ones for the humans to handle. He also grabbed up a crossbow and some extra bolts. "We're going to help with patrols. Looks like we're a little light on guards."

"But Morley—" Mrs. Grant's mouth slammed shut, into a grim line. She didn't need to be clued in, obviously. "Of course. I never doubted he'd stab us in the back."

"I'm not saying he has," Michael said. "I'm just saying he's not here. So we need to be sure that if things go wrong . . ."

Mrs. Grant rose from her chair, winced, and rubbed at a sore spot on her back. She looked tired, but very focused. "I'll get my men up," she said. "Should have known we couldn't do a whole night without some kind of alert. I just hoped for a miracle."

"How long have you been doing this?" Claire asked. "Fighting them off?"

"It wasn't all at once," the older woman said. "At first we thought the people we couldn't find were just sick— regular human sick. And they were clever at first, good at hiding out, picking off people who weren't paying attention. Like wolves, going after strays. By the time we knew, they came in force and took out most everybody

who could have gotten things organized against them. All told, I guess we've been living out of this library for almost three weeks now." She almost smiled, but it was just a bitter twist of her lips, really. "It seems longer. I can hardly remember what it was like before. Blacke used to be a real quiet town; nothing ever happened. Now . . ."

"Maybe we can get it back to that quiet town it used to be," Claire said.

Mrs. Grant gave her a long look. "Just you and your friends?"

"Hey," Shane said, snapping a shotgun closed with a flick of his wrist. "We're just trying to help."

"And stay alive," Eve added. "But trust me, this is not the worst situation we've ever been in." She sounded confident about that. Claire raised her eyebrows, and Eve considered it for a few more seconds. "Okay, maybe *tied* for worst. But definitely not the Guinness Record for awfulness."

Mrs. Grant looked at each of them in turn, and then just walked away to rouse her own men.

"Seriously," Shane said, "this kind of *is* the worst situation we've ever been in, right?"

"Speak for yourself," Michael said. "I got myself killed last year. Twice."

"Oh yeah. You're right—last year really sucked for you."

"Boys," Eve interrupted, when Michael started to make some smart-ass comeback. "Focus. Dangerous vampire attack imminent. What's the plan?"

Michael kissed her lightly on the lips, and his eyes turned vampire-bright. "Don't lose."

"It's simple, yet effective. I like it." Shane extended his fist, and Michael bumped it.

"I am *never* taking a trip with either of you ever again." Eve said. "Ever."

"Excellent," Shane said. "Then next trip, we hit the strip bar."

"I have a gun, Shane." Eve sighed.

"What, you think I actually loaded yours?"

Eve flipped him off, and Claire laughed.

Even now, things just stayed normal, somehow.

An hour passed, and nothing happened. Eve got anxious about Jason's absence, but Claire was starting to feel a little confident that nothing *would* happen tonight at the library, as the minutes clicked by and the night around the library continued quiet, with nothing but the wind stirring outside in the streets.

And then the walkie-talkie Mrs. Grant had given her squawked for attention, making her jump. Claire figured it would be Shane; he'd stationed himself on the other side of the building, apparently because she was so distracting (which really didn't disappoint her, when she thought about it).

But it wasn't Shane.

It was Eve. "I'm coming out," she said. She sounded breathless and worried. "You need to see this."

"I'm here," Claire said. "Be careful."

In under a minute, Eve was beside her, holding out an open cell phone. Not hers—this one, for instance, didn't have all the usual glow-in-the-dark skulls on it. Eve wouldn't have a boring cell like this one.

Oh yeah. It was the one Oliver had slipped into her pocket on the bus. The only one they had now, since the rest were probably still dumped in a drawer back in the Durram police station.

There was a text message on the phone. *Wounded*, it said. *Bring help. Garage.*

It was from Oliver.

And that was it. Just the four words. Claire had gotten the occasional phone call from Oliver, but *never* a text.

"Oliver texted me," Eve said. "I mean really. Oliver *texted*. That's weird, right? Who knew he could?"

"Mrs. Grant said the cell phones didn't work here."

"No, she said they went out. This one's working. Kinda, anyway."

"Michael!" Claire called, and he jumped down from the top of a bookshelf next to the window to land next to her, barely seeming to notice the impact. She didn't see him coming, either, which made her fumble the phone and almost drop it. "Hey! Scary-monster move! Don't like it!"

"I'll try to whistle next time," he said. "What?"

She showed him. He *did* whistle, softly, and thought for a few seconds.

"What if it's not him?" Claire said. "What if it's, I don't know, *them*? They got him, and they're using his phone to lure us in?"

"They didn't strike me as particularly clever with the planning, but you've got a good point. It could be a trap." He frowned. "But if Oliver is calling for help, it's about as bad as it gets."

"I know." Claire felt short of breath. "What do we do? He probably thinks Morley's here!"

"Well, Morley's not." Michael looked around at the library, at the cluster of kids sleeping on cots in the middle of the room. "I don't like leaving them, but we can't just ignore it. Not if there's a chance he's really in trouble. It's close to dawn, at least. That's good for them, bad for Oliver."

They found Mrs. Grant, who listened to them, read the text message, and shrugged.

Shrugged.

"You want to go, go," she said. "We held out before any of you got here. We'll hang on long after you're gone, too. This is our town, and we're going to be the last ones standing around here. Count on it."

"Yes ma'am," Claire said softly. "But—the kids—"

Mrs. Grant smiled bleakly. "What do you think we fight so hard for? The architecture? We'll fight to our last for our kids, every one of us. Don't you worry about

that. You think your friend needs you, go on. Take the weapons—we've got plenty. This used to be a big hunting town." Mrs. Grant paused, eyeing Claire. "In fact, hold on. Got something for you."

She rummaged in a closet and came up with something that was huge, bulky, and looked very complicated—but once Claire had it thrust into her hands, she realized it wasn't complicated at all.

It was a bow. One of those with the wheels and pulleys—a compound bow?

Mrs. Grant found a bag stuffed full of arrows, too.

"I don't know how to shoot it," Claire protested.

"Learn."

"But—"

"If you don't want it, give it back."

"No," Claire said, and felt ashamed of herself. "I'm sorry. I'll figure it out."

Mrs. Grant suddenly grinned and ruffled Claire's hair as one would a little kid's. "I know you will," she said. "You got spark, you know that? Spark and grit. I like that."

Claire nodded, not quite sure *what* to say to that. She clutched the bow in one hand, the bag of arrows in the other, and looked at Michael. "So I guess we're—"

"Saving Oliver," Michael said, straight-faced. "Maybe you'd better try shooting that thing first."

While Michael, Shane, and Eve straightened out whatever it was they were going to do to get to Oliver—who was, according to the map and Mrs. Grant, at an old adobe building near the Civic Hall called Halley's Garage—Claire set up a couple of hand-drawn paper targets on pillow-padded chairs, pulled one of the arrows out, and tried to figure out how to put it on the bowstring quickly. That didn't work so well, so she tried again, taking her time, then pulling back the arrow and sighting down the long, straight line.

It was surprisingly tough to pull the string back, *and* hold the arrow in place, *and* not waver all over the place. She didn't even hit the chair, much less the target, and she winced as the arrow hit the wall at least four feet away. But at least she'd fired it. That was something, right?

She picked out another arrow and tried again.

Twenty arrows later, she'd managed to hit the pillow—not the target, but the pillow—and she was starting to understand how this whole thing worked. It was easier when she thought of it in terms of physics, of potential and kinetic energy, energy and momentum.

As she was working out the calculations in her head, she forgot to really worry about all the physical things that were getting in the way—the balancing of the bow, the aiming, the fear she wasn't going to get it right—and suddenly it all just *clicked*. She felt it come into sudden, sharp focus, like a spotlight had suddenly focused on her, and she let go of the arrow.

That instant, she *knew* it would hit the target. She let the bow rock gracefully forward on the balance point, watching the arrow, and it smacked into the exact center of her crudely drawn paper circle.

Physics.

She *loved* physics.

Shane arrived just as she put the arrow into the center, and slowed down, staring from the target to Claire, standing straight and tall, bow still held loosely in one hand and ready to shoot again. "You look so hot right now," he said. "I'm just saying."

She grinned at him and went to pick up all the arrows. One or two had suffered a little too much from contact with the wall, but the rest were good to reuse, and she carefully put them back into the bag, fletching end up. "You just like me because I might actually be able to be useful for a change."

"You are *always* useful," Shane said. "And hot. I mentioned that, right?"

"You're mental. I need a shower, clean clothes, and about a year of sleep."

"Okay, how about a hot mess?"

"Let me be Eve for a minute," she said, and flipped him off. He laughed and kissed her.

"Not even close," he said. "Come on, we've got some cranky old vampire to rescue."

13

It was still dark outside, but it felt . . . different, as if the world was still dreaming, but dreaming about waking up. The air felt cool and light, and the darkness was just a tiny bit lighter than before.

"Not long until dawn," Michael said. "Which is good news and bad news."

"Good news for us," Shane said. "Present company excepted."

"You're such a bro."

"You start smoking, I'll roll you into the shade," Shane said. "Can't ask for more than my being willing to save your bloodsucking ass." They stood outside of the doors of the library for a few seconds, getting their bearings. Mrs. Grant had equipped them with sturdy LED lanterns, but it didn't feel like the light fell very far. There could be anything lurking ten feet away, Claire thought. And there probably was.

Michael shut down his lantern and just . . . disappeared. It was startling, but they knew he was going to do it, at least; the plan was that he'd get out ahead of the light and look for trouble. Kind of a cross between a scout and bait. Claire's walkie-talkie clicked a moment later—no voice message, just the quiet electronic signal. "Go," she said. "We're okay."

The three of them went at a jog, watching their steps

as best they could in the confusing jumble of shadows and harsh, flickering light. Blacke looked like a nightmare, or Hollywood's idea of a disaster movie—cars abandoned, buildings closed and dark, windows shattered. The big, Gothic Civic Hall loomed over everything, but there weren't any lights showing inside. The statue of Hiram what's-his-face remained facedown in the thigh-high weeds, which Claire thought really might have been the best place for it. At least it wasn't leaning over and threatening to fall on people. Especially on her, because that would have been the worst Darwin Award–qualifying death ever.

They made it to the sidewalk beside the Civic Hall. Shane pointed. "That way," he said. "Should be on that corner, facing the hall."

Michael suddenly zipped into view at the edge of the light. "They're coming," he said. "Behind us and to the left. Back of the Civic Hall."

"Run!" Shane said, and they took off, lanterns throwing crazy, bouncing light off broken glass and metal, turning shadows into ink-filled blots. The iron fence around the Civic Hall was leaning outward, into the sidewalk, and Shane had to flinch and duck to avoid a sharp, rusty arrow-point bent low enough to scrape his face. Claire almost tripped over one of the metal bars that had fallen loose from the fence. She kicked it out of the way, then paused and grabbed it, juggling the lantern.

"Don't stop!" Eve hissed, and pulled her on. The iron bar, with its sharp arrowhead top, was heavy, but straight, like a spear. Claire managed to hang on to it as they ran, but at the next curb she missed her footing and had to scramble. Her lantern broke free of her fingers and smashed on the ground. It flickered, brightened, then faded and died.

Out of nowhere, Michael was next to her, handing her his own switched-off lantern and grabbing the iron bar from her. "Keep going!" he said, and turned with the

iron bar to guard their backs. Eve looked back, her face pale in the white LED lights, and her dark eyes looked huge and terrified.

"Michael?"

"Don't stop!"

He fell behind in the dark after only three or four steps, lost to them. Claire heard something like a snarl behind them, and what sounded like a body hitting the ground.

Then came a scream, high and wild.

Up ahead, she saw a flash of what looked like faded pink. There was a leaning metal sign flapping and creaking in the predawn wind, and Claire wasn't sure, but she thought the rusty letters might have said GARAGE.

It was a square adobe building with some old-fashioned gas pumps off to the side that looked as if they hadn't worked since Claire's mom was a kid. The windows were broken and dark, but they were blocked up with something, so there was no way to see inside.

Shane arrived at the door of the building—a big wooden thing, scarred and faded, with massive iron hinges—and banged on it. "Oliver!" he yelled. "Cavalry!"

Funny, Claire didn't feel much like the cavalry at the moment. They rode in with guns blazing to save the day, right? She felt more like a hunted rabbit. Her heart was pounding, and even in the cool air she was sweating and shaking. *If this is a trap* . . .

The door opened into darkness, and a hand reached out and grabbed Shane by the shirt front, and yanked him inside.

"No!" Claire charged forward, lantern blazing now and held high, and saw Shane being dragged, off balance, out of the way. Not having time or room for the bow, she dropped it, grabbed an arrow out of the bag, and lunged for the vampire who was taking Shane away.

Oliver turned, snarling, and knocked the arrow out of

her grip so hard her entire hand went numb. She gasped and drew back, shocked, because Oliver looked . . . not like Oliver, much. He was dirty, ragged, and he had blood all down his arm and the front of his shirt.

There was a raw wound in his throat that was slowly trying to heal.

That was his own blood on his clothes, she realized. Something—someone—had bitten him, nearly killing him, it looked like.

"Inside," he ordered hoarsely, as Eve hovered in the doorway, peering in. "Michael?"

Michael appeared out of the darkness, racing fast. He stopped to grab up Claire's fallen bow, and then practically shoved Eve inside the building as he slammed the door and turned to lock it. There were big, old-fashioned iron bolts, which he slid shut. There was also a thick old board that Oliver pointed toward; Michael tossed Claire her bow and slotted the bar in place, into the racks on either side of the door.

As he did, something hit the door hard enough to bend the metal bolts and even the thick wooden bar. But the door held.

Outside, something screamed in frustration, and Claire heard claws scratching on the wood.

Michael wasn't hurt, at least not that Claire could see; he hugged Eve and kept one arm around her as they came toward Claire, who was still in a standoff with Oliver.

And Oliver was still holding Shane with a white, clenched fist twisted in the fabric of his shirt.

"Hey," Shane said. "Off! Let go!"

Oliver seemed to have forgotten he was even holding him, but as he turned to look at Shane, Claire saw his eyes turn muddy red, then glow hotter when Shane tried to pull away.

"Don't," she said softly. "He's lost a lot of blood; he's not himself. Stay still, Shane."

Shane took a deep breath and managed to hold himself steady, but Claire could tell it really cost him. Everything in him must have been screaming to fight, rip free, run away from that glowing red hunger in Oliver's eyes.

He didn't. And Oliver, after a few eternal seconds, let go of him and stepped back, then suddenly turned and stalked away.

Shane looked over at Claire, and she saw the real fear in his eyes, just for a second. Then he pushed it away, and smiled, and held up his thumb and index finger, pushed about an inch apart. "Close," he said.

"Maybe you're not his type," Michael said.

"Oh, now you're just being insulting." Shane reached out for Claire's hand, and squeezed it, hard. He didn't mind letting her feel the nerves that still trembled in him, but he wasn't going to let Michael see it, obviously. "So what the hell is going on in here?"

A vague shape loomed up behind him out of the shadows. Then another one. Then another. Shane and Claire quickly moved to stand back to back. So did Eve and Michael. Among the four of them, they were covering every angle.

"Lurking isn't answering," Shane said. "Oliver? Little help?"

Instead, one of the shapes stepped forward into the light. Morley. Claire felt relieved, and annoyed. Of *course* it was Morley. Why had she ever doubted it? He was the champion lurker of all time.

"What did you bring?" Morley rasped.

"Besides charm and beauty?" Eve said. "Why? What did you need? What are you doing here?"

"They've been helping us," whispered someone out of the dark. Eve turned up the power on her lantern to max, and the dim, cold light finally penetrated the shadows enough to show the people lying crumpled on the dirty floor of the garage. Well, *people* might have been a little bit misleading, because Claire realized they were

all vampires; their eyes caught the light and reflected it back.

She didn't recognize them. And then it finally occurred to her why she wouldn't.

These were the vampires of Blacke. The sick ones. And there must have been at least ten of them, in addition to another ten or fifteen of Morley's crew, crammed into the small adobe building.

"We went after them one by one," Morley said. "We've been at it for hours now. Some of them were a damn nuisance to bring here, let alone dose. But your witch potion does seem to work, little Claire. If we can get some of the crystals in them, they become rational enough to accept the cure."

Claire was stunned. Somehow, having seen how far gone things were, she'd never really expected them to be able to *save* people—but here they were, lying exhausted on the floor, shaking and confused. Unlike the vampires Claire had dealt with in Morganville, these were newbies, like Michael; people who'd been turned against their will in the first place, and made sick at the same time. For some reason, they'd been more susceptible to getting on the crazy train than Michael; maybe that was because he was originally from Morganville, and had some kind of better resistance. But they'd certainly gotten sick a lot faster, and a lot worse, than any vampires she'd ever seen.

Consequently, they were healing a whole lot more slowly. It hadn't taken Myrnin and Amelie and Oliver long to recover after taking their doses when Bishop was safely out of the way, but then, they were far older, and had already coped with being vampires.

Claire focused on a boy about her own age. He looked scared, devastated, and alone. He looked *guilty*, as if he couldn't forget how he'd been surviving these past few weeks or what he'd done.

"They're coming around," Morley continued. "But

the more we get of them, the more vulnerable we are; they can't get up and fight yet, even if we'd trust them to do so. And the others over there, they've tracked us here. Oliver did a gallant job, but they're no doubt on their way here now."

"Uh, I think we might have pretty much led them straight over," Eve said. "Sorry. Nobody specified stealthy in the message."

"I was hoping one would take it as implied," Oliver snapped. "I should have known better."

"And where the *hell* is my brother, you jerk?"

"He has orders," Oliver said. "That's all you need to know."

"Children, children, this anger gets us nowhere," Morley said, in a mocking, motherly tone. "There are about fifteen of them left we haven't been able to catch and give the cure, and sadly, we have very little left at this point. The ones we can't cure, we must confine, until we can get the drugs from Morganville."

Funny, Claire had never really thought of him as being a humanitarian—vampiritarian? Anyway, someone who put the best interests of others first. But getting out of Morganville—and away from Amelie—seemed to have done something good for Morley. He seemed to almost *care.*

Almost.

"Confine, not kill," Oliver said, and turned to come back toward them. His eyes had gone safely dark again, although Claire could see how tired and hungry he was in the sharp moves he made, and the tense set of his muscles. "And how precisely do you think we should do that, Morley? It's been difficult enough to trap these creatures singly and pacify them. Morning isn't far away, and in case you have failed to notice, you're down quite a few followers on your side."

Morley shrugged. "Some stayed near the library. Some simply wanted to go, so I let them. The whole pur-

pose of this exercise was to earn our freedom, Oliver. Even if you don't understand the concept of freedom in the slightest—"

"Freedom?" Oliver barked out a laugh. "Anarchy is what you want, Morley. It's what you always wanted. Don't dare to—"

"Hey!" Claire said, and stepped away from Shane, facing both vampires. "Politics later! Focus! What are we going to do, if they're coming? Can we hold them off?"

"This is the most defensible position in town, other than the library," Morley said, suddenly all business. "We can hold it with the men we have, even against the local talent."

"I'm sensing a *but* coming up soon," Shane said.

"*But*," Morley said, "we failed to bring much in the way of supplies. In fact, most of ours ended up stuck between the teeth of our friends across the way. And those who are recovering will need to feed, quickly."

There was a short, deadly silence. Oliver said nothing, but he looked drawn and weary.

"Wait," Eve said slowly. "What are you saying?"

More silence. Claire felt cold trickle down her spine. "You're saying we just volunteered to be blood donors."

"You are *not* serious," Shane said. "You are *not* snacking on us."

"Not all of you, obviously," Morley said. "The girl's exempt; she's Amelie's toy, and I wouldn't harm her for the world. Michael, of course, isn't the appropriate meat for our table. But you and our lovely living dead girl—"

"No," Claire said. "Never going to happen. Back off."

"My dear, do you think I'm actually offering you a choice? It's an *explanation*. An apology, of sorts. Oliver didn't send you the message. I held him down, took his telephonic device, and used it myself. Why do you think he's so badly mussed?"

It was weird, Claire thought, to feel so clear at this moment. So calm. "You're telling me you're going to take Eve and Shane and drain them."

"I could make them vampires when we're done, if you just can't face losing them. I'm terribly progressive that way. Then you would be the *only* breather in your little pack, Claire. How long do you imagine you'd last, especially if your boyfriend there declared his *undying* love?" Morley fluttered his eyelashes like a cartoon character and put both hands over his heart. "If I were you, I'd volunteer to join them. Being human is not precisely a clever plan."

"Yeah? How's this?" Claire, in one smooth, fast motion, pulled an arrow from the bag on her shoulder, slotted it home on the string, and pulled the compound bow back to full extension. She was aiming the arrow straight at Morley's crossed hands, over his heart.

He laughed. "You aren't serious—"

She fired.

The arrow went through both of Morley's hands, pinning them to his chest with the fletching at the end. He stared down in shock at the wood piercing his chest, stumbled, and went down to his knees.

Then just down, face forward. The arrow stuck up out of his back, like an exclamation point.

"I will," Claire said softly, and let the bow rock forward as she reached one-handed for another arrow and notched it home. "I'm not a really good shot, but this is a really small room, so let me make this very clear: the first vampire who tries to lay a hand on either of my friends gets a new piercing, just like Morley. Now, if you need food, I will figure it out. But you don't get to use my friends like vending machines. Are we clear?"

Around the room, vampires nodded, casting disbelieving looks at Morley. Even Oliver was staring at her as if he'd never really seen her before. She didn't know why; he'd known she could do it—hadn't he?

Or was she different, somehow?

"Shane?" Claire asked. He stepped up to her side. "Use Eve's phone. Call Mrs. Grant at the library. We need to organize something."

"What?"

"A blood drive," she said.

"Hang on—"

"Shane." Claire tilted her head up to look at him, and didn't smile. "They'll do it. These are their friends and family. They'll do it to save them. I'd do it to save *you*."

He touched her cheek gently. "I think you would," he said. "Crazy girl."

"Ask Morley how crazy I am," she said. "Oh, wait. You'll have to take the arrow out, first."

"Maybe later. Facedown is a good look for him." Shane gave her a quick, beautiful smile, and turned away to make the call.

Michael was shaking his head. Claire, without loosening her draw on the bow, gave him a quick, nervous look. "What?"

He laughed. "You," he said. "Jeez, Claire. If I didn't love you, you'd scare me."

"I don't love her," Oliver said acidly. "And if you *ever* point that arrow anywhere near me, Amelie's pet or no, I will take it away from you and introduce you to the sharp end, with great pleasure. Are we clear, girl?"

"Yeah," she said, and kept the arrow pointed away from him. "You got your butt kicked by Morley, and you're threatening me because I actually solved your problem for you. I think we're very clear. But don't worry. I won't hurt you, Oliver."

For a brief, deadly second, there was utter silence.

Then Oliver laughed.

It wasn't the bitter, angry, terrible laugh she expected. Oliver actually sounded almost *human*. He sagged back against the wall, still laughing, and sank down to a crouch, hands loosely braced on his knees. It sounded as

if he hadn't laughed that much, or that deeply, for a very long time. It was weirdly infectious; Eve giggled in little hiccups, trying not to; Michael started laughing at her struggle not to laugh. Before too long, even Claire was fighting to keep her aim steady on the arrow.

"Ease up," Michael said, and touched her arm, which was trembling with effort. "You made your point. Nobody's coming after us. Not in here."

She sighed, finally, and loosened the draw on the bow. Her shoulders were aching, and her arms felt like raw meat. She hadn't even felt the strain until it was gone.

"Claire," Oliver said. She looked over at him, suddenly alarmed and wondering if she had the strength to try to draw the bow again, but he was smiling. It gave his sharp face a relaxed look she wasn't really used to seeing, and his eyes held what looked like genuine warmth. "It's too bad you're not a vampire."

"I guess that was a compliment, so thanks, but no thanks."

He shrugged and left it at that. Still, Claire had a second's flash of temptation. *All those years. All those things to learn, to feel, to know . . .* Myrnin lived for the excitement of knowledge; she knew that. The only difference between the two of them, really, was that he could go on forever learning.

But despite all of that, despite all the shiny immortality and the fact that there were a few vamps she didn't actually hate—even Oliver now—Claire knew she was meant to be human. Just plain Claire.

And that was really okay.

As if to prove it, Shane slid his arm around her waist and kissed her cheek. "You rock, you know that?"

"I'm a rock star," she said, straight-faced. "I'm probably the saddest little rock star ever, though. What did Mrs. Grant say?"

"She says they'll set up a donation center there and bring it over in bottles. She's not risking her peo-

ple to bring it over. Somebody has to go pick up and deliver."

"Does she believe us?"

"She wants to," Shane said. "Her husband's in here, somewhere. So's her son."

And that, Claire thought, was why Morley had been right about this, even if he was a complete *vampire* about it.

You had to save what you could.

Amelie had understood that all along, Claire realized. That was why Morganville existed. Because you had to try.

Oliver ended up doing the blood pickup himself, maybe as a kind of offhand apology for putting Eve and Shane at risk in the first place, though that of course went unsaid. As the stuff was being passed around—one small plastic cup per vampire, to start—Claire knelt beside Morley's still body, rolled him on his side, and snapped the arrow off just below the point. Then she pulled it out of his chest and hands with one sharp tug, dropping it to the concrete.

Morley took in a huge gasp of air and let it out in a frustrated shout. He held up his hands and stared at the holes punched through them until the flesh and bone started to knit itself again.

He rolled over on his back, staring up at nothing, and said, "I was going to say you aren't a killer. And I still stand by that statement, because evidently I'm not dead. Only *very* upset."

"Here." Claire handed him a cup of blood. "You're right. I'm not a killer. I hope you're not, either."

Morley sat up and sipped, eyes narrowed and fixed on her. "Of course I'm a killer, girl," he said. "Don't be stupid. It's my nature. We're predators, no matter what Amelie likes to pretend in her little artificial hothouse of Morganville. We kill to survive."

"But you don't have to," Claire pointed out. "Right now, you're drinking blood someone gave you. So it doesn't have to be kill-or-be-killed. It can be different. All you have to do is decide to be something else."

He smiled, but not with fangs this time. "You think it's so simple?"

"No." She got up, dusting her knees. "But I know you're not as simple as you like people to think you are."

Morley's eyebrows went up. "You know nothing of me."

"I know you're smart, people follow you, and you can make something good happen for the people who trust you. People like Patience and Jacob, who've got good instincts. Don't betray them."

"I wouldn't—" He stopped, and looked away. "It doesn't matter. I promised to get them all out. They're out. What they do now is up to them."

"No, it's not," Oliver said. He was standing near them, leaning on a stack of old tires as he sipped from his own plastic cup. "You made yourself responsible for them when you left Morganville, Morley. Like it or not, you're now the patriarch of the Blacke vampires. The question is, what are you going to do with them?"

"Do?" Morley looked almost panicked. "Nothing!"

"Not an answer. I suggest you devote some thought to it." Oliver smiled, eyes unfocused as he drank with evident pleasure. "Blacke could be an ideal location, you know. Remote, isolated, little traffic in or out. The humans remaining have a vested interest in keeping your secrets, since their own have been turned. It could be the start of something quite . . . interesting."

Morley laughed. "You're trying to make me *Amelie*."

"Goodness, no. You'd look terrible in a skirt."

Claire shook her head and left them arguing. Dawn was rolling over the town's sky in waves of gold, pink, and soft oranges; it was beautiful, and it felt . . . new,

somehow. The destruction was still there; Hiram's statue was still facedown in the weeds; there were still a dozen feral vampires hiding out somewhere in the shadows.

But it felt as if the town had just come alive again. Maybe that was because across the square, the Blacke library doors were wide-open, and people were coming outside into the cool morning air.

Coming across the square to see those they'd thought they'd lost forever.

Shane was sitting on the curb next to the old, cracked gas pumps, eating a candy bar. Claire plopped down next to him. "Half?" she asked.

"And now I *know* you're my girlfriend, since you're not afraid to demand community property," he said, and pulled off the uneaten half to hand it over. "Look. We're alive."

"And we have chocolate."

"It's not just a miracle; it's a miracle with chocolate. Best kind."

Eve emerged from the garage doorway and settled down next to Claire, leaning her chin on her fists. "I am so tired, I could throw up," she said. "What's for breakfast? Please don't say blood."

Claire separated her half of the candy bar into two pieces and gave Eve one. "Snickers," she said. "Breakfast of—"

"Champions?" Eve mumbled around a mouthful of sticky goodness.

"Not unless it's competitive eating," Shane said. "So, Morley's staying? He's becoming King of Blacke?"

"I think it's more like Undead Mayor, but yeah. Probably."

"So can we ditch Oliver now?"

"Don't think so," Claire said. "He says we leave soon."

"How are we planning to do that, exactly?"

"No idea—"

She heard the engine first as a faint buzz, like a stray but persistent mosquito; then it built into a roar.

A big, black hearse slewed around the corner from the highway and skidded to a stop in front of the garage.

The window rolled down, and Jason Rosser looked out. He grinned. "Anybody need a ride? I figured I'd head back to Durram and grab yours, sis. Since it's officially legal and all. Oh, and I got your cell phones, too."

"Bro, you *rock*." Eve lunged up to her feet and ran possessive hands over the paint job. "Okay, creep, out of my driver's seat. Now."

Jason held the door open for her. As she started to get in, she threw her arms around his neck and hugged him, hard, even with the door between them. He looked surprised.

And so relieved, it hurt Claire a little to see it.

"Come on," Eve said. "We have to lightproof the back."

"Give me a sec," Jason said. "I need a bathroom."

"There's one in the library," Shane said. "Hey, how'd you get out of town?"

"I stole a tractor," Jason said.

"What?"

"A tractor. It took me all night to get to Durram. Wasn't sure if I'd ever make it, either. I ran out of gas two miles from where they'd towed the car."

"Huh." Claire could tell Shane was grudgingly impressed. "So you walked?"

"No, I flew on angel wings."

"Ass."

"How'd you get it out of impound?"

"Trade secret," Jason said. "But it involves not actually asking. Same with the phones. Speaking of which . . ." He dug in the pocket of his hoodie and came up with them, which he handed over to Shane. They didn't tap fists or high-five or anything, but Shane nodded, and Jason nodded back.

"No signal," Claire said, checking hers. "Man, the Morganville provider network sucks."

"It works when Amelie wants it to work," Shane said. "Apparently, she doesn't want it working right now."

"Michael needs to call the guy in Dallas. You know, let him know we're on the way."

"Let him know we got trapped in a vampire town and fought off a vampire zombie army, you mean?"

"I was thinking maybe car problems."

"Boring, but effective," Shane said. "I'll go see if we can make it work. Maybe cell phone wastage doesn't apply to vampires."

As they were talking, Jason walked across to the library, head down, looking like a thin stick in blue jeans. Claire wondered if maybe, just maybe, there was a chance for Eve's brother.

Not much of one, but . . . maybe.

EPILOGUE

"It's you," Eve said, and gave the wig a final tug on Claire's head, setting it just right. All of a sudden, it *looked* right—not just some random collection of plastic threads stuck on top of her scalp, but . . . hair. Pretend hair, sure, but, it looked . . .

Claire couldn't decide how it looked. She cocked her head first one way, then the other. Tried a pose.

"Is it cool? I think it's cool. Maybe?" The girl looking back at her wasn't just a mousy, skinny girl anymore. The new, improved Claire Danvers was taller, a little more filled out, and she was wearing a new hot pink shirt layered over black, a pair of low-rise jeans with skulls on the pockets, and pink and white hair. She was *rocking* the streaked wig. It flowed down over her shoulders in careless waves, and made her look mysterious and fragile and smoky, and Claire just knew she had never been smoky or mysterious in her entire life.

"That is absolutely so you," Eve said with a happy sigh, and jumped around in hoppy circles in her new patent leather black shoes with red skull imprints. "You have *got* to get it. And wear it. Trust me, Shane will go nuts. You look so *dangerous*!"

"Shane's already nuts." Claire laughed. "Did you *see* him in the T-shirt aisle? I thought he was going to cry. So many sarcastic sayings; so few days of the week to wear them. And I'm not sure I really feel comfortable looking, y'know, *dangerous.*"

Eve gave her a long, serious look. "You are, you know. Dangerous."

"Am not."

"It's not the hair. You just—you're something else, Claire. It's like when all the rest of us don't know where to go, you . . . just go. You're not afraid."

"That is so not true," Claire said with a sigh. "I'm scared all the time. Down to my bones. I'm lucky I don't run away like a little screaming girl."

Eve smiled. "That's my job. You're the heroic one."

"Not!"

"Oh, just shut up and get the wig already," Eve said.

"No."

"Get it get it get it!"

"Okay! Jeez, you're scaring the other freaks!"

They both broke into manic giggles, because it was true; a couple of very Gothy Goths were edging away, casting them both odd, apprehensive little looks. Being from Morganville gave you an attitude, Claire guessed. And that wasn't a bad thing, especially when you were in a scary-big city like Dallas, where everything seemed to move ten times faster than she was used to, including the traffic. She didn't know how Eve had managed to get them to the hotel, or get Michael to his studio appointment after dark, but she had, and it was *fabulous.*

The hotel rooms had free soaps and shampoos and *robes.* It was amazing. And they were all modern, with flat-screen, high-definition TVs, and beds so soft that sleeping on them was like sleeping on angel wings.

It was so not like the life she was used to living, which was, she supposed, what made it extra special cool.

"I am a rock star," Claire said to her reflection. Her reflection seemed to agree, although it still made her laugh inside to think it. She remembered Morley's surprise when she'd actually shot him, and Oliver's laughter, his genuine approval.

Maybe she was, a little *tiny* bit.

She flipped the hair over her shoulders and thought about makeup. "What do you think about heavy eye-

liner?" Claire asked, which was totally redundant, because Eve never went anywhere without heavy eyeliner. It was her number one fashion tool.

Instantly, Eve whipped out her Mac tools and began doing Claire's eyes for her. When she checked again, Claire looked . . . *really* mysterious. Her face had taken on depth, shadows, secrets.

Wow. It was amazing what a little change could do.

And a little sleep, Claire thought. She felt better than she had in *months*, knowing there was nobody lurking around the corner to kidnap her, munch her neck, or otherwise present a serious danger.

"You look absolutely fantastic," Eve said. "Drop-dead gorgeous."

"Not literally, hopefully."

"The idea is to knock *other* people dead, sweetie. I didn't think I really had to explain that part."

Shane rounded the corner of the aisle with a double armload of T-shirts, every one of them bound to offend *someone* in Morganville, and skidded to a stop at the sight of the two of them. His mouth opened and closed. Eve stepped away, but Shane didn't notice; his eyes were fixed on Claire, and he looked as if he'd been hit in the forehead with a two-by-four.

"How do I look?" she asked, which was a completely ridiculous question, given how he was staring at her.

He dropped the T-shirts and kissed her, long and sweet and hard, and she felt a fierce kind of joy blow into a storm inside, wild and crazy and *free*.

The Gothy McGoth twins, in their leather and spikes and dyed hair, sniffed and walked off, clearly offended by the sight of so much happiness in one place.

When Shane let her up for air, Claire said, "Maybe we should actually buy the stuff before we celebrate?"

"Why wait?"

And he kissed her again.

*   *   *

Dallas was *amazing*. All the lights, the dizzying buildings, the crazy amounts of traffic, the noise, the people. After a long morning of shopping, Claire was dog-tired, too tired and dazed to even properly admire how awesome their hotel was, with all the glass and marble and fancy furniture. Michael wasn't due to be in the studio until eight p.m., so she fell into bed and slept in her clothes, for a long time. When she woke up, Eve was just finishing her makeup—back to Goth Girl Gone Wild—and checking her lace skull-patterned minidress in the mirror. Her legs looked taller than Claire's entire body.

"Wow," Claire mumbled, and sat up. The mirror showed her just how horrible her bed head could be. "Ack."

"The shower is amazing," Eve said, and turned to the side, smoothing down her dress. "Is it too much?"

"For Morganville? Yeah. For Dallas? No idea. But you look fantastic."

Eve smiled, that secret little smile, and her eyes glittered brightly.

She was thinking about Michael, obviously.

Claire yawned, slipped off the bed, and went to try the shower. Thirty minutes later, her hair fluffed into relative cuteness, she was clean, dry, and dressed in jeans and her best cute blue top, the one Shane said he liked. She even stopped for a little makeup, although she knew it was a lost cause, considering Eve's outfit.

Shane rapped on their door ten minutes later, and when she answered, he looked sleepy but relaxed. Freshly showered, which was always a look she loved on him; his hair was even more insane than usual, as if he'd toweled it dry and then forgotten about it. She smoothed it down. He kissed her and called, "Yo, Eve? Crazy train's leaving the station!"

"I'm coming!" Eve yelled breathlessly, and came out of the bathroom, again, smoothing down her dress.

Shane blinked, but he didn't say anything. "Michael's waiting. He's freaking out that he's going to be late."

"Well, he won't be," Eve said. "Do I look okay? Like a rock star's girlfriend?"

"No," Shane said, and when she looked hurt, he laughed. "You look much better than that, scary girl."

She blew him a kiss and set off down the hall. Michael was pacing next to the elevators, crackling with nervous energy; his gear was piled next to the wall, and he had a strange, closed expression on his face that disappeared the second he saw Eve.

Claire sighed in sympathetic happiness as Michael kissed his girlfriend and leaned over to whisper something in her ear—something that made Eve laugh and cuddle even closer.

Shane rolled his eyes. "I thought you were in a hurry, man."

"Never in *that* much of a hurry," Michael said, and picked up one of the guitars.

Shane picked up the other and offered him a fist to bump. "Let's go rock it, Mikey." Michael just looked at him for a second. Shane held steady, and said, "Michael. You can do it. Trust me."

Michael took a deep breath, returned the fist bump, and nodded as he pushed the elevator call button.

There was a car downstairs—a big black town car, like a limousine only not as fancy—with a driver in a black jacket. He gave Eve a hand in, then Claire; Michael and Shane took the facing bench seat. The guitars, Claire assumed, went in the trunk.

Michael was looking pale, but then, when didn't he? He reached across the open space and took Eve's hand as the car began to roll. "Love the dress," he said.

"Love you," she said, very simply. His eyebrows rose a little, and he smiled.

"I was getting to that part."

"I know." Eve patted his hand. "I know you were. But

you're a boy. I thought I'd just cut to the chase. You're going to be great, you know."

They didn't say anything the rest of the short drive; the roof overhead was clear, and it gave them an amazing view of the tall buildings and the colored lights. Claire felt her heart pounding. *This was really happening.* She couldn't imagine what was going on in Michael's head—or heart. It seemed like a dream. *Morganville* seemed like a dream, one that had happened to someone else, and the idea that they'd leave this reality and go back to that one . . .

Shane didn't have to, Claire thought again. Of the four of them, he was the one who could walk away, and there was nothing in Morganville to hold him.

Nothing but her, anyway.

At the studio, which was in a plain-looking industrial building at the edge of downtown, the driver unloaded the guitars and saw them inside, where two people waiting immediately focused on Michael. Claire, Eve, and Shane suddenly became his entourage, which was funny and kind of awesome, and trailed along as the two recording people explained the process to Michael.

Shane carried both the guitars. He did it with a smile, too, that said clearly how proud he was of his friend. Michael looked fierce—he was concentrating on every word, and Claire could see him already putting himself into performance mode, that place that made him so different when he was onstage.

At the studio door, one of the two studio guys turned and held out a hand to Eve, Claire, and Shane. "You guys need to wait in the box," he said. "Through that door." He pointed to a thick metal door with a window inset, and took the guitars from Shane. Then he flashed them a quick grin. "He'll be great. Trust me, he wouldn't be here if he wasn't."

"Damn right," Shane said, and led the two girls into the box—which, it turned out, was the recording studio's

control room. A big man with frizzy hair was sitting at
the mixing board, which looked more complicated than
the inside of the Space Shuttle. He said hello and gestured for them to take a seat on the big, plush couch at
the back of the room.

It was an amazing place, the studio, full of people who
were all just really, really great at their jobs. The engineer
behind the giant, complicated mixing board was relaxed,
calm, and very easygoing, and the two on the other side
of the glass helped Michael get set up, did some sound
checks, and then left him alone to join the rest of them
in the control room.

"Right," the engineer said, and nodded to his two
assistants—if that was what they were; Claire wasn't
sure. "Let's see what he's got." He flipped a switch. "Michael? Go ahead, whenever you're ready."

He started out playing a slow song, head down, and
Claire felt the mood in the room change from profes-
sional to really interested as he settled into the music. It
flowed out of him, silky smooth, beautiful, as natural as
sunshine. It was an acoustic guitar thing, and it put tears
into Claire's eyes; there was something so soft and sad
and aching about it. When he finished, Michael held the
chord for a long moment, then sighed and sat back on
his stool, looking through the glass toward them.

The engineer's mouth was open. He closed it, cleared
his throat, and said, "What's that called, kid?"

"'Sam's Song,'" Michael said. "It's for my grandfather."

The engineer closed the microphone, looked at the
other two, and said, "We've got a live one."

How darkly hilarious, Claire thought. If only he knew.

"He's great," Shane said softly, as if he'd never actually realized it before. "Seriously. He's *great*. I'm not
crazy, right?"

"You're not crazy," the engineer said. "Your buddy
has insane skills. They're going to love him out there."

Out there. In the world.

In the real world.

Where Michael couldn't really go for long.

The booth door opened, and Oliver walked in. He was in a normal human mode, looking fatherly and inoffensive. The aging hippie, complete with tie-dyed T-shirt and faded jeans and sandals. Claire bet that if she'd told the engineer Oliver was a vampire, he'd have laughed and told her to lay off the crack.

Oliver perched on the arm of the sofa, listening. They all scooted over, because even Claire didn't really want to lean against him, no matter how nice he was apparently being. He said nothing at all. After a while, they all relaxed a little, as Michael continued to pour out the amazing rivers of music on the other side of the studio glass. Fast, slow, hard rocking—he could do it all.

When the last song was over, two hours later, the engineer hit the microphone into the studio and said, "Perfect. That was perfect; that's a keeper. Okay, I think we're done. Congratulations. You are officially on your way, my man."

Michael stood up, smiling, holding his guitar in one hand, and caught sight of Oliver watching him.

His smile almost faded, but then he moved his gaze over to Eve, who was on her feet, blowing him kisses. That made him laugh.

"Rock star!" Eve yelled, and clapped. Claire and Shane stood up and clapped, too.

Oliver sat quietly, no expression at all on his face, as they celebrated Michael's success.

It was their last night in Dallas.

Oliver had allowed them to have a nice dinner out, at a fantastically expensive restaurant where all the waiters were better dressed than Claire ever had been. He didn't go, of course, but somehow Claire could feel his presence, feel him watching.

It was still an amazing meal. She tried everything on her plate, on Shane's, even off Michael's and Eve's. They laughed and flirted, and after the dinner—which went on Oliver's credit card—they went to a dance club across the street, full of beautiful people and spinning lights. No liquor allowed for them, thanks to the glowing wristbands they didn't get, but they danced. Even Shane, although he mainly held on to Claire as *she* danced—which was fantastic. Hot, sweaty, exhausted, happy, the four of them piled into a cab and headed back to the hotel.

It was on the elevator ride up when Shane asked, "Are we really going back?"

It was a long ride; their rooms were on the very top floor of a very tall building. Nobody spoke, not even Michael. He rested his chin on top of Eve's head and held her close, and she put her arms around him.

Shane looked at Claire, the question plain in his eyes. She felt the heavy weight of it, the absolute vital *importance* of it.

The claddagh ring on her right hand felt cold, suddenly.

"Seriously," Shane said. "Can you leave all this? Just go back to *that*? Michael, you've got a future out here. You really do."

"Do I?" Michael asked. He sounded tired and defeated. "How long do you think I could last before something went wrong, man? Morganville's safety. This is—beautiful, but it's temporary. It has to be temporary."

"It doesn't," Shane insisted. "We can figure it out. We *can.*"

Before Michael could answer, the floor dinged arrival, and they had to get out.

Oliver was standing in the hallway, wearing his leather coat and serious expression. No more Mr. Nice Hippie, obviously. He was standing as if he'd been waiting for them for a while.

Creepy.

All four of them came to a sudden halt, staring at him; Claire felt Shane's arm tighten around her waist, as if he was considering moving in front of her. To protect her from what?

There was something odd about the way Oliver was looking at them—because he *wasn't* looking at them, exactly. It was not his normal direct stare at all.

Instead, he silently dialed a number on the cell phone in his hand and put it on speaker, right there, standing in the middle of the hotel hallway. All the plush carpet and lights and normal life seemed to fade away as Claire heard a calm voice on the other end of the phone say, "Do you have them all?" Amelie. Cool, precise, perfectly in control.

"All except Jason," Oliver said. "He's on an errand. He's not involved in this in any case."

Silence for a few seconds, and then Amelie said, "I want you to know I take no pleasure in this. I have made it clear to you, Claire, that I value your service to me and to Morganville; that you are important to us. Do you understand?"

"Yes." Her throat felt dry and tight, and her skin cold.

"Michael," Amelie continued, "I have spoken with you in private, but I will make this public: you must return to Morganville. This goes equally for Claire. You *must* return. There is no argument, no mitigation. Oliver understands this very well, and he is standing as my enforcer in this matter. No doubt the lights are very bright in Dallas, and Morganville seems far away. I assure you it is not. I don't doubt you have spoken of running away, of securing your freedom, but you must understand: my reach is long, and my patience is not infinite. I would much rather your parents continue in blissful ignorance of their danger, Claire. And yours, Eve. And even yours, Michael—even though they have left Morganville, they remain under my control, and always will."

"You bitch," Shane muttered.

"Mr. Collins, I will tolerate much from the four of you, including your occasional rudeness. I will allow you a great deal of freedom and latitude. But make no mistake: I will not let you go free. Make your peace with it as you can. Hate me if you must. But you *will* come back to Morganville, or suffer the consequences. You of all people know that I am quite serious about that."

Shane went pale, and Claire felt every muscle in his body draw tighter. "Yeah, I know," he said hoarsely. "Found my mom floating in a bathtub full of her own blood. I know how serious you can get."

Amelie was silent again, and then she said, "Morganville may not be paradise, and it may not be the future you believe you deserve. But in Morganville, you and your families will remain safe and alive while it is within my power to ensure it. I give you my word, as Founder, that this will be so. Is this understood?"

"You're holding our families hostage," Claire said. "We already knew that."

"And I wanted you to hear it from my lips, so there would be no mistakes," Amelie replied. "And now you have. I will expect you back tomorrow. Good night."

Oliver shut the phone off and put it away. He said nothing to them, just moved out of the way. For a few seconds the four of them just stood there, and then Shane said, "So that's it."

"Yes," Oliver said. "Tomorrow, we return. I suggest you make the most of the time you have tonight." He turned to leave, and then looked back over his shoulder—just one, fast glance. "And I am sorry."

Shane, without another word, took Claire's hand and led her to his room.

In the morning, with the sunlight falling over the two of them as dawn rose on their last day of freedom, Shane rolled over to look at her, propped himself up on an elbow, and said, "You know I love you, right?"

"I know."

"Because I suck at saying it," he said. "It's a work in progress, all this relationship stuff."

She hadn't really slept all night. She'd been too busy thinking, worrying, wondering. Imagining all kinds of futures. Imagining this moment. And she felt as if she were falling from a very tall building as she asked, "Shane? Are you—are you going to come back? To Morganville?"

Apart from Frank, his now-vampire dad, there was nobody Amelie could hold over his head . . . nobody but Claire and Eve and Michael, and, anyway, Amelie had never really needed Shane. *Claire* needed him, though. With every heartbeat she needed him more.

He looked at her, holding the stare for so long it felt as if the fall would go on and on, falling forever. . . .

And then he said, very quietly, "How can I not go back? How can I let you go, Claire? We all stay, or we all go back. I'm not letting you go on your own." He touched a fingertip to her nose, startling a laugh out of her. "Somebody's got to be your bodyguard."

She kissed him, and their skins warmed together in the sunlight; silently, Shane raised her right hand to his lips, and kissed her fingers and kissed the claddagh ring glittering there, that promise of the future that had so much meaning for him, in the past.

And then, one more time, while they were still completely free, he told her how much he loved her.

Afterward, going back to Morganville didn't seem so dark.

TRACK LIST

As always, music drives the creative bus for me, so here are some songs that rocked this little road trip. Feed the artists, please. They deserve your support.

"Good 2 U"	Dave Mason
"Fire"	Daniel Lanois
"Guilty as Charged"	Gym Class Heroes
"Call in the Cavalry"	The Shys
"Troubled Land"	John Mellencamp
"Luisa's Bones"	Crooked Fingers
"Looking Pretty, Pretty"	TAB The Band
"Post Blue (Dave Bascombe Mix)"	Placebo
"Running up that Hill"	Placebo
"Sister Rosetta (Capture the Spirit)"	Noisettes
"Circle the Fringes"	The Gutter Twins
"Nighttiming"	Coconut Records
"I Can't Do It Alone"	3OH!3
"Wish We Were Older"	Metro Station
"That Dress Looks Nice on You"	Sufjan Stevens
"Kill Kill"	Lizzy Grant
"I Love You Good-bye"	Thomas Dolby
"Prime Mover"	Steve Stevens
"I Don't Live in a Dream"	Jackie Greene
"Down Boy"	Yeah Yeah Yeahs
"People C'mon"	Delta Spirit
"The Future's Nothing New"	The Alternate Routes
"Snakes and Lions"	Melpo Mene
"Gift"	Curve
"World Can't Have Her"	Cobra Verde

"Go My Way (The iPod Song)"	Bacon Brothers
"Don't Let the Devil Take Your Mind"	Jackie Greene
"Keeper"	Butterfly Boucher
"Lonely Ghosts"	O+S
"Mama Told Me (Not to Come)"	Three Dog Night
"2080"	Yeasayer
"Wild Life"	Bacon Brothers
"Architeuthis"	Bacon Brothers
"On Fire"	JJ Grey & Mofro
"I'm Good, I'm Gone"	Lykke Li
"Disappearing"	Simon Collins

More playlists at www.rachelcaine.com

ABOUT THE AUTHOR

In addition to the Morganville Vampires series, **Rachel Caine** is the author of the popular Weather Warden series, which includes *Ill Wind*, *Heat Stroke*, *Chill Factor*, *Windfall*, *Firestorm*, *Thin Air*, *Gale Force*, and *Cape Storm*. Her ninth Weather Warden novel will be released in August 2010. She also writes the Outcast Season series, which currently includes *Undone* and *Unknown*. Rachel and her husband, fantasy artist R. Cat Conrad, live in Texas with their iguanas, Popeye and Darwin.

Web site: www.rachelcaine.com

Social networks: MySpace, LiveJournal, Facebook, and Twitter

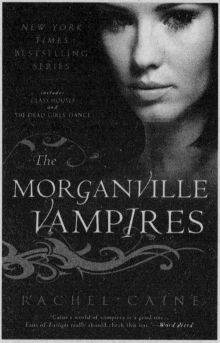